Praise for the novels of Beverly Connor

"Calls to mind the forensic mysteries of Aaron Elkins and Patricia Cornwell. . . . Chases, murder attempts, and harrowing rescues add to this fast-paced adventure." —*Chicago Sun-Times*

"Connor combines smart people, fun people, and dangerous people in a novel hard to put down." —*The Dallas Morning News*

"Outstanding. . . . Connor grabs the reader with her first sentence and never lets up until the book's end. . . . The story satisfies both as a mystery and as an entrée into the fascinating world of bones. . . . Add Connor's dark humor, and you have a multidimensional mystery that deserves comparison with the best of Patricia Cornwell." —*Booklist* (starred review)

"In Connor's latest multifaceted tale, the plot is serpentine, the solution ingenious, the academic politics vicious . . . entertaining . . . chock-full of engrossing anthropological and archeological detail." —*Publishers Weekly*

continued . . .

D0189454

Also by Beverly Connor

ONE GRAVE TOO MANY*
AIRTIGHT CASE
SKELETON CREW
DRESSED TO DIE
QUESTIONABLE REMAINS
A RUMOR OF BONES

*Published by Onyx

DEAD GUILTY

A DIANE FALLON FORENSIC INVESTIGATION

BEVERLY CONNOR

AN ONYX BOOK

ONYX
Published by New American Library, a division of
Penguin Group (USA) Inc., 375 Hudson Street,
New York, New York 10014, U.S.A.
Penguin Books Ltd, 80 Strand,
London WC2R 0RL, England
Penguin Books Australia Ltd, 250 Camberwell Road,
Camberwell, Victoria 3124, Australia
Penguin Books Canada Ltd, 10 Alcorn Avenue,
Toronto, Ontario, Canada M4V 3B2
Penguin Books (NZ), cnr Airborne and Rosedale Roads,
Albany, Auckland 1310, New Zealand

Penguin Books Ltd, Registered Offices:
80 Strand, London WC2R 0RL, England

First published by Onyx, an imprint of New American Library,
a division of Penguin Group (USA) Inc.

First Printing, September 2004
10 9 8 7 6 5 4 3 2 1

PUBLISHER'S NOTE
This is a work of fiction. Names, characters, places, and incidents either are
the product of the author's imagination or are used fictitiously, and any resemblance to actual persons, living or dead, business establishments, events, or
locales is entirely coincidental.

To Charles Connor

ACKNOWLEDGMENTS

I would like to give thanks to Judy Hanson and Terry Cooper for patiently answering my questions.

*"Rule number one of crime scene work:
If it's wet and sticky and it ain't yours, don't touch it."*

—Terry Cooper,
crime scene specialist, Georgia Bureau of Investigation

KNOTS

Bowline   **Figure Eight Knot**   **Stevedore's Knot**

Fisherman's Bend   **Handcuff Knot**   **Waggoner's Hitch**

Chapter 1

"If I'd known she was so afraid of snakes, I wouldn't have hired her," Diane Fallon muttered as she parked her car behind a patrol car on the hard shoulder of the small two-lane dirt road. She could hear the screams of her museum assistant director still ringing in her ears as she took her case from the backseat and climbed out.

Two guys and four young women dressed in cutoffs and tanktops stood in a knot talking to each other on the opposite side of the road between a beat-up pickup and a Jeep. A blonde, cell phone to her ear, stretched up on her toes, as if that would give her a better view into the woods. The words "See anything" leaped out of the crowd.

On Diane's side of the road, two men, tanned and athletic, stood next to a patrol car with what looked like surveying equipment in a pile at their feet. One of them appeared restless. He started to light a cigarette when the other stopped him, pointing to the dry weeds.

The onlookers turned their attention to Diane as a patrolman approached her, spawning a minicloud of dust with each step. He was a young freckled redhead, and he squinted at the sun though his dark glasses, his khaki shirt wet with spots of perspiration around his collar and under his arms.

"Nothing to see here, lady. Get back in your car." He motioned with his hand as though he was directing traffic.

"Forensic anthropologist." Diane held out identification that hung around her neck. "Sheriff Braden called."

The patrolman attempted a smile, nodded and pointed to the woods. "You have to work your way through the woods there. It's dense at first, but you'll come to a deer trail. Follow it about a quarter of a mile." He hesitated a moment, a grimace distorting his features as he nodded toward the two men next to his car. "They say it's not normal."

Not normal. The kind of death they called her out for usually wasn't. "My crime scene crew will be here soon. Send them down when they arrive."

"Sure thing. Spray yourself down good. Lot of deer ticks in these woods."

She thanked him, retrieved a can of bug repellent from her case and sprayed herself from head to toe before ducking through the underbrush. She followed orange tie markers through brittle flora until she found the deer trail.

About four hundred yards into the woods, a breeze brought a brief shot of relief from the heat but carried with it the aroma of death. Pushing her way through a thicket of wild shrubs, she saw the sheriff through the leaves. He and several deputies stood in an opening under large spreading trees, staring at the crime scene, muttering to each other. They looked in her direction and nodded as she came into the clearing— obviously glad to see her arrive.

At the familiar yellow-and-black tape she stopped to take in details of the scene. Like a grotesque image from *Alice's Adventures in Wonderland,* three bodies hung by their necks from ropes in the copse of trees.

The sheriff approached her, shaking his head, wiping his face with a blue bandana and fanning himself with his wide-brimmed hat. He was a tall, thin man with a round face and thick, wavy dark hair that was just beginning to gray at the sides.

"I don't know what they could have done to these people to make them like that," he said, motioning in the direction of the three hanging bodies. "When word of this gets out . . ."

Diane said nothing. She walked with the sheriff carefully around the perimeter of the yellow-taped crime scene. What had upset the sheriff and his deputies was not simply the triple death, but the horrid look of it. Bodies hanging still, as though frozen— their necks stretched from one to three feet in length.

The bodies looked very much alike, the way dead do. The kinship of the dead—skin black with decay, vacant eye sockets, exposed bones, mouths open and askew. They were each dressed in similar if not identical coveralls—navy blue, maybe dark gray, it was hard to tell, they were so stained with dried body fluids. One had long blond hair half plastered to its skull, with strands blowing gently in the breeze. The other two had shorter dark hair—brown maybe, or black. All had their hands tied behind their backs.

Without warning, the farthest body fell as the neck skin ripped apart. The head bounced on the ground and rolled a dozen feet from the torso, trailing a long piece of neck with it.

"Oh, Jesus," said one of the deputies, jumping back reflexively.

Diane watched the fall with interest. To her it was a process, and knowing the processes that work on bodies after death is to understand pieces to a puzzle of great consequence that she had to solve. The direction and distance a head rolls when it pops out of the noose is useful information for finding a missing skull. Knowing how long it takes for the head to separate from the torso in a decomposing hanging victim under specific conditions is valuable information for those interested in taphonomy.

She could see from the faces of the people here watching that this information was not of interest to them. She glanced at her watch.

The sheriff turned his gaze from the scene and mopped his brow again. "What do you make of this, Dr. Fallon?"

"We've been having a long dry spell," Diane said. He gave her a sideways glance. She crumpled leaves from a nearby bush in her hand and nodded toward the victims. "The dry air aids in this rather peculiar effect."

"You saying this is natural?" He said, "I've seen a few hanging victims, and I know the body stretches, but jeez . . . I've never seen anything like this."

"You just haven't seen them at the right time, or under the right conditions. The pull of gravity makes the bodies stretch, making them taller than they were in life. Sometimes you get this effect." Diane gestured toward the long neck of the victim closest to them.

"Well, I'll have to say that's a relief. We couldn't figure out how the killer could have done this—or why. Thought it must be some kind of perverted maniac—you know, as opposed to our normal maniacs we have running around."

Diane laughed with him, glad for any comic relief, no matter how mild.

She turned her attention back to the scene. Not many maggots on the corpses. But she didn't expect there would be. She turned her attention to the drip zone—an area underneath the bodies where liquified decay and bits of flesh dropped to the ground. Hundreds of maggots and their beetle predators made the surface of the ground move with a writhing motion. Soon they would find the fallen corpse, and if left alone they and other late arrivals would strip it bare.

"This is just disgusting," said one of the deputies.

Diane didn't recognize him. She didn't know all the deputies in this county to the north of Rosewood. He must be new. If he stayed with this job, he'd see things far more disgusting.

Hang 'em high. The words flitted through Diane's brain as she looked at the two bodies suspended from the leafy canopy. Even stretched long as they were, their shoes were still three feet from the ground. How had they been hung so high?

The killer—or killers—had to scout out a place with enough strong limbs for three hangings. Even in heavily wooded areas, hanging trees weren't that easy to come by. She glanced at the deputies milling around.

"Ask everyone to move back," she said to the sheriff. "There have to be vehicle tracks here somewhere." But looking at the underbrush and ground cover, she didn't see where a vehicle could have passed.

"You'd think so," said the sheriff, looking at the ground as though the tracks might be under his feet. "The perp had to use a winch or something." He motioned to the deputies. "All right, everybody. Let's move back, and watch where you step. We don't need to be trampling the crime scene."

"Those guys with the surveying equipment . . . did they find the bodies?" asked Diane.

The sheriff nodded. "They were doing a timber cruise for the paper company. This land belongs to Georgia Paper."

"Then the two men are familiar with the lay of the land around here."

"I'm sure." He turned to speak to a young deputy when he saw him spit out a chew of tobacco. "Dammit, Ricky, what the hell do you think you're doing? Pick that up."

"What?" The deputy looked around at the others, who shook their heads and tried not to laugh.

"That wad of tobacco you just spit out. Pick it up. This is a crime scene, not a sidewalk."

"Pick it up and do what with it?"

"Put it back in your mouth—I don't care, just don't throw it away here."

As they bantered back and forth, Diane fished a bag from her case and put a large red x on it and handed it to the sheriff.

The sheriff poked the deputy with it. "Here. Put it in this and take it back to your car. And while you're up there, talk to them timber fellas and see if there's a back road into here. Leon, you go with him and make sure he don't screw up."

The deputy picked up the discarded tobacco cud with a wad of leaves and stuffed the whole thing in the brown paper bag.

As he and the other deputy, Leon, were leaving, the sheriff shouted at them. "And don't piss in the woods on the way back." He turned back to Diane. "I tell you, sometimes I wonder how he gets through the day."

"Is the coroner here?" she asked, suppressing a smile.

"Not yet. You know we have a new one, don't you?"

"It's not Sam Malone?"

"No. He retired. Moved to Florida. Lynn Webber's the coroner. She's a medical examiner at the hospital too. Smart little girl. Real smart."

"Do I hear you talking about me, Mick Braden?"

Sheriff Braden's face lit up at the approach of a young woman dressed in designer jeans and a white lab coat. "Nothing but good things," he said. "Lynn, this is Diane Fallon . . ."

Lynn Webber was several inches shorter than Diane's five feet, eight inches, and her short, shiny black hair was much more neatly coifed than Diane's nononsense haircut. She extended her hand and gave Diane a smile that flashed bright bleached white teeth. "I just love the museum. I took my parents there while they were visiting. It kept them from thinking about what I do for a living for a whole day." Her dark eyes twinkled as she laughed.

"I suppose medical examiner isn't the job they picked out for you," replied Diane, shaking her hand.

"They wanted me to be a pediatrician." Lynn Webber looked up at the hanging bodies. "Good heavens. We've got something here, don't we, Sheriff?"

"I'll say." The sheriff nodded. "It was a relief, though, when Dr. Fallon told me this is natural."

Lynn lay a hand on his arm. "Bet you thought someone stretched them on a rack before stringing them up." She laughed again.

"Something like that," he said. "Lynn here caught a murderer that almost slipped by us. We all thought the Whitcomb woman died of a heart attack—including her doctor. Wasn't going to even have a postmortem—natural causes. Lynn just happened to hear the paramedics talking about the woman's rigor. Something about her position. What'd you call it— hyperextension? Suspected right away it was a poisoning."

"Sodium monofluoroacetate?" said Diane. She saw a momentary flash of disappointment in Lynn's eyes before she nodded.

"I'm impressed," Diane continued. "That's a tough one. I only know about it through my human rights work. It's the poison of choice among men in India who kill their wife because her dowry wasn't high enough."

Dr. Webber looked at her, speechless for a moment, pondering, perhaps, the self-centeredness of murderers. She shook her head and looked back at their corpses. "How'd the perp get them so high?" Her gaze darted around the crime scene. "A ladder, maybe. But it would've been hard to get their cooperation to just climb up and stick their head in a noose, wouldn't it?"

"The crime scene should show something. . . ." Diane began, then stopped.

Dr. Webber and the sheriff followed her gaze up to where, among the leafy branches, a fourth noose hung.

Chapter 2

"The one that got away? Or is it waiting to be filled?" said Dr. Webber, squinting up at the piece of hemp hanging in the tree. "It's not exactly a noose, is it? It's just a rope tied to a limb."

Diane had been studying the rope. It hung from a branch high off the ground like the others. Whoever put it there hadn't tied the familiar hangman's knot with tight coils above the loop. The noose was formed by a portion of the rope pulled back through a small loop tied on the end of the rope, creating a slip noose. Were it not for the small leafy branch that stuck its woody fingers through the loop, the noose would have slipped and vanished, leaving only an enigmatic piece of rope.

Diane looked carefully at the other ropes, paying particular attention to the one from which the body had fallen.

"It's like the others." Diane started to explain, when their attention was drawn to a rustling of the bushes, and her forensic team filed into the clearing.

"Well, this is weird." Deven Jin set down his case and stared at the two bodies in the trees and the one on the ground.

Neva Hurley stopped abruptly, her mouth agape.

"One of those flies is going to light on your tongue," said Jin, shoving her gently.

Neva snapped her mouth closed.

David Goldstein used a small set of binoculars to focus in on the bodies, then shifted to the leafy canopy. "I suppose you've seen the other rope," he said.

"Just now." Diane introduced her team to Dr. Webber and the sheriff. "Neva came to us from the Rosewood Police. Jin's from New York, where he worked crime scenes, and David worked with me at World Accord International as a human rights investigator."

They shook hands, muttered hellos and commented briefly on the strange state of the corpses.

Her team was anxious to get started. Jin, the youngest, was in hyperactive mode, his body moving even though he was standing in one spot, looking as if he was about to break into dance to some music only he heard. Diane envied his youthful energy. He snapped opened his case and began pulling out the marker flags, rope, wire stakes and drawing supplies. He shoved his straight black hair out of his eyes, pulled it back into a ponytail and donned the plastic cap that Diane required.

"David doesn't need a cap," Jin said. "He just wears one so people will think that fringe around the edges is a full head of hair." Laughing, he handed a cap to Neva.

David rolled his eyes and quietly took out his camera equipment.

Dr. Webber watched as he loaded it with film. "He doesn't use a digital camera?" she asked Diane.

"I use both, but I get greater depth of field and finer detail with the film," said David over his shoulder.

"David's actually quite an artist," said Diane.

David scowled. "Trying to be accurate isn't artistry."

"I'm talking about your bird photographs."

He cocked his head. "One might describe them as artistic."

Neva put on her cap and stood glancing from David and Jin to Diane, as if waiting for directions. Diane was torn between giving her some reassuring gesture or leaving her to manage whatever insecurities she was dealing with. Neva was one of the gifts Diane had to accept in her curious bargain with the Rosewood Police. She wasn't sure Neva really wanted to be here.

The ropes tied around the branches made a creaking sound as a breeze passing through the trees caused the bodies to swing slowly. The stench of dead flesh washed over them. Diane watched Neva hold her breath.

"You'll get used to the smell," Diane told her. "This is actually mild. Breathing through your mouth helps."

Neva looked horrified. Probably thinking about the flies and her open mouth.

"You should work with a decaying body that's in an enclosed space," said Jin. "I swear, the smell permeates your eyeballs. Your tears even stink," he added, grinning.

"The stench of adipocere formation is the worst," said David, swinging his camera to his side and turning toward Neva. "Absolutely the worst. One time, the smell just wouldn't go away. I had to have steroid shots in each nostril."

Neva looked miserable.

"You should have to autopsy those bodies," said Dr. Webber. "One of my first autopsies was on a bloated body found in an abandoned trailer. Like an idiot, I stuck a scalpel in the thing and it exploded all over everyone. I thought I could taste the stuff for a week."

That did it for Neva. She turned and headed for a tree, heaving. Diane followed and handed her a bottle of water.

"They're making fun of me, aren't they?" Neva pulled a tissue from her pocket and wiped her face.

"A little," said Diane. "You're the new guy, and they're just breaking you in. They mean no disrespect. We all had to have a period of adjustment to this kind of work."

"Did David really have to get shots in his nose?"

"No, he made up that little story. And the odor doesn't make your tears smell either. But bodies do blow up with gasses, and if you puncture them just right—well, you can imagine. But the pathologist always wears a face shield when autopsying decayed bodies."

Neva took several swigs of water and screwed the cap back on. "I'm all right."

"The trick is to focus on the work."

Neva nodded and walked back to David, Jin and Lynn Webber's good-natured smiles.

"Chuck over here"—the sheriff pointed to one of his deputies—"threw up so often when he was new, we all started calling him Upchuck."

Jin handed her a template and a pad of graph paper. "You can help me with the sketches," he said.

"We'll have the bodies ready for you as soon as we can," Diane told Lynn Webber.

Lynn nodded. "Do you want me to have the diener clean the bones?"

"Please. Unless we find their driver's licenses tucked away in their clothes."

"I'm not usually that lucky." The sheriff looked up at the two hanging corpses again. "Something tells me these are going to be hard to identify. Judging from the clothes they're wearing, I'd guess they might be some poor homeless people who crossed paths with a killer."

"You don't think it's a suicide pact?" asked the other sheriff's deputy, a hefty man who had been studying the woods, looking almost anywhere but at the bodies. "Ain't most hangings suicide?"

"Yes, most are," said Diane, "but how did they manage it without anything to stand on?"

"I guess you're right. But they could've climbed the trees and jumped."

Lynn Webber and Diane winced at the thought.

"Or maybe the fourth guy chickened out and, not wanting to leave a good ladder, took it with him."

"I'm sure the crime scene investigation and autopsy will sort all that out," said the sheriff.

"I'll leave you to it." Dr. Webber dusted her hands together, mentally washing them of the crime scene, even though she hadn't touched anything. "I need to clear my calendar for these new clients." She turned to Diane. "If you'd like to attend the autopsy, you may."

"Thanks. I'd like to collect the ropes and the insects inside the corpses."

"You're welcome to it. I hate collecting larvae. Though Raymond, my diener, doesn't seem to mind."

Dr. Webber left them and disappeared through the undergrowth up the trail. The sheriff's gaze followed her until she was out of sight.

She was replaced by the two deputies coming back

from the road. It was apparent by their faces they had
something to tell the sheriff.

"Edwards and Mayberry—that's the timber guys—
said they seen a place where it looks like a vehicle
mighta come through the bushes," said the taller of
the two, waving his hand to shoo away flies as he
spoke. "Said there's a place where the weeds was
kinda beat down."

"They's supposed to be some old timber roads over
yonder." The other deputy pointed northeast of the
bodies. "Right through there."

Diane motioned to the sheriff. "Let's have a look."
She turned to David. "After the photographs and
sketches are done, start a grid search under the
corpses. We need to clear a work space so we can get
the bodies down. Go ahead and collect the insects."

The sheriff ordered his deputies to follow David's
instructions and not get into trouble. He and Diane
walked to the edge of the clearing where the deputy
had pointed. A large fallen pine tree covered head
high in broken limbs, briars and loose brush blocked
the path. It was a place where Brer Rabbit might
have hidden.

The sheriff stooped and looked through the bram-
bles at the tree stump. "It was cut down with a chain
saw. And not long ago—I can still smell the pine."

"Could the timber guys have done it?" asked Diane.

He shook his head. "We can ask, but I can't see
why they would do it. They were counting trees, not
cutting them down. And why would they pile a bunch
of weeds and dead limbs on top of a fresh tree? A lot
of work for no purpose."

"So the tree was cut and brush was piled on top
of it to hide the crime scene, or block access to it,"
said Diane.

She took out her digital camera and snapped pictures of the blockade from different angles. The side leading away from the woods was as the timber surveyors had described: a ghost of a trail where tires had crushed the dry weeds.

Seeing the direction from which the tire tracks had come, Diane walked back through the brush, squatted and examined the ground on the side leading to the crime scene. She could see it now in the leaves covering the hard ground beneath the trees—faint impressions where a vehicle had passed.

"David," she called. "There's some tire marks through here. Be careful to record it before you search the ground."

A thorough ground search would require moving the forest litter, and with it, all signs of a passing.

"I knew they would have left some kind of trail," he said. "We'll take care of it."

Diane returned to the sheriff, who was studying the tire impressions in the crushed grass.

"From the width of the tracks, I'd say it was a truck or SUV. I suppose your people will measure it."

"We will. Where did the timber guys park their vehicle?"

"They said down one of the dirt timber roads. Their work's done on foot, you know. About like land surveyors."

Diane walked a hundred feet down the indeliberate roadway, turned and looked at the makeshift barrier. The crime scene was hidden. The barricade looked like an ordinary brush pile from that distance. Not an uncommon sight in this setting, but usually juxtaposed to a firebreak, a roadway cut or a clearing. This pile was at the end of a path through weeds and trees. These were the perpetrator's tracks and the perpetrator's doing.

"What you reckon this is about?" the sheriff asked
after he had joined her on the trail. He shook his
head. "I've seen hangings, but they were all suicides
in the victims' houses. Around here, if people kill
themselves in the woods, they do it with a rifle or a
shotgun. I've never seen multiple hangings like this.
It looks like a lynching. And why would they all be
dressed alike?"

As the words were out of his mouth, a deputy appeared from the bushes and trotted toward them.
"Sheriff, you gotta come take care of this. Word's
done got out about the hangings, and they're saying
there's been some lynchings. Elwood Jefferson from
the AME Church is here and wants to talk to you."

"What was I just saying? That's all we need. At
least it's Elwood. He's not a guy who shoots from the
hip like some I could mention."

At that moment a tall lean black man in a charcoal
gray suit came through the brush and strode purpose-
fully toward the sheriff.

Chapter 3

"Elwood, you know you're not supposed to be here." Sheriff Mick Braden regarded the man standing before him.

Elwood Jefferson was a head taller than any of them. Maybe in his sixties—his age was hard to tell— his smooth dark brown skin stretched over angular bones. His gray suit was well made and his trousers sharply creased. It was not a suit for tramping through the woods.

"We heard some black men have been lynched down here in Cobber's Wood. You know, Sheriff, if I hear a rumor like that, I've got to come see about it."

"Would you be here if . . ." the deputy began.

"Leon, let's not go there," said the sheriff.

Elwood Jefferson didn't look at the deputy, but at the sheriff. "You know when those black teenagers tore up the playground at the First Baptist Church, I brought them in myself."

"And you know that not everyone wanted them brought in," the deputy said. "You remember the stink Boden Conrad raised . . . making all kinds of excuses for 'em."

"Leon," the sheriff said, giving the deputy a look

that carried more weight than his words, "why don't you go see if the crime scene folk need some help."

Leon shot Jefferson a scowl before he reluctantly trotted back to the crime scene.

"After a body starts to decompose, the skin turns black," said the sheriff. "I'm sure someone up there on the road heard somebody say they were black and that's how all this started."

"I didn't come here to accuse," Elwood said. "I came to get information."

Sheriff Braden turned to Diane. "I know you haven't had a chance to examine them, but . . . I'm sorry. Diane Fallon, this is Elwood Jefferson. He's pastor of the AME Church up on St. Chapel Street. Dr. Fallon here is a forensic anthropologist loaned to us from Rosewood."

"I've been to the museum in Rosewood. You're the director there, aren't you?" He extended his hand, and Diane shook it.

"Yes, I am. I hope your visit to the museum was an enjoyable one."

"It was indeed." He nodded. "And you also work crime scenes. That's an odd combination."

"Yes, it seems that way to me sometimes."

"Is there anything you can tell me about the bodies?" he asked.

"One of the victims has long, fine blond hair. The other two have dark brown straight hair. That's not necessarily a defining characteristic, but I believe all three are Caucasian."

Elwood Jefferson shook his head. "I didn't get a look at the hair. All I could see was those necks. Who would do such a thing?"

"That was my reaction too," the sheriff said. "But

Dr. Fallon tells me that's a natural outcome of hanging by the neck for a long time in dry weather."

Jefferson raised his eyebrows. "Is that so? I've never heard of that. That's a relief."

"I'll have to ask you not to talk about the crime scene to anyone," said the sheriff. "We don't really know who or what might be involved here."

"You can rely on me. You'll tell me if anything changes in the identification of these poor souls."

"We won't hide the identities—you don't need to worry about that. I've got no interest other than getting to the bottom of this."

"And tell your deputy that we'll pray in church for the families of those victims just like we would if they were black."

"Leon can be a lot like Boden Conrad."

"Boden's just looking out for justice."

"I could say the same about Leon."

The sheriff walked Elwood Jefferson back. Diane stayed, looking toward the murder site, her eyes following the sheriff and the pastor as they disappeared through the underbrush.

She watched them, but her mind was trying to grab hold of the killer's thoughts. He had to know the area. He must have known he could come and go without being seen and be here for as long as he needed to hang three victims. Or was it four? How familiar was he with this place? Was he from here? Had he hunted here?

All the bodies were in the same state of decay. He'd probably killed them at the same time. That could have taken anywhere from half an hour to half a day. She tried to remember if she'd heard or read about murders involving multiple victims at one time.

Why hanging? That seemed like very risky business. Of the many methods of killing a person, hanging is one of the most difficult.

She'd been thinking about one killer, but there may have been more than one. More than one killer would have made the task a lot easier.

What would be the killer's motive? Were the hangings a message? A warning? Maybe it was a hit of some kind. Her mind flashed for a moment to the St. Valentine's Day massacre. Gang warfare? Not likely. Not here.

All three bodies were dressed the same. Did that have any special meaning? Did they work at the same place, belong to the same group, or were they dressed the same by the killer? For what reason?

"What I need is a victimology," Diane whispered.

For that she needed to know who they were. She doubted the bodies would have driver's licenses, credit cards or other identification on them, but there could be enough skin left on the hands to get fingerprints. If the sheriff was lucky, he wouldn't need her professional specialty to identify them.

Diane looked down the path in the other direction, away from the crime scene. There were spots where the trees grew so close together that a truck or SUV would have a tight squeeze. She followed the trail of the vehicle, inspecting the ground, the brush and the trees. The first narrow spot showed no sign of damage, but from where she stood she could see a light-colored gash on a tree ahead.

She was hoping for paint flakes or something scratched off the side of the killer's vehicle, but the gash appeared to be the result of a section of bark and wood cut out with a saw.

Could be the killer sideswiped the tree and stopped to cut out the evidence, leaving no paint to match up with his vehicle. Diane took an orange marker flag hanging from her belt and pushed the wire holder into the ground next to the tree.

She continued along, looking for more tight squeezes and surveying the ground, looking for anything.

About a quarter of a mile farther, she came to a rough dirt road filled with ruts and rocks the size of cantaloupes. In one direction the road was heavily overgrown with tall weeds growing down the middle. Erosion scars were deep and the woods thick.

In the opposite direction, the weeds in the center were shorter, the road better. An older Land Rover was parked in the middle of the road. As she walked toward it, she heard the sound of a motor, and a county deputy's car came into view. It pulled up behind the Rover and stopped. The two guys who had found the bodies got out and began transferring their equipment from the patrol car to the Rover. Diane quickened her pace.

"You lost, lady?" one of the men called out to her.

"No," she said as she approached their vehicle. "I need to ask you some questions."

"She's working on the case," said the deputy. He was the one called Ricky—the one who had to gather up his expectorated tobacco and take it to his car.

"I'm Diane Fallon."

"Chris Edwards and Steven Mayberry. We told everything we know to the sheriff."

Both men were young, not over twenty-five, Diane guessed. Chris Edwards had short, wavy light brown hair. He was athletic with a thin layer of baby fat between his skin and muscles, giving him a well-shaped, pudgy appearance. Steven Mayberry had dark brown straight hair that hung below his ears. He was more slightly built and leaner.

Both of them looked nervous, fidgeting with their equipment, dropping some of it on the ground. Chris put a hand to his face and coughed.

"Just a few questions," said Diane.

"Okay, but all we know is what we told the sheriff." Chris Edwards pointed to an instrument his partner had in his hand. "I was just calculating the height of a tree when I saw what looked like a body hanging in the distant canopy."

"Look," interrupted Deputy Ricky. "You need me to take you back to the scene? If you do, I'll stick around . . . but I need to get back. There's a crowd gathering up at the road."

"I'll walk back," Diane told him. "Thanks."

The deputy helped the two men with the last of their gear and drove off, backing all the way up the road. Whatever else Ricky was, he was a good backer. Diane watched as his car maneuvered down the rut-filled dirt road with hardly a waver.

"What exactly is a timber cruise?" asked Diane, leaning against the white vehicle. Perhaps a few mundane questions would put them at ease. The two did relax their stance.

"Basically, inventorying the trees," said Chris.

"You count them?"

"Yes—and determine the diameter, height and species."

"Surely not all of them."

"No, not on a parcel this size. It's six hundred and twenty-five acres. We do a point sample—count a tenth

of an acre at regular points on a grid." Steven pointed
to a rolled-up map in the backseat of the Rover.

"So you've been all over the woods. Or did you
just start?"

"No. We've been at it a while. Mainly in this section." He pointed to the woods on the side of the
road opposite the crime scene. "This section's mainly
soft woods and pine. The other side, where the bodies
are, is mainly hardwoods. It hasn't been cut in over a
hundred years," Steven added.

"Have you noticed anyone out in the woods while
you were working?"

Chris and Steven looked at each other wide-eyed.
"You mean the killer could be out here—now?"

"Probably not," said Diane. "I'm just asking questions I always ask. Did you see anyone?"

Both the men shook their heads. "No. But we found
some hoofprints thataways." Chris pointed to the
piney side of the road. "I'd say about a half a mile
in. For about a half mile you get these mostly thirty-
year-old trees you see here. After that, the parcel was
clear-cut about ten years ago. The hoofprints were
along a stream where the trees weren't cut. The timber
managers always try to leave a stand to control erosion along streams of any size."

"But you didn't see a rider?"

"No. Just the prints. If I was a tracker, I'd tell you
how old they were, but I'm not." Chris laughed, joined
by Steven. "I suppose they could be new or they could
be old. We haven't had rain in a while."

"Did the horses have shoes?"

They hesitated a second, surprised by the question.
"I don't know that I noticed," said Steven. "I'd say
yes. The print was crisp, as I recall."

"When you're doing your timber cruise, do you tag the trees in some way—make a cut in them?"

"Sometimes we use an orange ribbon to mark the center of the plot we're sampling, but you wouldn't want to make a cut. It'd be a way for diseases to attack the tree. Besides, these are valuable products. You don't go hacking them up," said Steven.

"She's talking about that tree over there." Chris pointed in the direction of the tree Diane had found with the gash. "We saw that. Somebody took a saw to it. No idea why. They wouldn't be checking for sap or anything. Maybe someone was trying to cut it down. Not doing a very good job of it, though."

"Near the crime scene, there's a tree that's been cut down and brush piled on top. Did you do that?"

Both of them shook their heads. "No," said Chris. "We saw that too. Maybe somebody was trying to hide what they'd done."

"Maybe. Have you noticed or found anything unusual while you've been out here?"

"Unusual? More unusual than those bodies?"

"Anything like the remains of a campfire, tire tracks, objects—anything not natural to the forest."

They hesitated a moment. Exchanged gazes briefly, and looked back at Diane. "Just the hoofprints," said Chris. "But we were mainly looking at the trees."

Steven agreed. "No one's supposed to camp here. Something like campfire smoke would've been noticed. They keep a pretty good eye out for forest fires, especially since it's been so dry."

"They?"

"The forest rangers. *Anyone* here 'bouts would take notice of smoke, for that matter."

Diane's gaze rested on the map in the backseat. "Could I have a look at your map?"

"We've got a copy we could give you," said Chris. He went around and opened the back and pulled out a cardboard mailing tube. "It's got our grid marked on it, but that shouldn't matter."

He pulled out the map and unrolled it on the hood of the Rover. That was when Diane noticed how marked up the side of the vehicle was. For a moment her heart skipped a beat. Of course their vehicle would be beat up. It was an old model and they used it on rough terrain—and she was sure the sheriff would check them out. They had found the bodies, and it would be routine to check them out. Still . . . She took a deep breath.

"We're right here." Chris pointed to a spot on the map next to a line marked as a road. "The bodies are here."

"We take a tenth of an acre sample everywhere the grid lines cross," added Steven.

"Where were the hoofprints?" asked Diane.

"That'd be right along here." Chris moved his finger along a blue line labeled as Cobb Creek.

"Give her that extra copy of the aerial photograph too," said Steven.

"Sure." Chris pulled it out of the tube and lay it out on the hood. "See, you can tell the kind of trees that grow here." Diane couldn't, but she nodded. "See over here where the stream cuts in? The trees are smaller. That's where it was clear-cut. Over here is where we did most of the cruise, and right here is the bodies." He rolled up the maps, put them back in the tube and handed it to her.

"I appreciate this."

"Glad to help . . ."

As he spoke, they heard the sound of a motor. *The deputy coming back,* thought Diane. But a dark blue SUV appeared over the rise.

"Oh, Jesus," said Chris.

Chapter 4

Diane knew what Chris and Steven were thinking. The same thought flashed through her mind—the killer. As the vehicle slowed to a stop, the letters WXNG on the magnetic sign attached to the side brought relief to Chris and Steven. But not to Diane. She crossed in front of the vehicle and walked to the driver's side.

"Can I help you?" she asked the woman who appeared as the window slid down.

"WXNG news." The woman, perhaps twenty-five with fine brown hair and eyes to match, looked Diane up and down a moment and spotted the identification that hung from a cord around her neck. "What can you tell us?" she asked.

"Not a thing. Have you seen the sheriff?"

"The deputy said he's at the scene. We heard it's a racial thing."

Thing, thought Diane. What a way to describe the horror of murder. Diane measured her words. She could see "No comment" appearing in the news, something like: "The authorities at the scene had no comment when asked if this was a racially motivated crime."

"What do you mean?" Diane asked.

"We heard that someone lynched three black men."

"You've been given incorrect information. For more than that, you need to talk to the sheriff."

"That's who we're going to see." She turned to her passenger. "I see a road down there. I think that'll get us to the crime scene."

"That roadway's part of the crime scene. You can't go there," said Diane.

"People around here want to know what's going on. It's my job to tell them, and I'm going to do it."

"Not by contaminating the crime scene, you're not. You get near that roadway, I'll impound your vehicle."

"You can't do that."

"Yes, I can. If you continue on after I've told you it's a crime scene, I'll have you arrested. You can get the information you want, just not through here. Drive back to the road. I'll call the sheriff and tell him you want to speak with him."

Diane took her phone and punched in the sheriff's number with her thumb, not taking her eyes off the woman. When he answered she told him about the reporter. She also asked him to send one of her team with some crime scene tape to rope off the roadway to the scene.

"Damn reporters," he said. "I suppose they've gotten on to this racial thing going around."

"Yes."

"You told them it wasn't, didn't you?"

"Yes. And I also told them that all other information had to come from you."

"You did, did you? I suppose I got to talk to them sometime. Tell them I'll meet them up at the road."

Diane relayed the message. The woman was reluctant. She sat in her SUV, not making a move to put her car in gear. "I need to pull down there so I can turn around." She pointed to the forbidden path.

Diane had the impression she was planning to make a break for it. "I'm sorry, but you can't. As I said, it's part of the crime scene."

"Well, where the hell do you expect me to turn around?"

"Not at the crime scene. If you back up several feet, there's a small turnaround between those trees."

"Back up?" She said it as though her vehicle didn't have a reverse gear.

"Yes."

She reluctantly put her car in gear and started to back up, then abruptly slammed on the brakes, throwing her passenger forward and backward. She stepped out of the car and turned toward Steven and Chris. "Who are you two? Are you the ones who found the bodies?"

The passenger, a tall lean man close to thirty, stepped out and shouldered his video camera and trained it on the two timber cruisers.

"You are the two who found the bodies, right?" the reporter asked again.

"We found them and called the sheriff. That's all there was to it," Steven told her.

"Tell us about the scene."

"The sheriff told us not to talk about it," said Chris.

"He can't order you not to talk."

"And you can't order us *to* talk." Chris shrugged. "As soon as we saw the bodies, we left and called the sheriff. That's it."

"How many bodies were there?"

"We can't say anything about it."

"What was it like, coming upon dead bodies?"

The two of them glared at her a moment. "What do you think it was like?" said Steven. "How many times have you found dead bodies in your workplace?"

Diane was glad to see that they were more reluctant to talk to the reporter than they were to talk with her.

As the reporter was trying to pull answers from Chris and Steven, Diane saw the two deputies, Chuck and Leon, coming up the trail from the crime scene to tape off the vehicle path through the woods. She walked down to meet them.

"I'm glad you're here. I fear I was going to have a hard time keeping that reporter from crashing the crime scene."

"That's Pris Halloran from that little TV station in Atlanta, WXNG," said Chuck. "She cruises around listening to her scanner. She's always trying to break a big story. Mostly, she makes a whole lot out of nothing."

"The guy's Kyle Anthony," said Leon. "He got fired from one of the big Atlanta stations after he was arrested for possession of cocaine."

"I think both of them's hungry for some kind of big news score," said Chuck. "I see she's giving the timber guys a hard time."

From the stiff posture Chris and Steven had taken, folded arms, head down, Diane guessed Chuck was right.

"Would you get that damn thing out of my face? You trying to get a view of my tonsils?" Chris' voice carried clearly down the road to where Diane and the deputies were securing the crime scene tape.

"Looks like Chris Edwards needs a little backup," said Leon.

The three of them walked up to them at a fast pace. "Everything all right here?" asked Leon.

"I'm just conducting an interview," said Pris Halloran.

"We've got to get back to work." Steven opened the door and slid into the driver's seat.

"You know," said Diane, "if the sheriff gets up to the road and you aren't there, you're not likely to get another chance to talk with him today."

That got the reporter and the cameraman moving. They jumped in their SUV and backed up to the turnaround and left before Chris and Steven could make their getaway.

"Fill me in," Diane said to Jin when she finally got back to the main crime scene.

Jin handed over the sketches he and Neva had made. "We found something interesting." He led her to the bodies through the path they had searched and cleared. "Notice anything funny?"

Diane scrutinized the corpse in front of her, tuning out the aroma of decaying flesh. She looked at the hands tied at the wrist, well on their way to becoming skeletonized.

"Well, damn," she said.

The killer had cut off the fingertips, leaving an open wound for the flies to lay their eggs and the maggots to infest quickly. The flesh on the hands was eaten away before the rest of the body.

"Damn's right," said Jin. "No chance of getting prints."

"I suppose the others are the same."

"Yes. Lots of good opportunities for getting something from the ropes, though. I'd like to watch you examine them. Been wanting to learn to do that."

"Finding anything on the ground?"

"Lots of bugs. David's got quite a collection. That's about all so far."

Neva stood up from the farthest grid square from Diane. "I have something here."

Diane crossed the grids that had already been searched and stooped to see what Neva had discovered.

"It's just a rope," she said, "but . . . well, there's a lot of rope here, and . . ."

The rope had been covered in leaves and lay in a loose tangle on the ground. It was hemp, like the death ropes, had no knots and showed signs of chafing in several places.

"This is good," said Diane. "The killer might have dropped it. Take a picture of it, do a sketch, but let me take it up."

"Sure."

"When you sketch it, take note of how the rope crosses itself."

Neva nodded. "David and Jin said you do forensic knot analysis. I've never heard of that."

"It comes in handy. It's amazing how many you run across in criminal investigations."

"Can you really find out anything from knots?"

"You can make some good guesses about the person who tied them. How good he is at tying knots, perhaps what kind of job or hobby he's had."

"I always thought a knot was a knot."

"Oh, no, there's a specific knot for every purpose. Some are commonly used, and some are rare."

"This rope doesn't have any knots in it. Will you be able to tell anything from it?"

"I doubt it, but you never know. There might be

bloodstains or fibers on it that'll give us information. If we're lucky, we might be able to find out where it came from. It's a good find."

Neva nodded. "I was afraid it might be just trash."

"There's no such thing as 'just trash' at a crime scene."

After Neva photographed the rope, she lay a grid over it and began drawing a sketch of it onto the graph paper.

Diane stepped out of the crime scene and walked around the perimeter toward David. She noticed that Neva occasionally cast nervous glances in her direction. Neva was a friend of Janice Warrick. Warrick's mishandling of the Boone family crime scene had resulted in her demotion in the Rosewood police department, a demotion that was blamed on Diane by almost everyone in the department.

"How's it going?" she asked David.

"We're ready to take them down."

He stood in the cleared area under the corpses, looking like he was about to be hanged himself. Diane understood. She hated this part—placing once living people into body bags.

Chapter 5

The only other time Diane had been in a hot autopsy room was in the South American jungle. Dr. Lynn Webber's lab in the regional medical center was stifling. The smell of death weighed over the room like a heavy blanket of rotting flesh. The metal tables, white glass-door cabinets, appliances and tools that went so well with the usual chill of the autopsy room looked out of place and dreadful here. Diane wanted to back out of the overwhelming stench and heat and go someplace else.

Through a window on the opposite side of the main lab Diane could see the isolation room designed for the autopsy of badly decomposed and infectious bodies. The diener, servant to the dead, stood by a table occupied by one of the hanging victims—extended on a shiny metal table, neck curved around the torso so that the head sat beside the shoulder.

Lynn was in her office on the phone, the door open. Her voice carried out to the autopsy room.

"I asked you two days ago to come fix the air conditioner." Pause. "I don't care if it's the vents, not the unit. The temperature is too high in here. I have dead bodies rotting on my tables. No amount of lemon juice is ever going to get the smell out of my hair."

Lynn tapped a pencil on a pad of paper as she listened. "I don't care if *both* your ankles are sprained. A man your age has got no business being on Rollerblades. Let me remind you that I'm a woman who knows how to kill and leave no evidence to show up in the autopsy. I want this problem fixed, and I don't mean tomorrow."

She hung up the phone and walked out into the lab. "I hate to talk to maintenance men. It's like talking to a blackmailer. They know they've got you by the balls."

She motioned toward suits of protective gear lying on the countertop. The two of them slipped on lab coats, face shields and gloves and entered the isolation lab.

The room had two tables, shiny metal rectangles atop bright white cabinets. Between the two tables hung scales for weighing organs. Across the room stood a series of cabinets, metal countertops and sinks. Everything sparkled, from the glossy blue floor to the metal surfaces—everything except the blackened corpse with stiff blond hair and an exceptionally long neck.

"I was so happy to get this new containment room. But it's been one problem after another."

"Can't the hospital administration do anything?" asked Diane.

"You're talking about Jack the Bean Counter." She sighed. "I'm sorry it's so unbearable in here. Right now we have to keep working and put up with it."

"My grandma found somebody hanging like this when she was a girl," said the diener. "Neck all long like a snake. She took it as a sign."

"A sign of what?" asked Diane.

"That she and her family should move to Atlanta."

"Did they?"

"Sure 'nuff, they did." He started toward the door, taking off his face shield. "I'll be right back."

Diane and Lynn watched the lean young black man walk out of the room.

"I never ask Raymond what he's doing when he gets that blank look on his face." Lynn shrugged, then shifted gears. "I'd like to start with the clothes. We'll have to cut the sleeves, but I'd like to inspect the body before the hands are untied."

The material was stiff and hard to cut. Maggots dropped from the body to the metal surface of the table as they worked. They were putting the clothes in a bag when the diener came back in. He put on his gloves and took the bag of evidence.

"I'll label. What we calling the body?"

"Blue," said Diane.

"Blue," said Raymond. "I guess that's as good a name as any."

"When we cut them down, we tied blue, red or green cord around both cut ends of the rope so we could match the ropes again after they were separated." Diane pointed to the blue string wrapped around the end of the rope that marked it and kept it from unraveling.

The noose was still tight around the neck, sunk deep into the flesh under the chin. Diane would hate for any family member to ever see their loved one like this. They would never be able to think of their relative again without seeing this image. She stood back and watched as Lynn and her diener tended to the painstaking external examination of the body.

Lynn talked into a hanging microphone as she described what they found. "The victim appears to be a female at this point . . ."

A pounding on the window startled Diane. The three of them looked up to see a man in his thirties standing in the outer autopsy room, looking through the window at them. He was dressed in gray trousers, white shirt and floral tie, holding a hand over his mouth and nose. Lynn flipped the intercom switch.

"What's going on in here?" he said. "Step out here for a minute."

"I'm in the middle of an important examination, Jackson. What do you want?"

Jackson bent over and gagged. "Why does it smell so bad in here?"

The three of them looked at Jackson with their eyebrows raised enough to make deep furrows in their foreheads.

"We have a rotting corpse on the table," said Lynn. "It would be a little better if the air-conditioning system were working, but it's not."

"The air conditioner is working in the rest of the building."

Lynn glared at him for a moment before she spoke. "Well, it's not working in here. What brings you here anyway? I don't think I've ever seen you visit the autopsy room."

"I was talking to a patron when this . . . this . . . horrific odor came into my office."

"The maintenance man said it's a problem with the vents. You'll have to talk to him."

"He's home sick." As Jackson spoke, he breathed through his mouth and tried holding his nose.

"Surely he's not the only person the hospital employs who can fix air conditioning."

"He's the only one who can look into this. We've had an injudicious use of vacation time, and the other man who does this kind of work is out of town."

"Then you'll have to call in someone from outside the hospital."

"We don't have the money."

"Then we'll have to put up with the smell until Marlon gets back."

"This is impossible."

"No," said Lynn. "Just difficult."

"I'll see what I can do." He hurried out of the lab. The door slammed behind him.

"Bean counter?" asked Diane.

"That's him. I won't ask you what you did, Raymond."

"That'd be best, Ma'am."

"Yes, well, getting back to Blue. We gave the clothes an initial inspection before you got here," said Lynn, speaking to Diane. "It's hard to tell, but the coveralls look relatively new."

"From Sears," said Raymond.

"Maybe at your lab you'll be able to pick up some more information," said Lynn.

"How'd a crime lab in a museum come about anyway?" Raymond asked Diane as he rolled the body over while Lynn held the head and neck.

"The Rosewood Police Department made me an offer I couldn't refuse."

"Uh huh," said Raymond.

"The city and county assessed the museum's property value so high it couldn't pay the taxes. The mayor and chief of detectives suggested that if we would operate a new crime scene evidence laboratory in the museum for the city, the city would arrange for the money from the real estate taxes paid to be returned to the museum for services rendered."

"Sounds to me a great deal like extortion," Lynn said.

"A deal with the devil," Raymond said.

"*Collaborative partnership* is the operative term."

"Yeah, we get that all the time here too," Lynn said. "Whenever I hear that, I know my money is about to be cut and my workload increased. Makes me want to gag more than this smell."

"From the mayor's point of view, it's a perfect solution. They get a new crime lab, and we get to keep the museum and the taxes we can't afford to pay. As an added bonus, they send us one of their employees."

"That would be Neva?" asked Lynn.

"She's kind of caught in the middle. She's not to blame."

"So, your forensic anthropology unit was swallowed up by the city's crime lab?"

"No. I wouldn't stand for that. The crime lab is separate. Half my salary and that of my forensic staff is paid by the city to operate their crime lab. It takes a team of accountants to do the paperwork. The one big downside of it is that on paper, I and a chunk of my staff are part-time employees of the city. Sometimes the mayor and the chief of police forget that it's only on paper."

"Bureaucracies are certainly wonderful," said Lynn. "I think I've found something on the ankle here—some kind of tattoo."

Diane walked over and took a look at the blackened skin with a barely visible darker design.

"I see it," said Raymond. "Can't tell what it is. Want me to get the lamp?"

"I think we have enough slippage so we don't have to burn off the skin. Get me a damp piece of gauze."

Raymond fetched the gauze and gave it to Lynn. Diane watched her gently rub the skin, removing a film of epidermis, revealing what looked like a yellow, blue and red butterfly.

"Nice," said Raymond.

"Let's go ahead and get a picture of this—use the large-format camera," said Lynn.

Raymond retrieved his Horseman VH Metal Field Camera from a closet.

"I want a close-up, and another that shows the entire ankle."

Lynn and Diane watched Raymond remove the bulky camera from the overhead mount and place it on a tripod. He put a metal ruler just under the tattoo, framed the shot and snapped the first picture. He moved in for a close-up. "Okay, you want some digital too?"

Lynn nodded. "Just to play it safe."

"Dr. Webber never expects pictures to come out."

"It's because I'm such a poor photographer," she said.

Diane retrieved more blue cord and a strip of plastic from her case while Raymond snapped photographs of the butterfly tattoo, duplicated all his shots with a digital backup, and filled out the photo log.

"Diane, I assume you want any internal insects when I go inside."

"Yes. If you think she may have been sexually assaulted, any larvae around the vagina might be useful."

"How's that?" asked Raymond.

"A rapist's DNA can show up in the maggots who have ingested it."

Raymond laughed out loud, a deep-throated laugh as if that was a joke played on the perp.

"Diane, why don't you go ahead and remove the rope. I really need to get her arms untied so I can go inside."

"Can Raymond make photographs of the process?"

"Sure."

"There's two ropes around the neck," Diane explained as Raymond set up her shots. "The noose and another loop of rope that leads down to the hands. If she moved around too much trying to free her hands, she'd only choke herself."

"Umpf," the diener grunted. "You want all the knots, right?"

"Yes, and I need you to show how the ropes around the hands and the neck are connected. You may have to angle the camera to see down through these loops on the hands to get a good view. It looks like the perp used multiple knots. Have you had much experience photographing knots?"

"None," said Raymond. "No, that's not right. There was that suicide that came in last winter. We don't usually see the rope."

"I need you to photograph me removing the rope. I need to have a record showing that the knots did not change as a result of my intervention."

"How 'bout I use the thirty-five millimeter for that."

"That's fine."

Diane began with the noose. First, tying the plastic around the knot to stabilize it. After securing the knot, she pulled the rope away from the skin, bringing bits of flesh with it. She slipped one end of the cord under the rope and tied it off. Three inches away she tied the other end of the cord around a section of rope. Each end of the cord had a tag that Diane labeled, indicating how the rope was oriented to the victim. As she worked, she heard Raymond snapping the camera over and over.

She cut the noose with a sharp scalpel. She slipped the noose off over the head. She placed the rope in a flat box and stuffed more plastic inside to hold it still and labeled it. She repeated the step with the second loop around the neck.

"You have to do that procedure with each loop of the rope, don't you?" said Lynn.

"I have to keep the rope as intact as I can. For tight rope arrangements like these on the hands, I made a plastic-covered, log-shaped form to slip through the loops to keep them from becoming tangled."

"I didn't realize ropes were so involved," said Raymond.

"There's a lot you can learn about the perp from them. This one is going to be more complicated," said Diane as she examined the ropes. "This guy knew his knots." She grinned up at Lynn and Raymond. "I love it when they know how to tie knots."

Chapter 6

"You really like analyzing knots, don't you?" said Lynn, her eyes widened in a puzzled stare.

Diane saw that reaction a lot—a knot is just a knot to most people. "Yeah, I do. They've saved my life more than once."

"How's that?" asked Raymond.

"I'm a caver. We rely on ropes and knots."

"Really?" said Lynn. "Have you explored many caves?"

"Quite a few. Not many in Georgia, even though I grew up here. But one of my employees at the museum is introducing me to some of the Georgia caves."

"I've always wanted to see the one in Mexico with all the crystals," Lynn said.

"The one on the Discovery Channel, right?" said Raymond. "It didn't look real, all those white crystals."

"The cave is called Lechuguilla," said Diane. "The formation you're talking about is the Crystal Ballroom."

"Yeah, that's it."

"Those are gypsum crystals. They're even more impressive in person."

"You've been there?" asked Lynn.

"Yes, I have. A couple of microbiologist friends invited me to go on an expedition with them. It's a protected cave. I was lucky to get the chance."

"It appears to be very beautiful," said Lynn.

"Stunning." Diane looked down at the decayed husk that used to house a young woman. "The line of work I'm in, it's very rejuvenating to be able to look at something so breathtakingly beautiful."

"What about this knot?" asked Raymond. "Is it something special?"

"It's a handcuff knot."

"Handcuff knot? I don't like the sound of that," he said.

"It's good as a handcuff and for hobbling horses. Our perp added a little twist. He took the working line and wrapped it around the vic's hands, tucking the end through the loops. I guess he didn't want her wiggling her fingers."

"Easier to cut them off," said Raymond. "Did he do that while they were alive?"

"I don't know," said Lynn. "I'm not sure I'll be able to tell."

"I think I can secure the outer loops without cutting them, but I'll have to cut the loops on the handcuffs," said Diane.

She took a blue cord and secured all the loops together and tagged each one. She treated each loop around the wrist in the same way she handled the noose around the neck—tying them off before cutting the loop free.

"It's like cutting an umbilical cord," said Lynn.

As Diane slid the rope free, a cool breeze eased through the autopsy room.

"I don't believe it," said Lynn. "They got someone to fix whatever was wrong."

"Just needed a little motivation," said Raymond.

"Oh, it feels good," said Lynn. She took in a deep breath, as if the cool air made everything smell better. "Let's get this done. What do you say, Raymond?"

She turned to Diane. "I hope you don't mind me running you off to the other room. I like to have as few people as possible in the room when I'm working on a body this decomposed."

"Believe me, I don't mind. I'll take these ropes back to the lab and start my team working on them, and then I'll come back. Do you intend to do the other two victims today?"

"I'd like to try. Raymond and I will collect the insect samples."

As Diane was going out the door, Lynn started the Y incision.

RiverTrail Museum of Natural History was housed in a beautiful gothic three-story granite structure that began its life as a museum in the late 1800s. The building was converted into a private medical clinic in the 1940s, and was now converted back to a museum. It had large rooms with Romanesque moldings, polished granite floors and rare wall-sized murals of dinosaurs painted at a time when everyone thought the huge animals dragged their tails behind them.

Diane had a sense of peace as director of the museum. It was a place of scholarship, learning and fun—and she ruled. Thanks to the late founder, there were no bureaucrats between her and what she wanted to do for the museum. It was idyllic, a dream career. She couldn't imagine going back into forensics—working with death and evil in places where evil won often and was rarely punished. But she'd found, oddly enough, after helping Frank Duncan find justice for his murdered friends, that she enjoyed the hunt, the puzzle. Good thing too, for it kept the wolves from the ornate wood doors of the museum.

It was 10:00 A.M. when Diane carried the evidence from Lynn Webber's autopsy lab to her crime lab on the third floor of the museum.

"Start on the clothes," she told Jin. "Wait on the rope. I'll bring more clothing and insect specimens later."

"Sure thing." Jin took the boxes and attached crime lab tracking labels to them. He and Diane signed the labels, and he locked the boxes away. "This is a big case. People are talking about it."

"We're going to be watched closely on this one. Both the mayor of Rosewood and the chief of detectives are going to be riding us pretty hard."

"We'll be brilliant. I'll start on the clothes right away. We can have some results for the sheriff by the end of the day."

Only a couple of technicians were in the lab, filling out papers. David's insect-rearing chambers sat in environmentally controlled containers in the entomology work space.

"David and the others in the field?" she asked.

"You know how he likes to take a final walk-through. He's got Neva with him. You've got her very nervous."

"I have?"

"She said you're the one who got Detective Janice Warrick demoted last year."

"Not me. Janice botched a case and contaminated

a crime scene. She's responsible for her own career situation."

"I guess Neva only knows what she's heard in the police department."

"How's she doing?"

"She's scared all the time."

"Of me?"

"You, but mostly the chief of detectives. Afraid she's going to screw up. She didn't want this job. He assigned her to it." Jin shrugged, clearly not understanding why anyone wouldn't want a plum job like this one. "David's got her out now. Showing her how to look for things. David's a good guy."

"Yes, he is." Diane didn't like hearing that about Neva. This was the kind of case they couldn't mess up. "I'm going to check in with the museum, then I'm going back to the autopsy."

Jin nodded. "Want me to have David call you?"

"No. I'll talk with him later."

"When you analyze the rope, I want to watch. I've never done that."

"You know anything about knots?"

"I was a Boy Scout."

"Can you tie knots?"

"Sure . . . some."

"Go to the museum library and get a book on knots. Study the types."

Diane left and went down to the first floor. The museum had been open for an hour and was filled with summer school students on a field trip. Loud excited chatter swept out of the dinosaur room as she passed it on the way to her office.

When she reached the main foyer, it was not the mixture of excitement from children and admonitions from teachers that caught her attention. It was the wooden anthropoid coffin lying on its back on a large metal cart next to the information desk.

Diane walked over to the large mummy case in the shape of a human figure and looked over at Jennifer on duty in the information station.

"They brought it in about an hour ago."

"They?"

"Some guys. Kendel—uh, Ms. Williams was with them."

At that moment a line of students with two adults at each end came into the museum.

"We're from the Rosewood Summer Library Program," one of the adults announced to Jennifer and then turned and cautioned the children—five girls and three boys—to stay together. They weren't listening. Their attention had immediately focused on the coffin.

"Is there a real mummy inside there?" asked a little girl.

That's what I'd like to know, thought Diane.

Jennifer, dressed in black slacks and a museum tee-shirt, stepped from the booth and greeted them. She nodded her head vigorously.

"Yes, there is. It just arrived, and it will be going up to our conservation lab. We're all very excited. We believe it's from the twelfth dynasty in Egypt. That was about four thousand years ago."

Jennifer was more forthcoming to the children than to Diane. That seemed to be one of her characteristics. She was good with children, somewhat absent with adults.

"Can we see him?" asked a blond curly-haired boy of about eight.

The docent arrived before Jennifer had to answer,

taking charge of the group in a way that was both firm and kind. The herd of children, pulling the adults behind them, skipped and bounced out of sight on the first leg of their tour.

Diane turned back to Jennifer. "What's this?" she began, just as Kendel Williams came through the double doors leading from the administrative offices.

Kendel had fine brown hair turned under in a 1940s style, cut to a length just above the padded shoulders of her gray tailored suit. She had brown eyes, straight posture, and a soft voice. Ladylike was how Andie had described her to Diane when Kendel had come to interview for the position of assistant director.

In looks and manner Kendel was the opposite of Diane—soft where Diane was hard. One of the things she had liked about Kendel was that her looks were deceptive. Like all the applicants, she had several years' of experience in upper museum administration. What Diane had discovered in the interview and from the people she called for references was that Kendal was tough when it came to championing her museum and acquiring holdings. What's more, Kendel knew museum culture.

That was a strength Diane didn't have. She understood the museum's structure and administration, but she was also an outsider among those career museum people who had come up through the ranks. Diane had been plucked from the technical field of forensic anthropology and hired as director. She knew that some people inside the museum culture resented that.

The relationships among museums were a mixture of intense competition and helpful collaboration. Kendel was familiar with most of the major museums and how they worked and who she could work with. Diane liked her. She'd never asked Kendel how she felt about snakes.

"Dr. Fallon," she said breathlessly, "I'm so sorry about yesterday morning. I don't usually go off like that."

"It's all right. I understand that you didn't expect to find a snake coiled up in your desk drawer the second day on the job."

The elusive museum snake had made a rare appearance—unfortunately, in Kendel's desk drawer—giving Diane another opportunity to rue the day she had told the herpetologists they could create a terrarium for live snakes.

"Only nonpoisonous snakes," she had told them. "And make sure the terrarium is escape proof."

At least they were able to keep one of her conditions. It was a harmless black snake that escaped. The only ones who ever ran across it were people who wouldn't think of trying to catch it. The herpetologist and his assistants hadn't even caught a glimpse of it.

Kendel was quickly followed by Andie Layne, Diane's assistant; Jonas Briggs, staff archaeologist; and Korey Jordan, head conservator. They gathered with Diane around the mummy case.

Diane looked at Andie. "I seem to remember saying something about not wanting to see any orders for mummies come across my desk."

Andie's Orphan Annie curly brown-red hair bounced as she laughed. "And you won't. This is a donation."

"Nice," said Korey. He placed a gloved hand on the case. "This is in good condition. Can't wait to see inside it." His white teeth were bright against his brown skin.

"It's from a James Lionel-Kirk," said Kendel. "Lionel-Kirk inherited it from his father in New York around twenty years ago. His father had inherited it from his grandfather in England, who inherited it from his father, we think. We're working provenance now."

"Is there anything in it?"

Jonas Briggs answered. Retired from Bartram University in Rosewood, and now the museum's only archaeologist, he had been the first to express a desire for an exhibit on Egyptology. At the moment, he was beaming. "There is indeed. There is a mummy inside."

"A mummy."

All nodded their heads vigorously. "We can't be sure it's the mummy that belongs with the case," Kendel warned. "At the time this was acquired, mummies were a popular tourist item and the Egyptian sellers did some mixing and matching of mummy cases and mummies."

"He's apparently unwrapped," said Jonas. "We think he—or she—was the centerpiece of a Victorian mummy unwrapping party. They were all the rage at one time."

"You're kidding."

"Not at all," said Kendel. "The guests would sit around and watch the host unwrap a mummy. We're lucky this one survived. Most from unwrapping parties were burnt as firewood."

"We were just about to take it up to the conservation lab and have a look," said Korey.

Diane motioned toward the elevator. "By all means. Let's have a look at our mummy."

Chapter 7

The conservation laboratory on the second floor was spacious, containing six shiny metal worktables, each with a microscope and a large swivel-mounted magnifying glass and light. Cabinets filled with chemicals used in conserving fragile objects of wood, paper, fabric, metal, and bone lined the walls. There were a fume hood, sinks, and more microscopes on the countertops. From the ceiling hung the framework for mounting cameras.

It was a cool, shiny, clean room managed by Korey. Three of his assistants were seated at tables, busy at work.

Across from the lab was the X-ray room, complete with used endoscopy and low level X-ray equipment—Korey's newest babies that he'd found at a medical surplus auction.

They wheeled the mummy case past the tables into the temperature- and humidity-controlled storage vault in the back of the lab. The small room was crowded with the five of them and the mummy. They all gathered around the case of heavy wood and inlay and lifted it onto a worktable.

"We'll lay the lid on the table," said Korey. "I checked it when it came in. It's not sealed. Okay, on three."

It was heavier than Diane had suspected but manageable as the five of them lifted the top off and laid it aside.

"Oh, this is nice," said Jonas as they looked into the coffin.

The mummy, a mixture of brown, red and dark gray, looked as if it had been fashioned from resin. The face was especially well preserved. The skin appeared as though it were pulled tight, and the outline of bones and ligaments could be seen under the flesh. The brow ridge and jawline looked male.

The arms were crossed over the chest. On its legs were piles of yellow-brown wrappings that looked like a bundle of well-worn rags.

"Other than some patches of fungi, he looks really good," said Korey.

"He does, doesn't he?" agreed Kendel.

"It's a *he*?" asked Andie.

"I believe so," said Diane.

"A pharaoh?" she asked.

"I doubt it," said Diane.

"We may never know," said Kendel. "However, his hands are crossed. That's significant."

"It is, indeed," agreed Jonas.

"How is that significant?" asked Andie.

"It's a royal burial position," said Jonas. "Plus he had a top-notch embalming job done on himself."

Andie rubbed her hands together. "I'll bet we got ourselves a king."

"Arrange a CT scan at the hospital," said Diane.

They all looked at one another, sharing the excitement, both surprised and pleased that Diane had decided to spring for the expense of a scan.

"Korey, you'll have to package him so he doesn't contaminate the hospital," Diane said.

"I can do that. I'll take care of any infestations first, then we'll wrap him in plastic wrap on a board."

"Plastic wrap?" said Andie.

"Sure. He'll be wrapped up like a mummy."

A groan from Andie. "Oh, please."

"We'll need tissue samples for dating and other analysis," said Diane. "Jonas, I'll depend on your knowledge of embalming techniques for the various dynasties to help us narrow in on the time and place of origin for this guy."

"Already been collecting my references," he said.

"Korey, let me know when you set up the scan." Diane left them excitedly discussing the mummy and headed for her office.

She sat down behind her desk, closed her eyes and listened to the water bubbling over the rocks of the fountain decorating the side table in her office. She had designed and constructed the fountain to remind her of the inside of a cave. When she closed her eyes and listened, she was in some deep dark grotto. She could almost feel the cool of the rock around her—the perfect peace.

"Damn, I'm sorry to disturb you."

Diane opened her eyes. Peace was always short-lived. "Mike. Can I help you?"

Mike Seger, graduate assistant to the geology curator, pulled up a chair and laid a folder on her desk. "Saw your interview on TV last night," Mike said

"Last night? Interview?"

"About the bodies in the woods."

"I didn't give an interview."

"It looked like file footage taken at the official opening of the crime lab. You talked about justice, the objectivity of evidence, the evil of murder—"

"Great. My mailbox will be filled with more complaints about the crime lab being in the museum."

A handful of people—including a few on her board—objected to having something as tawdry as a crime lab in the pristine learning environment of the museum, and they liked to E-mail her about it, having somehow gotten her private E-mail address.

From the look of her mail, she was right. Amid E-mail from various members of her staff was some from people she recognized as dissenters.

"I have photographs of the model in progress," Mike said. "Of the Journey to the Center of the Earth exhibit."

"Have you shown it to Kendel?"

"Yes. But since it was your idea . . ."

Mike's light brown eyes glittered with what looked to Diane like mischief. She processed her E-mail as Mike laid out photographs of the model he and the exhibit designers were constructing.

There was a message from a man who lamented that everywhere he turned there was forensics—books, movies, TV networks, learning channels, and darn it all, now his museum. And an E-mail from a woman who insisted Diane resign rather than serve two masters—the sublime and the grotesque. Another one began with something about an eye for an eye, and what did a museum director know about evil? And several wanted her to include the crime lab on the museum tour. She hesitated a moment, wondering whether to forward the messages to Andie for reply, or simply delete. She deleted all of them.

Mike was enthusiastic as he arranged the photos.

"It'll look just like they're descending through layers of the earth. It will be especially cool when they get to the fossil layer."

"This is what I had in mind," she said. "I like it."

"I thought perhaps we could discuss it over dinner sometime."

"If the exhibit designer would like to, you don't need my permission. You can meet anywhere you want."

Mike grinned broadly. For a moment she thought his teeth actually sparkled.

He leaned forward with his forearms on her desk. "That wasn't exactly what I had in mind."

"No?"

"I thought you and I could discuss it."

"I haven't the time or the inclination to micromanage the exhibits. Most of my people know their jobs. I like to leave them alone."

"All right, I can handle that. How about going caving?" He gave her a one-sided dimpled smile and pulled a folded paper from his shirt pocket and handed her a list. "These are some good caves to start with. Some of us from the Bartram Caving Club's been to all of them."

Diane read the list. Blowing Cave, Climax Caverns, Glory Hole Caverns, Kingston Saltpeter Cave Preserve. She cocked an eyebrow. "You're kidding."

"What?" He took the list and studied it for several seconds before he burst out laughing. "I didn't name them."

"Which one do you suggest we start with?"

"Glory Hole Cavern's really beautiful but not a lot of fun for someone who hasn't had much experience. Didn't you say one of your crime crew wants to come along?"

"Neva Hurley. She's visited caves as a tourist, and a few as an explorer, but she doesn't have much experience."

"Climax is a good cave. Great geology. Lots of fossils. The front rooms are pretty easy. It gets harder farther in."

"Where is it?"

"Near the Florida border."

"Anything closer?"

"There is a cave I've been interested in visiting." He stuffed the list back in his pocket. "It's not easy to get the owner to allow people in. It's a big cave and not too hard, I've heard. Some of the deeper rooms and tunnels are for experienced cavers. It also has some good geology. It's only twenty miles from here."

"Do you think you could get permission?"

"Yeah, I think so. A guy in my caving club is tight with the man who manages the property. We'll have to take him."

"That's fine. Do you know if it's been mapped?"

"Some of the tunnels, but I haven't seen the maps. You thinking about mapping it?"

"If it's an interesting cave and hasn't been mapped, yes. That'd be fun."

"I'll let you know something in a couple of days." Mike stood up and started for the door, hesitated, smiled, turned again and went out the door.

Diane looked through the papers Andie had left on her desk. Nothing that couldn't wait. She needed to get back to the autopsies.

Chapter 8

The diener was placing another of Diane's bodies on the table when she reentered the autopsy containment room, suited, masked and gloved, her hair under a plastic cap. The rooms were cool now, the odors manageable, the way they should be.

This victim was called Green, after the color of cord Diane had used to secure the ends of the cut hanging rope. Green had hung fifteen feet from Blue.

Lynn and Raymond were chatting away about the Braves as they cut away the clothing. The only part of the conversation Diane understood was Raymond saying, "Unh unh, ain't no way."

Lynn looked up and nodded as Diane approached. "This one is about the same age as Blue," she said. "I'd say in his early twenties, maybe late teens."

"Too young to die," said Raymond.

"We have some insect specimens for you from Blue." Lynn motioned toward the counter where several jars sat. "We collected live larvae as well as dead husks. Raymond enjoys that sort of thing, don't you, Raymond?"

"You going to hatch those bugs?" asked Raymond.

"That's the only way the entomologist can be certain about the species of the larva and how long the life cycle is. It'll help fix the time of death."

"They haven't been there long. I'd say just a couple of weeks, from the rate of decay," said Lynn.

"They were hanging off the ground," said Diane.

"Shouldn't make that much of a difference," said Lynn.

This was the first time Diane had cause to question Lynn's competence. But she didn't say anything, remembering that earlier on at the crime scene Lynn had shown a sensitivity to being contradicted or outshown.

However, to be fair, it takes experience with hanging victims to realize that it can indeed make much of a difference. Rate of decay is highly dependent on the environment. Bodies decay differently in Alaska than in Hawaii, or the Sahara, or Portobelo. And they decay differently out in the open, or hanging, or sealed in an enclosed space, or buried shallow, or buried deep, or buried in a limestone environment. It also makes a difference if they have open wounds, such as the cutoff fingertips.

It's a matter of the body tissues being accessible to the insects and microbes that cause decay. And the presence of chemicals or elements that interfere with microbial and insect action by causing the body to dehydrate or to become preserved.

There are so many permutations and combinations that unless you've had experience with them all, there is no way to just know. Had these bodies been discovered at a later date and had Red, the corpse Diane witnessed fall, lain on the ground where the insects could get to him, he would appear to have died earlier than the others, even though their time of death might be the same.

Diane thought of explaining, but it would just sound like a lecture, it would offend Lynn's sensitivity and it would make Lynn look bad in front of Raymond. She'd simply use what information David collected from his reared insects and make her estimates of the time of death.

Diane removed the rope from Green the same way she had from the first victim. Raymond took the photographs. Green was tied in exactly the same way as Blue—hands behind the back in a handcuff knot with the standing end of the rope in a loop around the neck and the extra rope from the working end wrapped four times around the wrists with the end tucked between the loops.

The noose was tied the same way as on the first— a bowline to make a loop to pull the rope through to create a noose that tightens under tension. She hadn't expected the knots to be any different, and they weren't. She carefully packed and labeled the rope.

"I was wondering if you would take me caving sometime," said Lynn. "A simple cave for a rank beginner."

"Neva wants to go caving too. She's also a beginner. We should be able to find a good starter cave we can go to."

Lynn grinned. "I have always loved caves, underground lakes, all those things. One of my favorite movies is *Journey to the Center of the Earth*. Loved that underground lake."

"Caving's not usually that eventful," said Diane. Both Raymond and Lynn laughed.

"You wouldn't catch me going down a black hole," said Raymond. "Heard about too many people getting themselves stuck. You sprain your ankle and it's hell trying to get you out."

"You learn to be careful," Diane said. "Knowing your ropes and knots helps too."

"I think he's had his appendix out," said Lynn. She rubbed the area with a damp piece of gauze. "Let's get a photograph of this, Raymond. Have you ever had to be rescued?" she asked Diane.

"No, but I have been on a rescue team. It can be a dicey situation, for certain." Diane collected several surface specimens of insects while Lynn and Raymond continued the external examination of the body.

Green was male. Taller than the woman, though it would be hard to tell exactly until Diane could measure the bones. Now, from his head to his feet his stretch length was eight feet seven inches.

"Other than the appendix scar, there are no visible external markings. No needle marks or signs of defensive wounds that are visible." Lynn talked into the recorder in a monotone voice, quite different from her conversational tone.

Lynn didn't run Diane out for the autopsy this time. Diane stayed and continued to collect insect specimens.

At the crime scene and on the bodies a full range of insects were present—insects that feed on flesh, and insects that fed on the flesh-eating insects. The only kind she didn't see were the ground beetles that feed on dried flesh. All the dried flesh was hanging well out of their reach.

Lynn made the Y incision and pulled back the flaps of tissue, increasing the putrid smell in the room. Lynn was petite, even looked delicate next to the autopsy table, but she had no problem cutting away the chest plate, gaining her access to the block of organs.

"You know," said Lynn, "I really prefer fresh bodies."

Diane had to agree as she watched Lynn and Raymond locate the subclavian and carotid arteries.

"Go ahead and tie them off, Raymond—if you can.

I'm getting a lot more decay in this one than the Blue girl. Let's get these organs out and, Diane, you're welcome to any insects you can find."

Raymond did most of the cutting to remove the organs and took them to the other autopsy table for Lynn to examine. There were very few insect larva in the chest cavity, but Diane found several good specimens in the lower abdomen.

"Go ahead and get at the brain," Lynn told Raymond. "I hope it's not mush."

As Lynn examined the organs, Diane told them about the unexpected mummy.

"So he just kind of showed up on your doorstep?" said Raymond. "Now, that's cool. Dr. Lynn, I'm going to cut the neck, if you can . . . never mind, I think I can manage it. These long necks are a mess to deal with, I'm telling you."

"So you'll be opening an Egyptian exhibit?" asked Lynn.

"At some point perhaps. We've got a lot of research to do before then."

"Oh, this fellow had a heart condition," said Lynn.

Diane looked over her shoulder at the darkened heart Lynn had opened up.

"See here?" Lynn pointed her scalpel at a valve. "He had a mitral valve prolapse. You know," she turned her head toward Diane, "this might show up in his bones."

"You think it may be associated with skeletal abnormalities?"

"It's observed in about two-thirds of patients with this condition."

"Would he have been under a physician's care?" asked Diane.

"It's not severe, so he may have been basically asymptomatic. That's not uncommon. He may have had to take antibiotics when he had dental work."

The sound of the Stryker saw was of short duration. Raymond was skilled. The sound of the calvarium being removed didn't have the characteristic pop of a fresh body.

"Pretty soft," said Raymond. "We may be able to fix it."

Out of the corner of her eye Diane saw him carefully remove the jellylike brain and put it in a jar of formalin.

Little by little they were collecting bits of information about the victims—tattoos, scars, bad heart valve. There was a good chance that all these things would add up to a critical mass of information leading them to the identity of the victims.

Surely, someone was missing these people—unless they were the lost people, the invisible class that slips through the cracks and becomes easy prey for killers.

It was almost 9:30 P.M. by the time they finished the third autopsy and Diane arrived at the museum with the evidence for her crime lab. David was there, taking notes and checking on his insects.

"I called the weather bureau. It's been pretty redundant for the past couple months—dry and hot. I've duplicated the environment for my babies here." He pointed to his rearing chambers.

"Here's some more insects. Larva and bug parts." She handed them over and began logging in the clothing and rope she had collected from the autopsies.

"Discover anything new?" David asked.

Diane sat down in a chair and stretched out her legs in front of her. "Some. Right now the vics all look to be in their twenties. Blue is a female and has a tattoo of a butterfly on her ankle. Green's a male. He's had his appendix out and has a heart condition. Not serious. Red's another female. She has a tattoo of a hummingbird on the right side of her lower back and another one of a rose on the upper part of her left breast."

"Good tattoos?"

Diane thought a moment. "Yeah, they are. Very intricate."

"Expensive, then."

"Could be."

David ran his hands through what was left of his hair—a thick curly fringe around his head. "That'll help."

"Did you happen to find any fingertips?" Diane asked him. "None of the bodies had theirs."

"Nope. We did find where a truck was parked. From the cable marks on the tree branches, I'd say he hoisted them up with a winch."

"How's Neva doing? Jin said you took her out for a walk-through."

He wavered his hand from side to side. "She's about fifty-fifty. Hasn't decided if she likes this work yet. They just assigned her here, you know, didn't ask her if she wanted it. But she's no different than any other newbie I've trained."

"How are you doing?" asked Diane.

"You don't have to watch me. I'm not going to self-destruct."

"I'm not worried about your sanity, just your happiness."

David Goldstein had shown up literally on Diane's doorstep, asking for a job. The massacre of their friends at the mission in South America had left him, like her, on the edge of sanity—burnt out and with no place to go. Diane's loss of her daughter had so overwhelmed her she didn't really see the grief the others were feeling from losing their friends. David was adrift when he arrived in Rosewood. Diane was glad to be able to give him a job. It surprised her that he requested to work in her new crime lab.

"Are you sure you want to do that?" she had asked him. "Don't you want to get away from everything we've seen?"

"Don't you?" It was a reasonable question. "Diane—you know how it was. You stand in those concrete rooms splattered with dark stains you know are going to be blood, and you look at the shackles and dirty rusted tables and you know that no matter how many people you interview, how many depositions you get, those responsible will never be put on trial. Most of the time, the best we could hope for was to have some poor schmuck arrested who was just guarding the place.

"But this here . . . a big percentage of the time, we'll bring the killers to justice. I need to do that. Bring killers to justice. I need to know that what I'm doing will make a difference."

"Our record out there was a little better than that," Diane had whispered almost to herself, but she knew what he meant. Rarely did they get to the top of the food chain.

"I'm doing okay," he said finally. "What's nice about the museum here is when things get tough with the crime evidence, I can go look at rocks, or shells or the big dinosaurs. I particularly like the shells. The colors and the curved shapes are very soothing. Remember how Gregory liked to go look at beautiful paintings, particularly the Vermeers, whenever we were near a museum? It's like that."

Gregory had been their boss at World Accord International and a mentor to Diane. Gregory even carried postcard-sized representations of famous paintings. The everyday scenes painted by Vermeer were his favorite. He could look at them for hours.

She had adopted Gregory's love of looking at beautiful art when she needed a break from the grim realities of human rights violations. She understood what David meant about the museum. It was a refuge for her too.

"What's that new medical examiner in the next county like?"

"Dr. Lynn Webber. Nice. Hospitable."

"And that means?"

"Just what I said. Seems pretty competent."

"You don't like her?"

"I didn't say that."

"You didn't have to. I was listening to your ringing endorsement."

"I got the impression that she kind of likes to be the star." Diane hesitated a moment. "I think she's going to get the time of death wrong. She doesn't have much experience with hangings."

"And for that you don't like her?"

"I didn't say I don't like her. Just that she reminds me a little of Leah."

"A cherry bomb waiting to go off?"

Diane made a face. They had worked with Leah for a while in South America. She was a bit of a prima donna, albeit a competent one.

"I shouldn't have said anything. She's been very gracious. Even wants me to take her caving."

"You going to take her?"

"I thought I'd ask Mike about some easy caves."

"Mike? Mike Seger? I thought you're dating Frank Duncan."

Diane was taken aback. "I'm not dating Mike. We're just talking about going caving. He's an employee."

"Don't you guys have to take your clothes off to cross a body of water in a cave—to keep the water clean?"

"You can leave your underwear on."

"So, do you wear Victoria's Secret or those cotton jobs?"

"I think I'd better go home. See you tomorrow."

It was well after ten o'clock before Diane got home. She was tired and couldn't wait for a shower. After letting the water run over her for a long while, she ran a warm bath, put a capful of lemon juice in the water and just lay and soaked with her head resting on a folded towel on the back of the tub. She was tempted to stay the night there, just soaking in the water, letting the smell of death become overwhelmed with clean pure water. She would have stayed if her telephone had remained quiet.

Diane followed the directions to a small house in a clump of trees about a half mile from the Bartram University campus. The house, a bungalow with white wood siding and fieldstone columns and steps, looked like it might have been built in the late 1920s.

She parked her car on the side of the road and walked across the yard. She looked briefly up at the second-floor gabled window and leaning rock chimney. It looked like housing rented to students. Maintained enough to keep the roof up, but not enough to rent to anyone looking for a family home.

She showed her badge to the officer guarding the door, slipped covers over her shoes and went in.

A girl was sitting on a futon sofa in the living room, sobbing. The room was in disarray, drawers pulled out of a desk, their contents emptied onto the floor, couch pillows scattered about, chairs overturned.

Douglas Garnett, chief of detectives of Rosewood, and Whit Abercrombie, county coroner, were standing at the entrance to a room off the living room. Whit was Lynn Webber's counterpart, but he wasn't a medical examiner. He was a taxidermist with a master's in biology. They nodded to Diane.

Chief Garnett was a large, lanky man in his midforties with a full head of salt-and-pepper well-kept hair. He had a deep crease between his abundant black-and-gray eyebrows.

"In here," he said.

The body was on its knees, leaning forward against a rope around the neck and tied to the clothes rod in the closet. The closet door stood open, and the full-length mirror showed a side image of the gruesome scene. Diane looked at the purple swollen face with its dead stare and protruding tongue. Even with the distortion of death, she recognized the face.

"Oh, my God," she whispered.

Chapter 9

"You know this kid?" Garnett asked.

"I know who he is." Diane shivered—not from the gruesome scene—the room was cold. She tore her gaze away from the dead face and looked at Chief Garnett.

"It's Chris Edwards. He's one of the two men—the timber cruisers—who discovered the bodies hanging in the woods."

She looked around the bedroom, the single bed with its sheets pulled away, the chest of drawers open with its contents spilled out over the sides and onto the floor. A bloody hand weight lay in the middle of the bed.

"We need to contact the other man who was with him."

Chief Garnett moved to the living room and directed his attention to the woman sobbing on the couch.

"Miss . . . Beck, Kacie Beck?"

She pushed her blond hair out of her face and rubbed her red-rimmed eyes with the tips of her fingers.

"Miss Beck," said Garnett, "do you know . . ." He turned to Diane.

"Steven Mayberry," supplied Diane.

"Steve? . . . Yes."

"Where does he live?"

"Over on Udell. He has a trailer over there."

"Do you have his telephone number?"

"Telephone number? No . . . Chris knows it." She started sobbing again.

Garnett pressed a rapid-dial number on his cell phone. "Steven Mayberry, did you say?"

Diane nodded. She motioned to Whit as Garnett called for the address.

"We need to get Miss Beck out of the crime scene. She can sit in my car until Garnett questions her. I'll call my team to start working this. . . . And I'll need a warrant."

"Garnett has one coming." Whit pushed his straight black hair from his forehead as he glanced back at the bedroom. "You think this is connected with your other case?"

"I don't know. If not, it's an amazing coincidence."

Whit was escorting Kacie out of the house when Garnett got off the phone.

"Got an address. I called for backup to meet us there."

Outside, Diane slipped off the shoe covers and rang David.

"Yeah?"

David obviously had been asleep, as Diane wished she was.

"David, Diane. I need you again tonight."

"Gee, Diane, if I'd known you're this demanding, I'd have gotten myself a woman with less energy. What's up?"

Diane explained, and he was quiet for a moment.

"Can't be a coincidence."

"I'll call Jin. You'll have to wait for a warrant before you can go in."

"Sure."

A young woman answered Jin's phone. "Just a minute."

Her voice sounded sleepy, and Diane heard the rustling of covers as she waited for Jin to get on the phone.

"Yo?"

"Jin, this is Diane. We have another crime scene. I need you and David to work it tonight." She gave him the address. "I'm sorry to do this to you."

"No problem." Jin sounded wide awake.

Diane turned to the chief. "I'd like to ride out to the Mayberry house."

He gave her a curt nod, and she climbed into his Lexus and buckled herself in.

"These murders . . ." Garnett paused a moment. "It's going to be a test of our new crime scene unit. I don't need to tell you how important it is to get it right."

Several ways of answering him flitted through Diane's mind. Sarcastic was right up front, considering that it was he and the mayor who had virtually blackmailed her into housing the new crime lab and heading it up. But when she opened her mouth, it was her good friend Gregory's wisdom that tempered her tongue.

"It's a good unit with good people. We'll find all the evidence that's there to find."

That seemed to satisfy him. He said nothing for the remainder of the trip. Instead, he tapped the steering wheel with his fingers as he drove. Diane was glad it wasn't a long ride.

As they rounded a corner and turned into a drive leading to the trailer park, Diane saw a police car parked out front. The single trailer was lit, revealing silhouettes of two uniformed officers moving through the length of it.

As Diane and the sheriff stepped out of the car, the two uniforms emerged. One was Janice Warrick.

Good thing her eyes aren't phasers, thought Diane as they came face-to-face. Warrick held her chin high and jaw clenched and addressed the chief of detectives.

"He's not here."

"How's it look inside?"

"A mess," said Janice Warrick. "Chairs overturned, drawers pulled out and emptied. We're looking for Mayberry now. Officer Wallace is calling his parents and friends, and we have an APB out for his car."

"Did you see any blood, drug paraphernalia . . . ?" Garnett asked.

Janice shook her head. "Nothing but the mess. We only did a casual look through. That's all we could do." Her eyes darted in Diane's direction and back to Garnett.

"Stay here and see if he shows up. We need to find him," said Garnett. He turned to step back into his car.

There was nothing for Diane to do but go back to the crime scene. With three people working, perhaps it wouldn't take the entire night.

"Sorry, guys," Diane said to her crew.

"No problem. Who needs sleep?" said David.

The warrant had arrived in her absence, and Jin and David, clad in head and shoe coverings, had already started. David was photographing the body, and Jin had begun a fingerprint search, starting at the front entryway and following a path to the bedroom. Whit stood just outside the bedroom door watching David. Garnett stopped beside the body. Whit wore gloves and shoe coverings. Garnett did not.

On the porch, Diane had donned a hair cap and fresh shoe coverings. Now she slipped on a pair of gloves and examined the knots in the rope that bound and strangled Chris Edwards. Of particular interest was the knot tied in the middle of the rope between the clothes bar and Chris Edwards.

"Get good photographs of the knots."

"Of course," said David.

"What about the knots?" Garnett stepped up behind her.

Diane wondered if he had decided to take the lead in the investigation. Janice Warrick hadn't yet been replaced, and Garnett had stated to the press when he accepted the appointment as chief that he was going to take a hands-on approach.

She handed him a pair of latex gloves and covers for his shoes. He looked at them quizzically for a moment before he slipped them on.

"The rope and knots are different from the ones used with the other victims," said Diane.

"That's significant?"

"It is indeed."

"Diane is an expert in knots," offered David, snapping another photograph. "In that she has had to hang from them herself on many occasions."

David was good at keeping conversational tones, treating people like Garnett as if he was one of the team and not an adversary—which was the way Diane saw him.

"Uh, you'll have to explain that," said Garnett. He gave Diane a sidelong glance.

"I'm a caver," she said. "I work on rope a lot." Diane sniffed the corpse's hair. "Shampoo. He'd just come out of the shower. I take it Miss Beck found the body. Why so late?"

"She just got off work," said Garnett.

Diane studied the body. Chris Edwards was clad only in briefs, and there were bruises on his face, abdomen and arms. Despite the discoloration of his face resulting from the strangulation, bruises were still evident on his right temple and the right side of his jaw, as well as his arms. Dried blood was caked on his nose, down around his mouth and in his hair. He had put up a fight.

"He looks like he was kicked." Garnett pointed out the bruising on his side.

"It looks like it," Diane agreed. "Who's going to get the body?"

"Rankin. He's our medical examiner. You thinking maybe he should go to Webber because of the connection to the other victims?"

Yes, she wanted Webber to do it. If the cases were related, it would be better if one examiner did them all.

"I think it would be a good idea." When the words were out of her mouth, she wondered if she sounded too curt.

Garnett thought for a moment. "Webber would make sense, especially if this turns out to be truly connected to the others. However, we don't need to offend Rankin."

Diane could see that Garnett was going to make a political decision, and started to say something, but Whit beat her to it.

"We'll send them to Dr. Webber."

Garnett looked sharply at Whit Abercrombie, as if forgetting for a moment that it was Whit who had the power to make that decision. Whit's black eyes sparkled as he returned Garnett's gaze, and his teeth gleamed against the border of his short black beard.

"I'll talk to Rankin," Whit said. "I'm sure he won't mind."

Garnett nodded. "If you have everything under control here, I need to see about finding Mr. Mayberry."

Diane was glad to see him go. He might be the lead detective, but his presence was like a guest who arrived uninvited for a dinner party and you didn't quite know where to put him.

"How did you get mixed up with the Rosewood police?" Whit asked when Chief Garnett was safely away. "Last time I heard, you weren't on their Christmas card list."

Diane explained the complicated scenario.

"So you got blackmailed into it, and Rosewood got free space for a crime lab."

"That's about the size of it. I have to admit, I rather like it. But I can't tell the mayor or the chief of detectives that."

Whit laughed. "I understand. It's like, 'Please, Brer Fox, don't throw me in that briar patch.' "

"Thanks for making the call on Lynn Webber."

"It makes sense," said Whit. "Rankin won't mind. He's not as political as the people around him."

Lynn Webber arrived with the medical technicians to transport Chris Edwards' body to the morgue. Diane asked the technicians to wait on the porch while Lynn examined the body and Diane and Jin finished processing a path to the door.

One of the technicians, a white man about twenty-five with brown receding hair and dark blue eyes, asked if it was all right to sit down on one of the porch chairs.

"It's been dusted," Jin yelled from the living room. "Might get powder on you."

The other, a black man of about thirty, told him he'd best remain standing. "No telling what you might sit on at a crime scene." The two of them talked to each other about football while they waited.

Lynn twisted the neck and jaw of the corpse, and then moved his arms as far as the rope would allow. "Whit tells me I have you to thank for this."

"I hope you don't mind. They may be related."

"This looks different from those in the woods," said Lynn.

"But this is one of the men who found the victims in the woods."

Lynn looked up at Diane sharply. "What's going on?"

"I don't know."

Lynn shook her head, pushed her thermometer into Chris Edwards' liver and looked at her watch. "Ninety-four point five. Rigor's . . ." Lynn looked around the room. "Who's the detective on the case?"

"Chief Garnett's taking the lead," said Diane. "This guy's partner, Steven Mayberry, is missing—the one who was with him in the woods when they found the bodies."

Lynn's frown deepened. "This just gets worse. Any idea what this is all about?"

"Maybe we'll find out when Mr. Mayberry is found."

Dr. Webber stood up. "At a one-and-a-half-degree

drop an hour, it's possible he died two and a half hours ago. He's already into rigor. That's a little early, but it looks like he put up a fight and that would hasten it."

"His girlfriend put the call in about two and a half hours ago," said Whit. He was standing back from the body, watching Dr. Webber examine it.

"I suppose Chief Garnett needs to talk with her," said Dr. Webber. "I'm done here."

She turned to Diane. "Raymond has one skeleton for you. Blue Doe. He's delivering it today. He'll have Red and Green done shortly."

"Good. Perhaps we can find out who they were." Diane pulled out a coil of orange string to tie off the rope for cutting.

"If this keeps up," said Lynn, "you're going to run out of colors."

Chapter 10

"Looks like autoerotic asphyxia," said the black technician when he saw the body. "I had one about six months ago. Just a kid."

Jin stopped an examination of the chest of drawers and walked over. "Most instances of autoerotic asphyxia are adolescents," he said. "This doesn't look like it. Wouldn't you say, Boss?"

"I think we don't need to speculate," said Diane.

"His hands are tied awful tight," said the other assistant.

"Maybe he had help," his partner suggested. "The rope is tight around the front where he's leaning into it, but there's a lot of give in the back." They held the body while Diane tied off the yellow polypropylene rope with orange string and cut it.

"He sure looks trussed up around the neck like that kid. The kid's mother moved all the porn he had in the room," the technician continued. He looked around the bedroom. "Friends and family will do that, you know." The technician didn't want to give up his diagnosis.

"Let's get this poor boy out of here," said Lynn Webber. She stripped off her gloves as the technicians placed the remains of Chris Edwards in the body bag.

"Be careful of the ropes," said Diane.

"Will do." The black man smiled at Diane. "Pete and I always give our guest a good ride. Don't we, Pete?"

"You bet. We've never had any complaints." The two of them laughed.

Lynn left, telling Diane she wouldn't be getting to the autopsy until the afternoon, so Diane could come then and retrieve the ropes.

Whit stayed until the body was removed and Lynn was gone. Diane walked him to the door.

"I had a talk with his girlfriend before letting her go home," said Whit, leaning close to Diane and speaking low, though only she and her crew were in the house.

"She said there's usually a key under the mat. It was on the desk when she got here. I asked her if anything was missing that she could see. She said she thought his laptop was gone. He usually keeps it on the desk along with a DVD player."

Whit pointed to a pine table against the wall flanked by two speakers. The table was empty, but the dust pattern showed that something had sat there.

Diane looked around the room for any other ghosts of missing objects. It was a sparse room with walls painted the color of sand. The furniture consisted of a brown futon couch and two chairs, one stuffed and slipcovered in brown corduroy, the other a cane-backed rocker. The coffee table was a large rough-hewn cross-section of a tree trunk with glass covering the top. The some-assembly-required computer desk sat against one wall.

On the wall opposite the couch, a tall bookcase held a television and books on forestry and stacks of *National Geographic*. Beside it was the table where the DVD player had sat. The hardwood floors were bare.

"Jin took the girlfriend's—Kacie Beck's—fingerprints before she left. She was very cooperative," he said.

Diane nodded. Whit's dark eyes looked sympathetic as he took a final look toward the bedroom.

"Young guy." He shook his head. "I'm not sure why I ran for this office. I'm thinking of bowing out the next election."

"Working with murder is certainly wearing on mental health," said Diane. "Sometimes it seems like people have become so used to it, they've lost their perspective on the horror of it."

"Dad thinks it's movies and television, but I don't know what it is." He shook his head again as if to shake the thoughts from his mind. "Tell Frank I said hello."

Frank, thought Diane. He's due back from San Francisco. She wondered if she'd ever have time to see him again. She wondered if she'd ever have time to get back to the museum again. She sighed as Whit went out the door.

Neva came marching up the steps just as Whit drove away. She stopped in front of Diane. Diane had seen her drive up and waited for her on the porch.

"I heard it on the scanner. Were you going to call me?"

"No. I try not to overload new people with death the first week on the job."

"I can handle it."

"It wasn't aimed at you. It's just my policy. However, I'm glad you're here. It's going to be a long night, and I fear we may have another crime scene soon."

Diane assigned Neva the kitchen. "Jin's taking fingerprints. David's taking photographs, and you and I are doing evidence searches. Start with the back door. We believe he entered through the front door. He may have left through the back."

Neva nodded. "Vic let him in?"

"Probably got the key from under the mat. The victim may have been in the shower. He's one of the guys who found the hanging victims in the woods."

Neva's eyes widened. "Oh, my God. What's going on?"

"I don't know. Hopefully, by the time we finish, we'll have enough evidence to at least know if they are connected."

"They have to be connected, don't they?"

"Coincidences do happen."

"Yeah, but . . ." Neva glanced into the bedroom, where Jin and David were working. "This is some coincidence."

Diane began a spiral search of the living room beginning at the tree trunk coffee table. As she worked, the house made noises. Beyond the creaking of the floors and the sound of wind against the windows, the refrigerator turned on and off; so did the air-conditioning. Things that were normal now seemed odd, almost ghostly, with Chris Edwards dead. *Someone should tell the house that it can rest now,* Diane thought as the refrigerator once again came on.

Jin came from the bedroom. "I need to turn the lights out," he said. He was carrying a filter and black light to check for fingerprints.

"You're going to like this, Boss," said Jin. "I found the infamous bloody glove in the bedroom—at least its print. It looks like the index finger on the glove had a tear on the surface of the leather."

"Leather?" asked Diane.

"Looks like it. We can ID this baby if we find it. There's a lot of prints on the coffee table here, but I bet they belong to the victim and his girlfriend. You think maybe they were involved in some kind of kinky stuff that got out of hand? I heard what you guys said about the time of death."

"You think she also hit him with a hand weight?"

"I did a crime scene in New York where the victim suffered an astounding amount of consensual abuse. What is it that happens to a person in childhood that wires the brain to like that kind of stuff?"

"I don't know, and we don't know what happened here."

They worked all night and into the morning— searching, dusting, collecting. The smell of fingerprint powders and reagents mixed with the smell of death that always lingered.

"Heard we have a mummy."

Despite the fact that the crime unit wasn't techni-cally connected to the museum, David and Jin claimed the museum as theirs. So did the technicians Diane had hired to work in the lab. Neva was the only one who didn't appear to feel any connection with the mu-seum yet. Diane didn't know if that was good or bad.

"We apparently inherited one while my back was turned."

"Know anything about it?" asked Jin.

"Kendel said the mummy case appears to be from the twelfth dynasty. But that doesn't mean the occu-pant is from that time. From what Kendel and Jonas have told us, there was a flourishing trade in mummies in the 1800s, and European adventurers and Egyptian entrepreneurs were eager to supply the tourist trade. That included taking stray mummies and playing musi-cal mummy case."

"They also made new mummies for customers," said David. "Are you sure it's even ancient? It could be just a couple hundred years old."

"Right now, we don't know anything about it." Diane found a smear of blood on the metal base of the desk lamp. "I need a photograph in here, David. I believe it's Jin's bloody glove."

David took several shots of the smear using lighting in various positions to enhance the pattern.

"What are you going to do with the mummy?" said Jin, who was waiting to lift the print when David finished the photographs and Diane collected the sample.

"After Korey cleans it up, it goes for a CT scan," said Diane.

"Cool. I'd like to see that."

Most of the night they worked in silence, occasionally interrupted by small bits of conversation about the museum, Jin's music, and David's bird photographs. Neva said very little, and Diane realized that they didn't know much about what she did outside of work. They did discover that she liked to model small animals from polymer clay.

Just before dawn the radio came on in the bedroom and startled everyone.

"That got the old heart pumping, didn't it?" Jin laughed.

"I think I wet my pants," David said. "Must have been set by the victim. Time to get up."

"Won't be getting up this time," Jin said.

Diane went to the kitchen to check on Neva. She found her in the pantry picking up and shaking cans of food. Neva looked up sheepishly.

"I, uh, just . . . you know how some people keep their valuables in fake cans of soup? Whoever it was apparently checked out the kitchen drawers, and I just thought . . ."

"Good idea. I wouldn't have thought of that. Find anything?"

Neva looked relieved. Her whole body relaxed and she smiled. "Nothing in the groceries. Jin found plenty of prints, but they were in places you'd expect in a kitchen that's used for cooking. He said they were probably from exemplars. I've collected some fibers from the doorjamb. That's one good thing about these old houses: The door frames are apt to be splintered—good for grabbing at clothing."

"It looks like the perp wore gloves," said Diane. "I don't think we'll be getting any of his prints." She looked out the kitchen window and down at her watch. "It's getting to be daylight. When you finish, I want you and David to work the outside, around the house."

Diane and Jin worked the bathroom. It was this room that told a big chunk of the story of what happened to Chris Edwards.

She stood in the middle of the bedroom, her brow wrinkled, recreating in her mind scenarios of what might have happened. She was fairly certain it wasn't anything sexual. He'd just showered—his hair had smelled of shampoo and the bathroom towels were damp—and put on his briefs before he was hit, apparently with the hand weight. First in the nose—the blood spattered on the sink. He may have been hit again on the temple at that time. He fell, smearing blood on the floor.

He was half-pulled and he half-walked out of the bathroom—there was a bare bloody footprint on the floor. Blood was on the soles of his feet.

His hands were tied behind him and a rope was tied around his neck. It was possible they hadn't meant to kill him straightaway because, as the morgue technician noticed, the rope wasn't tight around his neck. He had to lean into it for it to choke him and cut off the blood supply to his brain.

One thing Diane did know: Whoever tied these knots wasn't the same person who tied the ones on the hanging victims in the woods.

Chapter 11

When Diane walked into Lynn Webber's autopsy room, Lynn was examining the surface of Chris Edwards' body with a scope on a rope. The scope transmitted a magnified image onto a computer screen, making visible any puncture marks, fibers, or other minutiae that marred or clung to his skin.

"We'll be finished in just a minute," Lynn said.

They were in the main autopsy room. The isolation room was just a wall away. Diane could see the shiny metal tables through the large window.

Odd, she thought, she didn't mind the closed-in feeling of a cave. She rather liked it. But the isolation room was a different matter. Being confined with a decaying body wasn't her favorite way to spend an afternoon.

Chris Edwards' corpse looked as if he had just died. He lay on his side on the table, dressed the same way he had come into the world, with the exception of the yellow rope that now tied his hands behind his back. The rope that had been so tight around his neck, that had cut off not only his air passage but the blood supply to his brain, was now loose, the weight of his body no longer pressing against it.

Just two days ago, Diane had talked with him. He had thoughts, a personality . . . life. Now everything he had been was gone. Only the dead flesh and bones remained.

She tried thinking back to when they had spoken, if he had said anything or acted any way that would give a clue to what happened to him afterward. Both he and Steven Mayberry had been edgy, but that was understandable. They'd just found three dead bodies. Nothing from her memory of her brief interaction with him enlightened her.

"You come to get the rope?" asked Raymond.

Diane almost sighed. "Yes. I've come to get the rope, and anything else you have for me."

"I delivered Blue Doe to your lab this morning. I've got Red and Green Doe ready for you to take back."

"That was quick work."

"Raymond likes his work," said Lynn. "He especially likes to skeletonize the bodies. He doesn't get to do that too often."

"They're much prettier in their bones. Skin doesn't wear well, especially hung out to dry like that." He grinned.

"You seem happy today," said Diane.

"Like Dr. Lynn says, I like my work." Raymond didn't take his eyes off the screen. "I got it," he said. He used his tweezers to pluck something from the body and placed it in an evidence bag.

"We have some fibers and a couple of hairs for you that we've collected from Mr. Edwards," said Lynn. "The blood in his hair is interesting."

Diane walked over and looked where Lynn parted his hair to reveal the scalp.

"The blood didn't come from his head. I think it

was on the perp's hand—or his glove. See this irrita-
tion on his scalp? I think the perp held his hair to
pull back his head. Like this." Lynn illustrated by pulling on the hair.

"Releasing the pressure on his neck to let him
breathe," said Diane. "Might have been an interrogation technique."

Lynn nodded. "That's what it looks like to me.
Okay, Raymond, let's let Diane get her rope."

Diane took this rope the same way she had the
others, first securing the knot, though it was tied tight
into a granny knot and pretty well secure on its own.
She tied the noose off with string before cutting it.

"This is different rope," said Raymond.

"The rope on the other victims was hemp. This is
polypropylene. It makes good outdoor carpet and
rope. Boaters like it because it doesn't absorb water—
and it floats."

"You know your rope," said Raymond.

"Rope is one of the most versatile tools in history.
It's good stuff."

"Not too good for our boy here," said Lynn.

After the noose was off, Diane took the rope off
his hands. This was more difficult, for the rope was
tight and bit into his skin. As she worked, Raymond
snapped pictures.

"I'll get these to you as soon as I can. I put the
other photographs with the bones," he said. "They
turned out real good."

"Raymond also gave you copies of the photos of
the tattoos. Maybe they'll help in making an
identification."

Diane didn't wait around for the autopsy. Even
though she'd met Chris Edwards only briefly, it was

not easy to watch someone she knew being dissected. As she took a last look at the body, she wondered where Steven Mayberry was. Dead like Chris? Or was Steven the killer and on the run?

Diane took the bones of Red and Green Doe, the rope, and all of the evidence Lynn and Raymond had collected for her back to the crime lab. David looked up from his microscope when she came into his lab.

"I'm looking at fibers from the door frame of the house now," he said. "It's mostly white cotton from tee-shirts and blue cotton from jeans. Jin got some good prints of his bloody glove."

"Speaking of blood . . ." Diane said.

"Neva drove the samples to Atlanta."

"I'm glad none of you people need any sleep."

"Sleep? We get too much sleep." Jin, wearing jeans and a black tee-shirt that said M.E.S ARE ON THE CUTTING EDGE, came bopping into the lab, holding a folder. "You know, if we live to be a hundred, we'll have spent over ten years asleep. I checked out the prints we found. All are exemplars, except maybe the glove print."

"Got anything on the clothes from the Cobber's Wood crime scene?"

Jin nodded. "Lots of carpet fibers. Orange nylon. I found them on all the rope too, including that piece found on the ground. I'll have the brand of carpet soon. There was some brown shed human hair, but no roots."

"All the blood samples are delivered." Neva entered the lab and stood for a moment, looking embarrassed. She held a brown bag in her hand from which she took three boxes, and handed one to each of them.

"Hey, what's the occasion?" asked Jin.

"No occasion. We talked last night about my work with clay, and . . . well, thought you might like some."

Diane opened her box. Nestled in white tissue paper was a tiny figurine of a gray squirrel on a log, holding an acorn. It was small enough to hold in the palm of her hand, but the details—the fur of the squirrel, the bark on the tree, the cap of the acorn—were remarkable.

"You made this?" said Diane.

"Yes. It's very relaxing."

"Relaxing?" said David. "Look at this. You must have had to do each leaf separately." His figurine was a tree with a bird standing on a branch next to another bird sitting on a nest. "Those feathers look real."

Jin's was a raccoon peering out of a hollow tree. "Cool," said Jin. "Do you sell them?"

"I go to craft fairs occasionally. Mostly, I make them for friends and family. Mom calls them dust catchers."

"It's heavy," said Diane, weighing hers in her hand.

"I put nuts or BBs in the bottom of the clay to keep the center of gravity low. Even though they're small, they're pretty good paperweights."

"These are great," said Diane. "Thank you. This had to take hours to make."

"As I said, it's very relaxing."

"I'll have to introduce you to the people who make models of planned exhibits. They'll love this."

Neva seemed pleased with the reception of her gifts. Diane was relieved that Neva was making an effort to identify with the team. The intercom squawked with the receptionist's voice announcing that Sheriff Braden and Chief Garnett wanted to see her.

"Buzz them in."

That must be a pair, thought Diane. She knew that Sheriff Braden and the chief weren't the best of friends. But neither were she and Garnett. These days, it seemed that Garnett was trying to rebuild a lot of burnt bridges. The two of them looked cordial enough as they walked into the crime lab.

"The sheriff was discussing with me a possible link in our murders, and I thought I'd bring him over to see the lab."

Sheriff Braden scrutinized the room as he approached. "This looks real modern."

"We're proud of it," said Diane.

"It has the latest equipment," said Garnett.

"You do DNA work here too?" asked the sheriff.

"No. We send that to the GBI lab in Atlanta."

"I know you aren't finished analyzing all the evidence yet," Garnett said, "but we'd like to see what we have so far."

It appeared that Garnett wanted to get down to business before the sheriff asked about any other procedures they didn't do.

"Sure," Diane said, "but perhaps the sheriff would like a tour of the facilities first."

Diane didn't wait for a reply, but immediately began showing the sheriff the labs and the glass-walled work spaces. She explained to him how each of the different microscopes revealed hidden characteristics in all manner of trace evidence. The sheriff nodded as she explained to him about opaque material versus transparent material and the type of microscopes they required, about polarizing and phase-contrast microscopes.

"The museum has an electron microscope that we

contract to use," said Garnett with pride that suggested that it was his own piece of equipment. Apparently, this made up for not doing DNA analysis.

"We contract with the museum for several processes," said Diane. "Pollen analysis, soil analysis, questioned and damaged documents. It's one advantage of being in a museum."

"But don't your researchers here do some DNA work?" said the sheriff. "During the museum tour last year, some of the biologists said they were working with DNA."

"They're heavily involved in their own research projects," said Diane, "and what they do is very different from what we need. They're not set up to process crime scene evidence."

Diane hoped the gas chromatography, spectral analysis and electrostatic detection and the amazing range of national and international databases—AFIS for fingerprint identification, CODIS for DNA identification, databases for fibers, shoe prints, cigarette butts, bullet casings, tire treads, paint, hair, plus all the software that matched, categorized, imaged, mapped, and, correlated—was sufficiently interesting to get him off his DNA analysis obsession. The last stop was David's bug-rearing chambers.

"These are the insects from Cobber's Wood. They'll give us a pretty good estimate of time of death."

"Dr. Webber said the bodies had been out there about a week," said the sheriff.

"More like three," said David.

The sheriff laughed. "Three weeks in this climate gets you bones."

"Hanging slows decomposition."

"I've found that Lynn Webber is always right on the money," said the sheriff, still smiling.

"We'll grow out the bugs and give you a report," said Diane.

"You do that, but I have to tell you, I respect the mind of a human more than I do the mind of a bug."

"When it comes to brains, so do I," said Diane. "But we're talking about sex, and bugs are very predictable in that area."

Laughter broke the contentious mood that threatened.

"We're just starting to process the evidence," said Diane, "but we'll tell you what we can about the murders."

Chapter 12

Diane led Sheriff Braden and Chief Garnett to a round table in the corner that she and her crew used for planning and debriefing. She sat across from them. Her crew filled the remaining spaces around the table; David and Jin to her left between her and the sheriff. Neva was the last to sit down. She pulled out the chair between Diane and Garnett and hesitated a moment before she sat, leaving a wide space between her and Garnett.

The metal top of the table reflected a fuzzy image of all of them. Chief Garnett put his hands on the table and looked at his reflection for a moment. The sheriff's gaze still shifted around the room, looking through the glass partitions at the equipment—no doubt wondering how much everything cost.

"What more can you tell us about any connection between these two crime scenes?" asked Garnett when they were all settled. "It's an amazing coincidence that the man who found those bodies was himself hung a day later. Are we looking at the same perp, or were Edwards and Mayberry involved in the woods murders in some way?"

Diane didn't know the answer to that question, and

she guessed that Garnett didn't really expect an answer.

"I can tell you that the person who tied the knots on the hanging victims was not the same person who tied the knots for Chris Edwards."

"How can you possibly tell that?" asked Garnett. "I know you're some kind of expert in knots, but . . ."

"My examination is not yet complete, but I've seen enough to know that the same person probably tied Blue, Red, and Green Doe, but not Chris Edwards."

"Blue, Red, and Green Doe?" said Garnett.

"Until we determine their identities, we refer to them by the color of cord used to secure the rope when we cut it from the victims."

Garnett's mouth twitched into almost a smile. "Go on."

"The nooses on the Cobber's Wood bodies were tied by first making a loop with a bowline knot, then pulling the other end of the rope through to make a noose. I haven't yet looked at how the rope was tied to the tree limb."

Jin jumped up and left the room. It was such a quick movement, they all looked after his retreating back.

"He's going to get something," said Neva. "You get used to his energy after a while."

Diane's cell phone vibrated in the pocket of her gray blazer. She fished it out and looked at the caller ID. Denver, Colorado. Who did she know in Denver? She didn't recognize the number. Probably wrong. She let the voice mail pick it up.

"I hate those things," said the sheriff. "They're always ringing at the wrong time, but you can't do without them. They cause a lot of automobile accidents."

"Actually, more accidents are caused by drivers not

keeping their eyes on the road. Cell phones are way down on the list," said David.

"You don't say?"

Jin came back and handed Diane a stack of photographs. She flipped through them until she came to zooms of the rope tied around the tree. It showed the rope wrapped twice around the limb with the standing end of the rope going under the two loops around the tree. It had an interesting twist—a stopper knot on the end to make sure the rope wouldn't slip back through and release under the weight of the victim. The perpetrator had also tied a stopper knot on the end of the bowline knot and one on the end of his handcuff knot. The stopper knot was set—tightened. She had not yet examined what kind of knot he used for the stoppers, but she'd bet they were all the same knot.

"Okay," she said, "this is an anchor bend used on the limb, also called a fisherman's bend—it was at one time used to tie anchors to ships."

She handed the photos to the sheriff and Garnett. The chief of detectives smiled as he exchanged photos of the knots with the sheriff. Diane had observed that talking about knots did that to people—it made them smile, as though they were gaining secret knowledge about a really cool skill.

David and Jin noticed it too. It was one of the things she valued about the two of them. They observed everything. Jin, especially, could maintain pleasant eye contact, all the while taking in subtle information about a person.

Neva sat very still with her hands clasped in front of her. She mostly looked at the table, occasionally making eye contact with Jin or David.

Diane handed her the stack of photographs. "Have you had a chance to look at these?"

She felt that giving Neva something to look at and study might help her be less self-conscious, a quality that would make her a better criminalist. Neva took the photographs, glanced at Diane, and began looking through them.

"The rope that hung Chris Edwards was tied with a granny knot, both on the closet rod and on the loop that made the noose. It wasn't a noose that tightened. It was made so that when his head was raised, he would stop choking.

"I suppose Dr. Webber told you that there was blood in his hair. She believes the killer may have grabbed him by the hair and pulled his head back to stop him from suffocating as part of an interrogation or torture. I think she's right." Diane saw the sheriff give a subtle nod.

"His hands were tied together by coiling the rope three times around his wrist and securing it with a granny knot. The hands of the three victims from Cobber's Wood were all tied with handcuff knots. And several coils of rope were wrapped around their hands, securing their fingers and thumbs."

Diane turned to David. "Have you had a chance to check the ropes for blood?"

David nodded. "All the ropes that bound their hands had blood."

"So it appears probable that at some point after he bound their fingers up tight, he cut off the fingertips." The sheriff and Garnett winced.

"He also added another twist, so to speak. The rope from the handcuffs had a noose in the end that looped around the victims' necks. They were tied so that if they struggled and tried to get their hands loose, they'd choke themselves."

"Wasn't taking any chances," observed the sheriff.

"I still don't understand why you're saying the woods victims and Edwards weren't tied by the same person," said Chief Garnett.

"Significantly different knots," said Diane. "The person who tied the knots on the Cobber's Wood victims had knowledge and skill with knots. He knew how to set them and finished them off so they wouldn't slip. The person who tied Chris Edwards' rope used granny knots. A granny knot is an incorrectly tied square knot. Even if he had tied a square knot correctly, it wouldn't have been the right knot for that situation."

"What do you mean?"

"Square knots slip easily. That would make it easier for the victim to untie himself. The person who tied the hands of the Cobber's Wood victims with handcuff knots wouldn't have used a granny knot on Chris Edwards."

"Maybe he was in a hurry," said Garnett.

Diane shook her head. "If you know how to tie a handcuff knot, it's just as fast to tie as wraps of rope secured with a granny knot."

"If I'm not mistaken, aren't granny knots hard to untie? That seems like it would be an advantage," said the sheriff.

"A good knot doesn't slip under pressure, but is not impossible to untie. Knots such as the handcuff knot and the bowline knot are used by people who know their knots because they work best for what they do."

Diane could see Garnett wasn't convinced. The magic of knots was evaporating rapidly for him.

"All the victims were hung and all had their hands tied behind their backs," Garnett said. "The perp had a lot of time in the woods to get his knots right. He was in a hurry at the Edwards house."

This time it was David who rose from his chair—more leisurely than Jin—and came back with props. He handed Diane a length of rope. She took the rope in her right hand and maintained eye contact with Garnett and the sheriff. They watched her fidget with the rope.

"It doesn't matter if he was in a hurry. It's not faster to do it wrong if you know how to do it right, and our Cobber's Wood guy knew how to do it right."

She held up the knot she had just tied. "This is a bowline. It's called the king of knots because it's very useful—it holds well and is easy to untie. It's a personal favorite of mine.

"I'm not someone who is extraordinarily gifted in knot tying. I'm a caver, and sometimes we have only one hand free to tie a knot, and sometimes we're in very low light or darkness while we're tying them, and our lives are depending on a good knot. Cavers learn to tie knots with one hand without looking. I believe our Cobber's Wood perp was good at knots. He could have done it under stress and in a hurry."

"Are you saying he may be a caver?" asked Garnett.

"No. I'm just trying to convince you that people who know how to tie knots know how to tie knots."

The sheriff laughed. "Then are you saying that expert knotters never make mistakes?"

"No. We certainly do, but rarely do we tie granny knots. All I'm saying is that the person who tied Chris Edwards didn't know knots or rope. The rope he used was old and worn, and there was an overhand knot in the middle between Edwards' neck and the clothes rod from which he was hanging."

"So," asked Garnett, "what does that mean?"

Diane took the rope and tied an overhand knot, pulling it tight. "I just decreased the strength of this rope by fifty percent."

"You're kidding." Garnett spoke in a way that suggested all his ropes had knots in them.

"No, and in a worn rope, that's significant. Chris Edwards was a husky, athletic young man, and a big portion of his weight was going to be on that rope that was barely adequate. It was another bad choice, like the square knot. The perp didn't know what he was doing."

"But it didn't break," said Garnett.

"No, it didn't, but it was too close to the breaking point to be a safe choice."

"Well, you've convinced me about the ropes," said the sheriff. "But that still doesn't tell us if the murders are connected."

"No, it doesn't," said Diane. "The evidence we've looked at so far seems to indicate it might have been a single perp at the Edwards crime scene. But we don't yet have any indication from Cobber's Wood to point to a single perp or more than one."

"Could have been a whole gang of 'em," said the sheriff. "And for reasons we don't know, one of them might have killed Chris Edwards. It might not be the same one who did the rope work in Cobber's Wood."

"But the evidence does give us an MO for the person who tied the knots on Chris Edwards," said Diane. "He probably always ties knots the same way because he doesn't know any other way."

"I see what you mean," said the sheriff. "If we find

something all tied up in a suspect's house, for instance, the way he ties his knots might connect him to one crime scene or the other."

"Yes. It can't be the only evidence, but . . ."

"But it'll give us and the suspect something to talk about in the interrogation room," said the sheriff.

"I have to agree with Chief Garnett," said Diane. "It's too big a coincidence that Edwards was killed just after he and Mayberry discovered the bodies. Have you found Steven Mayberry yet?"

"No. Nor have any of his friends or relatives seen him. Frankly, we don't know if he's on the run or if he met with the same fate as Edwards. Have you found anything else interesting from the Cobber's Wood crime scene?"

"Orange carpet fibers. Jin's working on the brand. We'll be able to tell you something about the sequence of events when we're finished looking at the tracks and other impression evidence. We also found brown shed human hair."

"Shed hair," said the sheriff. "So you can't do anything with that. As I understand it, you can't get DNA from shed hair—you need the root. Is that right?"

Jin glanced over at Diane. He raised his chin and eyebrows so slightly that probably only she and David noticed. She knew what he was urging her to tell them. He'd been talking about it ever since he read the article, and now here was a chance to give it a try. *Well, why not?* she thought. The sheriff was apparently enamored with DNA.

"Tell me what you know about DNA," she asked the sheriff.

Sheriff Braden shifted in his chair and gave her a long stare. "Now, I've always heard you can't get

DNA from hair that's been shed because it doesn't have the root, and that's where the DNA is. Are you saying that's not true?"

"It's not precisely true. Shed hair does have nuclear DNA, just not much of it. The root of a hair has about two hundred nanograms of nuclear DNA. The shaft has less than ten—not enough even for a normal PCR test. Added to that little difficulty is that the pigments in the hair can inhibit the PCR reaction."

"PCR—that's the test that copies DNA?" said Garnett.

"Yes," the sheriff answered. "That's it."

"Polymerase chain reaction," said Diane. "It's a powerful method that can be used on degraded and small samples of DNA. However, some samples are just too small."

"Like shed hair," said the sheriff.

"Yes," agreed Diane. "Shed hair does have more mitochondrial DNA, but that type of DNA doesn't have the identifying power that nuclear DNA has. It's too heterogeneous and doesn't have the poly-morphisms."

"I can see how that would be a handicap," said Garnett.

Diane smiled. This was the first time she'd witnessed that Garnett had a sense of humor. "Polymorphism is the occurrence of several phenotypes linked with its alternative form. . . ."

"Well, that certainly clears it up," said Garnett. There was laughter around the table. "But what I'm hearing you say is just what the sheriff started out saying. You can't get DNA from shed hair."

Jin leaned forward as if he was having a hard time waiting for Diane to get it out.

"Not presently," she said. "However, a crime lab in California is developing a procedure for in situ amplification."

Jin couldn't wait. "You fix the cells on special coated slides and the PCR is done on the slide itself, using special equipment. You see, no need to extract the DNA. That's where you lose some of it."

"The in situ method has been done on tissue samples for other applications," said Diane. "It's experimental. They're still working on the protocol for forensic use."

Garnett's phone rang. He plucked it from his belt and looked at a message on the screen and put it back in his pocket. He gave Diane a long stare. "I assume it's not cheap." Garnett glanced over at the sheriff, an apparent DNA analysis-phile, and saw that his interest was piqued.

"No," said Diane. "It probably won't be cheap, even if we can get it done. As I said, it's experimental."

Garnett seemed to look inward a moment, then his gaze rested on Jin's tee-shirt. Jin had numerous forensic sloganed tee-shirts—for M.E.s, criminalists—all with varying degrees of humor, gore, and double entendre. Today he had worn one that caught Garnett's eye—M.E.S ARE ON THE CUTTING EDGE. Diane could see him make up his mind.

"Why don't we give it a try? We can carry the bulk of the cost for your county, Sheriff."

"I'd like to do that, I sure would," said the sheriff.

Garnett rose. "I just got a message saying they found Steven Mayberry's truck on a back road. It's empty. No sign of foul play, but you'll have to look at it."

Diane nodded and turned to Neva. "I want you to process it, Neva."

Neva stared back at Diane and started to speak, but Garnett spoke first.

"This is real important."

Diane held his gaze, but she could see in her peripheral vision that his words had stung Neva.

"Yes," Diane said. "I know it is."

Chapter 13

Diane watched Chief Garnett pause before he left, looking as if he wanted to say more about her choosing Neva for this assignment. She guessed he was stuck. Garnett was the one who had given Neva to Diane's crime scene unit. He could not very well say now that he doubted Neva's abilities. She was wet behind the ears and had a little trouble with rotting bodies, but Diane had examined her qualifications. Neva's file showed a good training record in evidence analysis.

Neva collected her equipment and rushed to catch up with Garnett, casting a glance back that looked like a combination of determination and fear. Jin went whistling into his office to call crime scene researchers in California. The sheriff lifted his lanky frame from his chair, looking suddenly abandoned.

"Let David tell you more about his insects," said Diane. "I want you to understand how we fix the time of death. We can't go solely by rate of decomposition. Insects can't eat what they can't get to. If they aren't eating, decomposition is slowed. Wind and dry weather can stop decomposition altogether and start a mummification process. The Cobber's Wood bodies showed a combination of light insect infestation and slight mummification. Our best clue may be the life cycle of the fly larva—telling us how long they have infested the body."

He was silent a moment, holding his hat in one hand and studying the floor as they walked to the maggot room, as David liked to call the small cubicle.

"The inside of this building is not the same thing as outdoors," said the sheriff, looking at David's maggots.

"My rearing chamber is similar to the climate at the crime scene," said David.

As David explained about insect succession and life cycles, Diane could see that the sheriff hadn't relaxed the rigid pose of his shoulders.

"I guess time will tell," he said. "I have to tell you, the sooner we get to the bottom of this, the better. I know our boy Garnett is"—he gestured toward the door where Garnett left—"just real excited about having a high-profile case for you guys to work on. But it's been a pain in the butt for me." He shook his head. "Fortunately, Lynn Webber released information identifying the victims as white. The last thing I needed was rumors of a lynching flying around and having people stirring up trouble."

"I imagine it was the description of the bodies that bothered Reverend Jefferson," said Diane. "He's old enough to remember his parents and grandparents telling about spectacle lynching. Those images must have been raised in his mind when he heard about the condition of the bodies."

"Spectacle lynching?" asked Jin, returning from his office with his thumb up, indicating his success with the call to California. "Sounds like an oxymoron. Weren't illegal hangings done in secret?"

"Lynchings were not only hangings," said Diane. "Any death by a mob is called a lynching. Spectacle lynchings were just that—they were spectacles. They would be announced on the radio and in the newspaper and lasted all day. The mob often tortured the victim, castrating him, cutting off his fingers and toes, burning him with hot pokers, dragging him behind a car or wagon—then they would hang him."

The description of spectacle lynchings was not news to David. He was familiar with all manner of human rights violations, but the sheriff's and Jin's jaws dropped.

"Sometimes the mob would get themselves in such a frenzy," added David, "they would take out after any black they saw on the street, or they might break into the homes of black people and drag them away."

"No one tried to put a stop to it?" asked Jin.

David nodded. "Many tried. In several instances, white employers tried to protect their black employees, but it was at their own peril."

David paused, leaned against the table, crossed his arms, and gave them a soft smile. "One lynching produced an oft-repeated movie line. A man named Dick Hinson told about a mob that gathered outside his livery stable, where his father had hidden several blacks. When the mob leader told Hinson they were coming in, through him if necessary, Hinson took out his gun. The leader laughed and told him that he couldn't shoot all of them. Hinson said sure enough he couldn't—just the first man who came through the door."

"And?" asked Jin.

"No one wanted to be shot. No one came through the door."

"How long has it been since this kind of thing happened?"

"The 1920s and '30s were the height of it. The spectacle aspect began to die out in the midforties."

The sheriff shook his head back and forth. "I guess I'll go see Elwood and try to reassure him." He sighed and stared at the maggots. "I don't want to rush anything, Dr. Fallon, but when do you think you might have me something on the skeletons?"

"I'm starting on them today. They're a priority. I'll work as quickly as I can."

"Interesting stuff about the rope. It'll be more interesting if it actually leads us to the killer. I'd appreciate a call when you find out anything I can use." He put on his hat and headed for the exit.

Diane watched him go past the lab receptionist and into the special elevator they had installed for the crime lab.

"I don't think we convinced him about the time of death," said David.

"Maybe," Diane said.

"He's got it bad for Dr. Webber," said Jin.

"Apparently. What arrangements did you make about the DNA, Jin?"

"The California folks are going to send their protocol to the GBI lab sometime today. I'll take the shed hair over tomorrow. Good thing I wore this shirt, huh, boss?" Jin grinned, showing white, even-edged occluded teeth.

"Yes, it is. Much better than the one that says CRIMINALISTS DO IT EVERYWHERE. I'll be in the osteo lab."

The first thing noticeable about her bone lab was the number of tables—eight large shiny tables lined up in two rows of four, spaced with plenty of room around each. Diane liked space to work. One of the most frustrating things about working in the field was

cramped space in inaccessible locations. Here she had
room to spread out. She had countertops lining the
walls. She had cabinet space to spare; she had sinks.
It was a good room.

The cabinets held her measuring instruments—
sliding and spreading calipers, bone board, stature
charts, reference books, pencils, forms. On the counter
space she had a series of microscopes. A metal framework for mounting cameras hung from the ceiling
above the tables. Standing mutely in the corner were
Fred and Ethel, the male and female lab skeletons.

Her workroom had the essentials of a well-stocked
anthropology lab. Much of her analysis with bones was
manual labor—concentrated scrutiny, measuring and
recording observations. It was a room she could work
in even if the electricity went off, as often happened
during the frequent springtime and summer thunder-
storms.

Despite her fondness for lowtech, Diane had some
dazzling equipment in the vault, the secure, environmentally controlled room where she stored skeletal
remains. In it she also kept her computer and forensic
software, and the 3-D facial reconstruction equipment
consisting of a laser scanner for scanning skulls and
another dedicated computer with software for recon-
structing a face from a skull.

She hadn't invited the sheriff and Garnett to see
the vault. Technically, it was part of the museum, and
she didn't want Garnett to think he had free reign in
this lab.

Blue Doe's skeleton was resting in a transparent
plastic storage box on the table closest to the vault.
The rope Diane had removed from Blue Doe at the
autopsy sat in a separate box beside the remains. An-

other box containing the corresponding rope from the trees sat on top of it. A set. Bones and rope. Victim and weapon. Red and Green Doe were on separate tables, paired with their ropes.

Diane started with Blue by laying out her bones in anatomical position on the shiny metal table. This initial process Diane found relaxing. It was a chance to get an overview of the skeleton—how much was there, its basic condition, anything outstanding.

She rested the skull on a metal donut ring at the head of the table. She took the broken hyoid bone pieces from a small separate sack and lay them just below the skull. The hyoid is the only bone in the body that isn't connected to another bone. In the body it anchors the muscles that are used in speech. It also supports the tongue and, like this one, is nearly always broken during strangulation.

She set the vertebrae in position—atlas, which holds the world, axis which rotates that world, and the spinal column (cervical, thoracic, lumbar, sacrum, coccyx) vertebra by vertebra. Followed by ribs, shoulders, pelvis, long bones, fingers and toes.

Blue had strong white bones. The internal framework of her body was quite beautiful now that it was cleansed of rotting flesh.

Diane began her detailed examination with the pelvis—the main bones needed to reliably sex the individual. Lynn Webber had already judged that Blue Doe was female, and Diane confirmed that the pelvis was indeed that of a female.

Blue had slim hips, almost androgynous—hardly wider than those of a male her age. Diane ran a thumb along the fine line representing the epiphyseal union of the iliac crest with the flared innominate bone. Fusion occurs anywhere from fifteen to twenty-three years of age. The iliac crest was not completely fused.

She turned the pelvis in her hand and examined it for marks or distinguishing characteristics. There were none. No weapon marks, no sign of injury or disease. Nor was there sign Blue had ever been pregnant or given birth, though stress on the pelvis from pregnancy doesn't always show. The rugged ridged look of the pubic symphysis conveyed an age of eighteen or nineteen—consistent with the epiphyseal fusion. So very young.

Diane measured the bone at all of its landmarks and recorded the information. So far she'd found nothing that would help her identify the remains, but she hadn't really expected to in the pelvis.

After the pelvis, she went to the skull, picking it up gently. The mandible was detached now that the muscle and ligaments were gone. She picked it up, held it in place and looked into the bone face. Blue had no cavities, a slight overbite, smooth high forehead, slight cheekbones, a pointed chin—and a nose job.

The nasal spine, the spike below the nasal opening that acts as the nose's strut, had been modified. A portion of the bridge of the nose had been removed. Blue had undergone extensive rhinoplasty.

A satisfied feeling gripped Diane's brain and extended down to her stomach—one step forward in identifying Blue Doe.

She went about the meticulous task of measuring the crainometric points on the skull until she had virtually a mathematical definition of the face—the length, width, the measurement of each feature and its distance from every other feature. It was a narrow Caucasian female face.

Diane examined each of Blue's bones for signs of healed breaks, disease, pathology, cuts from knives or chips from bullets. Other than having the tips of her fingers cut off and a shattered hyoid bone from the hanging, there were no other diagnostically important marks.

With the sex and race established, Diane measured several of Blue's long bones on the bone board. From one person to another, bones are relatively consistent in their size relationship to each other. The length of any of the long bones when referenced on the stature tables for age and race gives a reasonably accurate estimate of the height of the individual.

Blue was a five-foot-five-inch woman, girl really, probably between 18 and 23, but not older than that. She was of good health and strong body—attested to by her prominent muscle attachments. The beveling on the glenoid cavity of her right scapula suggested she rotated her right arm in its socket more than the left, and so was probably right-handed. She'd had good enough dental care and hygiene to have avoided cavities. She had no orthodontia, and her third molars, the wisdom teeth, hadn't yet erupted. Blue had expensive plastic surgery. These did not appear to be the bones of a homeless waif, as the sheriff thought.

He—whoever had killed Blue—had taken her fingertips, so all the terminal phalanxes were missing. *Trophy or practicality?* She took the medial phalanxes to her dissecting microscope and examined the distal ends. All showed damage. The surface was cut enough on three of them that she could see a striation pattern—two lines, one thicker than the other, perhaps representing a flaw on the cutting edge of the tool. She photographed the images.

After recording the information that now defined Blue Doe, Diane turned to the ropes that had bound her. She took them from the box and laid them out on the table next to the skeleton. The rope was relatively new and made from hemp. It was rough and stiff in her hands. The loose fibers pricked her sensitive fingers.

Diane's tender skin made her realize how long it had been since she'd been caving. As a caver she didn't use natural fiber rope but the stronger nylon. Even though she wore special gloves when she caved, her hands were hardened when she was regularly on rope. They had gotten soft.

She examined each knot in detail. They were as she had described to the sheriff and Garnett—handcuff knot and bowlines backed up by a stopper knot. Diane teased the rope until she loosened the stopper knot.

Personally, she used a figure eight when she needed a stopper. Whoever tied Blue used a stevedore's knot—similar to a figure eight but with an extra twist. Further examination showed that he had also tied a stevedore's knot on the loose end of the bowline that made the neck noose, on the end of the anchor's bend around the tree limb, on the end of the handcuff knot, and on the end of the loop from the handcuffs to the neck.

Diane bet to herself that he used the same pattern in all of his knots with the other two victims. Not a significant MO, but certainly one that could help tag a suspect if the sheriff found one.

Green Doe was at the next table, lying in his clear plastic box with his rope next to him. She opened the boxes and took out the ropes. Bowline, handcuff knot, anchor's bend—all tied the same way and all with a stevedore's knot as stoppers. She was right. He made a habit of tying knots a certain way. Another little piece of the puzzle.

As she stood looking at the knots, basking in the pleasure of her discovery, something about the profile of Green Doe's skull peeking out from its plastic container caught her attention.

Chapter 14

Diane cradled the back of Green Doe's skull in her hand and inspected his face, drawing a finger over the long nasal bone. The nasion, the place between the eyes where the nasal bone meets the frontal bone, the topmost landmark that defines the height of the nose, was only slightly indented. The bridge of the nose connected with the frontal bone, making an almost flat plain. Below the nose opening, the anterior nasal spine was quite long. Green Doe had a large nose. What she found interesting was not the size of the nose, but that if Green Doe had decided to have a nose job, it would have been of the same type that Blue Doe had. Odd.

Diane glanced at her watch. It was late. If she expected to get any sleep, she didn't have time to do another skeleton, no matter how loudly this one now called to her.

"Damned interesting," she muttered to herself as she reluctantly put the skull back in the box.

She locked the osteo lab and walked back to the crime lab. She was glad to see that her crew was gone. They all needed sleep. The night operator was settled behind her desk reading a book. Diane waved as she left by the museum entrance.

Diane rarely used the lab's private elevator that allowed her to come and go and never set foot in the museum. Walking through the large exhibit rooms gave her psyche a rest after dealing with all the grim aspects of crime.

When she stepped out of the third-floor crime lab wing and closed the door behind her, the change in ambiance was startling. The shiny metal antiseptic furnishings and white walls were replaced by dark, rich wood walls, granite floors, vaulted ceilings and the sweet smell of wood polish. She crossed the overlook that allowed a view onto the huge first-floor dinosaur room, where she saw the silhouette of David sitting on a bench in the dim light. Looking at the wall paintings, no doubt. The pictures of dinosaurs didn't exactly have the soothing quality of Vermeers, but she herself often unwound by sitting quietly and looking at them—or at any number of wonderful things in the museum.

She took the museum elevator to the first floor and joined David in the dinosaur room with the skeletons of the twenty-five-foot-long *T. rex*–looking *Albertosaurus,* the suspended pteranodon with his bony wings nearly spanning the width of the room, the aquatic tylosaurus, the three-horned triceratops, and the newly arrived brachiosaur.

She sat down beside David on the bench. "Relaxing?"

"Looking at that little unicorn."

The museum's wall paintings were done in a style of dated realism that gave them a charming antique quality. A distinctly unique characteristic of the twelve wall murals was the tiny unicorns hidden in each painting. Diane never tired of looking at them. Apparently, neither did David, for she often found him sitting with the Mesozoic Era dinosaurs or in the Pleistocene room.

"What are you thinking about it?"

"Some days I think he's going to get trampled. Other times, I think he's just going along with the big guys."

"They never get trampled," said Diane. "They're magic."

"That's good to know. Sometimes I worry about them."

"You don't have to worry."

David's voice was calm, quieter than usual. "My divorce became final today," he said.

Another casualty of our work, Diane thought.

"You okay with that?"

"Actually, yes. I don't feel much about it. It's not that I don't still love Carolyn, but . . . I don't feel it anymore—if that makes any sense whatsoever."

"I guess I can understand that."

"I thought we might get back together. She was excited when I got a job at a museum."

"Then she discovered you would still be doing crime scenes?"

"Yeah."

"You know, David . . ."

"I need to do this. I need to see justice done. Despite all the little political undercurrents, this is a good place to work."

"Yes, it is, despite all the political undercurrents— as long as you can swim."

David smiled. "That was a good thing—sending Neva to work the car. She just left here a while ago. Found some blood. A few fibers and some miscellany. She's getting a warrant to go over Mayberry's trailer."

"Blood's not good."

"There wasn't much of it. So who knows? We may yet have a happy ending. What do you think's going on?"

"I don't have a handle on it yet." Diane told him about the discoveries she found on the skeletons.

"Interesting about the noses. What you figure?"

Diane shrugged her shoulders. "Coincidence, maybe? Perhaps a familial relationship? Maybe they met each other in Blue's doctor's waiting room?"

"It'll be interesting to compare DNA. The M.E. did take samples, didn't she?"

"Sure. But you know how DNA is. Good chance it's all degraded. I'm going home to get some rest. You head home too."

Diane left the dinosaur room, walked down the hallway past the museum store and cut through the primate section to the main lobby of the museum. Chanell Napier, the museum's head of security, was at the desk.

"What're you doing here this late?" asked Diane.

Chanell was slender and athletic. She had dark skin, a round face and black hair cut close to her head.

"I like to rotate out with the night guards once in a while. Keeps me up to date on what goes on at night. I get to know the night custodial staff."

"I hope not a lot goes on here at night." Diane laughed.

"It's pretty quiet. Just a lot of polishing of these shiny floors and walls. I like things quiet."

"So do I. Carry on." Diane passed through the double doors that led to the private area of the museum where she and many of the other staff had their offices. The office corridors were empty. The carpeting looked freshly vacuumed, so she guessed the custodial staff had already cleaned here.

She unlocked the private door to her office. On her desk was a stack of mail Andie had left for her. She sifted through the letters and placed them in stacks according to how urgent they were. Some she simply threw away.

Kendel had put a stack of requisition forms from the museum curators with notes attached to each request saying whether she thought it had merit.

"I think this is a good idea. Good price," read one note.

Diane looked at the form. The paleontology curator had found a small museum that was selling its collections. They had two casts of velociraptor skeletons for what really did appear to be a good price. The casts were damaged, but the paleontologist assured Diane that this wasn't a problem.

Velociraptors were the speedy, vicious villains of *Jurassic Park*. Everyone who came to the museum wanted to see one. They were not nearly as large as the *Albertosaurus* or brachiosaur, but the movie gave them a long-lived reputation. Diane wrote on Kendel's note to tell the paleontologist to purchase the skeletons. When they were assembled, it would mean another round of good publicity for the museum.

The next item was another memo from Kendel. She discovered that members of the family who gave them the mummy had amulets that had come from the mummy's wrapping. She thought she could negotiate a good deal on them. Diane agreed with that too. As long as they had a mummy and a case, it would be good to have everything that went with it. They certainly couldn't afford an entire Egyptian collection.

The last item was from Korey. He had X-rayed the mummy, and she could come up to the conservation lab at any time and take a look. He had also scheduled an MRI for next week.

Things seemed to be going along nicely at the museum. So far, working two jobs hadn't been too much of a problem—and she really didn't need that much sleep. She wrapped up the museum business and left her office, walking directly into the Pleistocene room.

She liked the museum at night. The cavernous rooms were dark except for a few low-level lights fixed close to the floor so that one could navigate through the museum at night without running into the exhibits. Museum lighting was its own problem, light being a destructive force, yet completely necessary. The lighting of a museum must take into consideration angle, distance, strength and type of light, and requires more mathematics than one might think possible for what for most people is a commonplace matter. The light must have destructive UV rays filtered from it, but it also must render accurate representations of color. Diane had staff whose only job was to take care of the lighting.

Her footfalls echoed a hollow sound on the granite floor. Walking though the Pleistocene hall was like being in the twilight area of a cave—that place where only a small amount of light filters in from the entrance and gradually diminishes to total darkness. Here she could see only the silhouettes of the skeletons of the mammoth, the giant sloth, the huge short-faced bear.

Caves are places of dramatic opposites. Some rooms and passages are so small you have to suck in your breath just to get through. Others, Diane could have fit her entire museum inside. The big rooms of mapped caves have glorious names—the Chandelier

Ballroom, Pellucidar, Cathedral Hall, Grand Ball-room, Throne Room, or sometimes simply Big Room. Diane had the same love of the museum as she did for caves. It was calming to her, which was why she always took the museum route out of her crime lab.

She opened the huge doors to the Pleistocene room and entered the main lobby again. Chanell wasn't at the front desk. Probably making her rounds. Diane unlocked the outside doors and walked out into the hot night air. Her car was parked almost alone in the middle of the lot. As she walked toward it, an uneasy feeling crept over her.

She looked around, wondering what might be caus-ing the feeling. The lights from the high poles illumi-nated the entire parking lot. Beyond the lights was darkness. It never bothered her before. She scanned the dark border, looking for something that she might have subconsciously seen from the corner of her eye. Nothing. *Silly,* she thought, as she clicked the button that unlocked the driver's side door of her Taurus.

Chapter 15

When the car door unlocked, the dome light illuminated the interior. As she reached out to open the door, she saw a bouquet of red roses lying on the backseat. Diane smiled. Frank must be back. She looked around the lot but didn't see his car. Why hadn't he come into the museum? She took the flowers into her arms and smelled one of the roses, a bud just barely open. *Nice*. The card was slipped between the flowers and the tissue wrapping—no name, simply two words printed in a script font that read: TO JUSTICE.

Frank's side must have won the case, she thought.

Diane slid onto her car seat and put the flowers on the passenger's seat. The aroma of the bouquet filled the car. It was odd, though, not like Frank to just leave flowers. Perhaps Star, his adopted daughter, put him up to it. Diane started the engine and drove home.

She lived in a huge old Greek revival house converted into apartments. It had a good feel to it. Once inside, she put the flowers in a vase of water, kicked off her shoes and headed for the shower. The cool water felt good, a relief from the heat. The landlady still had not fixed the air-conditioning.

Out of the shower, Diane turned on the ceiling fan, slipped into a nightgown and started to set her radio alarm for the morning when she noticed the red blinking light on her answering machine. She crawled in bed, hit the replay button and lay back to listen to the messages. The first was from Frank.

"Hi. Since you're not there, you're probably working yourself to the bone, so I won't try your cell phone. I'm still in San Francisco, but I'm catching a plane tomorrow. I'll call. Get some sleep."

If he was still in San Francisco, who sent the flowers? Diane wondered as she listened to the next message play nothing but road noise. She deleted it, and the machine cycled to the third message. A deep male voice she didn't recognize spoke.

"Why won't you talk to me? I've tried your cell phone, your E-mail and your home. I need to talk to you."

Wrong number? She checked the caller ID. One call came from San Francisco; that was Frank. The next two were from Denver, Colorado, and Omaha, Nebraska.

Denver. "I wonder if that's the same number as the cell phone call earlier at the lab," she said aloud. "Who do I know in Denver?"

Couldn't be a wrong number; he had tried both phone numbers and her E-mail. She didn't know anyone in Omaha either.

She shrugged, deleted the message and lay back in bed, thinking that perhaps Frank had the flowers delivered. But who put them in her locked car? Andie? Made sense. Had she given Andie a key? She drifted off to sleep.

Diane awakened abruptly at the sound of the ringing telephone. She looked at the clock—6:00 A.M. Her radio came on as soon as she reached for the phone. She shut it off as she picked up the receiver.

"Yes?"

"Diane, this is Lynn Webber. I hope I didn't wake you."

Lynn's voice sounded strained, and Diane was suddenly wide awake, wondering if something else had happened.

"No, you didn't. Have they found another body?"

"I had a very disturbing conversation with Sheriff Braden yesterday."

Diane waited.

"He told me you contradicted my time of death in the Cobber's Wood murders. That was very inappropriate."

"What? What are you talking about?"

"Those bodies were not far enough advanced to have been out in the woods more than a week."

"Why are you calling?" said Diane.

"My reputation is important to me. I am very conscientious in my work. To have someone who's not even an expert go to the sheriff and contradict me is unacceptable."

Diane was so surprised at the outburst, she didn't quite know what to say.

"I didn't go to the sheriff. The chief of detectives brought him by the crime lab to discuss the two cases. I simply brought him up to date on what we had discovered so far."

"Now Sheriff Braden doesn't know what to think."

Then I made progress with him, thought Diane, but figured it would not be a good idea to voice that thought.

"I'm sure he'll read both reports and come to his own conclusion." Diane wondered if she should be biting her tongue so hard.

"You're simply wrong about the time of death. This isn't even your field of expertise."

Time to quit biting.

"I'm not wrong, and yes, it is in my purview of knowledge and authority. If you like, I'll send you some research on the retarding of decay in hanging victims."

"Sarcasm and insults are unnecessary. I'm just telling you, when it comes to matters of time of death on bodies that lie on my autopsy table, my conclusion takes precedence and you are to fall in line."

Dr. Webber hung up before Diane could respond.

"Great," said Diane to the dead phone. "She's in a snit and will probably call Garnett, upset him, he'll call me and worry me to death about how we can't make any mistakes and definitely cannot offend anyone of importance."

While Diane had the phone in her hand, she checked caller ID for the number Frank had called from, dialed his hotel and asked for his room. When she heard his sleepy voice, she remembered the three-hour time difference. *Shit.*

"I'm sorry. I forgot about the three time zones."

"Diane. You sound good—anytime."

"I got your message. Did you by any chance send me flowers?"

"Flowers? Was I supposed to? Did I miss an anniversary, birthday—no, not birthday. Okay, what was it?"

Diane felt the laughter rising up through her body until it reached her face and made her smile. How that must sound—calling him at three o'clock in the morning all the way across the country, asking if he sent flowers. She scooted back into the pillows of her bed and crossed her legs.

"No. You didn't miss anything. Someone left flowers in my car yesterday. I found them in the backseat. I assumed they were from you."

"Was there a card with them?"

"All it said was 'To Justice.' "

"To Justice? I'm not much of a romantic, but I could do better than that." Diane laughed again. The whole thing was silly, and silly felt good.

"Must be from a secret admirer. Do you have one?" he said.

Secret admirer. "No . . ." She thought of Mike. Of course, Mike Seger must have left them.

"You do, don't you? I'll bet it's that guy—the one with the hair. What's his name?"

"The one with the hair?"

"You know. That modern, just-got-out-of-bed, cool kind of style. I think he's a geologist."

"Mike? Why do you think it's him?"

"That challenging-the-alpha-male look he gives me. Admittedly, I haven't gotten the look for a while, now that I've been an adult for a number of years, but I remember that provoking stare with a touch of amusement behind it. You and he go caving, don't you?"

"Well, yes."

"Yes. It was him, though I figure he could also do better than 'To Justice.' Don't you keep your car locked?"

"It was locked. Someone must have borrowed my key from my office, or opened the door with one of those things. . . . What do you call them?"

"A slim jim?"

"Yeah, one of those. Oh, maybe I forgot to lock it. I've had a lot on my mind."

"That's interesting."

"How are things in San Francisco?"

"Nice. Good weather. Looks like they'll convict our guy, unless the jury's just nuts. I'm looking forward to getting home. I hear you've been busy."

"We've had a few murders."

"Scuttlebutt says you have a serial killer."

"Too early to tell, but it doesn't feel like it. But I didn't wake you up in the middle of the night to talk about murder."

"Really. Phone sex?"

"Funny. So, you're coming home tomorrow?"

"I hope. I like it by the ocean here, but it'll be good to get back home."

Diane didn't talk long. Guilt for waking him up gnawed at her throughout the conversation, but he'd made her laugh and she liked to start the day laughing.

Andie was already in the office when she arrived. She wore a tailored denim suit and had her abundant curls pulled up on top of her head, and they shook and jiggled as she zipped about in quick little movements.

"Andie, do you know anything about a delivery of flowers to me yesterday?"

"Nope. Somebody send you flowers?"

"Yes. The card wasn't signed. I thought maybe you were here when they came."

"I was here, but I didn't see them."

"Doesn't matter. Someone will ask about them sooner or later."

"Wasn't Frank, was it?"

"No, I talked to him this morning."

"Wasn't Mike, was it?" she said, with a wink and a teasing grin.

"That's what Frank said. Why does everyone think it was Mike?"

"Oh, nothing. You know, just the way he's ga-ga around you."

"That's ridiculous. There is nothing there. He's just a kid."

"All right. I believe you," said Andie. "He's too young for you anyway."

"Now, wait a minute."

"Just teasing," said Andie, laughing.

She handed Diane a cup of coffee with chocolate, the way she liked it. Diane took a sip and sat down behind her desk.

"I saw you approved the velociraptor casts. That's exciting. I like those guys," said Andie.

"It's a good price. The shopkeepers tell me the velociraptor is the best-selling model after *T. Rex* in the museum gift shop, so maybe having some on display will generate more visitors." Diane turned on her computer. "Call Kendel and Jonas. I'd like them to go up with me to take a look at the X-rays of the mummy."

"A lot of stuff is happening about the mummy. You're getting a ton of mail. I've sorted it and put it on your desk."

"How is that possible? We just got it."

"I think there must be some kind of mummy grapevine out there."

"What are they writing about?" Diane said, mainly to herself.

While Andie called Jonas and Kendel, Diane began

reading the E-mail. The first was a request for a piece of the mummy for DNA research. She had fifty-two messages. Several others were from researchers about the mummy. "I had no idea," muttered Diane.

Her phone rang as she was scrolling through the E-mail.

"Dr. Fallon, Dr. Fallon?" The voice was high-pitched and nervous sounding. "I've been trying to reach you. Did you get my letter?"

"Who are you?"

"Dr. Earl Holloway, Indiana University."

"Indiana?" Not Colorado or Nebraska.

"Yes. Yes. It's important that I have access to your mummy. It's so hard to find mummies these days, despite the fact that there are millions of Egyptian mummies. They are so jealously guarded. People have such parochial ideas about dead bodies. It's almost like the days when medical schools had to resort to resurrection men."

"Exactly what do you want?"

"Haven't I said? Haven't you read my letter?"

Diane rummaged through the letters until she came to one from Dr. Holloway.

"Your letter just arrived on my desk. I haven't even had a chance to open it."

"Yes. Well, you would see, Dr. Fallon, if you had read my letter, I'm a paleoparasitologist. I'm doing postgraduate research here. A groundbreaking pilot study analyzing mummy tissue for drugs and diseases. It's a prelude to a proposal to the mummy tissue bank."

"The mummy tissue bank?"

"Yes. Most researchers are looking into the courses of diseases in ancient mummies. But I'm looking specifically at Egyptian mummies, since they came from a culture which had a more sophisticated practice of medicine. I'm hoping I can discover what they used to treat ailments we now know were caused by parasites, such as schistosomiasis, and evaluate the efficacy of their treatments."

"Have you thought about looking at the practices among the native peoples of South America? Though not technologically advanced, they have a tradition handed down from ancient times and have made pretty sophisticated use of the native plant life for medicinal purposes."

Diane wasn't sure why she said that. She didn't usually question researchers on their methodology, certainly not on something that wasn't her field. She supposed it was some gut reaction to defend the skills of the South American Indians, with whom she was very familiar.

"Yes, well, I don't really want to argue the point. My research design requires Egyptian samples, so you can see why I'm interested in your mummy."

"Yes. You and many others. We just acquired the mummy. How did you find out about him?"

"A few months ago, a friend told me about him. I couldn't get access, but I kept in touch with its disposition. I assure you, my research isn't frivolous."

"No. I'm sure it's not. I'm just surprised at the interest in him so soon. I'll read your proposal."

Andie led in Mike Seger who was carrying a large three-paneled poster board. They began setting it up on the desk in Diane's office. Andie stepped back to look at it.

"Look, Dr. Fallon," Holloway continued, "I sent you my list of publications. You don't propose to evaluate my research. . . . You are a small museum. . . ."

"I assure you, size doesn't matter."

This assertion caught the attention of both Andie and Mike. They looked at each other, then at Diane, eyebrows raised, amusement written on their faces. Diane rolled her eyes.

"I didn't mean to suggest," said Dr. Holloway. "Of course, I recognize your competence, but . . ."

"Dr. Holloway, if you know about the mummy, then you know he is without provenance. We don't even know if he is actually an ancient mummy or of more modern origin."

"I understand that, but there are tests . . ."

"Yes, and we are in the process of running them. Right now, I'm not prepared to address your request one way or the other."

"You aren't saying no, then. That's good. We'll keep the lines open, then."

"Kendel said we'd be getting requests from re-searchers," said Andie when Diane had hung up the phone.

"Apparently, they're calling my cell phone and my home." The calls had nagged Diane, but she felt better knowing they were probably from researchers. "Just a moment," she told Andie and Mike.

Diane decided to return the calls while she was think-ing about it and refer them to Kendel and Jonas. She di-aled the Colorado number and got a recorded message:

"You are returning a call to a prepaid calling service system, and the party cannot be reached at this number."

The Omaha number gave her the same message.

"That's odd."

"What?" asked Andie.

"These calls . . ." Diane explained the calls and the recorded message she just reached.

"Calling card," said Mike. "It's a standard birthday and Christmas gift my parents give me, hoping I'll call more often."

Andie nodded. "One of a handful of cities comes up on the caller ID every time you use it."

"Oh."

She'd just have to wait until they called her again. She rose and walked from behind her desk.

"What do you have here?" she asked Mike.

"An illustration of the earth science exhibit," said Mike. "The entrance starts here." He pointed to the upper-left part of the poster. "The crust is divided into the horizons. We're working on mechanical devices—kind of like Disney World stuff—that look like insect and parasitic life found in the soil. It will be large—the visitors will seem like they've shrunk."

"I like that," said Diane.

"Next we have the mantel, the convection currents, then the core. It's all pretty straightforward. The exhibit designer and I are trying figure out the best way to display all of this. One option is to have it on video as they descend the exhibit. But we also had the idea of building a mechanical device that will move a viscous substance around in a tank to illustrate the mantel, its convection currents and how the crust floats on top. We plan to reference everything with the current exhibits in the geology hall."

"Cool," said Andie.

"I'm thinking something like the tunnel in an aquarium," said Mike. "A place where the visitor can descend into the exhibit and have the earth all around him."

"You need to make it wheelchair accessible," said Diane.

"We know. We've discussed a winding ramp, an elevator sort of thing. We have a lot to work out."

Diane looked at the depiction of the soil layers, fossils, the molten mantel, the dense core. Mike had made notes on the display indicating what would happen to you if you were able to actually journey to the center of the earth—becoming very hot and finally turning into something the size of a marble under the enormous pressure of the core.

"This is coming along nicely. I don't suppose you have a cost?"

Mike winced. "No. Not yet."

"Okay. Tell the designer that I like the plans. Just remember the budget as you work."

"Sure."

The phone rang, and Andie ran to her office to answer it.

"I'm looking forward to seeing the model when it's built. By the way, did you leave anything in my car?" asked Diane.

"Your car? Like what?" Mike was a head taller than Diane and stood just at the edge of her comfort zone. He smelled of aftershave.

Diane backed up a step. "Like anything."

"No. Was I supposed to?" He raised his eyebrows and smiled. He actually had dimples. She didn't remember noticing them before.

"No. I was just asking."

"Was something left in your car?"

"Have you talked with the guy about the cave?" she asked.

"I'm meeting him tomorrow for lunch. I think it's a go. Would you like to come to lunch with us?"

"I'll probably still be analyzing skeletal remains."

"How are two full-time careers working for you?"

"Keeping me busy."

"Too busy for a social life?"

"I have a social life."

"Can't be much of one." He gave her that look that Frank might have described as challenging.

"Kendel and Jonas are going to meet us in the conservation lab," Andie called from her office, saving Diane from answering the challenge.

Chapter 16

They all met in the conservation lab on the third floor. Jonas Briggs, his blue eyes twinkling, entered carrying a folder. Kendel came in soon after. She was, as usual, impeccably dressed, today in a pearl gray suit with pearls at her throat and clipped onto her ears. Whereas Andie had several body piercings, Kendel didn't even have her ears pierced. She was carrying a package, an amused expression apparent on her face.

Korey emerged from his office. "You're going to like this, Dr. F." He led the four of them into his newly refitted X-ray lab. Highlighted by the view boxes that lined one wall, four X-rays of a skull stood out, as in relief.

"I have some good pictures here." He dimmed the lights.

Diane looked at the first X-ray of the front view of the face of a man who was possibly four thousand years old. He had distinct cheekbones, square jaw, rounded forehead. She examined each X-ray in turn before she said anything.

"Is that what I think it is?" said Jonas, pointing at a dark area surrounding tooth roots in the maxilla.

"If you think it's evidence of an acute periapical abscess, it is," said Diane.

"That doesn't sound good," said Andie.

"It wasn't," said Diane. "I'm sure it caused him a tremendous amount of pain. Look here at the fistulas above the left first and second premolars and first molar."

"Fistula?" asked Andie.

"It's a pathway the body creates to drain bacteria from an infected area, in this case, the roots of at least three teeth."

"Oh, gross."

"Do you think it was bad enough to have caused his death?" asked Jonas.

"Yes, this could very well have been what killed him."

"Well, we made quick work of that," said Andie. "Now, can you tell how old he was?"

Diane traced the tooth line with her fingernail. "He has his third molars—his wisdom teeth—so that's at least past twenty-one. His other teeth are worn pretty badly, which pushes his age upward. The sutures on his skull"—Diane pointed to the X-ray showing the side view and ran a finger along a faint line—"these irregular lines here, are almost fused. That pushes the age up considerably—say, at least past forty. I'll need to examine the entire set of X-rays, but our mummy was well into middle age."

"I want to know what's in that package you brought with you, Kendel," said Jonas. "You've had this little smile on your face since you got here."

Kendel sighed. "A member of the family that gave us the mummy sent this." She opened the box and dug around in the bubble wrap. "They said it belongs with the mummy."

She pulled out a cut glass jar with a lid that appeared to be sealed with wax. Something was inside the jar, and Diane and the others looked closely.

"Is that his finger?" said Andie.

"No," said Jonas. "Definitely not his finger."

"Oh, my God, that's not his . . ."

"Apparently, it is," said Korey. "Must have broken off during the unwrapping."

"That's terrible," said Andie. "The poor guy expected his body to be safe throughout eternity, and he ends up the main attraction at a party where he loses his jewels. At least they put it in a pretty jar."

"How confident are we that this belongs to him?" asked Diane.

"His is missing," said Korey.

"The fact that this is a Victorian pickle jar . . ." began Kendel.

"A pickle jar?" exclaimed Andie, as if this added insult to injury.

"Yes. It's authentic, so the time frame is right."

Diane remembered that jars and their history were an expertise of Kendel's.

Korey took the jar and held it up. "This looks like an old seal. We'll need a DNA sample from both to be sure."

"Why don't we just kind of put it with him when we wrap him back up?" said Andie.

Jonas cleared his throat. "That organ is the best place to find good blood residue. If we want to look for certain parasites and the like."

"Parasites? In his . . ." Andie couldn't finish.

"That's true," said Kendel. She handed the jar to Diane. "Your forensic lab should be able to sample it for us, shouldn't it?"

Diane held the heavy leaded glass container in her

hand. "Yes. We can handle it." The thought of explaining this to Garnett flashed through her mind.

"We'll be able to get some good samples of flesh when we endoscope him," said Korey.

"We are more likely to get a good DNA sample from the root of a tooth," said Diane. "We'll extract one when we do the endoscopy."

Andie looked horrified.

"We're doing the least invasive tests on him," said Diane. "He will be completely intact, for the most part, when Korey rewraps him."

"I know," said Andie. "It's just that this isn't what he expected from his death."

"I know, but we will treat him with respect," Jonas told her, "and we will be getting a lot of useful information from him about ancient illnesses." Jonas shifted his gaze from Andie to the X-rays of the skull. "The dead can have a lot to say, and I think it's important to listen to them."

"Andie, I need you and Kendel to go through the mail from people wanting access to the mummy and tell them that we will be glad to share with them the information that we gather."

"Will do," said Andie.

"We need to make a form letter," said Kendel. "These requests will continue."

"Okay. I'll rely on you to say something diplomatic," said Diane. "Speaking of form letters, Andie, I've been getting another round of complaints about the crime lab being attached to the museum. Look through the ones I haven't deleted and send that E-mail we generated the first time—the one thanking them for their concern, et cetera."

"I'll get on it." With a last incredulous glance at

the Victorian jar in Diane's hand, Andie bounced out
of the lab.

"I'm going to Virginia to the home of one of the
relatives of our mummy donor," said Kendel. "They
have a collection of amulets that purport to have come
from the mummy wrappings. I'm going to take a look
and try to wheedle them away from them. Failing that,
I'll get pictures." She hurried to catch up with Andie.

"If anyone can wheedle things away from people,
it's Kendel," said Jonas. "I don't know if you've noticed, but after you've talked to her awhile, you really
want to please her."

"Yeah," said Korey. "Underneath that soft femi-
nine exterior, she's tough. You kind of get the idea
she can be ruthless if she needs to be."

"I'm glad you two approve of my choice," said
Diane.

"She can sure get the job done," said Korey. "She's
got a set of lungs on her too."

Jonas raised one of his white bushy eyebrows.
"Lungs?"

"You were here when she found the museum snake
in her desk drawer," said Korey. "Her voice carried
all the way up here."

"Well, it was a shock," said Jonas. "And speaking
of getting the job done, I'm in the process of translating the case our mummy friend came in. I'm working
with an Egyptologist friend from the University of
Chicago."

"Is there any way we can date the case?" said Diane.

"I took the liberty of taking a few scrapings from
the inside to send off for analysis. The translation will
also tell us something. I've sent photographs to my
friend."

Diane looked from Jonas to Korey. "It looks like all of you have all this well in hand. I'll be in the lab if you need me to sign something."

Before Diane went back to the other bones in her lab, she asked Korey to send the X-rays to her office so she could study the complete set on her light table that evening. She was getting as excited about the mummy as the others. It felt good. She would like to have explained to the people who didn't want a crime lab next to the museum that for the people working in the lab, the museum was a welcome oasis.

Jin looked through the glass into the jar and back at Diane, his face somewhere between amazement and laughter. "Nice piece of glass he's in," said Jin.

"I need a blood sample. My people in the museum tell me that this is the best place to get it."

Jin nodded. "All that vascular tissue it has is needed to—" He grinned. "Well, you know."

"Indeed. Will you take care of it?"

"You came to the right place. Did you break it off?"

"No. He came to us in that condition."

"Want me to let you know if it was whacked off or broken?"

"Please."

"I knew there would be perks in working here," said Jin, taking the Victorian pickle jar to his work-station.

Diane started back to her lab, but abruptly turned and went to Jin's desk—a large work space with microscopes, glassware and chemicals. It could have been the space of a mad scientist.

"Jin, did you leave anything in my car?"

"Leave anything? Like what?"

"Like anything."

"No. Was I supposed to?"

"No. Just asking."

Diane didn't really believe that Jin would have sent her flowers, but you never know.

She laid out the bones of Green Doe in order, head to toes, on the shiny metal table. As with Blue, she started with the pelvis, measuring, recording and observing. The pattern of Green Doe's pubic symphysis, the front articulation of the two sides of the hips, was similar to Blue's—rough and unworn. He hadn't lived the years it takes to smooth out the ridges and increase beveling along the margins. Green was around the same age as Blue Doe. Young—late teens or early twenties. There were no markings on his pelvis, nor were the muscle attachments overly prominent. He hadn't been a particularly muscular fellow.

She went to Green's skull, which had strikingly interesting facial features. Her mind flashed to the clay models that Neva had presented to them. The fact that she was an artist wasn't on her vitae—it wasn't something that Neva thought employers would find important. But it was important to Diane. She picked up the house phone and rang the lab. David answered.

"Jin showed me the mummy's crown jewels. Interesting," David said.

"I imagine it will generate all manner of conversation among my staff."

"How could it help but?"

"Is Neva there? Would you send her to the bone lab?"

"Sure thing."

"Oh, and David. You didn't happen to leave anything in my car, did you?"

"No. What did you find there?"

Diane told him about the flowers and the card. "I didn't think you or Jin sent them, but so far, no one I know has."

"That's really odd. I take it Frank didn't send them, or Mike?"

"No, they didn't."

"Maybe you should get one of us, or museum security, to walk you to your car for a few days."

"It's odd, but I don't think it's ominous."

"Nevertheless . . . it doesn't hurt to be careful. I'll send Neva over."

Diane met Neva at the entrance to her lab and let her in. Neva stopped at the entrance and gazed around the lab and over at the table where Green Doe was laid out.

"I haven't seen this lab. It's big," she said. "You didn't put it on the chief's tour."

"No, I didn't. Technically, it's part of the museum."

Neva looked uncomfortable . . . a little embarrassed. "I want to thank you for sending me to process the car by myself."

"I had confidence you could do it. And now—why I asked you in here. You're about to discover that there are hazards in letting your employer know you have a talent."

Chapter 17

Neva's frown deepened as Diane said the word *hazard,* as if bracing herself for a dressing-down, but by the time Diane reached the end of the sentence, Neva simply looked puzzled.

Diane smiled. "Let me show you another room that wasn't on the tour."

She picked up the skull of Green Doe and led Neva into the vault. Neva's gaze moved over the room, resting on each piece of equipment, then on Diane.

"What is this room?"

"This is where I keep my special toys."

Diane turned on the computer and equipment and set Green Doe on a platform in front of a machine.

"This is a laser scanner. The laser reads the topography of the skull as it rotates on the pedestal and generates a matrix of points. It looks like a wire frame on the computer screen. Other software uses a skin-depth database to reconstruct and display a texturized face."

Diane turned on the computer and called up an image. "This is a reconstruction I've already done of

Ethel—Fred and Ethel are the skeletons in the corner of the lab."

She showed Neva the sequence of images for Ethel from the wire frame to the reconstruction of a thirty-year-old woman with dark hair and eyes, a small nose, thin lips and high cheekbones. The face had the masklike, lifeless look of a computer-generated face, but it was a remarkably detailed face.

"Wow. This is some incredible software."

"It is. It's the absolute state of the art."

"You want me to run it?"

"I'm assuming that if you can do the detailed sculptures that you do, you can also draw."

Neva nodded. "I wanted to take art, but my parents discouraged it. They said you can't make a living with art."

"Well, you are about to. There are several problems with facial reconstructions. One is characteristics that the bones don't show—the shape of the eyes, lips and tip of the nose. And these are the things that trigger recognition. People recognize the tip of Karl Malden's nose without seeing any other feature."

"Who's Karl Malden?"

"Someone whose nose you would recognize if you were my age. I don't suppose you know who Jimmy Durante is either."

Neva held up a hand as if she held a hat, quivered, and sang "Hot-cha-cha-cha-cha!" in so perfect an impression of Jimmy Durante that Diane almost fell off her chair laughing.

"I used to entertain my relatives as a kid with that. Amazing what you can get by with as a kid."

"Your talents are apparently endless."

Diane shook her head and returned her attention to the computer-generated photograph of Ethel.

"We could show this to Ethel's mother and there is a good chance she wouldn't recognize her. Her mother knew her as an animated person, with mannerisms, facial expressions, and gestures. She knew all the details of her daughter's face, and this just doesn't have all those fine details that make up the person she knew as her daughter.

"However, if we were to show this to a store clerk who bagged Ethel's groceries, he might recognize her. He may not remember what the tip of her nose looked like, but he remembers the general look of her. What we need is pictures that both a mother and an acquaintance can recognize. What I would like you to do is take an image like this and draw a more realistic picture."

Neva put her hands to her face and pressed the bridge of her nose. "Okay. I can do this."

"It means you will have to learn the software."

"I'm good with computers."

"Good. Start by looking at Fred's and Ethel's computer-reconstruction files to familiarize yourself with how it all works. Then we'll do the three hanging victims. After we get a CT scan of the mummy, I'll show you how to use the information from the scan to reconstruct his face."

Neva nodded.

"You'll also have to learn the bones of the skull and how the bones affect the look of the face," said Diane. "And you'll have to pay attention to other details too. Sometimes knowing things like the person walked with a pronounced limp might give you a hint about how to portray a facial expression. Or if a toxicological report on a decayed victim comes back showing a certain kind of thyroid medication, you might guess that the victim has a bug-eyed look that is a side effect of some of those medications. A big part of this work is intuitive."

Diane watched her look at the skull sitting on the platform.

"I've seen how they do those skin-depth points to make a sculpture of a face. But I've never understood how they know what the nose looks like."

"You can't know the shape of the tip. However . . ." Diane took the skull and sat down at a desk, motioning Neva to draw up a chair. "The width of the nose is indicated by the size of the nasal opening. The bridge of the nose and the nasal spine—this sharp projection at the bottom of the nasal passage—determine the length of the nose. A large nose needs a strut to hold it up. That's what the anterior nasal spine does. If you draw a line coming off the end of the nasal bone and one coming from the nasal spine, where the lines meet gives you an idea how long the nose was. The angle of each line can suggest the tilt of the nose."

Neva nodded. "That makes sense."

"Another effect of a long nasal spine is upward angling of the skin between the upper lip and the nose. Notice what happens when I pull on the lower part of my nose." Diane pulled the bottom of her nose forward, stretching the skin above the lip. "In a shorter nose, that part of the face is parallel to the plane of the face, but in a long nose it angles forward."

"So this guy would have that characteristic," said Neva.

"I believe so. Look how far the tip of the nasal spine is from his maxilla—where his upper teeth are."

Neva nodded and reached out and touched the skull with her fingertips, along the spine and down the maxilla. She stopped abruptly and drew her hand away. "This is one of the hanging victims, isn't it? How did his bones get so clean?"

"Yes, he is one of the victims. The diener at the morgue cleans the bones after we take all the samples we need from the flesh."

"What a job—I'd hate to have to do that."

"He seems to enjoy it. Having the proper equipment helps."

Neva laughed nervously. "But it has to be a mess."

"Not a lot messier than dealing with his clothes—and you had to do that."

"That's·true. Thank God for latex gloves."

"And Febreze," said Diane.

"Oh, God, yes. When we got out of the woods, I had to spray myself down good with Febreze to kill the odor. You'd think the woods would be well ventilated."

"Another feature that is a consequence of a large nasal spine like this one is nostrils that appear arched. That shape exposes a larger-than-normal portion of the inside of the nose—the surface of the septum."

"Yeah, I've seen that in people."

Diane touched a point on the bridge of the nose directly between the eyes. "This is the nasion. It's a craniometric point. Here just below the opening of the nose is the nasospinale. For physical anthropologists, the length of the nose is measured between these two points. However, the relative position of the bones as they are situated in the face determines how we perceive the length of the nose."

Neva furrowed her brows, looking hard at the skull as Diane continued.

"See how the bridge of the nose stands away from the face, forming a straight line from the forehead to the nose? It's different from, say, mine." Diane rubbed her finger across the nasal bone of the skull and then touched her own.

"His is kind of like those Roman statues."

"Exactly. That would make the nose look longer. In this kind of nose there is a perception that the nose is longer than it actually is because your eye sees the nose as starting at the forehead, rather than where the nose actually starts."

"Okay, I see. What about people with a bump on their nose, like the mummy? What would the bone look like?"

"The nose is supported by bone and cartilage. You see the bone here in Green Doe's skull, but the cartilage was destroyed by the cleaning of the bones. When a body decomposes, the cartilage decomposes—though more slowly than flesh. The bump on the nose in the mummy resulted when the supporting cartilage decomposed and collapsed following death, and the nose drooped, revealing the end of the nasal bone—making it look like a bump. The mummy wrappings have pressed the nose down so that the nasal bone has a prominence that it wouldn't have had while he was alive. Looking at all the pictures of Egyptian mummies in our reference books, it's easy to think that Egyptian pharaohs all had nose bumps—making them all look alike."

"That's funny. I did think that all those pharaohs had bumps on their noses."

"Bet you thought they were old and lean, too."

Neva grinned. "Yes, I did."

"In more modern skeletal remains, you can tell from the upward angle of the lower part of the nasal bone that some noses probably had a bump. A person can appear to have a bump on their nose if they have damaged the cartilage supporting the tip of the nose, like from an accident or just getting hit hard in the nose."

"And that would show up in the skull?"

"Not necessarily. You might see a break in the nasal bone, but you wouldn't know how the break manifested itself. Is that more than you wanted to know about how to determine the shape of the nose from the skull?"

"No. This is good. I've seen all those nose types in people. It never occurred to me that it had anything to do with their bones. How about the eyes and lips?"

"Those are more of a problem. You know how far apart the eyes were because you have the sockets. But you don't get much help beyond that. Information about gender and race helps, along with knowledge of the geometry of the face—like where the corners of the lips are in relation to the other features. And age plays a big part. As you get older the eyelids sag, the lip line isn't as distinct. As I said, much of this is intuitive. You do the best you can with the information you have. But you go as far as you can with the bones."

The phone on Diane's desk rang, lighting up the in-house line. Diane reached and pressed the speaker button.

"Fallon, here."

"Dr. Fallon, it's Andie. I've been going through your E-mail, and there's one that's kind of strange."

"Strange? How?"

"I'll read it to you. It says: 'Sometimes the dead are guilty.' " Neva and Diane exchanged glances.

"The dead are guilty? What does that mean?" asked Neva.

"I don't know. I'm going downstairs. You stay here and work with the software."

Diane left her lab and headed for the elevators. Andie was sitting at her desk when she entered the private door to her office.

"What do you think they're talking about?" said Andie, giving up her seat at Diane's computer.

Diane looked at the message. *Sometimes the dead are guilty.* That was all, no signature, no explanation. Diane looked at the sender. JMLndrmn23. It wasn't anyone she recognized. But then, who did she know that would send her a message like this?

Sometimes the dead are guilty. A prank? An uneasiness began creeping up Diane's spine to the back of her neck.

"Are you going to respond?"

Andie's voice startled her. She'd forgotten she was still standing there by the desk.

"I don't know." But she found herself clicking the REPLY button, and she wrote a simple note, *What do you mean?* and hit the SEND button.

"What do you think it does mean?" asked Andie.

Diane shook her head. "Probably some self-righteous person who doesn't like the museum being connected to the crime lab."

She also was beginning to think that it wasn't such a good idea. But Rosewood had her between a rock and a hard place on that one.

Odd, in any case. Something else she had recently

described as odd. Oh, yes, the flowers. That was odd too.

David appeared at the door, interrupting her thought. "Garnett just called. We have another case."

Chapter 18

Diane drove her car to the address David had given her. Briarwood Lane was a cul-de-sac of old frame houses and large mature trees in a mixed neighborhood of Hispanics, whites, and blacks, many of whom were standing in their yards, looking in the direction of the asphalt-roofed house with gray shaker siding where several emergency vehicles were parked.

David, Jin and Neva had arrived just ahead of her and were just emerging from their van. Chief Garnett, Sheriff Braden, Whit Abercrombie, and several others were standing beside a car that Diane recognized as Lynn Webber's. *Great,* thought Diane, *another confrontation—and this isn't even Lynn's jurisdiction.*

As Diane approached, Garnett turned toward her and she caught sight of Allen Rankin, Rosewood's pathologist. She stopped abruptly when she saw Lynn Webber sitting sideways in the driver's seat with her feet on the asphalt road, sobbing.

"I don't understand this," Lynn was saying. "What is this about?"

For a moment Diane thought that Lynn was, of all things, under arrest . . . and it hit her all of a sudden. The neighborhood. Lynn Webber sobbing. She looked at Garnett.

"It's Lynn's diener, Raymond, isn't it?" She didn't even know his last name.

Garnett nodded. "Raymond Waller. He came home for lunch and didn't come back. When he was late, Dr. Webber called his home and his cell. When she couldn't get in touch, she came to his house and found him."

"She came to his house?"

"She said she has several bodies backed up, and he was always reliable." Garnett lowered his voice. "She can get kind of feisty when she's let down. I take it she was going to bring him back to work."

Diane had experienced some of her feistiness. It wasn't how she would have described it. "Was he murdered?"

"Yes. Hit on the back of the head. Somebody threw water in his face. Maybe an attempt to revive him."

"This is really odd." There it was, that word again.

"Odd . . . at least. Look, I have no idea what's going on here, but I want everyone involved with those hanging victims to be extra careful. I'm going to send a squad car by everyone's home, but maybe you can get your museum security to help with your people."

"We'll come up with a plan. Chief, I've had a couple of other disquieting things happen."

Garnett frowned as she handed him the note she had printed out and told him about the flowers. While she spoke, her gaze darted at the various people watching, looking to see if she recognized anyone she might have seen in the museum or the parking lot. No one looked familiar.

"You replied to the E-mail. You should have talked to me first."

"I thought it was museum business."

"And you don't know who left the flowers?"

"I've asked everyone that I know. . . . I just assumed you didn't," she added, with half a smile.

Garnett chuckled. "No."

"Why are you two laughing? You think this is funny?" Lynn Webber flew out of her car and stood before them, anger flashing in her red-rimmed eyes.

"Dr. Webber—" began Garnett.

"I'm sorry, Lynn," said Diane. "We were just trying to deflect some of the tension. We are very disturbed by all this. I met and worked with Raymond and liked him. Of course I don't think it's funny. Neither does the chief."

Lynn Webber shook her head, as if trying to shake out some thought. "I know. I'm sorry. I don't know what's wrong with me."

"Why don't you let me take you home?" said Sheriff Braden. "You don't need to see any more of this, and those bodies in the morgue can wait a day or so. They aren't going anywhere. I'll ask one of the policemen here to follow in your car."

"That's a good idea, Dr. Webber," said Garnett. "We'll keep you apprised."

Lynn nodded. "Raymond has family in Philadelphia. I'll call them. It would be better coming from me."

The sheriff left with Lynn; Officer Warrick followed in Lynn's car.

"Why is the sheriff here?" said Diane. "This is Rose County."

Garnett shook his head. "He must have heard the call on the radio and wanted to come to Dr. Webber's rescue. I assume his interest in her hasn't escaped your notice."

"No, it hasn't."

"I need to ask you—about the hanging victims' time of death . . . you can back up your numbers?"

"Yes."

"Webber's real certain."

"So am I."

"When are you going to be finished with the bodies?"

"Today. My team will work this crime scene. I'm going back to the lab. I'm going to do some analysis that will tell us which region of the country they grew up in, and that will take longer. But we'll have a report and facial reconstruction for the sheriff shortly."

"Facial reconstruction? You can do that?"

"Of course . . . I assume that's why you sent me Neva Hurley."

"Neva?" He stopped a moment and looked at Neva, who was donning a pair of gloves. "Oh . . . yes . . . of course."

Diane smiled inwardly, but made sure it didn't reach her face.

"Any sign of Steven Mayberry?" she said.

"No. And I'm worried. We can't afford to have wholesale murder going on and not be able to do anything about it. The media will jump all over this."

"Perhaps they won't know where the bodies were autopsied."

"Why wouldn't they?" said Garnett. "It looks like the murderer did."

"I know this is quite a coincidence," said Diane. "But I just don't see any reason behind the murders that would establish a connection. Not yet."

"Neither do I. Perhaps it is just that. A coincidence." He did not sound convinced.

"The evidence will tell us if there is a connection. I'm going back to it."

Diane gave her team instructions and left for the lab, relieved not to have to look at Raymond's dead body. It would be bad enough when she looked at the photographs. She drove back to the lab and parked in the crime lab parking area, a gated lot to the side of the enormous museum building. She took the lab elevator to the third floor, bypassing the museum.

Suddenly, it looked like she was bringing crime into the museum, and that was something she had no desire to do and couldn't afford to do. She would close the lab and take Rosewood to court about the taxes before she would allow that to happen.

But crime labs are not dangerous places. She knew of no cases where perps had targeted crime labs or the people who worked in them. After all, the people just analyze data. Why, then, was this happening? Perhaps it wasn't. Perhaps the flowers were from someone connected with the museum, or even a fan of the crime lab. Perhaps the E-mail note meant nothing.

Green Doe was where she had left him, waiting for her on the table. She measured the skull, made notes of his orthodontic work, examined and measured his long bones. His left radius had been broken and healed well. She examined the ribs and each vertebra. There were no nicks or cuts on any of his bones, except, as in Blue, his terminal phalanxes were missing. Of the damaged medial phalanxes, only one showed the surface striations that she had seen on Blue. But that was enough. Diane entered all of Green Doe's data into the computer.

Her team hadn't returned yet. They could be out all night. She went to her office. Andie was gathering her things to leave for the day.

"Hey, you got a message back from that weird E-mail about the dead being guilty. I printed it out." She grabbed it off Diane's desk and handed it to her.

Diane read it aloud. " 'I didn't send this. Who are you anyway? Don't bother me. My father's a policeman.' Well, this is interesting. Sounds like a kid."

"That's what I thought," agreed Andie.

"Hey, anybody home around here?"

"Frank. When did you get in?" Diane gave him a hug and held him a little tighter than she felt comfortable with in front of Andie.

"My plane landed a few hours ago. I stopped by to see Star and Kevin."

His thirteen-year-old son, Kevin, lived with his mother. Star, his new daughter, stayed with them while Frank was gone.

"Cindy wanted Star to stay the weekend so that she and David could go out. I thought maybe we could get some dinner. Have you eaten?"

"No, and I'm starved. The museum restaurant is open for a while yet. Mind if we eat there?"

"I'll see you tomorrow," said Andie, going out the door. "Good to see you, Frank. Miss you at karaoke."

"Bye, Andie. Thanks," called Diane.

"You want to eat at the museum? Sounds like you're planning a late night working."

He stepped close and drew her into a kiss. Frank felt good—and safe, like home. She wanted to hang on to him, but she let go.

"I've got to get the last skeleton done."

As Diane checked her E-mail and looked through the messages Andie had left for her, she told Frank the whole story—the Cobber's Wood hanging victims, the timber cruisers who found the bodies, and now Raymond, the diener. She tacked on the E-mail note to her narrative.

"Damn. I can't leave you alone at all."

"Can you trace the E-mail?"

"Probably."

"I'd appreciate that . . ." The ringing of her office phone cut her off. Diane grabbed it midring. "Fallon?"

"Finally. We can talk. You're a hard woman to reach."

The voice was rough textured and unfamiliar to Diane. He talked slow, with a south Georgia accent.

"Who is this?"

"Did you like the flowers?"

Chapter 19

"You put the flowers in my car?" Diane looked at the caller ID on her office phone. NO DATA. She had picked up the receiver too soon. "Why didn't you sign the card?"

Frank stood, took his cell phone from his pocket and backed out of her office while he dialed. She assumed he was having the call traced.

"It was unnecessary."

"What does 'To Justice' mean?"

"Just that. I saw on TV that you are a sincere woman. I want you to know that I understand that, but you don't have the whole picture."

"Is that why you're calling—to make sure I understand?"

"The thing you said on the TV—about all murderers being evil."

"That's not exactly what I said."

"It's close enough. That's what you meant. You can't say things like that without knowing all the circumstances. Sometimes it's the so-called murder victim who's evil. The so-called murderer is just seeing that justice is done."

Diane tried to stall for time. "First of all, you need

to know the television interview was some old stock footage they had from when we opened the crime lab. I was talking about murder in general."

"I know. That's just the thing. You can't talk about murder in general, unless you know all the circumstances all the time, and you don't."

"I know that everyone deserves their life."

"Then you don't believe in giving murderers the death sentence?"

"I believe in following the law."

"You're just playing with words."

"It sounds like you have some personal experience . . ." She heard a click. Damn. She hadn't handled that well.

"I'm sorry," she said as Frank came into the office. "I couldn't hold him on the line any longer."

Frank took a pen and scribbled a number on Diane's desk calendar. "The call was made from this pay phone at the Rest Aplenty Motel out on 441."

"You had time to trace it?"

"That business about losing the trace if you don't keep people talking for several minutes is just a device used by the movies to keep the detectives from finding the killer too quickly." Frank pulled his chair closer to Diane and sat down. "Phone companies have been able to trace a call in a matter of seconds for more than twenty years."

"You're kidding."

"No, I'm not. You just have to know who in the phone company to talk to. I called the police and asked them to check it out, but I imagine he's gone by now."

"I didn't know there were any pay phones anymore."

"There's a few still left, but they're disappearing. So, what did this guy say?"

"Not much."

Diane related the conversation almost verbatim. She watched Frank as she talked. He listened, leaning forward in his chair, his elbows on his knees, hands loosely clasped together. His short salt-and-pepper hair looked steel gray under the lights of her office. He looked good in his blue jeans and white shirt with the sleeves rolled up to just below his elbows. Frank seemed to listen with his blue-green eyes—he narrowed them in a way that made them glitter. He'd been gone for a couple weeks, and she realized it seemed like a couple of months. She was glad he was back.

"Do you think he's the perp?" Frank asked.

"I don't know. He hasn't mentioned the murders specifically. Just allusions to justice. We've had a lot of people contact me to protest the location of the crime lab in the museum." Diane threw her hands up. "For all I know, I could have picked up a stalker when I appeared on television."

"You need to get some rest."

"Does it show?"

"I wasn't going to mention it."

"You just did."

"No. I said you need to get some rest." He gave her a broad smile.

"The key to solving this is the identity of the victims. I need to finish the last set of bones."

"Why don't I stay with you, drive you home when you're done?"

"You must be exhausted after your trip back from San Francisco."

"Don't you have a comfortable couch in your office up in that fancy lab of yours?"

"Yes. But . . ."

"There you have it. Problem solved. Let's eat, then go identify a skeleton—I've always wanted to learn how to do that. I'm pretty good at recognizing clavicles now. I'll betcha I can tell the left from the right."

Diane called David at the Waller crime scene first to check up on her team.

"How's everything going?" she asked.

"Going fine. I sneaked some pictures of the people watching."

"Good for you."

"We found a secret closet."

"No. A secret closet?"

"It was next to the main closet, with a bookcase for a door. You can imagine what ran through our minds as we were opening it."

"Collections of fingertips."

"That's what we all were thinking."

"Well, what was in it?"

"His collection of memorabilia from the old Negro Leagues. I'm sure he was keeping it hidden from burglars. You know he's got a bat signed by Josh Gibson? He hit over nine hundred home runs in his career, eighty-four in one season. I actually held a ball signed by Satchel Paige. I mean, you should see the stuff the guy had."

"You think it was a burglary gone bad?"

"That's what Chief Garnett thinks."

"Was Raymond tied up like Chris Edwards?"

"No. His hair, face and chest are wet. That's what Garnett is keeping back."

"Do I detect a note of disagreement? Is there any evidence this is connected to Edwards or the Cobber's Wood victims?"

"Not exactly. But . . ." Diane heard sounds of David walking. She assumed he was going someplace where Garnett couldn't hear him. "The place is tossed like Edwards'. Chris Edwards was caught unawares in his bathroom, dazed by a blow to the head and then tied up, but he was able to put up a fight. I think there's a possibility that the killer tried the same thing with Raymond, but hit him a little too hard, tried to revive him, but he had killed him."

"The perp could still have been looking for the baseball stuff."

"Yes, he could. We'll see if there's anything in the trace evidence similar to Edwards."

"Keep up the good work. I hope we are all able to get some sleep sometime this week."

"Sleep? You don't still do that, do you?"

"Call me if you need me."

"Frank not back yet?"

"As a matter of fact, he is."

"Does he know about the flowers?"

"The flowers. It turns out the person who left them called."

"Oh, who was it?" David had asked about the flowers in jest, but he sounded cautious now. Diane briefly told him about the caller. David whistled. "Okay, this isn't good."

"It could be completely innocent . . ."

"Normal people don't act like that—only crazies or people guilty of something."

"Can you hand your phone to Garnett."

"Sure."

After a moment, Garnett's voice came on the phone and Diane related the story a third time.

"I don't like this. You say you kept him talking long enough for the phone company to trace the call?"

Diane hesitated a beat. "Yes. A policeman went to check it out, but I imagine he's long gone."

"I'll call and tell them to talk to anyone who might have seen anybody using that pay phone."

"I got an answer from the E-mail. You know of a policeman named Lenderman or something like that?"

"There's a Marty Lenderman. You saying it's him? He's a very down-to-earth guy. I can't even imagine it's him."

"The person who replied said they didn't send the message and not to bother them, that their father was a policeman. The address was JMLndrmn. I just added some vowels to what looked like it might be the last name. Does he have a kid with the initials J. M.?"

"Sure does. Jennifer Marie. She's only about sixteen. You think she did this as a prank?"

"I don't know. Can't spammers hijack E-mail addresses?"

"I'll talk to Marty. In the meantime, I'll have someone trace where the E-mail message came from."

"I can probably do that here."

"Okay. All this may be just some prank, but be careful anyway. I think Raymond was probably killed for his collection. It's pretty valuable, according to your guy David."

"I heard him drooling over the phone."

Garnett laughed. "I haven't heard of most of the guys except Satchel Paige, but that ball by itself should be worth some money."

*　　*　　*

The museum restaurant was a maze of tall archways made of salvaged bricks that looked like it could have been an ancient monastery library, and yet for all its vaulted height and medieval atmosphere, it felt cozy. Five dark rough-hewn wood tables sat in each of the five chambers made by four contiguous archways at right angles to each other. Booths in arched brick alcoves lined the walls. Diane and Frank chose a booth.

Near the entrance in another recess sat a line of four computers—for all its Old World museum look, the restaurant was also an Internet cafe.

The restaurant was known for its great salad and fruit bar. It also had a varied menu. Diane made herself a chef salad with a fruit side dish and took it back to the table. Frank ordered a steak.

"How's Star?" Diane asked as she sat down opposite Frank.

He tore off a piece of bread and dipped it in herbed olive oil. "She's like that little girl with the curl in the middle of her forehead."

"She's not really horrid, is she?"

The waitress brought Frank's steak. As Diane ate her salad, she was beginning to wish she'd ordered a piece of red meat too. She felt the need for a lot of protein.

"Star's doing pretty good, considering her family was murdered a year ago. She wanted to go with me to the West Coast—insisted that she didn't need anyone watching her while I was in court. Can you imagine me letting her loose by herself in San Francisco? Want some of my steak?"

"No, go ahead and eat," she said, but Frank cut off a piece on the tender side and put it on her salad. "Frank, that's the best part."

"If you're going to insist on burning the candle at

both ends, you need to eat. So, tell me about your mummy. Know anything about him yet?"

"So far, we've X-rayed him. Jonas is translating the sarcophagus, though it's probably not his."

Diane related what they had discovered, skipping over the details of what abscesses were like at a time when dental care was not what it is today. Frank was laughing over the story of the Victorian pickle jar when Diane took the last bite of her fresh pineapple.

Chapter 20

"Nice place," said Frank, looking around Diane's osteology lab.

The white walls and overhead lighting did make the room look bright, as the shiny tables, sinks and microscopes made it look new.

"You've been here. You're one of the few who've had the grand tour."

"I suppose I'm surprised it hasn't fallen into that dingy hospital look. Do you paint the walls every few weeks?"

"I'm very neat in my work. I clean all the blood spatters off my walls every day. You remember where my office is?"

Diane led him to a corner door, unlocked it and turned on the light. The small office had pale off-white walls that, if she remembered correctly from the paint can, was called Candle Glow. The floor was green slate, the desk and filing cabinets a dark walnut. A long burgundy leather couch sat against one wall, its matching chair close to her desk. There was adequate space, but no more.

Although she needed a private office in the osteology lab, it was her second office, and she hadn't wanted to use more space than absolutely necessary. She chose the leather and wood furniture so the room wouldn't look as hard-edged as the lab with its stark metal tables and impersonal equipment, but something about the room was still cold. Perhaps it was the lack of a carpet. She didn't have a carpet installed because she wanted neither the static electricity nor the fibers it would generate. The walls were mostly bare—one lone watercolor of a wolf hunting in the wild.

"You can rest in here, if you need to," she said.

"Actually, I got a lot of rest on the plane. Why don't I watch you work?"

"All right. But it's like watching paint dry."

"I think you underestimate yourself." He drew her into another kiss. In the privacy of her office, Diane didn't feel obliged to break off as soon. "You know," said Frank, when he pulled away, "this looks like a real comfortable couch."

"It is. If you need to rest, I'm sure it'll be soft enough. I have to look at Red Doe now. If we can find where these people belong, we can discover who killed them."

Red Doe sat in the box on a table, waiting. As Diane laid out the bones, Frank walked around the lab looking at the microscopes, wall charts, books and various other lab paraphernalia. When she started the examination, he wandered back over and watched.

"Male or female?"

Diane looked up at him silently.

"Sorry, I've never seen you work before and I'd like to know how you do it. You know, in case I come across some bones." He grinned.

"If you come across any bones, you call in an anthropologist," she said. A moment passed before she spoke again. "It's female. You can tell by the pelvis."

The pubic symphysis had more wear than the other two, but not enough to throw it into another age category. All the victims were around the same age. Red may have been a little older, but she also may have been more active. The muscle attachments on her pelvis were more developed than Blue's—and Green's. Interesting.

Red Doe's face was orthognathic, with an almost flat profile. Her cranial index—the ratio of breadth to length—was the lowest number in the mongoloid range. In fact, all her cranial indices measured at the low end of the mongoloid range. Red's teeth had even-edged occlusion, but she did not have shovel-tooth incisors. Like Blue and Green, Red had no cavities. They all had grown up with fluoride and regular dental checkups.

"She's Asian," said Diane.

Frank squinted at the skull. "How can you tell?"

"There are certain features you look for, but mainly it's in the math. There are indices calculated from measurements of precise points on the skull. The index numbers fall within ethnic ranges. There are also differences in the rest of the skeleton that fall within ethnic categories. That's why accurate measurement is important and why I must do so much of it."

"Looks like there'd be computer programs that would compute these things."

"There are and I have them, but I still have to do the measuring."

"Your fancy machine doesn't take the measurements?"

"It does make external measurements for the skull, but I still have to make all the other measurements on the skeleton the old-fashioned way and put the numbers into the program. In the end, I'll have a very detailed mathematical description of the three skeletons to give Sheriff Braden.''

"These bones look nice and clean," said Frank.

"Raymond . . ." She paused. Her mind went back to the autopsy, his good humor, his competence, his interest in what she did. "Raymond Waller, Lynn Webber's assistant, cleaned them."

"You all right?"

Diane met Frank's gaze and realized he didn't know anything about Raymond. "He died tonight—he was murdered."

"Is that the crime scene your team's on?"

Diane nodded.

"That's certainly a coincidence—him having just worked on these bodies."

"Especially when you consider that one of the men who found the bodies was also murdered and the other one is missing."

Frank stared at her a long moment. Having said it out loud to Frank, it didn't sound like it could possibly be a coincidence, even though she had been kind of buying into Garnett's theory that Raymond's murder had to do with his collection of Negro Leagues baseball memorabilia.

From the look on Frank's face, she could tell he didn't think it was a coincidence. But Frank never believed in coincidences. In his universe, everything was connected; you just had to follow the train of consequences of that butterfly flapping his wings.

"That's certainly interesting. And you're getting calls and E-mails about the murders?"

"I don't know that they're about the murders. Neither the E-mails nor the caller mentioned any of the murders."

"I'll trace the E-mail account for you tomorrow."

"Garnett's working on it—I think."

"I'll have a look too."

"The murders could be a coincidence, couldn't they?" said Diane, not really believing it herself.

"Not in a town this size."

His comment just hung in midair, effectively ending this part of the conversation. Diane returned to her measurements.

As she examined the postcranial skeleton, all the bones except the skull, Frank watched everything she did with a keen interest.

"Red Doe may have been a ballet dancer," Diane said, breaking the silence.

"How's that?" asked Frank.

"She has very well-developed attachments from her calf muscles, greater than any other part of her body. That's a major muscle used in ballet dancing."

"Calf muscles, that'd be the gastrocnemius," said Frank.

"Very good. You know your muscles?"

"You have them on the chart over there."

"You memorized the chart while I was laying out the bones?"

"I just saw a couple of names I recognize. Besides, anyone who ever lifted weights knows the names of the major muscle groups—you know, deltoids, pectoral, biceps, six-pack."

Diane laughed and shook her head.

"There must be more evidence than that—I mean, maybe she just did a lot of calf exercises."

"Red Doe's had some serious inflammation in her right flexor hallucis longus, probably due to the plantar flexing involved in being *en pointe*."

Frank stared at her a moment, amusement dancing in his eyes. "Okay, she had sore muscles from dancing on her toes."

"Frank, you surprise me. That wasn't half bad."

"Well, I know what flexing means, and jumping around on your toes can't be good for you—besides, I'm a detective."

"The hallucis longus tendon starts on the fibula, one of the lower leg bones, goes under the foot and connects to the big toe. That constant hyperflexed position can do damage to the tendons severe enough to leave lesions on the bones. You're right—it's not good for the toes or any of the joints. During a dance, the dancer can increase the forces on her joints as much as ten times her body weight.

"Red Doe's toes show signs of stress from that kind of pounding. That goes along with other lesions I found on the left femur, where she had chronic tendinitis of her psoas tendon from the repetitive turn-out position of the leg. I suspect, but don't know, that Red went *en pointe* too young."

"Why in the world would anyone put their body through that?"

"Would you like to discuss football?"

"Yeah, well, that's different."

"Right."

Frank finally took her up on the offer to nap on her couch and Diane worked in silence, examining, measuring and recording each bone—along with any identifying characteristics that manifest themselves in the bones. She looked for nicks or perimortem breaks that might be associated with an injury inflicted by the murderer. She found none.

As she examined the vertebrae, she found a stress

fracture on the pars interarticularis of the fifth lumbar vertebrae. More evidence that Red Doe had been a ballet dancer. The arabesque position places an inordinate amount of stress on the lower spine, and fractures on one of the lumbar vertebrae are not uncommon.

Finally, Diane examined the cut end of the phalanges under the microscope. Four bore the mark of the same tool that was used to cut off the fingers of the other two victims.

She was taking photographs when Frank came back, sleepy eyed. "Don't you ever go to bed?"

"Is that an offer?"

"Yes, definitely."

"Okay. Let me take a look at the rope and I'll let you take me home."

"Rope?"

"The rope they were hung with."

"Oh."

Diane took Red's rope to the table and laid it out. The red string that tied the cut ends together looked as if it had been dipped in fresh blood. She examined each of the knots again. They were identical to Blue's and Green's, down to the stevedore's stopper knot. Definitely tied by the same hand.

She decided to leave the bones and the rope out on the table and get David to help her finish the photographs tomorrow. She looked at her watch. Today. Damn, she'd hardly get any sleep. As she started to leave, she saw the other box with the single piece of rope that they had found on the ground at the scene. She took out the rope and lay it on the table. It was full of kinks and covered with worn places. No knots for her to analyze. She laid it on one of the empty tables.

*   *   *

Diane fell asleep with her arm around Frank's waist, his body nestled against hers. Despite the hot night, his body felt good and safe, like home. The last thing she thought of before going to sleep was the lone rope she left lying out on the table in the lab.

Chapter 21

When Diane arrived in the crime lab, Neva approached her anxiously and handed her drawings of Fred and Ethel. The drawings looked as if Fred and Ethel had sat for them. They were similar to the computer graphics, but didn't have that computer graphic look. Both were Caucasian. Diane noticed the noses right away. They had the most distinctive detail. Neva had taken to heart the lesson Diane gave her.

Ethel was young, midtwenties, with dark hair falling below her chin, oval face, slight nose, eyes wide apart. Fred was older, midforties. Neva had drawn his hair neither short nor long, but a median length for males. His face was square and his nose almost pug, with a prominent dip between the nasal bone and the frontal bone between the eyes. Their lips were neither thin nor thick. Fred and Ethel, who never knew each other in life, were now "married" skeletons, given a new life in Neva's drawings.

"Very good," Diane told her. "This is exactly what I'm looking for. We'll have to frame and hang these." A museum exhibit had already begun playing out in the back of her mind.

Diane unlocked the lab and the vault for Neva.

While she waited for David, she set up the camera equipment.

"If this rate of mayhem keeps up, you're going to have to hire a second crime scene unit," said David as he came through the door.

"Maybe we can put an ad in the paper notifying everyone that the county has reached its quota of murders for the year, so they can't commit any more."

David took over the task of setting up the cameras, and Diane laid out the bones for the photographs. As he helped her photograph Red Doe's bones, David briefed her on the crime scene and the latest gossip.

"You certainly gave Neva a boost—sending her to process the car by herself, then assigning her to reconstruct the faces." He spoke in a low voice, even though there was no way Neva could hear them from inside the vault room. "She was much more confident—and friendly—at the crime scene."

"She just needed experience—and someone to counteract Garnett. That Janice Warrick thing last year apparently touched all the women working in the department."

"Garnett asked us to take Raymond Waller's collection to keep safe in the museum until Raymond's family could claim it. He didn't want to leave it in the house. I took everything to Korey. I thought some of the items might need special care."

"That's fine. Korey will know how to care for them. Nice of Garnett to take care of things for the family."

"He's not a bad guy," said David. "A little too political. Acts like he's always looking over his shoulder."

"Probably is. Have you met the mayor?"

"No, but I understand that you've had a conversation with him."

Diane smiled as she placed Red Doe's fourth lumbar vertebra on the stand to be photographed. "Yes. We had a conversation."

David laughed, snapped the pictures and removed the camera from the stand. "That's the last one, isn't it?" Diane nodded. "We're processing the Waller evidence as quickly as we can. There wasn't much there. We collected fiber samples from the furniture that had been ripped up. When we find the perp, he's bound to have gotten fibers all over him."

"Someone was obviously looking for something," mused Diane. "You don't think it was the collection?"

David shrugged. "Maybe. That seems the most obvious. It's just that . . ."

"There are those other murders," finished Diane.

"Yeah, those other murders. And why would he rip up the upholstery in search of baseball bats? Doesn't add up."

David cast a glance at the lone rope lying on the table, the one found on the ground at the Cobber's Wood crime scene. "You going to be able to do anything with that?"

"I don't know. It was tied in knots long enough to leave kinks in the rope. I thought I might be able to do something with those."

"What can you possibly do? The knots are gone."

"But they were there."

"So was my hair, but we can't reconstruct where the cowlick was."

"It was on the front right side, opposite where your part was."

David opened his mouth, then shut it, and stroked his bald head as if feeling for something. "How could you know that?"

Diane took a rope she had purchased that morning

and laid it beside the crime scene rope. "You forgot, I've seen pictures of you as a kid."

David threw back his head and laughed one loud *Ha!* "You had me going. Good thing you told me. I'd have been thinking about that all day."

"You'd have figured it out. The point is, there's always evidence."

David went back to the crime lab, shaking his bald head, leaving Diane to study the rope. Near one end was a cluster of six kinks about an inch to an inch and a half apart—some kinks were more crimped than others. Fifteen inches down, there was a larger kink with significant wear on the inside of the curve. Two and a quarter inches from there, another series of worn places. The wear was not continuous, but in patches down the rope.

She photographed the rope and measured all the places where it was kinked and worn. Altogether, there were eleven kinks of varying sizes and seven places where the rope had been worn, some quite extensively, some barely noticeable. Sometimes the wear was inside the kink, other times it was alone.

Diane lay her new rope beside the crime scene rope—called the "lone rope" in her notes. She took red and green Sharpies and began marking the new rope to match the lone rope—green signifying a kink, red signifying wear.

"Okay, smarty," she muttered to herself, "what kind of knot was tied in this rope?"

The obvious first choice—obvious to her, at least—was a sheepshank. Perhaps the person wanted to use the rope, but was worried the worn places had weakened it. A sheepshank is a method of strengthening a rope by tying it in such a way as to take the strain off the weak areas. It shortens a rope, but is a good way to use a damaged rope in a pinch.

She tied a sheepshank several times, each time trying to match the green kinks to the turn of the knots and placing the red worn areas where they would be strengthened by having good rope on either side. Even after numerous attempts, she never got close to matching her red and green points to the turns of the sheepshank.

The initial failure made her more determined. *Okay, the kinks are the turns of the knots—or . . . where the rope looped around an object. And so where does the wear come from—from rubbing against an object, or itself?* Diane fished a handful of colored rubber bands out of a drawer and dropped them on the table next to the experimental rope.

First she located each green kink with no red wear on the inside, made a bight—a loop—and placed a yellow rubber band around it to hold it in place. She took the kinks with inside wear and did the same thing. Where the rope showed several kinks close together, she didn't bother with how the knot was actually tied, but simply looped them together and held them with a blue rubber band. *Okay, now it looks like a mess, but that's all right.*

Diane examined the crime scene rope again and studied the red wear marks on her experimental rope. She tried several ways of folding the rope so that the wear marks—the red marks on her experimental rope—touched each other. Each way was a tangle of rope with no significant pattern.

There was about a foot and a half where several spots of wear spiraled around the rope. She folded her arms and frowned at the two pieces of hemp lying on the table. The lone rope had been twisted in some way. She made a loop at the widest space between wear marks and then twisted the rope so that all the wear marks touched, securing it with a red rubber band. It now almost looked like something. But what?

Neva came out of the vault, stretching her arms. "I thought I'd break for lunch," she said.

Diane looked at her watch. She'd been at this damn rope far too long, and what was it going to tell her anyway?

"I didn't realize it's getting so late. How's the reconstruction going?"

"Good, I think. I'll have something by the end of the day. If people will refrain from killing each other for a while, I'll get all three done pretty quickly."

"What's your take on the most recent murder?" asked Diane.

"We don't have that many murders here, and now we have a cluster of five, maybe six. It doesn't look like a serial killer to me. Not that I've had any experience with serial killers, but the last two killers seemed to be looking for something. I'm kind of thinking it may be Steven Mayberry. And he, Chris Edwards and Raymond Waller were involved in something." She shook her head. "But none of them have any criminal record that we know about, and as far as I know, they were all decent, hard-working guys."

Diane nodded. Not a bad analysis, she thought. "Fortunately, the who and why are Chief Garnett and Sheriff Braden's problem. We just uncover the evidence."

Neva looked at the tangle of rope. "What are you doing here?"

"I'm trying to figure out what kind of knot was tied in the rope."

"You can do that?"

"So far, no. But that hasn't stopped me. I'll leave it alone for a while. Maybe something will come to me if I get my mind off of it."

Diane faxed her initial report on the analysis of the skeletons to Sheriff Braden, letting him know that photographs and copies of the report would arrive by messenger in the afternoon. By the time all that was taken care of, she was starved. She brought tomato soup in a Styrofoam cup and a chef salad back to her museum office. As she sipped the soup and ate her salad, her gaze rested on envelopes containing the mummy's X-rays sitting in her in-box. It made her smile. Diane was getting into the mummy thing like the rest of her staff. She quickly finished her lunch, disposed of the remains and sat down at the light table.

She selected the X-rays showing the thorax—the midsection—of the mummy. As was her custom, she started by examining the pelvis. It was a male pelvis. That was no surprise. The innominates, the large flat hip bones, showed signs of thinning. It looked as though he had suffered inflammation of his ischial tuberosities—the site of several muscle attachments as well as the place where he sat.

However, it was the mummy's lumbar vertebrae that were the most interesting. She pulled out two other X-rays, a side and back view, from the envelope. He also suffered from vertebral scoliosis, and on the margins of the body of his lumbar vertebrae there was a significant degree of lipping.

Interesting. While the condition of Red Doe's lumbar vertebrae was caused by excessive arching of her back, the mummy's condition was caused by a prolonged position in the opposite direction. The mummy, whoever he was, had spent long periods bending over in a seated position.

Diane stared at the X-rays, but saw the mummy and tried to visualize the person. What came to mind was a small Egyptian statue she had seen—a scribe in a cross-legged seated position. The kind of inflammation in the ischium was also called weaver's bottom, because of the prolonged sitting in front of a loom that weavers had to endure. Could the mummy have been a scribe? Or maybe he was some artisan, like a jewelry maker, who was seated over his work for hours a day. She liked both of those possibilities.

Diane examined the remainder of the X-rays and found more evidence of arthritis, but no other conditions. Perhaps when they discovered when he had lived, her observations would have more meaning.

Andie brought in more mail for Diane to go through.

"Probably more requests for mummy tissue," said Andie. "Want me to go ahead and deal with it?"

"Please." Diane handed them off to Andie.

"You've been looking at the X-rays. What did you find?" Andie pulled up a chair and sat with her elbows on the desk and her chin in her hands.

Diane went into detail about all of the conditions and her speculation about what they meant. "We should get even more information from the CT scan."

"This is so cool. Do you think he could be a pharaoh? Maybe one with a hobby?"

"I hope not. We'll have to give him back to the Egyptian government if that turns out to be the case. They like to keep their heads of state."

"Oh, I never thought of that. Well, scribe is good.

Maybe he was an architect. Did they spend more time drawing up plans or building stuff?"

"I have no idea. You'll have to look to Jonas and Kendel for details of Egyptian life. I'm going to have Neva draw his face from the data we get from the CT scan."

"Okay, now, that is really neat. This is as much fun as when they were assembling the *Albertosaurus*."

Diane nodded. "It is, isn't it?"

Andie went back to her office, and Diane returned to her paperwork. She checked her E-mail and was relieved to find no more messages from whoever sent her the flowers. Probably just a crackpot.

She reviewed several proposals, signed several order forms for everything from pens to chemicals and answered queries from her board members. As she worked, an idea came to her about the lone rope from the crime scene. She jumped up from her chair, looked on her shelf for her book on knots and headed for the lab, telling Andie where she would be as she flew out the door.

Chapter 22

Diane's museum office was in the opposite wing from the crime lab. She enjoyed the walk across the museum, even when she was in a hurry. She liked seeing the visitors going from room to room, looking at the exhibits, and hearing children's delighted voices squeal upon seeing a display upon which the museum staff had worked hard. But today Diane's mind was focused on a nagging problem, and she bypassed the crowd and took the east wing elevator to the third floor and hurried across to her osteology lab. David met her in the hallway coming from the crime lab.

"Andie said you were on your way up."

"Yes. I have an idea."

"Chief Garnett called. He traced the E-mail and talked to Officer Lenderman and his daughter."

Diane's cell rang and she held up a finger motioning David to wait while she answered it. The ID showed Frank's work number.

"Hey," he said. "Loved seeing you last night."

"Me, too. Frank, I'm . . ."

"I traced the origin of the E-mail. It was from inside the museum."

Diane stood there, dumfounded. "Inside the museum?"

David began nodding in agreement.

"You need to tell Garnett," said Frank.

"I will, Frank. Thanks. David's here, and I think he has some more information on it."

"Good. Call if you need me."

"Inside the museum?" Diane asked David.

"Yes. Garnett talked to the daughter. She's a student at Bartram and comes to the museum to work on a paleontology project. She said she sometimes uses the computers in the restaurant—that's where the E-mail originated from."

"She sent it?"

"She says not. She remembers sending some messages and leaving the computer for a minute or two when she saw some friends come into the restaurant. That's when someone must have hijacked her E-mail account. She was still logged on."

"Damn. Does she remembering seeing anyone?"

"No. I think she was very focused on herself and her friends."

Diane put her hands to her face. "Not the museum. This is my worst nightmare."

"Wait a minute," said David. "Why are you worried about the museum? Whoever this guy is, he's focused on you."

"But he's coming into the museum. I can't have that. Did Garnett have anything else to say?"

"Yes, he wants you to meet him at his office in about an hour. He's meeting again with Sheriff Braden. I have a file full of reports you can take to each of them."

"Good. I prefer going over there to them coming here."

"They're talking to Kacie Beck," David said.

"Kacie Beck. Isn't she . . ."

"Chris Edwards' girlfriend."

"Why is that?"

"She was there very close to the time of death. They've discovered a witness who puts her there even earlier than she reported—a lot earlier than her 911 call."

"I can't see her hitting him over the head, dragging him to the closet and tying him up like that. She weighs what, a hundred ten pounds at the most?"

"They're thinking maybe she had help—like Steven Mayberry. Edwards' partner. But there's another problem."

"What's that?"

"It was in the report, but I'm not sure it registered with them. On Chris Edwards' nightstand we found a digital thermometer—the under-the-tongue variety that keeps the last temperature reading. Whoever used it had a 103-degree fever."

Diane pictured Lynn taking the liver temperature at the crime scene. She had commented on the early rigor. "If it was Chris who had the temperature, that changes the time of death by several hours."

David nodded. "Three hours earlier at least."

"Well, damn. That's all I need is to tell Lynn Webber she got another time of death wrong."

Jin came bopping through the hallway from the crime lab and stopped when he saw Diane and David.

"You tell her about the time and temperature thing?"

David nodded. "Just now."

"The babe at the scene didn't have a fever," said Jin.

"You sure about that?" asked Diane.

"Sure, I'm sure. How you going to break it to Doc Webber?"

"Gently," said Diane. She thought for a moment. "Okay, she's sure to have noticed at the autopsy if Edwards had any kind of infection."

"One would think," said David.

"The medicine on the nightstand with the thermometer suggests that it was upper respiratory," said Jin.

Diane recalled Chris Edwards coughing a time or two at the Cobber's Wood crime scene.

"Lynn Webber probably hasn't alerted Chief Garnett about any possible change in the time of death, so here's what I want you to do. David, call her at home if she is taking time off, and tell her about the thermometer and the fever, and you are concerned about someone else being in the house and you want to know if Edwards was sick. That ought to give her enough of a nudge to call Garnett herself."

"You're going to tell him too?" asked Jin.

"Of course," said Diane. "I'm just trying to keep the peace." She shrugged. "I probably shouldn't bother, and just let the chips fall."

"Speaking of letting things fall," Jin said. "It was cut clean with a sharp knife."

Diane stared at him for a moment. "What was?"

"King Tut's jewels." Jin pushed his hair out of his eyes.

"Ouch," said David.

"It was postmortem." Jin grinned broadly. "That must have been some unwrapping party," Jin continued on his way through the museum. "I've sent a sample of his blood off," he called as he went through the doors into the museum proper.

"Garnett wants to see me in an hour?" said Diane. David nodded. "Okay. I have just enough time to test an idea about the rope."

"Don't tell me you discovered what kind of knot was tied."

"Maybe."

"This I gotta see." David followed Diane into her lab.

Diane flipped to the index of her handbook and looked under *hitches* until she found the knot she was looking for. She found the page and lay the book down next to the rope that she had trussed up with rubber bands.

"They sort of look alike—in a way," said David, comparing the illustration in the book and the rope on the table, tilting his head as if that would give him the ability to see the resemblance more clearly.

Diane took the rubber bands off the experimental rope and looked around the lab for a place to tie the hitch. The cabinets. She studied the rope a moment, looking at the green and red marks that represented kinks and chafes. She secured one end of the rope to the handle of the cabinets above the counter. Then she made a crossing turn at the first green mark and a bight farther down at another green mark. After several complicated twists and loops, she placed one of the loops over the handle of the bottom drawer, tightened the rope, and stood back, surveying her work.

The knots matched up with her green marks. The red marks along the rope also met up with each other, showing that they had rubbed against each other. The loop around the lower cabinet handle also fit with her color coding—a kink with chafing on the inside made by rubbing against something it was looped around.

"Okay, what is it?" asked David.

"A waggoner's hitch. It's not common, but when

I noticed how the chafing spiraled around the rope, something nagged in my brain and I finally thought of this hitch. It's a hitch for tying down a load in a wagon. It's kind of a cool knot. It's very secure under tension. But once the tension is released, the hitch comes loose easily. It has to be tied and set properly for it to work right. One of its characteristics is that if the knot is repeatedly tied in the same place, it really wears down the rope by the friction against itself from movement."

"I'm impressed. I really didn't think you could re-create the knot in that scrappy piece of rope. However, not to rain on your parade, does this get us anywhere?"

"It was once used by waggoners. Some truck drivers still use it."

"Okay, that does get us somewhere."

"It doesn't mean he's a truck driver, but he did use this piece of rope often. That's why it's in such bad shape. It is the same kind of rope used in the hangings, and it was found at the crime scene. It's at least suggestive."

"Truck drivers travel quite a bit—perfect occupation for someone who wants to hide what he does in his spare time. Sheriff Braden's going to like this."

"Would you photograph this? I'm going to pay a visit to the Rosewood Police Department."

Chapter 23

The Rosewood police department was housed in a new building constructed in a more modern style than the red brick 1900 courthouse to the left and the 1960s pink granite post office across the street. From the time Diane walked in, she could feel the unfriendly looks in her direction.

Even Frank's friend, Izzy Wallace, looked sheepish when he saw her. He still didn't like her. He no longer had a reason. Before, he at least had the excuse of the untruths told about her. Now he apparently just couldn't break the habit. He turned from the officer he was talking to and forced a big smile onto his fleshy face.

"Why, hey, Diane. What brings you here? How's Frankie boy?"

"He's back from San Francisco. Convicted his guy, so he's happy. How are you doing?"

"Just fine. Just fine. I understand that's quite some crime lab you have over there at the museum."

He grinned, and Diane thought she saw some of the policemen look at each other and snicker. They probably knew she was pressured into housing it at the museum. Diane smiled sweetly.

"We're very proud of it. Good to see you, Izzy." She turned to the sergeant on duty. "I'm here to see Chief Garnett."

She showed him her identification, and he nodded and pointed up the stairs.

Homicide squad took up the entire second floor of the building. She passed reception and entered the main squad room. It was an open area with desks marking each detective's work space. One wall of the room was a giant magnetic dry-marker whiteboard for attaching photographs, drawing interaction patterns, social networks, or for simply giving pictures to thoughts.

The board held photos of the three hanging victims from Sheriff Braden's jurisdiction, photographs of the Chris Edwards and Raymond Waller crime scenes, a list of similarities, a photo of Steven Mayberry's car, and a map indicating the location of each crime scene. It was not unlike the display she had in her own lab.

As Diane passed various detectives and staff, some were friendly and spoke; others frowned upon seeing her. She had no idea what motivated either of the two camps. She smiled at all of them.

Chief Garnett ushered her into his office, where Sheriff Braden sat in a chair near Garnett's desk, twirling his hat in his hands. Diane had expected Garnett to have an ornate office, but it was basically utilitarian with faux leather and chrome chairs, metal desk and a long wood conference table. Hanging on sand-colored walls were diplomas, awards, photographs of Garnett shaking hands with numerous politicians and framed newspaper clippings. Diane wondered briefly if he had sprayed the clippings with a deacidifier so they wouldn't yellow. She smiled inwardly at herself.

"Good to see you again, Sheriff."

The sheriff rose and shook her hand. "I got your fax. That's a lot of good information about those victims. Impressed me. We ought to be able to identify them real quick. It doesn't look like they were homeless after all, does it?"

"No," agreed Diane. "They seem to have been well off."

She sat down at the table, and the sheriff pulled his chair around so that he was opposite her.

"You say you'll be able to give me pictures of their faces?"

"Neva Hurley is working a reconstruction now. She says she'll have them done quickly."

"Now, that'll be just real helpful."

Garnett sat down at the head of the table, with the sheriff to his right and Diane to his left.

"We keep as up to date with techniques as we can," he said, claiming a resource he only recently knew he had. Garnett looked down at the folder in front of him before turning to Diane.

"I thought it would be good for you to go over what you have so far. I've included the sheriff because there's a good chance the crimes are connected and I think it would benefit all of us to cooperate."

Of course you do, thought Diane. For Garnett and the mayor to make Rosewood the crime-solving center of the region, they had to have the cooperation of the surrounding counties. What better way than to cooperate with them first?

"We're holding Kacie Beck right now," Garnett continued. "By her own admission, she was there right at the time of death. She called nine-one-one at eleven eighteen. M.E. put the time of death close to eleven. A witness saw Miss Beck drive up at a little after nine.

It doesn't look good for her. I'm thinking that if she didn't help kill Edwards, she knows who did."

Diane took the folder from in front of Garnett and thumbed through the reports. She pointed to an item.

"My team found a thermometer showing a temperature reading of 103 degrees on Chris Edwards' nightstand, along with cold medications. If he was running a temperature that high at the time of death, it will push back the time of death estimate to around seven P.M. The M.E. didn't have that information when she took a liver temperature at the crime scene."

Garnett took the report back from Diane, removed a pair of glasses from his pocket and examined it as if for the first time. "We don't know that this was Edwards' temperature."

"Not now, but we took a swab from the thermometer . . ." began Diane. She reached over and pulled out the autopsy report on Chris Edwards. "Dr. Webber indicates he had congestion in his lungs." Diane looked for attachments. "His blood work is not back yet."

Garnett started to speak, but was interrupted by his phone. From the one-sided conversation, Diane knew it was Lynn Webber. Diane wasn't sure why she had bothered with this elaborate ruse. It wasn't a desire to spare Lynn Webber's feelings or reputation that motivated her. What she wanted was to keep on good terms with the sheriff—and Garnett, for that matter. Both seemed rather swept off their feet by Webber.

"That was Dr. Webber," said Garnett, returning the phone to its cradle. "She said the blood work came back on Edwards showing he had an infection and that he probably had a fever. That corresponds to what you were telling us."

Diane merely nodded.

"That doesn't mean that Miss Beck isn't good for it," continued Garnett. "But we'll have to let her go."

"No sign of Steven Mayberry?" the sheriff asked.

"No. He seems to have vanished. He'll turn up sooner or later—I hope alive."

"I just finished the rope analysis." Diane explained about the waggoner's hitch.

"Well, I'll be," said the sheriff. "You got that from that old piece of rope?"

"It doesn't mean he's a truck driver," said Diane.

"I understand. But it's a place to start," said the sheriff. "Who'd've thought you could find anything in an old piece of rope like that?"

"You sure that rope belongs with the crime scene and it wasn't one that just happened to be in the woods?"

Garnett didn't seem to be criticizing, but rather the evidence appeared to excite him and he didn't want it to evaporate by being irrelevant. Everything that Diane did in the crime lab that impressed Sheriff Braden—or anyone else—was a feather in Garnett's cap.

"It has the same orange fiber on it that was on the clothes of the victims and on all the hanging ropes. The fourth noose and the Cobber's Wood crime scene also had the orange fiber, but no skin cells around the noose. It was never used."

Garnett nodded, looking satisfied.

Diane reviewed the evidence, crime scene by crime scene, starting with Steven Mayberry's truck, which was found on a dirt road near a small lake. "There was blood on the steering wheel and some smeared on the seat. We don't have the lab work back yet, so we can't say whose it is."

"It could be Chris Edwards', then?" said Garnett.

"Could be anyone's. We found Mayberry's finger-prints on the steering wheel. Some were in the blood, indicating the prints were left when the blood was fresh. His fingerprints were also on the dash, the seat, the gas cap, and the back gate of the truck. Chris Edwards' prints were on the passenger's side dash, the inside and outside door handles and the glove compartment. On the passenger's side we found another set of unidentified prints. They were smaller and could be female."

"Miss Beck?" said Garnett.

"No. We have her prints and these don't match. Inside the car we found three beer bottle caps, and a parking ticket issued by the Bartram campus police. He had parked in a faculty lot at the university library. The ticket had a boot print on it that matched Chris Edwards' left boot. We also found carpet fibers that matched Mayberry's trailer carpet. There were also cotton fibers, but we won't be able to provide any distinguishing match for those."

"I don't suppose there were any orange carpet fibers?" said Garnett.

"No matching orange carpet fibers found anywhere yet. So far we haven't been able to physically connect any of the crime scenes. The only connection is the coincidence of Edwards and Mayberry finding the bodies and Waller assisting with the autopsy."

"So it could all be a coincidence," said Garnett. "And one murder doesn't have a damn thing to do with the others."

Diane briefly went over the other crime scenes, except Raymond Waller's. They had covered them in the previous meeting, but it helped her to repeat the evidence. She suspected it would help Braden and Garnett too.

Both Sheriff Braden and Chief Garnett were silent when she finished her summary. Each sat back in his chair like they were digesting a large meal.

"The perp was looking for something in both the Edwards and Waller crime scenes," said the sheriff, after a moment.

"In Mayberry's trailer, too," said Diane. "It was tossed like the others."

"So what do you think the perp, or perps, was looking for?" asked the sheriff to neither of them in particular.

"Waller had a significant baseball collection," said Garnett. "I don't know that our other two boys had anything valuable."

Diane gave Garnett copies of the newest reports on the Chris Edwards scene and gave the sheriff the photographs of the Cobber's Wood skeletons.

"I'll send you information as it comes in," she said. "For the sheriff's case, identifying the victims is the key to the solution. If the crimes are related, then that may shed light on the others."

"If not, it'll have to be the old-fashioned way of interviewing everyone the vics knew," said Garnett. "I've got detectives doing that right now. So far, it looks like Edwards and Mayberry didn't have an enemy in the world. They were just two recent graduates from the forestry department working as timber cruisers. Raymond Waller didn't have any enemies either. He went to work every day and never got into any trouble. The worst we could find out about him is that he may have given a funeral home or two a heads-up on deaths that came through the morgue."

Garnett turned to Diane. "Do you think it was the killer who called you?"

"I don't know. Every time the news shows that interview with me the day we opened the crime lab, I get all kinds of mail and phone calls from people who don't like it. It could very well be one of those people with some strange take on justice. However, the flowers bother me."

"Flowers?" asked the sheriff.

Diane explained to him about the flowers, the E-mail and the phone call.

"This changes things a bit. You say you occasionally have this problem from people who see the interview?"

"None have ever sent flowers before."

"The guy who called from the motel on 441 says he sent the flowers, and he also E-mailed you from inside the museum."

"I don't know if the E-mail was the same guy—but the themes of justice and guilt seem to be similar. So it wouldn't be a stretch thinking it's the same person."

"Then if we watch you, we're likely to catch the killer," said the sheriff.

"For which crime?" asked Garnett.

"Who knows?" began the sheriff.

He was interrupted by a detective who stuck his head in the door.

"Chief, we got an emergency call from Dr. Lynn Webber."

Chapter 24

Garnett and the sheriff dashed out the door. Diane wanted to go with them, but there was no reason for her presence. She stood in Garnett's office a moment with a chill in the pit of her stomach. What was going on? She was beginning to feel responsible for not solving the murders. Maybe there was something she and her team had missed.

As she started out the door, Janice Warrick appeared suddenly, blocking her exit. She had on her blue police uniform, her light brown hair pulled back into the same French twist she wore when she was a detective.

"I know you think I blame you," Warrick said, "and maybe I do a little, but Neva tells me you treat her fairly and take up for her with him." She nodded toward Garnett's office.

"I try to treat all my employees fairly. Neva does a good job."

Janice Warrick stood for a moment, still in front of Diane, hesitating. "There's something that's been bothering me. I'm not usually a cruel person, but I said something cruel to you that had to do with your daughter being adopted—about your picking up strays.

It's weighed on me." She hesitated a moment and Diane thought she might actually get teary. "I'm sorry about that. I was sorry as soon as I said it." She turned abruptly and walked off before Diane could respond.

Diane left Garnett's office and wove her way through the squad room. She stopped at the whiteboard a moment, looking for anything they might have thought of that she and her team hadn't. But there was nothing, no pattern or startling revelation jumping out at her.

On the steps outside the police station, she ran into Kacie Beck. Her blond hair hung in limp sections, and she pushed a lock of it out of her eyes when she saw Diane. Her blue eyes looked bluer, set in her blood-shot sclera. She looked at Diane a moment, as if not remembering where she had seen her.

"I was at the crime scene," offered Diane.

"I didn't kill Chris. If you think I did, you're letting the real murderer get away."

"I don't think anything. I just worked the crime scene. Can I ask you some questions?"

"I've told the police everything I know. I'm tired and I want to go home."

"I can see you need some peace. I just have a few questions."

Kacie looked around. "Shit, I don't have my car." She dug in her purse and brought out her phone and scowled at the display. "They let the damn thing run down. The least they could do was turn it off for me."

"Let me take you home."

"Why not? But you aren't going to get me to admit to anything I didn't do."

Diane led her to her car, and Kacie got in on the passenger's side and sat slumped in the corner. She looked even smaller than she did sitting on Chris Edwards' couch at the crime scene.

"Buckle your seat belt," said Diane.

"What does it matter? It would at least end it if I went through the windshield."

"Maybe not. You might just end up scarred and brain damaged. Besides, if we're involved in an accident, you might flop around inside the car and hurt me."

Kacie laughed despite herself and clicked her seat belt in place. Diane drove to a Waffle House close to Kacie's apartment. Inside, Diane selected a booth in the rear of the diner. Kacie ordered a hamburger. Diane ordered a slice of pie and coffee.

When the waitress left the table, Kacie said, "I gotta go to the bathroom and wash my hands and face. I've never been in a jail before. What a nasty, stinking place."

After several minutes, Diane wasn't sure she was coming back. But eventually, Kacie slid back into her seat, looking marginally better. Little strands of moist hair bordered her face. As they waited for their order, Kacie nervously turned the engagement ring on her finger.

"That's a nice ring," said Diane.

Kacie stopped turning it and looked at the ring—a diamond solitaire set in either platinum or white gold.

"Chris gave it to me the morning before he died."

It looked like a rather large diamond to Diane, but she didn't know jewelry and it had been quite a while since she had an engagement ring. The waitress brought their food and drinks. Kacie nibbled at her hamburger, put it down and picked up a fry.

"I'm sorry about Chris," said Diane.

"I hate this. The police don't know what they are doing. Sometimes they acted like Chris was involved in something and caused this himself."

"They're just trying to find out what happened to him."

"It looked like one of those home invasions to me."

"Did Chris have a lot of valuables? Do you know what they might have been looking for?"

Kacie shrugged her shoulders and nibbled on her fry. Diane tried another tack.

"He must have paid a lot for that diamond. Does Chris have a lot of money that the thieves may have been after?"

Kacie looked at her ring. "He said he was going to show my parents. They don't really like Chris."

"Why not? He was a nice guy with an advanced degree. He had a job."

"My parents consider forestry blue-collar."

"Ah, they must know my parents."

Kacie looked up at Diane, her blue eyes puzzled.

"My parents consider anyone not a doctor or a lawyer to be blue-collar—unless he owns a Fortune 500 company."

"That's sort of my parents." She smirked. "It's not going to look good in the hometown paper that I was arrested for his murder."

Diane guessed that Kacie really was looking forward to it coming out in the hometown paper.

"You don't have any clue who might have done this? Could Steven Mayberry have killed him?"

"Steven? The police asked that. No. No more than I could. We're students—we don't kill people."

"I thought Steven and Chris had graduated."

"They've finished their course work. They both

have to finish their thesis, but they're almost done—were almost done."

Diane wasn't getting anywhere talking to Kacie. She now believed Kacie had no idea why her fiancé was killed.

"Do you have any idea where Steven Mayberry might be?"

"He has family. Haven't the police contacted them?"

"I'm sure. But I thought you might know some place he would go."

"If he's not with family, then . . ." She let it trail off.

"Why did you go over there so late?"

"Chris'? I had to work late. I didn't get off till eleven."

"A witness said you were there earlier than eleven."

"That's what the police kept asking me. I was there, but I didn't go in—not all the way in. I had a twenty-minute break, and I ran over to check on him. He'd been coming down with something. I knocked, opened the door a little and called out. The house was dark. When he didn't answer, I thought he was asleep and I didn't want to wake him up." Tears sprang up in her eyes. "I thought he needed rest. Maybe if I'd gone in, maybe— I always lock the door when I'm there. Chris never did. If I'd been there and had the door locked, whoever it was wouldn't have gotten in and he'd still be alive."

"There was nothing you could have done. Don't blame yourself."

"You don't think I did it?"

Not without a lot of help, she thought. "No, I don't think you did."

Kacie wasn't very hungry. Diane had Kacie's meal

put in a carryout. She dropped her off at her apartment and walked her to her door.

"Try to get some sleep. Do you have a friend you can call?"

Kacie nodded. "I'll be all right."

Diane spent the remainder of the day working at her museum job, doing something she liked the least—meeting with the board. She handed out budget and income reports for them to review, including a report on the initial findings on the mummy, hoping that would keep them busy and off any discussion of the crime lab. Board members also got some of the crank E-mails whenever she appeared on television in connection with the work of the crime lab.

She needn't have worried. All they could talk about was the mummy, as if having one made the place a real museum, as if all museums worth their salt had to have an Egyptology exhibit.

"So, do you know what he did for a living?" Laura Hillard was one of Diane's oldest friends. They first met in kindergarten, and remained friends even after Diane moved away with her parents when she was in eighth grade.

"I know he spent a lot of time sitting slumped over. There are a handful of jobs in ancient Egypt that would have kept him long hours in that position. Jonas and Kendel will be giving us more information. I just know about the bones at this point."

"And where is Miss Williams?" asked Madge Stewart, another member of the board. "I haven't met her yet. I was really hoping she would be here." Madge looked around the room as if Kendel might be sitting in a corner keeping quiet.

"She went to Virginia to try to acquire some arti-facts that belong with our mummy."

Diane explained that mummies of a certain time were wrapped with amulets that represented luck, pro-tection and help in getting into the underworld after death.

"Family members of the donor are reported to have some in their possession. I'm told that sometimes there were as many as a hundred such amulets. They would add a lot to the value of the mummy."

"This is so exciting," said Madge. "An Egyptian exhibit will be so good for the museum."

"We have a CT scan scheduled next week for him. That may give us more information about who he was."

Thankfully, all the conversation was taken up with the mummy and Diane was able to adjourn the meet-ing in a good mood. She counted herself lucky. Per-haps in time the board members who were queasy about the location of the crime lab inside the museum would become proud of the work that was done there.

Madge took Diane's arm as the board members were dispersing. "When we open the Egyptian exhibit, we must have another party. You know I missed the one for the museum opening."

Madge gave Diane that I-wasn't-told-about-the-party look that she adorned her face with on any occa-sion she could bring it up. Diane had stopped ex-plaining to her that it was she who wrote the wrong date on her calendar. Diane simply smiled and told Madge a party would be a great idea.

Diane went back to her office to finish some more paperwork—and to see if Garnett had left a message. She hadn't heard what happened with Lynn Webber. Perhaps no news was good news.

Andie was getting ready to leave as Diane arrived. She had changed from her more conservative museum uniform to her clubbing costume, as she described her various forms of dress.

"Got a date?" asked Diane.

"Yes. In the middle of the week—can you believe it? We're going to a jazz concert on campus."

"Sounds like fun. Have a good time. Did I get any messages?"

"They're on your desk. Just routine stuff, nothing out of the ordinary."

Diane laughed. She was sorry that life at the museum was such that "ordinary" and "out of the ordinary" were frequent distinctions Andie had to make.

"Perhaps things are settling down." At her desk, she called up to the crime lab. David answered. "Isn't it time for you to go home?" she asked.

"Just seeing about my bugs."

"Any messages from Garnett?"

"No, it's actually been pretty quiet around here. Neva's been working on some stuff you'll be pleased with. She's already gone, but I think she works on the artwork at home."

"I think I've gotten Garnett off her back. Maybe she can settle down and be comfortable around here."

Diane told David how her meeting with Garnett and the sheriff broke up.

"Damn," exclaimed David. "Someone went after Webber? What's this about?"

"I don't know. Go home and take care. I mean it."

When she hung up, Diane dialed Garnett's cell phone.

"This is Diane Fallon," she said when he answered. "I was concerned about Dr. Webber."

"She's fine. It turned out to be a false alarm."

"False alarm?"

"She was on the second floor of her condo and saw some guy who looked like he was trying to break into her back door. Turns out it was a new neighbor who just moved in. He was trying to open her screen to knock on the door. The poor guy and his wife are probably going to move again after all the grilling they got."

"I'm relieved."

"So were we. Lynn . . . Dr. Webber was still shaken. We need to clear this up as quickly as we can."

"I agree."

We who? thought Diane when she hung up the phone. She leaned back in her chair and closed her eyes. She had almost dozed off when the ringing of her phone jerked her awake. *Frank,* she thought and looked at the caller ID. It said Denver, Colorado.

Chapter 25

Diane steadied her hand as she reached out to pick up the phone.

"Hello." She hoped her voice was calm.

"It's me again. Are we alone?"

"What's your name?"

"I can't tell you that."

"Okay. What do you want?"

"I want you to understand. I want to talk about what you said about killing being evil."

"As I recall, I said something about it taking a dedicated community of criminal investigators to combat the evil of murder . . ."

"Yes, but I saw your eyes when you said 'the evil of murder,' and it bothered me." The man's voice was both deep and soft and had a sincere quality to it that was sad.

"What bothered you?"

"The way you put all killings in the same load."

"You say you want me to understand you, but you seem to be talking around the main point. I want to understand you. Can you be more direct?"

"Is there no one in your life that if you had them in your crosshairs, you would pull the trigger and feel justified?"

Ivan Santos, the man who murdered her daughter, came to mind. *He must know quite a lot about my life,* she thought.

"There's a difference between gut-wrenching emotion and becoming the law."

"Why?"

"Because there's a difference in what you know and what you believe. Everyone acts on what they believe, few on what they really know. Taking the law into one's own hands can lead to ghastly mistakes. That's why we need an objective process to find the truth." The man wanted dialogue; she would give him dialogue.

"*Objective.* That's just another word for rich-lawyer tricks."

"I've tried to answer your questions. Will you answer a few for me?"

"Shoot."

"Did you send the E-mail that said sometimes the dead are guilty?"

"You know I did."

"I believed you did."

He let out a soft chuckle. "Okay. You said you had a few questions? Do you have another one?"

"Did you hang the people in Cobber's Wood?"

He hesitated only a beat. "This is just a conversation. You shouldn't read so much into it."

"Is that a yes or a no?" But she was talking to dead air.

She dialed Chief Garnett's cell phone again. He had told her he was going to tap her phones; she hoped he had one in place.

"I just got a call again," she said when he answered. "If the phone is tapped, then you'll have the complete conversation."

Garnett was silent for a moment. "You think it's our guy?"

"Yes."

"What does he want?"

"I'm not sure. He seems to want to confess, but he never gets around to it."

"So, we do have ourselves a nutcase. Okay, I'm going to have a stakeout put on your apartment. Maybe we'll get lucky. I'll call Braden."

Yes, maybe we'll get lucky and he'll come after me, thought Diane. She hung up the phone and sat for a moment, musing over the phone call. He didn't sound violent. He sounded calm. Many killers are calm. In fact, it is often the killing that calms them.

She shook her head. Time to take a rest from crime. She grabbed her purse and left her office. Maybe tonight she could get a good night's sleep.

Halfway to the lobby she had an idea. Instead of going out the door, she headed for the second floor to the geology section. If she was lucky, someone would still be working there.

She got out of the elevator and walked across the overlook into the Pleistocene room. The visitor lighting was still on in earth science, so someone was probably still working.

The earth science room was a warren of display alcoves and partitions. She passed an alcove designed to look like a cave. Facsimiles of stalagmites guarded the entrance. Inside were pieces of real stalagmites and stalactites, gypsum crystal formations that looked like snowflakes, a display on the anatomy of cave fill showing the geological history of the area, a lesson on cave mapping, giant photographs of the major caves in the United States, a virtual tour of Lechuguilla and

Carlsbad caverns. Diane liked the exhibit, but it needed more work. It didn't quite capture the beauty and mystery that she saw in caves. She continued past the exhibits on volcanoes and plate tectonics and one on the water cycle before she entered the rock room.

The rocks and minerals room never grew old. It dazzled her every time she entered. In the center stood a deep purple amethyst geode so enormous she could fit into it. Off to the side stood an equally large agate geode sliced and polished, highlighting a rainbow of silica bands. All the rocks and minerals on display were equally stunning—every color of quartz crystals, golden pyrite in its varied crystal habits, tourmaline, feldspar, olivine, spinel—minerals with names as beautiful as their appearance. It was a room designed to make visitors catch their breath. She looked over the labels of each as she worked her way to the gem section.

"Boss. What brings you here?"

Diane looked up from the display case. "Mike, hi. Working late?"

"I'm making some thin sections for Dr. Lymon."

"You wouldn't happen to know anything about gemstones, would you?"

"My speciality is mainly sedimentary stratigraphy and crystallography. However, as it happens, I do know quite a bit about gemstones. What stone are you interested in?"

"Diamonds."

"Nice choice. What about them do you want to know?"

Diane was glad he didn't make that girl's-best-friend joke. She would have been disappointed in him. "Expensive, aren't they?"

"Can be very expensive. Depends on the quality. Diamonds are graded for their cut, clarity, color and carat weight. In diamonds, size does matter." He grinned. "You in the market for a diamond?"

"This information is for the crime lab."

"Great. Does this mean I can put forensic gemology on my resume?"

"Depends on how helpful you are."

"I'm here for you, Boss. What you need to know?"

"I suppose I want to know if the person who purchased it could afford it, however, at the time, I didn't think to ask the woman how much it cost."

"Okay, we'll start with the easy stuff. What color was it?"

"Diamond colored."

"You don't know about diamonds, do you? Never had an engagement ring?"

"Yes, I have. It belonged to my ex-husband's grandmother and was a ruby with two diamonds on either side."

"I didn't know you were married, Boss."

"When I was very young—still a university student. It didn't last long."

"One of those quick, passionate affairs that fizzled?"

"No. He was a lawyer selected by my parents. It turned out I didn't like him very much."

"Your parents selected your husband? What century are you from?"

"It was the last time I tried to please my parents. It was a lost cause. I was simply the black sheep of the family, and I learned to accept it. Now that you know my history, can we get back to the diamonds?"

"Your history? That was just the teaser."

"Mike."

"Okay, Boss. Come this way." He led her into the geology lab adjoining the rock room.

"This is part of our reference collection of gems. Have a seat and I'll give you a lesson in Diamonds one-oh-one." He went into the storeroom and came out with a large flat drawer and set it on the table.

"With some exceptions, white diamonds in general are the most valuable, and they're graded on a color scale from white—colorless—to yellow," said Mike. "They do come in other colors, but for the most part they aren't as valued, unless the color is quite brilliant. For example, the pink diamonds from Australia, and some of the high-carat famous diamonds like the Hope diamond are very rare and very valuable. A red diamond can be a million dollars a carat. But here, I take it, we're dealing with the white diamond."

"Yes."

"Did it have a yellow cast that you noticed?"

Diane shook her head. "No. It was really a beautiful stone. It had a traditional round cut."

He shook his head. "Cut doesn't refer to shape, but the quality of the cut. Not all diamonds are cut kindly."

"You are enjoying this, aren't you?"

"I am."

"Doesn't the rock room have a computer exhibit on diamonds?"

"Yes, it does, but it's not nearly as interactive as I am."

Diane shook her head and laughed.

"I made you laugh. I'm making progress." Mike took a clear plastic container from the tray, removed a stone and held it in his hand. "Diamonds have a high refractive index. You want a cut that reflects the light out of the top of the stone and doesn't let light leak out the bottom."

"Leak out the bottom?"

"It has to do with the angle each facet is to the others. In an ideal cut, the arrangement maximizes the light's ability to disperse throughout the stone and reflect back out the top. A good-quality diamond can be ruined by a bad cut. When you said the diamond looked like a really good diamond, you were probably referring to how it glittered."

Diane thought a moment and met his gaze. "You're right. It sparkled."

"How large was it?"

Diane looked at her hand, visualizing Kacie's ring. She was fairly good at estimating measurements, having measured so many skeletons.

"About seven or eight millimeters in diameter."

"That's about a carat. That is a respectable diamond." He lay the stone in his hand out on a piece of cotton batting he took from the drawer.

"This is a carat diamond."

"It was about that same size. Do you have something black you could put it on?"

Mike shook his head. "You don't want to view diamonds against a black background. Black makes all diamonds look white, and you'll miss the light yellow tinge of a lesser diamond."

"I'm getting all kinds of useful information."

"That's what the museum's here for."

Diane caught a twinkle in his light brown eyes. "You're right about that," she said, smiling in spite of herself. Diane picked up the diamond and put it against her skin. "That's about the size of the one I saw. How much is this diamond worth?"

"This is a particularly good diamond. It's one

carat—carat refers to weight, by the way. It's actually weight that matters and not size. This one is pretty much clear of flaws. It has what's called an ideal cut and is rated a D on the color scale, which is at the top of the colorless range. On the market, this would cost around ten thousand dollars."

Chapter 26

Diane looked up at him sharply. "Ten thousand dollars?"

"Good diamonds are expensive."

"I didn't realize that diamonds are that rare."

"They're not. But over three-quarters of the world's diamonds are controlled by one company, and they're very good at making diamonds seem rare."

Diane picked up the diamond and studied it in the palm of her hand. "That's a lot of money for a diamond."

"You don't think your guy could afford that?"

"I haven't seen his bank account, but I would have thought it unlikely."

"Then it may not have been a diamond. We've been working on the assumption that the stone was a diamond, but it takes an expert to identify one."

Mike reached in and pulled out several more plastic containers and lined up five stones on the batting. He dropped one of the lids on the floor and it started rolling. Diane reached down and picked it up before it got across the floor.

"I could have sworn you did that on purpose," said Diane when she rose and placed it back on the table.

"I did. I rearranged the stones. I thought I'd let you pick out the diamond."

Diane looked at the row of stones. They were all beautiful, all about the same size, and very similar.

"What if these get mixed up? Can you tell them apart?"

"Sure. I know in what order I placed them, and I have photos of their internal structures. Besides, I've got this sweet little device that'll identify them for me if I get mixed-up."

"That's good to know." Diane went down the row of stones, picking each one up, twisting it from side to side with her fingers, looking at the sparkle. She pushed one back. "I don't think it's this one."

"Very good. That's a white sapphire. The value is, I think, around a hundred thirty dollars."

She examined the remaining four again and moved another back and looked at Mike, who watched her closely with an amused glint to his eyes. "Cubic zirconia. Maybe fifteen dollars," he said.

Diane moved another stone away from the line.

"Very good," said Mike. "That's a synthetic diamond—retails for about three thousand dollars."

"A lucky guess. They all look so much alike. But it had a slightly yellow cast to it. You're right. You'd have to look at it against a white background to see it."

Two were left. Diane picked them up and looked at them side by side. She moved them under the light. Weighed each in her hand, though she didn't know why. She had not a clue what it would mean if one were heavier than the other. It was the sparkle, she realized, she had used to eliminate the others. She took another look at the stones, twisting

them under the light. She set them down and moved
a stone back in line with the others she had eliminated, and looked at Mike. His eyes still cast that
amused sparkle.

"Well?" she asked.

"You just eliminated the diamond."

"And I was almost sure."

"Nope. You were looking at the fire, weren't you?"

"Yes."

"This." He picked up the one remaining stone.
"This is a moissanite—costs about three hundred dollars. It has a higher refractive index than a diamond
and is almost as hard."

"I've never heard of a moissanite."

"Silicon carbide crystals. It's named after Henri
Moissan, a scientist from Paris. In 1893 he discovered
the crystals in a meteorite. Naturally occurring moissanite is rare, but a way to manufacture it was developed in 1995."

"Her diamond might have been any one of these."

"You have to look at the diamond's internal structure. Think she'll let you borrow it?"

"About as much chance as a snowball's in hell, I
imagine. Although, if she thought it could help catch
Chris Edwards' killer, maybe."

"Today, a lot of good diamonds are engraved on the
girdle—on one of these tiny facets around the girth of
the stone—with a serial number and a logo for where
it came from. They are also fingerprinted—in a manner of speaking. The internal structure of each diamond is unique. People who deal in real diamonds are
very concerned about distinguishing their product
from the man-made variety."

"Tell me, if these nondiamonds are so much

cheaper and you have to have a special machine to tell them from the real thing . . ."

"Why do people pay so much for diamonds? They are the stones created a billion years ago in the bowels of the earth—the mantle, actually—and were spewed out of the earth by a volcano in molten lava. It's the mystique, and very clever marketing by the diamond companies."

He picked up the diamond. "Besides, diamonds are cool stones. If the temperature and pressure had been a little less when it was being formed, we'd be writing with this in a pencil."

"I do know that graphite is carbon, and that diamonds are formed out of carbon."

"Did you know when light passes through a diamond, it slows down to half its speed?"

"I would have been more impressed if it speeded up," said Diane.

"You're a science fiction fan, aren't you? So am I. Another thing we have in common." Mike began putting the stones back in their marked containers. Instead of putting them back in the drawer, he set them aside in a tray. "Since they've been out of their boxes, I'll check all of them to make sure I didn't mix them up." He took them back to the storage room.

"I didn't know we have such valuable gemstones," said Diane, when he returned.

"Kendel's been helping to increase our number of reference gems. I tell you, if I'm ever on a scavenger hunt where my life depends on the outcome, I want that woman on my team."

Diane nodded and smiled. "I've been very pleased with her. Did she acquire the diamond we just looked at?"

Mike nodded. "She got it out of Mrs. Van Ross. We decided to keep it in the reference collection rather than exchange it with the one on display in the rock room. The one on display is a larger diamond but not near the quality, but with the lighting it's a little more impressive because of its size."

"It's on a black background, isn't it?"

Mike grinned. "Yep."

"Mike, I appreciate the lesson in diamonds." She stood up to go.

"Have you eaten?"

"Mike . . ."

"Come on, Doc. You have to eat. We could eat in the museum restaurant. We'd just have to walk downstairs."

Diane thought for a second. "Oh, all right. I am hungry."

"Great! Besides, I have something I need to ask you."

Between the sets of huge double doors at the entrance to each wing of the museum, Diane had added a new door that led down a long hallway to the restaurant that remained open after the museum closed. She and Mike took one of the elevators across from the rock room down to the first floor. It let them out at the midpoint of the hallway.

Photographs of pieces from the museum hung along the long walls—the inside spiral from a chambered nautilus, starfish, sea horses, seashells, rocks, minerals and gemstones, dinosaurs, wolves, butterflies, birds and flowers. A preview of what the museum offered. Diane had framed several copies for her apartment. There was nothing as peaceful and soothing to her as a seashell.

Several couples were walking down the hallway to the restaurant when Diane and Mike emerged from the elevator.

"Oh, the museum is still open. Let's go look at the jewels." A dark-haired woman in a black spaghetti-strap silk dress decorated with stylized white butterflies punched the UP button several times. "It's out of order." The man she was with and another couple stopped and waited.

"The museum isn't open," said Diane. "This bank of elevators is locked down for the night."

The woman looked Diane up and down. "How did you ride it?"

"I have a key."

"How do you get a key?"

"By being the director, Evelyn. This is Diane Fallon," said the man. From the wedding rings on their fingers, Diane guessed they were husband and wife.

He shook Diane's hand and introduced himself, his wife and friends. "You spoke at my club for lunch last month."

"Good to see you again," Diane began, but was cut off by the wife.

"So, you run the museum. What about this crime lab attached to it? That is just so strange. Should you be doing that?"

"Evelyn." Her husband sighed and smiled. The other couple examined the granite floor around their feet.

"Well, I want to know," she said, still looking at Diane for an answer.

"Rosewood had a need, and I was happy to be able to help," said Diane.

"I'm sure, but to think of autopsies being performed at the museum while people are looking at the exhibits. That's not going on now, is it?"

"We don't do autopsies. They are performed at the hospital. We examine trace evidence—fibers, fingerprints, that kind of thing."

"I know I heard someone say that you examined bodies here."

"Perhaps they meant skeletons. I'm curator of the primate skeletal collection and I'm also a forensic anthropologist. I do look at bones here."

"Bones. I see. Well, we are so glad to have a restaurant of this caliber here, but I have to say—"

"Evelyn."

Evelyn ignored her husband, which, Diane imagined, was something he was accustomed to.

"I can't say I like those computers there."

"We have a number of students who come here and use them during the day."

"In the restaurant? Why don't you give them a room to do that in?"

"I'll ask the staff to look into it," said Diane.

The woman smiled brightly. "You see, Burt, it never hurts to ask." They turned and walked down the hall to the restaurant.

"You did that well," said Mike. "I thought we were going to be stuck here in the hallway the rest of the night."

"She just wanted me to tell her she was right," said Diane.

"See, that's what I like about you. You know how to deal with things."

They were seated in a booth on the opposite side of the restaurant from Evelyn and Burt's party. Diane liked the low lights and quiet of the room. She was more tired than she realized.

"This is good. I was afraid we were going to be seated near that woman," said Mike.

Diane eyed him over her menu. "That wouldn't have happened."

"Why? Oh, they always seat you away from everyone else, don't they?"

"When they can. They know I like calm with my meals." She looked at the flow of restaurant customers coming in. "It looks like the restaurant is filling up quickly tonight."

The waitress came, and Diane ordered steak. Mike, it turned out, was vegetarian. He ordered a portobello mushroom, spinach and cheese dish.

"Really," he said. "You handled that well. I wouldn't have been so patient."

"A visitor to the museum is like a guest in my home."

"Nice sentiment, but it's good you know how to handle people."

"Actually, I don't, but I picked up a few things from my last boss, who was a diplomat. What was it you wanted to talk to me about?"

"The caving club." Diane was surprised. She'd expected something personal.

"What about it?" She was a member of the Rosewood Speleological Society, but she often wasn't able to attend the meetings.

"We lost our meeting place at the student center—we weren't a big enough group. Somebody needed the space and the administration chased us out of our room. Of course, one of our more prominent members could have spoken up for us, but she doesn't attend meetings that often."

"We have a prominent member in the club?"

"Yeah, we do. Big director of the museum in town. Anyway, in the absence of this director, we all came up with the idea of meeting in her museum."

Diane nodded. "At least I would be able to attend the meetings if we met here."

"That's a yes, then?"

"We can meet in the main auditorium or one of the geology rooms. It would mean that you will have to meet the group at the door to let them in. I can alert the security staff to watch out for latecomers."

"Great. I think the earth science room would be a good place to meet. We already have that small auditorium where we show the Volatile Earth series."

Diane hadn't realized she was as hungry as she was until her meal arrived. She was going to have to remember to eat more. She took several bites of her fillet and baked potato before she said anything else.

"I really am sorry I haven't been able to attend more meetings."

"I can understand, with two full-time jobs. By the way, we do have a new member. One of your staff from your other job. Neva Hurley."

"I'm glad she joined. I encouraged her to."

"She seemed to feel a little out of place, but I think it's because she's the least experienced member. I have the plan for the cave we're visiting. It's a great cave, really. There's an easy way and a wild way through it. I thought we'd start with the easy way and later take a trip back and explore the wild part of the cave. That section has to be explored on rope, so it's not for beginners."

Diane ate and listened to Mike talk about the cave

they were going to visit. She heard the low tone of her phone ring. She fished it out of her purse and answered without looking at the display.

"I thought maybe we could finish our talk. I hope I'm not interrupting your dinner," the voice on the phone said.

Chapter 27

"Are you watching me?"

The interior darkness of the restaurant that had been as comfortable as a familiar blanket now closed in around her. She searched the faces of the diners nearest her, but all she could see was flickering faces illuminated by the table candles. The diners just beyond were merely shadows with spots of light, the faces swallowed up by the darkness. Diane fished a pad and pen out of her purse and began scribbling a note to Mike, who looked at her, frowning.

Frank? he mouthed.

Diane shook her head.

"I'm not a maniac," the voice said. The sound was urgent—as in "please believe me." "It's around a lot of people's dinnertime. I thought you might be eating." That sounded more rational.

Diane handed Mike the note and watched his eyes widen and jaw drop as he read it in the candlelight. He jumped from his seat and walked out of the restaurant.

"What exactly do you want?" asked Diane.

"I told you. I want you to understand."

"You say that, but you never get to the point. What is it that you want me to understand?"

"That the law doesn't always work. Sometimes it can't work. Sometimes the terrible things people do aren't against the so-called law." His voice was getting louder and his words were coming faster. The rationality that he managed to grasp a moment ago was turning to a panicked anger.

"Okay. I understand that in theory. Can you give me an example?"

He hesitated so long, Diane thought he had hung up, then he spoke in a calm voice. "An example?"

"An example of a terrible thing people can do that isn't against the law."

He paused for a long moment. "Oh, I could give you a hundred examples. Gossip comes to mind—and bullying, to name just two."

"There are legal remedies to both of those."

"Right. Not when you're in school. Besides, legal remedies are expensive. For most of us, it's a choice between a so-called legal remedy and a roof over our head. There's no legal remedies for normal people."

"So sometimes you have to make your own remedies. Murder seems a harsh remedy for gossip and bullying."

"Who said anything about murder?"

"You did. This conversation started from you objecting to my calling all murders evil."

He chuckled softly. "Yes, you're right. I did. And you're right that killing is too harsh for my examples, but they were just examples. It's what you asked for."

"Then perhaps I wasn't specific enough. Give me a good example of a justified killing."

"I have to go now. I'll call again and we'll talk some more."

Diane's gaze eased around the room, looking for

anything out of the ordinary, anyone leaving, something out of place. Everything looked right.

Mike returned a minute later, still wide-eyed, but with a serious look on his face. "That was . . . you were actually talking to the killer?"

"I don't know. Were you able to get hold of Chief Garnett?"

"Yes. He said he'd get on it."

Diane wasn't sure, but unless they were already on it they would miss the opportunity. Surely, they included her cell in the surveillance.

"What did the guy want?" asked Mike.

"I think he wanted me to tell him he was right."

"See, that's why I'm attracted to you."

"Mike, explain that to me. I confess, I don't understand why."

"It came as a surprise to me too, I'm not usually attracted to older women. But you're . . . interesting."

"Interesting?"

"Yeah. Smart—not just intelligent, but clever. You're adventurous, you do things, map caves, solve crimes—nothing scares you."

"Lots of things scare me."

"Maybe, but you have it under control. Like just now when that guy called. You were so calm." He grinned a boyish grin that deepened his dimples. "You look good, too. So how about it—will you go out with me again?"

"Again? This is not going out. It's eating together at the museum. And no, I can't go out with you. We can go caving together, but we can't date."

"Why?"

"Three reasons. I'm dating someone else, I'm your boss and I'm older than you are—by too many years.

Any one of those reasons, for me, is a nonstarter. All three—well, it isn't going to happen."

He put a hand on his chest. "You've broken my heart."

"I doubt it. It's the hunt you like. Besides, the anticipation is often better than the reality."

"You know, for guys that isn't true."

Diane laughed. She had been so tense, all her muscles were still ready for fight or flight. She relaxed. The release felt good.

The remainder of the meal, Diane asked Mike questions about the cave he had arranged for them to visit.

"You say it hasn't been mapped?" That information excited her. She loved cave mapping.

"None of the wild sections have." Mike pushed his plate to the side and tried to talk Diane into dessert.

"You've tried to tempt me enough, I think."

"We could share."

"Definitely not. Who in the caving club has mapping experience?" she asked.

"I think most everyone has done a little traversing. If you're talking serious mapping, you've had the most experience. I've had some, and there's Stan. I know several would like to learn."

"Maybe that can be one of our goals." Diane pushed her plate back and gave the waitress her credit card as she appeared at the table.

"I'll get it," said Mike, putting his wallet on the table.

"No. I appreciate the information on the diamonds."

"Then let me leave the tip." He fished out several bills and left them under his tea glass. "If you can get the woman to come in, I'll have a look at her diamond."

"I'm not sure how I'd manage that." Diane signed the receipt the waitress brought back, and stood up, retrieving her purse. "I do appreciate the information, and I'm sorry about the phone call."

Mike's smile disappeared. "That was strange. Do you think he's watching you? I'll walk you to your car."

Diane shook her head. "I'm going to my office first and give Garnett a call. I'll be fine. I've given security a heads-up."

They threaded their way through the tables. As they passed the trellis garden, an outdoor part of the restaurant, Diane heard her name called from the darkness. She turned, peered into the flickering shadows and made out Izzy Wallace. He sat at a small table on the terrace, dressed in slacks and a short-sleeved shirt, across from a woman that Diane guessed was his wife. She tried to recall her name, but she couldn't remember what Frank said it was.

"Izzy. How are you?"

He stood and introduced his wife, who nodded and patted her mouth with her napkin.

"We just love this restaurant. Such atmosphere," she said.

"We're very proud of it. You should come in the daytime sometime. They have a wonderful salad and fruit buffet and, of course, the museum is open in the daytime."

Izzy kept eying Mike, so Diane introduced him. "This is Mike Seger, one of our geologists here at the museum."

"That was a lot of excitement at Dr. Webber's house," he said. "Poor guy nearly wet his pants."

"Izzy!" cautioned his wife.

"This business has everyone in an uproar," said Izzy. "The chief's hanging a lot on the forensics."

Diane felt Izzy was trying to draw her into a conversation about the crime scene. Even if it wasn't inappropriate, Izzy wasn't someone she confided in.

"Is he? Well, you two enjoy the rest of your dinner. The chocolate cake is to die for."

She left them and walked as far as the entrance with Mike. He continued on out the door, and she used her key to enter the primate room and crossed over to the lobby. She waved at the security guard on duty and went back to her office. Before she called Garnett, she wrote down the conversation with John Doe Caller, as she named him, as accurately as she remembered. When she finished, she dialed Garnett's number.

"There was a little miscommunication with the surveillance guys. When they tapped your phone, they didn't make arrangements for your cell. What did he want?"

"I wrote it down. I'll fax it to your office tonight."

"That'd be good. I'll have it first thing. We've hired a profiler to come and take a look at the evidence. He used to work for the FBI. Supposed to be real good. He'll want to talk to you."

"Sure." It appeared to Diane that Chief Garnett had taken over the sheriff's case. As she hung up the phone, she wondered how Braden felt about that. He couldn't mind too much; he'd allowed it.

It wasn't as late as she feared it might be when she finally left for home. She'd still get a good night's sleep and have time to get up early and exercise. Several people were working late—not just the security and custodial staff. She saw three of her curators' cars in the parking lot. And of course, the cluster of cars belonging to restaurant patrons. When she unlocked her car and her dome light came on, she automatically checked the seat, expecting to see another gift, but both the front and backseat were empty. She got in the car and drove to her apartment building. As she pulled into her regular parking space at the curb under the limbs of a large overhanging tree and turned off her car lights, her phone rang.

"Hey. It's Frank. Want some company tonight?"

"Frank, I'd love . . ."

Crack!

At first Diane thought someone had fired a gun. A moment later when she saw the crack in her window, she thought a limb had fallen on the windshield. A split second after that, another crack shattered the windshield. She saw a dark shadow wielding a baseball bat.

Chapter 28

Diane recoiled reflexively from the banging on her car that rang like gunshots inside her head. He was now outside her driver's side door, flailing with a baseball bat against her window. Guttural sounds—like some moaning, barking, struggling animal—came from his throat. The end of the bat crashed through the shattered side window. Diane dodged forward in her seat and screamed at Frank to call the police. She still held the car key in her clenched fist. *Put the key in the ignition.*

She tried repeatedly with her shaking fingers to insert the key in the slot in the steering column but kept missing it in the dark. He shoved the bat through the hole in the window again, missing her head but striking a painful glancing blow off her left shoulder. She saw another thrust coming, ducked low in the seat to avoid it, and dropped the key somewhere in the dark. She ran her hand over the floor searching, trying to hold back the fear inside her. Under the accelerator her fingers touched the plastic remote. She clutched it and pressed the red panic button. The persistent blaring horn added to the frenzy, and she had to remind herself that it was on her side.

"Where are you?" She heard Frank's voice shouting from the phone that now lay on the passenger's side floor.

"Home," she yelled, jerking open the glove compartment, looking for anything that might be a weapon. "Inside my car."

A gloved hand reached through the hole in the window, feeling for the door handle. She grabbed at his arm. He caught her hand and yanked. Diane stabbed repeatedly at his hand and wrist as hard as she could with the key clenched in her fist, digging for bone and tendon. He cursed and pulled his hand back. More angry than before, he beat at the window furiously with the bat until the entire glass was broken out.

"Get out of there, you stupid bitch!" he yelled above the blaring horn. "Get the fuck out of there now! I'm going to beat your damn fucking head in!"

"The police are coming," she yelled.

Diane had no weapon in her car. Not a tire iron, not a pocket knife, nothing. She had to start the car. She made for the ignition again, aiming at it with the key just as he reached in and caught the door handle. The key slipped in the slot at the same time the door swung open. Diane turned the key and the car roared to a start. He cursed her and grabbed her jacket in the grip of his right hand. She jerked the car in gear and pressed the accelerator. The car moved forward, pulling him with it. He ran alongside, holding on to her clothes through the open door, breathing hard. Thank God her seat belt was still buckled.

"You can't get away. I'm goin' to kill you, you bitch," he said in as menacing a voice as she had ever heard.

She grabbed at the stocking he wore over his face,

pulling it until it stretched. He punched blindly at her with the bat. Diane ducked and hit the accelerator and the car sped forward, and then she slammed on the brakes. The door swung wide open. She put the car quickly into reverse and stomped the accelerator. The suddenness of the move caught him running forward, hit him with the open door and knocked him to the ground. Diane wanted to run him over as she backed up her car and saw him lying in front of her. The temptation was almost too much to resist. While she hesitated for a second, he scrambled up off the road, ran toward a Crown Victoria across the street and jerked open the door. She turned the steering wheel in the direction of his car and floored the accelerator. But her car responded sluggishly, haltingly, and his car sped off in the opposite direction before she reached it.

Diane managed to turn her car half around and started to pursue. She pressed the brake instead. He was going too fast, and she had no business becoming involved in a high-speed chase. She sat in her car crossways in the middle of the road, breathing hard.

"Diane, are you still there? The police are on their way. Diane."

She found the phone on the floor half under the passenger's seat. "Frank. I'm here. He's gone."

"Diane, are you all right? I'm almost to your apartment. Are you all right?"

"Yes. I'm fine. I'm going to have to get some new windows for my car, though."

At that moment an unmarked police car came over the rise, lights flashing, but no siren, and stopped opposite her in the road. Two policemen jumped out, drew their guns and pointed them at her car.

"Get out of the car. Put your hands on your head."

"Frank, the police are here. Apparently, they are going to shoot me. I have to go."

Diane dropped the phone on the seat, unbuckled her seat belt and got out of the car with her hands on her head. She recognized the two policemen, and tried to recall their names as they walked slowly toward her.

"You're Dr. Fallon," said one of the policemen. Both of them lowered their guns. Diane dropped her hands to her sides.

"Yes, I am. I was attacked in my car. The man left, driving west in a light-colored Crown Vic. I couldn't get his tag number. You probably just passed him."

Frank's car came to a screeching halt at the curb.

"That's Frank Duncan. He's an Atlanta detective and a friend," she told them. "He's the one who called you."

She was the one shaking inside, and she felt that they were the ones who needed calming.

Frank walked up and showed his badge. "You okay?" he asked, pulling her into a hug.

"Scared witless, but other than that . . ." She leaned against him. "I need to move my car out of the street."

"Sure," said one of the policemen. "Go ahead. We'll call an APB on the Crown Vic."

"I'll move your car," said Frank. "You get out of the street."

As Diane watched Frank get in her car, she saw that both tires on the driver's side were flat. Sometime during his frenzied attack, the perp had managed to slash her tires. Her car looked totaled, the windshield was caved in, the driver's side window was nearly gone. The front headlights had been smashed. The dents in the body were too numerous to count. The attack seemed so quick to have done all that damage.

Frank parked her battered Taurus against the curb just as Chief Garnett drove up in his car. He jumped out and hurried over to Diane and the policemen, scowling. Diane noticed her landlady and some of her neighbors gathered in front of the apartment building. The apartment house stood mainly by itself on the small street. Good thing. She'd have hated having the whole neighborhood out looking at her.

"You were supposed to be watching the house," Garnett said to the policemen.

Diane understood now why the two policemen looked nervous. They hadn't been where they were supposed to be.

"We got a call . . ." began one of the policemen.

"You got a call? We'll discuss this down at the station. In the meantime, I want you parked out here all night. Is that understood?"

"Yes, sir."

He turned to Diane. "Are you injured?"

"No, I'm fine. I'd like just to go up to my apartment and get some sleep."

"Of course. Do you think it was the guy who's been calling?"

"I don't know for sure. But I got a sense that the caller was frustrated with the way our conversations have been going."

"Did you give his description to the officers?"

Diane nodded. "I described his vehicle. He was dressed in dark clothes and had a stocking over his head, distorting his features. He had dark hair, about six feet tall, well built."

"You call it in?" Garnett snapped at his officers.

Both of the policemen nodded.

"I tried to get his tag number. I couldn't see it."

"We'll find him."

Diane turned and took a step toward her apartment. "Oh, I met Kacie Beck as she was leaving the police station and gave her a lift home. I noticed that she had an engagement ring with what looked to me like a pretty large diamond. If it was real and of good quality, my geologist said it could be worth upwards of ten thousand dollars. It might be worth checking out."

Garnett whistled. "Where would Chris Edwards get that kind of money?"

"It could be synthetic, but it looked real and she thinks it's real."

"Like you said. It's worth checking out. Go ahead and get some sleep. We'll talk in the morning."

Diane nodded. Chief Garnett was being awfully solicitous, especially for someone who only last year was among those who would like to have run her out of town. She glanced up to her apartment building at the knot of neighbors looking in her direction. How was she going to explain this to her landlady?

Frank returned with Diane's purse in hand and guided her up the sidewalk to her building.

"What's going on?" This was from one of Diane's newest neighbors, a young couple from the ground floor.

"What's all that noise? How are we to sleep with all that noise?" Mrs. Odell and her husband, who lived across the hall from Diane, stood with their arms crossed and their chins in the air.

"Hate those car alarms. There ought to be a law against them. They go off for no reason at all." Mr. Odell added, with a sharp nod of his head.

"What happened?" asked the landlady. "Why are the police here?"

"As I was parking my car, someone came up and beat my car with a bat," said Diane, trying to sound calm. "They ran off."

"Why would anyone do such a thing?" said the landlady. "I tell you, it's those hoodlums you read about. They're everywhere. I keep telling my nephew that . . ."

Diane nodded and made her way up the stairs to her apartment on the second floor. The last thing she wanted to do was get her landlady started on one of her stream-of-consciousness conversations. The Odells came up the stairs behind her.

"You know, you should move somewhere else," said Mrs. Odell. "This was a quiet apartment building until you moved here."

Diane opened her door. "Good night, Mrs. Odell. I'm sorry you had your sleep interrupted."

Once Diane's apartment door closed behind them, Frank asked, "Those are the people you were telling me about? The ones who had seven children die, and whose only joy in life is going to funerals?"

"That's them. Mrs. Odell was the one who broke into my apartment looking for a cat, and I almost clobbered her with my cornbread pan."

"Maybe you should move."

Diane laughed. "You're probably right." She collapsed on the couch. "I'm so glad to be home. It was a rough day at the office."

Frank sat down and pulled her against him, cuddling her in his arms. "I don't think I've ever been so frightened—listening over the phone, not knowing what was going on."

"How did you call the police?"

"I used my car phone. So you think that was the man who's been calling?"

"I don't know. I'm afraid it might be."

"Why is he fixated on you?"

"He may be fixated on all of us who had anything to do with the Cobber's Wood victims, or . . ." Diane rubbed her eyes with her finger. "I don't know. I don't know what the hell is going on."

"What's Garnett doing about these calls?"

"They were supposed to have someone outside my building, but they apparently slipped up."

"You mean, there were supposed to be policemen posted in front of your house? Dammit, where were they?"

"I don't know." What Diane wanted to do was forget about the whole thing for just a few hours. "Where's Star tonight?"

"At a concert with a friend. She's spending the night with her after the concert."

"On a school night?"

"It's summer."

"Of course it is. God, I'm losing track of time. You're letting her go to a concert? Aren't you nervous?"

"Nervous doesn't quite describe it. All I can think of is all those drugs floating around and how vulnerable she is."

Diane's back was against Frank's chest and his face was close to her ear. His breath was warm and smelled like cinnamon.

"Her friend's a good kid and I know her parents. I let Star go to a concert last month. She checked in with me when she arrived and was home on time, so

I'm letting her go again. I don't know. In another year, she'll be old enough to strike out on her own. I'm just trying to give her some experience being responsible, but I feel completely out of my depth."

Diane wove her fingers into his and relaxed a bit, nestling further against him. "She seems to be doing well."

"Most of the time. We have some pretty big disagreements. Cindy helps. She's good with Star. She lets Star stay with her and her husband when I'm away. It's good for Kevin. It's like having a big sister." He moved his arms from around her and stood up, pulling her with him. "Let me fix you something. Have you eaten?"

"At the museum. I bought Mike dinner tonight."

Frank raised his eyebrows. "Mike. That's . . ."

"The geologist."

"You bought him dinner?"

"He gave me some information about diamonds."

"He doesn't get a salary for that?"

"This was after hours."

"Okay, this just gets better. This is the guy who's got a thing for you?"

"Yes."

"So you admit it now?"

"He admitted it."

"I see."

"It's not serious. I believe it's just the challenge. I told him that I was not only seeing someone else, I was his boss and old enough to be his mother, though I didn't put it quite like that."

"Only if you had him when you were twelve. That's not that big an age difference."

"It is to me. I thought you were going to fix me

something. I could use a cool glass of wine when I get out of the shower. There's some white zinfandel in the refrigerator.''

Frank put his arms around her. "You doing okay?"

"I'm still shaking . . . and praying that this was just a random act of violence. Frank, I don't know how to handle that guy. It's like he wants to talk to me, but he won't say anything. And now this. Garnett said he hired a profiler.''

"Do you know who?"

Diane shook her head. "Some consultant who used to work for the FBI. I hope he's good. We need someone to make some sense out of all this. I sure can't.''

Chapter 29

Her car looked worse in the light of day than it had that evening under the streetlight. She shook her head as the tow truck drove off with it.

"I don't think I'll be able to have that fixed," she said to Frank.

"It's all cosmetic, really," he told her.

"Cosmetic. It looks totaled."

Before Diane left for work, she took coffee and hot egg and bacon sandwiches out to the policemen on her stakeout. They were surprised and grateful.

"Will you be relieved soon?" she asked.

"In an hour," they assured her.

Frank drove her to the museum. She bought a paper on the way in and leafed through the pages, dreading what she would find. Another thing she'd have to deal with now—bad publicity for the museum, with her name attached.

"I don't see anything," she said.

But there it was in the police blotter—one line. CAR REPORTED VANDALIZED ON EAST ELM STREET.

"I don't believe it. Hardly a mention. With any luck, that'll be the end of it."

She was already letting go of the image of the phone

calls, E-mails and letters about the attack—and the *I-told-you-so*'s from her board members.

"Dinner?" asked Frank, stopping in front of the museum.

Diane got out and leaned into the passenger's side of his car. "Yes. Let's go some place quiet."

"How about my place? Star will be there, but she'd enjoy seeing you."

"I'd like to see her too."

"You going to be all right today? That was quite an ordeal last night."

"I'll be fine. Thanks for the rescue."

"I didn't do anything."

"Yes, you did."

Diane went straight to the crime lab. Jin, David and Neva were already there. David peeked his head around the corner from where his rearing chambers were located.

"Aren't you due to give birth soon?" asked Diane.

"Yep, got lots of babies here now. We're coming along nicely. I'll be able to give you a good time of death soon."

Jin came out from his work space when he heard Diane's voice.

"I have an ID on the orange carpet fiber."

"More good news," said Diane. "What is it?"

"It's an inexpensive make and, unfortunately, it's plentiful. Made by a company in Dalton, Georgia."

"I can't imagine that there is an expensive version of orange carpet," said Neva.

"I'll have you know that I have orange carpet, and it looks quite nice," said David.

Diane and Neva looked at him with raised eyebrows.

"In case you're wondering, it's the expensive variety. I had Jin take a sample from it to document that we haven't contaminated anything."

"It is a nice carpet," said Jin. "Thick, low pile, soft. It's more of a burnt orange color. Our guy's carpet is bright orange, almost the color of a safety vest."

Diane and Neva laughed at the two of them talking about carpet.

"Neva has something to show you," said David, pointing to the conference table.

They all gathered around the table and looked into portraits of Blue, Red and Green Doe, first rendered by the computer, then as drawings enhanced by Neva. She had drawn a full face and profile of each victim. She had done as Diane asked, turning a computer graphic into realistic portraits of a Caucasian female and male and an Asian female. They looked like people. They looked like someone their mothers would recognize.

"These are great," said Diane. "I mean it. This is really good."

"I made the two whites look too much alike. I tend to do that when I'm drawing faces freehand—make them all look alike. I must subconsciously still be doing that."

"The computer renditions of them look a little bit alike around the eyes and brow," said David.

"What I didn't tell you," Diane said to Neva, "because I didn't want to influence you, is that Blue"—she put a finger on the corner of Blue's drawing—"had a nose job."

Diane pointed to the profile of Green Doe with his large nose.

"If he had a nose job, it would have to be the same

kind that Blue Doe had in order to reduce the size, and they would look very much alike. We'll have to see the DNA report, but I suspect they may be related—perhaps cousins, or sister and brother."

Neva looked at her, wide-eyed. "Then I did do it right."

"Way to go, Rembrandt," said Jin, bumping into her, shoving her slightly. "I told you they're good."

"Go to the archives department in the museum and make several copies. Use the color copier. Even though these aren't color, the color copier will give you a better image," said Diane. "Then run a set to Garnett and Braden. Leave a couple of sets of copies here, and store the originals."

Neva nodded and gathered up her drawings.

"Before you do that, I need to tell all of you something."

Diane described the attack on her the previous evening—the shadow furiously wielding the bat. The three of them listened with varying degrees of open mouths.

"Last night?" said David. "After you left here?"

"Yes. Have any of you noticed anyone following you—anything out of the ordinary?"

The three of them shook their heads. "Nothing," said David. "And I'm paranoid."

"No," said Neva. "I would have noticed."

"Me too," said Jin.

"I want all of you to be extra watchful. I'm going to hire security to watch your homes until we solve this. Jin, I want you to process my car. It's in the police impound. I doubt you'll find anything useful, but you never know. Maybe the bat left some kind of distinctive paint or something. He slashed my tires.

See if you can find a tool pattern that we could match to a knife."

"Sure, Boss," said Jin.

"I didn't see anything in the paper," said David.

"The police blotter had a one-liner," said Diane.

"The vandalism on Elm Street?" said David.

"That's it. I consider it lucky. The last thing I want is for this to be connected to the museum. I'm surprised the media didn't pick up on the story."

"That's because Chief Garnett ordered that any calls concerning you, the lab or the museum be handled off radio and on telephones so police scanners can't pick them up," said Neva.

Diane looked at her for a moment, puzzled, then it dawned on her. Garnett was as protective of the museum as she because he wanted to protect the crime lab. He knew that if push came to shove, she'd cut the lab loose from the museum and find some way to deal with the tax problem.

"I see. I hope this doesn't come back to bite us in the ass," she said. She sent Neva to the copying services, Jin to the police station, and she went to her crime lab office and settled down with a file on each of the murders, determined to find something that would help.

Diane was in the middle of the Cobber's Wood file when Neva came in with the copies of the drawings.

"You're right. The color copies are really good. I can't tell them from the originals." Neva lingered in front of the desk after she gave Diane two sets of copies.

"Is there something else?"

"Weren't you scared last night?"

Diane motioned for her to sit down, and Neva pulled up a chair.

"Yes. Terrified."

"Down at the department, they say you don't have any fear."

Diane couldn't contain a laugh. "What?"

First Mike and now Neva. What kind of impression was she giving people?

"That what happened to you in South America took all your fear away. Some say you have very little emotion about anything."

"Where in the world did that come from?"

"The mayor's office."

"The mayor's office?"

Diane remembered now. Her encounter with the mayor when he tried to threaten her politically. She laughed again.

"I'm not afraid of the mayor, but a maniac wielding a bat in the darkness made my heart race."

"But you dealt with it."

"Yes."

"How?"

"Practice, apparently." Diane shrugged. "Fear's just an emotion. You deal with it."

"I did pretty well in my police training. I do pretty well confronting suspects. It's authority figures I can't handle. Garnett terrifies me."

"I know."

"I know you know, and I appreciate your helping me out with him."

"You can help yourself out by dealing with him in a straightforward way."

"How?"

"Just pretend you aren't afraid of him. What can he do to you anyway?"

"He can fire me, for one thing."

"So. Is that the worst?"

"Well, yes."

"You could walk out of here today and find another job. Perhaps a better one."

Neva shook her head as though she didn't believe her. "It isn't that easy—to pretend you aren't afraid."

"Yes, it is. You haven't tried it. It's harder to think about than it is to do. It starts by building confidence in yourself."

Neva smiled. "Some of the guys at the station say you're arrogant."

"Perhaps they're right, or perhaps I'm just pretending."

"I don't see how you do it."

"Do what?"

"I mean, you have two really big jobs—two major careers going at once."

"I couldn't if that was the American Museum of Natural History out there," Diane said as she gestured in the direction west of her office, toward the museum, "and if this was a New York City crime lab. But RiverTrail is a small museum—large building, but small as holdings go. And Rosewood doesn't have a high crime rate. As it is, I'm pretty much at the limit of what I can do."

"Still . . ." Neva was interrupted by a knock on Diane's office door.

Chief Garnett entered the room with a man who looked like a college professor. He wore a brown tweed sports coat and slacks, had a respectable head of brown hair and a short well-trimmed beard to match. He was slightly built and moved with an air of confidence.

"This is Ross Kingsley," Chief Garnett said. "He's going to be doing some profiling for us."

"I'd like to interview you, if you don't mind." He held out a hand to Diane, and she shook it.

"Certainly. Before we start, Chief, Neva has finished her drawings of the Cobber's Wood victims."

She handed a set to him and watched as he and Kingsley studied them.

"This looks good," Garnett said, casting an approving glance at Neva.

"They are," agreed Diane. "The sheriff ought to be able to find someone who knew them."

Neva stood and eased herself out the door, clearly not picking this day to confront her fear of Garnett.

"We found what we think was the Crown Vic. Stolen, of course. That Asian guy—Jin—I've asked him to process it too."

"I figured it was stolen," said Diane. "Maybe Jin will be able to find something."

"I'll leave you two here," said Garnett. "I'll be in the lab if you need me."

Diane motioned for Kingsley to sit down. She felt oddly uneasy about being interviewed by him. So much for the myth of her fearlessness.

Chapter 30

Ross Kingsley let his gaze wander around her office before bringing his attention back to Diane. Diane's eyes never left Kingsley.

"Your office is very Spartan," he said.

Interesting choice of words, she thought. *Sparse, bare, cold,* perhaps, but not *Spartan*—the places to sit were far too comfortable.

"It's relatively new," she said.

"Garnett told me you suffered a great tragedy doing human rights investigations in South America."

"Yes."

"And you don't want to revisit it. I can understand. What do you do for fun?"

"Why are you profiling me?"

Kingsley shifted in his chair. "Because this man who may be the killer has focused his attention on you. I want to know why, so I can understand him."

"I enjoy caving."

"Exploring caves?"

"Yes." •

"You like dark places, then."

"I always carry at least three sources of light."

He laughed. "But caving is dangerous."

"It can be."

"What is it that you like about it?"

"I enjoy cave mapping. I like exploring a new world. I also like dangling on the end of a rope."

He laughed again. "Why do you think your office is so devoid of personal items?"

"Because I haven't put any in yet. I spend more time in the labs here or in my other office."

"Other office? At the station house?"

"How much about me did Garnett reveal to you?"

"Not a lot. That you are a forensic anthropologist who used to do human rights investigations. We listened to the tapes of you and the caller. Most of my time so far has been spent looking at the reports of the crime scenes."

"I have an office in the museum. That's where you'll find personal items, including a rather nice photograph of me dangling on the end of a rope."

"In the museum? This one connected to the crime lab?"

"Yes. I'm the director."

That caught him by surprise. Diane wondered why they hadn't told him. Perhaps Garnett just hadn't considered it pertinent. She could almost see Kingsley revising his profile of her.

"I see. Well, that's certainly interesting. You must be a busy woman."

"I am."

"You don't have any cognitive"—he waved a hand in the air—"dissonance switching from one job to the other?"

"No. Actually, they go together better than you might expect. I have within a couple of floors experts in a great many fields—geologists, biologists, entomol-

ogists, archaeologists. Sometimes my duties overlap.
For instance, we just inherited a mummy. He's getting
the same analysis that a modern body would. For me
and my forensic staff, being next to the museum has
very definite benefits. After working a gruesome crime
scene, it's amazingly calming to go look at the collection of seashells, or at the giant dinosaurs."

"I'll bet it is. This is interesting. Very unexpected.
So, why do you think this guy is calling you?"

Diane wasn't fazed by his abrupt change of subject.
She suspected that was why he did it—to see if she
really could switch attention on a dime.

"I don't know. He says he wants me to understand
his position. It sounds like he wants my approval. I
don't know why."   •

"Do you think it was he who attacked you last night?"

"In the last conversation with him, I had a sense he
was frustrated that I wouldn't tell him he was right. I
assumed it was him, but I don't know. Nor do I know
who else might have done it."

"That's a good question. Did you get a sense of
how old the caller is?"

"Twenties was my impression. I'd say not much into
his thirties, if that old. But that is just an impression."

Kingsley looked at his notes. "You say that the person who tied the ropes that hung the people in the
forest wasn't the same person who tied the ropes that
hung the guy in the house. Is that something you're
sure of?"

"Yes."

"Would you explain that to me?"

Diane went through the same explanation that she
gave Chief Garnett and Sheriff Braden about how the
knots were tied.

"So the person who tied"—he looked down at his

notes—"Chris Edwards' knots did not know how to tie a proper knot?"

"No. He tied a granny knot."

Kingsley referred to his notes again. "You mention that all the knots tied by the person who tied the hanging victims in the forest had . . . what did you call it? . . . a stopper knot on the tail end of each?"

"Yes."

"Would you call this compulsive behavior? I mean, why did he do this with all the knots he tied?"

"No, I wouldn't call it compulsive. One thing you have to make sure of is that the end of the rope doesn't slip through the knot you just tied when weight is put on the knot. That's what a stopper knot is for. This guy used a stevedore's knot. I use a figure eight when I need a stopper knot. A stevedore is like a figure eight, just with an extra turn. It might say something about where he learned to tie his knots."

Kingsley nodded. "And this length of rope you found. You actually re-created the knot that was once tied in it?"

"I found a knot that I could make correspond to the kinks left by previous knots and that also corresponds to a specific spiral wear pattern on the rope. That's not to say I am right."

He smiled. "I appreciate your careful use of words. Say you were right. You mention that it is a knot used by truckers."

"I don't know how commonly it is used by them, but it is a knot used by that group. It's a knot for tying up and securing a load. When the tension is released, the knot is easy to untie. In knots, being able to untie them is almost as important as being able to tie them."

"I find this interesting. This is the kind of thing I

don't usually get from evidence. Tell me this. Suppose
for a moment that the person who is calling you is the
one who killed the victims in the forest. Is he smart
enough to try to fool you?"

"Dr. Kingsley, anyone is smart enough to try to
fool me."

"I guess you're right. Let me rephrase. What I'm
getting at is, would this person tie the wrong kind of
knot on purpose at a second crime scene just to throw
you off track?"

"He could, but how would he know that we would
even look at the knots?"

"Perhaps in the TV interview . . ."

Diane shook her head. "I never mentioned the
knots—just bones. Most people don't even know there
is such a thing as forensic knot analysis."

"Good point." He rose. "According to the report I
read, you haven't found any physical evidence that
links any of the crimes together."

"That's true—none."

"You have been very helpful. I assume I can call
on you if I need any more information?"

"Of course."

Diane opened a drawer and handed him a card. On
it she wrote her cell phone number.

"Another thing. I don't think this was in any of the
reports exactly, but it just occurred to me. He seems to
know how to avoid having his calls traced to him—that
is, he uses calling cards, or someone else's E-mail account. That took some cheek—one of the E-mail messages came from inside the museum in the Internet café
downstairs from here. He apparently waited for someone to leave their computer a moment and just slipped
in and sent his own E-mail. I understand he knew
enough to erase it from the person's sent file."

"That's interesting. You're right, that wasn't in the report—not in that way."

"Why do you think he is calling me?"

"I think you are right and that for some reason he wants your approval. I don't know if you remind him of his mother, sister or the nun who used to rap his knuckles. He might simply think you look like a sympathetic person. I'm not sure yet."

"How should I handle the conversations? Should I push him for information?"

Kingsley hesitated for a moment. "Handle it the same way you've been doing it—as the firm but kind teacher. I may change my mind when I've been over everything."

They shook hands, and Diane walked with him to the lab, where they found Chief Garnett engrossed in what was apparently a lengthy explanation from Neva of how one arrives at the shape of a nose from skeletal remains.

Diane had to go to a funeral that afternoon—Raymond Waller's. She'd borrowed Andie's Honda and left the museum just before noon to go home and change into a dark navy suit. Elwood Jefferson of the AME Church was conducting the funeral. When she arrived, she sat down by Lynn Webber.

"Raymond had a lot of friends," said Diane.

"He did," said Lynn. "I'm proud to count myself among them. You know, I work with death all the time and I still don't understand it. Why do people do it? It's not something you can take back." She shook her head. "Raymond was just the nicest, funniest man."

"Yes, he was." Diane gazed around at the people gathered to say good-bye to Raymond Waller. Most of the people she didn't know. About a third of them were white and the rest black. There were several people from the neighborhood that she recalled seeing standing on the side of the road. She saw Chief Garnett and Ross Kingsley in the back. She wondered if Raymond's murderer was there.

Reverend Jefferson gave a stirring eulogy about Raymond's life and the wickedness that took him early. As moving as it was, Diane was glad when it was over.

The small church was hot, and Diane was relieved to finally get outside. The church had its own cemetery, and that was where Raymond was buried. A little less than half of the congregation left before the graveside service. Diane stayed. She and Lynn walked together to the grave site and stood across from the family. There weren't many of them. An older man and woman who looked like they were probably husband and wife. Two younger women with men who were probably their spouses, and a boy of about thirteen.

After the family said their last farewells and the casket was being lowered, Diane walked with Lynn to give their condolences to the family.

"Have you met them?" asked Diane.

"No. Raymond didn't talk about them much. I got the idea that not everyone got along."

Diane held out her hand to the first family member, a very pretty woman dressed in a black cotton suit. She had a head full of dark spirals, brownish green eyes and skin slightly lighter than Raymond's. She looked like she was probably in her early-to-midthirties. Diane introduced herself and was in the middle of expressing her sympathy when the other woman, who appeared to be an identical twin, stepped forward.

"I heard somebody tell us to get in touch with you. You have Raymond's things. I want you to know, we expect to get them back. Don't think you are going to get away with them—no, ma'am, we're going to get them back."

"Hello," the first woman interrupted. "I'm Katherine Markum and this is my sister, Elisabeth—also known as my evil twin. We're Ray's cousins. Momma here was Ray's momma's sister. We appreciate your not leaving his valuables in the house to get stolen."

"Speak for yourself," said Elisabeth.

"They're at the museum. My head conservator cataloged them when they were stored," said Diane. "We also have Mr. Waller's journal of photographs describing his holdings."

"We had no idea that Raymond had anything valuable," said Katherine.

"One of my employees tells me that it's a very good collection."

"Don't you be thinking you're going to get your hands on it."

"Elisa, please," said her uncle. "This is Ray's funeral."

She ignored him. "I've already had people call wanting to buy them. We'll be picking them up right now."

"We who?" said her sister. "Ray has a will, and I know he wouldn't leave anything to you. It's not like you and he were friends." Katherine turned to Diane. "I am sorry to be airing our dirty linen in front of you, a perfect stranger, but at least you don't have to live with her."

Diane was beginning to regret telling Garnett that it was all right to store the baseball collection at the museum.

"One thing I don't understand," said Katherine. "Why did the museum work Raymond's crime scene?"

Diane started to explain when a tall middle-aged black man stepped forward and spoke to the family.

"Excuse me. I'm Russell Keating, Raymond's attorney. I have his will. You should have gotten a letter from me. We'll be meeting tomorrow in my office." He turned to Diane. "I think, right now, a museum is a good place to hold his collection. I understand you have it in an environmentally controlled room."

"Yes, we do."

"Humph," said Elisabeth. "We have air-conditioning."

Katherine lowered her head. "Please, Momma, tell me I don't have the same DNA as this woman."

"Kathy, I'm getting really tired of your snide little comments," said Elisabeth.

"We can clear all this up tomorrow," said Keating. "In my office at ten A.M."

Diane gave her condolences to the rest of the family and walked with Lynn Webber to her car.

"Well, they're a pair," said Lynn. "I've never seen twins who look so much alike and are so different. Raymond told me a little about them. He liked Kathy, couldn't stand Elisa." Lynn stopped at her car and opened the door. "I'm glad I'm not going to be at the reading of the will. He told me he wanted the Negro Leagues Baseball Museum in Kansas City to have his collection."

"You're right. I'm glad to be missing that too. I

have an appointment at the hospital in about thirty minutes to have a CT scan done on our mummy. Would you like to attend?"

Lynn stared at her for a long moment. "A mummy? Oh yes, you told us about him."

"We inherited him. We don't have any provenance on him, but we're all excited just the same—hoping he doesn't turn out to be a fake."

"That'd be interesting." Her eyes misted over. "That's the kind of thing Raymond would have just loved. He'd have had me and him front row seats before you even knew you had a scheduled date. I am sure going to miss him."

As Diane spoke with Lynn, she caught sight of Garnett and Kingsley as they got in Garnett's car to leave. She wondered if Kingsley got any information of importance from the gathering.

Garnett reached for his cell in his breast pocket and put it to his ear. She felt her phone vibrating in her purse. She took it out and looked at the display. It was David.

Chapter 31

Diane said good-bye to Lynn Webber and headed toward her car a few feet away, punching up David's cell number as she walked.

"What's up?" she asked.

"We have another murder."

"Anyone we know?" Diane was half joking, half expecting it to be Steven Mayberry.

"It's Kacie Beck."

Diane was stunned. "Kacie? I just spoke with her."

"I'm on the way to work the scene. Neva's with me. The two of us can do it. Don't you have an appointment at the hospital for the mummy's CT scan?"

"Yes, but . . ."

"You go on with that. Give us a head start on the crime scene. Maybe we'll know something by the time you get there."

"Okay. I'll be there as soon as I finish at the hospital. David, she was wearing a diamond engagement ring when I saw her. Look for it."

"Will do."

Diane got in her borrowed car and sat there for a moment before starting the ignition. *Damn,* she thought. *Damn. Another murder victim with a connec-*

tion to the Cobber's Wood murders. What's this about?
Surely the killer left some piece of physical evidence
that would connect at least some of the crime scenes.
But she hadn't been able to find it.

The caller had her believing he was a serial killer.
Run-of-the-mill killers usually don't try to engage the
crime lab director in dialogue. But Diane had a sense
that there was something more to it than just a
crazy person.

When she arrived at the radiology department,
Korey was already there with Jonas, waiting in the
hallway with the mummy. Korey leaned against the
wall, and Jonas sat on a chair that he apparently
dragged from an adjacent waiting room. Next to the
wall on a gurney was the mummy, strapped to a board
by several layers of plastic wrap that enveloped him
from head to foot.

"I imagine you caused a stir bringing him in," said
Diane

"We did indeed," said Jonas. "Everyone here is
quite excited."

"So, this is your mummy." Lynn Webber arrived,
changed from her dark dress to a white lab coat and
slacks. "I've never seen one up close." She stood over
the gurney and scrutinized him. "Nice clothes. I like
these plastic wrappings much better than the dingy
linen ones you usually see on them."

Diane introduced everyone to Lynn Webber. Jonas
stood and offered her a seat.

"No, please stay seated."

But Jonas rose and joined Lynn next to the mummy,
explaining to her what they had discovered so far and
how it came to be in their possession.

Korey handed Diane a file. "Jonas and I examined

him with an endoscope. We took these pictures. We also took some tissue samples and sent them off for analysis."

Diane opened the folder and flipped through the photographs. "These are good."

"I thought we got some real clear images," said Jonas, turning from the mummy. "Notice that the brain is removed. That places him in the late Middle Kingdom or after." He explained to Lynn how methods of embalming changed over time. "See this incision here?" He pointed to a cut in the mummy's abdomen on the left side. "It was here up through the eighteenth dynasty. After that, the incision point was from the hip to the pubic region."

"We went into the incision and had a look around," said Korey, pulling out a photo from the rest and showing Diane. "As you can see, we didn't see much. I couldn't find a way in and I didn't want to do any damage. But this looks like one of the kidneys."

"Didn't they remove the organs?" asked Lynn.

"Yes," said Korey, "except the kidneys. I'm not sure why."

"One of the interesting things," said Jonas, "is the position of the hands."

"Position of the hands?" repeated Lynn. She placed one of hers on Jonas' arm and gave him her full attention.

Diane could see that he was falling under her spell just as the sheriff and Garnett had—though she had to admit, she thought the bloom was off the rose with Garnett.

"From his bones, it appears he may have been a scribe or some worker who had to sit for hours hunched over his work. However, his hands are in the royal position." Jonas crossed his hands over his chest. "Rather than by his side, or crossed in a lower position."

"Royal position. Why, I'm glad to know that, Jonas. I'm going to put that in my will. When I die and they put me in the casket, it's going to be in the royal position." She crossed her hands over her chest. "I know a lot of people who won't be surprised by that."

Diane had to force herself to attend to Korey, Jonas and Lynn's conversation. She watched them, feeling guilty—they were so excited, and all she could think of was Kacie Beck. She should have asked Kacie about the ring. She should have probed deeper about Chris Edwards and why he was murdered. Kacie had known something, and Diane had just dropped her off at her apartment. What was she missing?

"Diane." Jonas' voice penetrated her thoughts. "What do you think?"

Diane hesitated a second, recalling the conversation that had managed to filter through her own thoughts. "I don't . . ." She saw Kendel coming through the doorway. "Here she is. We don't have to guess—let's ask her if she was able to acquire the artifacts."

Kendel waved to them as she walked down the hallway. Her hair was twisted up in a clip. She wore white capri pants, a sleeveless turquoise shirt and tan leather wedge slides on her feet. Kendel had the ability to look dressed up in the most casual of clothes.

"You're back," said Jonas. "That was quick. How did it go?" He had the beginnings of a frown, as if a quick return might have meant failure.

"I got back an hour ago." Kendel grinned. "We are

now the owner of a collection of twelfth-dynasty amulets that is most likely from our mummy's wrappings."

"You did it. Good for you, girl," said Jonas. His face broke into a broad smile.

"Well done," said Diane. "How much did it cost us?"

"I came in way under budget. People still want immortality. The collection will be called the Robert Lyon Rider Collection." She made a frame in the air with her hands. "We'll have a wonderful gold plaque labeling the room and the collection."

"Good job. You said they are twelfth dynasty? The amulets support that date for our mummy, then?" said Diane.

"Yes. I was very happy when I saw them. There's a couple of lovely scarabs, a beautiful collection of carved fish, several figurines. I'm still establishing a paper trail to our mummy, but it's looking good. The Riders had wills describing the artifacts and even a letter that described the unwrapping party, with"—Kendel paused dramatically before she spoke again—"a mention of our Victorian pickle jar."

Jonas rubbed his hands together. "That's just great. More than I expected."

"Well done, Kendel," said Diane. "Very well done."

"I was thinking on the way back that we should concentrate just on the twelfth dynasty in the exhibit—something like Everyday Life in Twelfth-Dynasty Egypt."

"Good idea," said Diane. "That tight focus is a good way to make the most of the handful of items we have. I'd like to see a time line that shows what was going on in other parts of the world during that same period. Set up a meeting with the exhibit planners and we'll start on it. It would be good if we can make the opening dovetail with a fund-raiser."

"Do you want me to put feelers out for other acquisitions?" asked Kendel.

"Let me look at the budget. It might be better to use the resources to do a fine exhibit with what we have. We can always branch out later."

Diane introduced Kendel to Lynn, who stood between Jonas and Korey, observing Diane's assistant director.

"Good to meet you. Love your shoes," said Lynn. "Gucci?"

"Michael Kors," said Kendel, holding out her hand to Lynn.

A technician came out to the corridor. "We're ready for our patient."

He took the gurney into the imaging room and directed them into the viewing room where several staff from the hospital had assembled to watch. The mummy was a celebrity. Someone had even called the newspaper. A reporter, a young woman who looked like she might still be a journalism student and an equally young photographer hurried through the door just behind Diane and her staff.

"Thanks for asking me," said Lynn. "This is a nice thing to come back to after burying Raymond."

"I'm happy to have you look at the scan and offer any ideas on what you see."

The viewing room was actually too small for the crowd gathered there. It was already getting hot, but no one but Diane seemed to notice. When they were all settled, Jonas repeated the story of the mummy to the reporter and the crowd of technicians, nurses and doctors. Diane imagined that he must have been a great lecturer. He took all the bits and pieces of information they had discovered so far and wove a fascinating story. As he spoke, Diane watched the technicians lift the mummy from the gurney onto the CT platform. The photographer snapped pictures as the mummy started his journey into the circle.

"Chevron one encoded," said the technician at the viewing screen. A few of the onlookers laughed, some rolled their eyes, most looked puzzled.

"You're a *Stargate* fan," said Diane.

"Ya, sure, ya betcha," he quoted from the TV series.

"Me too," said Diane.

The mummy moved back and forth through the CT ring, and images of the skull cavity began appearing on the monitor.

"Look at that."

"Amazing."

"That had to hurt."

Everyone commented at once when the upper jaw and its abscesses were revealed.

"You're right," said Lynn. "That must have been what killed him."

"Why didn't they just pull the teeth?" asked one of the doctors.

"I don't know," answered Jonas. "They had dentistry methods, but they rarely did extractions."

A cell phone rang and three-quarters of those present turned at once, searching for the offender.

"You are supposed to turn those off in the hospital," said a nurse. "They interfere with the equipment." She had zeroed in on the culprit, the journalist.

The young woman smiled and shrugged. "It won't be but a minute."

"Now!" said the nurse.

But the young woman wasn't listening. She had crumpled to her knees in tears.

Chapter 32

Diane was the first to her side. She put an arm around the sobbing girl and took the phone out of her hand. She read the text message before she turned off the power.

OH GOD, WHERE R U? KACIE MURDERED! AMY

"I'll take care of her," said Diane, pulling the woman to her feet and helping her out the door. The photographer started to put down his camera and leave with her. Diane turned to him. "You stay and finish."

He stopped in his tracks. "Oh, okay, sure."

Diane took her to the nearest lounge and sat her down in a chair. She found a paper-cup dispenser and got her a drink of water.

"What's your name?" Diane asked, after the woman took a drink.

"Madison. Madison Foster."

Madison had blond hair arranged back in a single braid. She pulled at her short khaki skirt as she talked. Her white tee-shirt had a drop of blood on it.

"Your nose is bleeding." Diane dug in her purse for a tissue. "Put your head back and pinch your nose."

"I've always gotten nosebleeds. It happens when I cry." She put the tissue to her nose and put her head back.

"Do I need to get a nurse?"

"No. This happens a lot. It'll go away soon."

Diane gave her several moments before she said anything. When the bleeding seemed to have stopped, she spoke to her in a low, calm voice.

"Madison, are you a student?"

"Yes. A journalism student at Bartram."

"You knew Kacie Beck?" asked Diane.

Madison looked at her for a long moment. "You read the message?"

"Yes."

"Kacie was my best friend." She took a deep breath and seemed to collect herself. "I need to call Amy. Maybe she's playing some kind of trick. She has an odd sense of humor sometimes."

"No, Madison, it's not a trick."

Madison's brow puckered into deep furrows as she looked at Diane. Wondering, no doubt, how Diane could possibly know.

"I'm head of the crime lab for Rosewood."

"Oh, I think I knew that."

"My team is over at her apartment now."

"Oh, God, it's true." She started sobbing again.

Diane handed her another tissue, went to the bathroom and came back with wet paper towels. Madison wiped her face with the towels and took a deep breath.

"I don't believe this. Who would want to kill her? Right after her fiancé, Chris. And them arresting her. Oh, God. Why did this happen?"

"Madison. I would like to ask you some questions. It will help us find out who did this."

Madison nodded.

"How well did you know Kacie?"

"We grew up together in Columbus, Georgia. We came to school here together."

"Did you know Chris Edwards?"

"We met him up here."

"Kacie had on a ring."

"I saw it right after he gave it to her. She was really proud and couldn't wait to show it to her family. They didn't like Chris very much."

"Why?"

Madison shrugged. She dabbed her nose with a wet towel. "It's not bleeding again, is it?"

"No."

"Her father's a doctor. They wanted her to marry a doctor. Her parents are real snobs. They're nice, but snobs."

"Do you know if it was a real diamond?"

Madison looked at her wide-eyed. "Why wouldn't it be?"

"Diamonds are expensive. Do you know how Chris was able to buy it?"

"I just assumed he put it on his card."

Madison wasn't being much help. Diane thought perhaps she wasn't asking the right questions. She should have just passed her along to Garnett, but she really didn't think he would fare much better.

"Did Chris have a second job?"

"Besides his forestry job? I don't think so. He was working hard on his thesis and his job—and seeing Kacie. He didn't have time for much else."

"What did you think of Chris? Did you think he was good enough for Kacie?"

"Oh yeah. He was a great guy. Sweet. Good sense of humor. He wasn't self-centered like most guys."

"Do you know his friend, Steven Mayberry?"

"Steve. Yeah, sure. A little. We've gone out a couple of times."

"What is he like?"

"Not like Chris. He talks about himself a lot. Has big plans for getting a job in his uncle's paper company. He always talks like he has a lot of money, but I don't think he does. At least he never spent any on me. We ate out mostly at fast food places."

"Who are Chris and Kacie's other friends?"

Madison shrugged. "I don't know, really. The guys in their department, I suppose."

"Do you know if they had any friends who are missing?"

"Missing? What do you mean? Like Steven, you mean?"

Diane had made smaller copies of Neva's drawings to carry in her purse. She pulled them out and showed them to Madison.

"Do you know any of these people?"

Madison looked carefully at each one. "They don't look familiar. Who are they?"

"Have you heard from Steven lately?"

"Not for about a week—since he's been missing. What's all this about?"

She looked at Diane with large, liquid brown eyes—she wanted answers, Diane could see. She needed some meaning to all this. Diane needed meaning too.

"When was the last time you spoke with Steven?"

"Spoke with him? Not for a long time. He left a message on my voice mail about a week ago. He wanted to go out, said something about having a ship come in. I have no idea what he meant. I didn't call back. I really don't like him very much."

Ship come in. That was the first sign that anything was going on. She was surprised at the sense of relief she felt. Finally, something.

"Did Chris or Kacie mention anything about what he might have meant?"

"I didn't tell them. It was just a voice message. It didn't really mean anything."

"Did you get a sense that Chris was about to come into some money?"

"Well, he got the ring—but then, I just thought he charged it."

"He'd need one big credit limit."

"When you're a student, that's pretty easy. They send you cards in the mail by the dozens with huge limits. My dad's an accountant, and he's lectured me from the time I was three about owing money, so I don't use them big time, but some people do."

"Did Chris seem especially happy about something?"

Her face brightened. "Yes, now that you mention it. Kacie did mention that he'd been really happy lately—almost manic. She didn't know why—she figured he'd gotten a really good job and was going to surprise her."

"Did any of them seem to be frightened of anything?"

"No. Just after—you know—Chris died, Kacie was a basket case, as you can imagine. She had nightmares and was taking Valium."

"Were her nightmares about anything specific?"

Madison looked at Diane as if she were an idiot. "She found Chris."

"I know, but I thought her dreams might have some clue that her subconscious was trying to bring to the surface."

"She didn't say. It was always about finding Chris like—like that."

"Madison, if you remember anything, however small, give me a call." Diane fished a card out of her purse and wrote on it. "I put my cell number on here, and the number of Chief Garnett. He's the detective in charge. Call him or me if you remember anything or need to talk."

Madison took the card, turned it over and looked at the numbers. She nodded. "I will, I promise."

Her tears had dried and her nose had stopped bleeding, but Madison looked profoundly sad. Diane wanted to say something that would help, but she felt completely helpless in the face of grief. She should know a lot about grief, and she did, but she didn't know how to make it go away.

"Do you have someone to stay with?"

"I think I'll go home—to Columbus. Jerry, the cameraman, will drive me. He's been after me for a date. I guess I'll see what kind of stuff he's made of."

They were almost finished with the CT scan when she returned. The image on the monitor was of the abdominal cavity.

"We're thinking he had a tumor on his kidney," said Lynn. She pointed to the screen. "You know, if we could just get a piece of that tissue."

"I can try again with the endoscope, now that I know where to look," said Korey.

"We'll have you a great three-D image of your

guy," said one of the doctors. "You going to do one of those facial reconstructions?"

"Yes," said Diane. "It'll be a lot of fun to know what the guy looked like."

"Well, we are happy to be of help. Interesting case."

Before she left, Diane thanked the hospital personnel for their help. She thanked Lynn and asked her if she had time, if she'd like to write a report. Diane had a couple of motives. One, she genuinely wanted her expert input. She also wanted to pat down her ruffled feathers. As long as Lynn stayed at her job, Diane would have to work with her. If she could build up some good interactions, when the inevitable disagreement came about time of death, or whatever else that ticked off Lynn, they'd at least have established a good rapport.

Diane went from the hospital to Kacie Beck's apartment. Garnett was there, along with David and Neva. The body had been removed. *We probably passed somewhere along the way,* she thought.

Kacie had a small one-bedroom apartment close to campus. Diane had seen it from the outside, but hadn't gone inside. Perhaps she should have. Was someone waiting for Kacie in the dark? The thought sickened her.

Diane shook her thoughts and looked around the room. Kacie's decorating tastes included import shops. She had carved end tables with a scroll design, a carved wooden elephant coffee table with a glass top, several colorful silk throws of fuschia, lime green and blue tossed on the chairs and sofa along with a multitude of ornate throw pillows. The apartment smelled of death and incense.

Kacie had been found in her bed—strangled, beaten

and raped. This one didn't look anything like the others. Except someone had gone through her drawers. They had also taken her ring and had skinned her finger pulling it off.

Diane told Garnett about Madison Foster and related the information she had gained from her.

"She was at the hospital reporting on your mummy?" He shook his head. "It's about time some of the coincidences worked in our favor," he said.

Diane was relieved. She feared that she was going to have to explain to him just why she was interviewing witnesses.

"So there was something the boys were into," said Garnett, almost to himself.

"It appears so. Have you any leads on Mayberry?"

"None. We still don't know if he's dead or alive."

"Where's Ross Kingsley?"

"He's in his motel room working on his profile."

"What's his thinking?"

"Different from mine, especially with the new information. I think our boys were into something with the three Cobber's Wood victims. They had a falling-out, and Edwards and Mayberry hung them. Then Mayberry and Edwards had a falling-out, and Mayberry killed him. I'm thinking that Edwards tied the knots for the Cobber's Wood victims and Mayberry tied the knots that strung up Edwards."

"What about Kacie? Mayberry do her too?" asked Diane.

"Either that, or this really is a coincidence. She was raped. This could be a rapist who also steals."

"That sounds reasonable," said Diane, "but there's one thing."

"What's that?"

"Who's calling me? I spoke with Mayberry at the Cobber's Wood crime scene, and it wasn't him."

Garnett winced. "Maybe that's someone else too. You said you get lots of E-mail every time they run that interview."

"Yes. That's true. I do."

"Damn, all this is too complicated." Garnett ran a hand through his thick hair.

"What's the profiler saying?" Diane asked.

"That the Cobber's Wood victims were done by a serial killer who's probably done some people before. We're looking for similar killings in other states now."

"And the other murders?"

"Separate. He said something about Cobber's Wood being an organized scene and Edwards' scene being disorganized. He thinks Raymond Waller was killed for his collection. He talked to one of your curators or conservators, or whatever you call them, and it seems that the collection is real valuable. We ran a check on Waller's finances, and all his spare money for as far back as we can check has gone into the collection."

"That makes sense too," said Diane.

But something she couldn't put her finger on bothered her. Looking at all the crime scenes was like looking at an illusion and not being able to perceive the alternate point of view. If she could just see through the illusion.

"You're right," she said. "This is too complicated. Perhaps we should quit looking for a connection and look at each scene as separate until we know better."

As she spoke, Jin showed up at the door. "Hey, Boss. I thought you'd like to know, I've connected two of the crime scenes."

Chapter 33

Jin gathered up his hair and doned a cap just before he stepped into the room. He picked up a pair of latex gloves and put them on. "I just finished with the Crown Vic, and I tell you one thing, we can find this guy by looking to see who's walking around with a handheld vac. He's cleaned that sucker up. Obviously been watching too many crime scene shows."

"You said you've discovered a connection," said Garnett. He sounded a little testy, but Jin ignored that.

"Sure did. You know the bloody glove print with the tear we found at the Chris Edwards crime scene? Well, I found that same glove print on the left front fender and on the left front door of your car, Boss. He's the guy who attacked you."

Diane must have looked dumfounded. Garnett certainly did. He stood there in his suit that he'd worn to Raymond's funeral, his mouth hanging slightly open.

"I thought you'd be surprised," said Jin.

"Are you serious?" said Garnett.

"As a heart attack," said Jin. "It's the same glove. Still had traces of blood on it."

"Well, now we've got something," Garnett said. "Okay, where does that leave us?"

"The person who attacked Dr. Fallon is the same person who killed Chris Edwards," said Jin. "He is also the same person who stole the Crown Victoria."

"That means, if you're right on the voice recognition, Diane, that it was not Mayberry who killed Edwards. This is beginning to get as complicated as one of those logic problems that my daughter likes to work in her game magazines," said Garnett.

"I love those," said Jin. "Can't get enough of them. I've even had a few of my own published in those mags." Garnett looked at Jin as if affronted by his intelligence. Jin, obviously enjoying the moment, pressed on. "If he's the same person who's been calling you, Boss, then that makes for a very interesting problem."

"How's that?" asked Garnett.

"Because," said Diane, "the person who's been calling me said he was inspired by the television interview—that was shown before Chris Edwards died."

Garnett looked surprised again and fell silent. "Okay," he said. "He was contemplating killing someone, picked out Edwards from the interview to kill, and you to call and chat about it."

Diane was tempted to laugh, but she could see Garnett was serious.

"You need to give this information to the profiler," she said. "He'll need it before he gets too far into his analysis. And I have an idea. See if the university has someone in the linguistics department who specializes in recognizing accents and dialects. We have the caller on tape. Maybe we can place where he grew up."

"That's an idea. What department would I call?"

"Anthropology and English. They both teach linguistics. I'll ask my archaeologist if he knows anyone. You also might try someone in speech. Sometimes they have someone with that skill."

"That's a good idea."

"It's about time for some of the chemical analysis on the bones and the toxicology reports from the autopsies to come back. That could give us a lot of information."

"We've finished here." David and Neva came from the bedroom, carrying an armload of evidence bags.

"Find anything useful?" asked Garnett.

"Won't know until we get back to the lab," said David. "By the way, I'm sending you and Sheriff Braden a copy of my report on the insects. Diane was dead-on about the time of death for Cobber's Wood. Twenty-one days before they were found. My insects don't lie."

Garnett nodded. "Well, Dr. Webber will be sorry to hear that. I guess you know she pitched a fit when you disagreed with her." Apparently, Garnett didn't like women who pitched fits.

"I got a call from her myself," said Diane.

"I need to go talk to Ross Kingsley," said Garnett. "When you have time, come by my office. I need to talk to you about something."

Diane looked at her watch. "How late will you be there?"

"Late. Just call my cell." He went out the door and to his car.

"How'd the mummy thing go?" asked Jin, removing his cap and gloves outside the door with Diane, David and Neva.

"I'm going to keep the crime scene seal on," said David. "I'll release it when the parents get to town."

"All right," said Diane. "The mummy thing went well. Found a tumor on one of his kidneys."

"Poor fellow," said Jin. "Suffered all those abscesses, a tumor, lower back pain, and the indignity of a Victorian unwrapping party."

"Kendel did find the amulets that were inside his wrappings and acquired them for the museum."

"Cool," said Jin.

"When I was little," said Neva, "my grandma used to have these party favors she called surprise balls. It was a crepe paper streamer wrapped into a ball. As she wrapped the crepe paper, she'd put little trinkets in the wrapping, so that we'd find things as we unwrapped the ball. It sounds like the idea came from the Egyptians."

"I've heard of those," said David. "Be interesting if the idea did come from the Egyptians—by way of the Victorians, maybe?"

Diane looked at her watch. "Damn, I've got to get Andie's car back to her so she can go home."

"Need some wheels, Doc?" asked Jin.

"I should have some coming from the insurance company. If not, I suppose I'll be spending the night at the museum."

"If you need a ride, we all have cars. Doesn't the museum have a fleet?" said David.

"Yes, but they are not for my personal use. Neva, we'll have the CT data on the mummy sometime tomorrow. I'll show you how to use the data in the facial reconstruction software."

Neva grinned broadly. "That'll be fun. I'm looking forward to seeing what he looked like."

"How do you feel about doing a sculpture of him? The museum will pay you."

"Yes. I'd like that very much."

"Cool," said Jin. He waved and went to his car.

Diane rushed back to the museum. Andie was busy at her desk.

"I hope you didn't think you were going to be stuck in the museum," said Diane.

"I knew you'd show up sooner or later." Andie grinned and grabbed her purse.

"Andie, thank you so much for letting me use your car."

"Not a problem. Glad to do it." She handed Diane a set of keys. "Ford Explorer down in the lot. Bright candy apple red. Can't miss it."

"Is this from the insurance company?"

Andie nodded. "Nice. Only a couple of years old. Very clean inside."

"Thanks. I appreciate everything you do, Andie."

"Good. I'm working on being indispensable."

"You are. I'll see you tomorrow. Oh, did they tell you about the mummy scan?"

"Kendel and Dr. Briggs came up and told me about it. Also about the amulets. They said we're going to do a three-D reconstruction of the face?"

"Yes, Neva Hurley will be doing it."

"This is going to be so nice. Dr. Fallon, I had this idea. I've been looking at Egyptian stuff and what their houses looked like with that adobe-looking wall around the front yard and all, and I thought it would be fun if we could re-create one in the museum. If we can't do a life-sized one, maybe a miniature city."

"Andie, I think that's a great idea. Tell Jonas about it tomorrow."

"See? Indispensability—that's who I am. See you tomorrow."

Diane envied all her staff who were going home. She sat down at her desk to have a look at her mail and remembered that she was supposed to be having dinner with Frank tonight. She looked at her watch. He wouldn't be getting home from Atlanta for another hour. She'd have time to go see what the heck Garnett wanted, then go to Frank's.

She gave her mail a brief look. Most of it was things that Andie could take care of—or already had taken care of. She looked at her E-mail and responded to messages from two of her curators.

Her final message was one line, no signature. I THINK WE SHOULD MEET.

A chill ran through her. She stared at the message for several moments and realized that she was holding her breath. She exhaled and started to type a response, and stopped. What would she say? What did he want? To give up? She didn't respond. Maybe she and Garnett could set something up. *Right,* some inner voice said, *put your life in the hands of the Rosewood police. That's a plan.*

She shut down her computer and headed out the door. The candy apple red Ford Explorer was parked in front of the museum. It was indeed very red. Hard to miss. She got in and drove to the police department, calling Garnett on the way to tell him she was coming.

She showed her identification to the policeman at the duty desk. Of the four policemen who were there, all of them smirked at her. Even the sergeant on duty was trying hard to make his face an objective mask. One of these days, she'd have to sit them down and ask what the hell their problem was.

In the detective's squad room she was met with more amused stares and half heard a comment that someone would like to be a fly on that wall. Great, Kingsley probably profiled her out to be an axe-murdering maniac. She knocked on Garnett's door.

Chapter 34

Garnett rose from behind his desk as Diane entered his office. "Diane. Please sit down." He motioned toward his conference table as he pulled out a chair and sat down. Diane pulled up one of his chairs and sat down opposite. He formed his hands into a steeple and looked very uncomfortable.

"Diane, I don't want you to take this the wrong way."

"Douglas, I pride myself in always taking things the right way."

He was taken aback for a moment. He looked at Diane as if there might be some coded message in what she said. Or perhaps it was her uncustomary use of his first name. But he was making this sound like a trip to the principal's office, and she was going to stay on equal footing.

"Yes, of course. It's come to my attention . . ." He paused.

Come to his attention. Hadn't she had this conversation before . . . with the mayor? Perhaps that's why he looked so uncomfortable.

"Appearances are very important."

Okay, she thought, *am I not wearing enough makeup . . . too much?*

"Yes, appearances are important, among many things."

"What I mean is, when you get on the witness stand, you must not only be above reproach, but appear to be above reproach."

"Like Caesar's wife."

"Who?"

"Never mind. Is there something you're trying to say?"

"Defense attorneys look for the least sign of impropriety to impugn the character of a witness in order to win a case."

"Some do. Where are we going with this conversation?"

"It has come to my attention that you are . . ." Garnett seemed to be searching for the right words. ". . . Dating men half your age."

Diane threw back her head and laughed—which did bewilder Garnett. He looked at her with a frown. She hardly knew where to begin her response to such an asinine statement.

"I won't even address the point of view that a woman dating younger men somehow impugns her character. I'll simply cut to the truth of what has come to your attention. Frank Duncan is two years older than I am. Now, I realize that spending all that time in the jungle sun put a few wrinkles on my face that I wish I didn't have, but really, Douglas, I don't think I look almost eighty."

Garnett opened his mouth, then closed it and opened it again. "I don't mean Frank."

"He's the only man I'm dating."

"You've been seen having a romantic dinner with a much younger man who works for you."

Garnett settled back in his chair and from the look

on his face, he did realize how ridiculous it sounded for him to call her into his office for such a nebulous thing. She was sure when it was reported to him, probably through Izzy's boss, it came out something like she was some slut robbing a cradle, putting moves on her underlings.

"Define romantic."

"Well, romantic, candlelight . . ."

"I think I see where this originated. I ate dinner with one of the geologists who works in the museum. We belong to the same caving club and we were discussing caving business. The restaurant was the one at the museum. It's on the same floor as my office, and I use it frequently. In the evening all the tables have candles. It never occurred to me to blow it out, but then I'd have been sitting in the dark.

"If your informant had seen me a week earlier, he'd have seen me having dinner in the candlelight with my head conservator, who's about the same age as the geologist. However, he's black and has dreadlocks, so I suppose that would have caused quite a stir with your informant. A month ago, I had lunch with one of the docent interns. He's nineteen. One of the children in his party hid in the museum and he couldn't find him for an hour. It upset him greatly, and I had to calm him down. We ate lunch on the terrace, so that could have been construed as romantic. About once every two weeks I have lunch or dinner with my archaeologist, and we often play chess together. Of course, he is much older than me and I suppose the reversal of ages doesn't impugn my character, so my association with him doesn't count.

"Douglas, I have had dinner or lunch with over half the people I work with. I'm head of the museum, and it is not a nine-to-five job for anyone. We often work over dinner. I will not stop interacting with my employees because it offends some busybody's sense of propriety. If it comes up in court, I will handle it."

Diane had managed to keep her voice calm and even during her whole diatribe. When she finished, Garnett sat for a long moment without speaking.

"I think I was probably misinformed," he said.

"Is that the only reason you wanted to see me?"

"We're under a lot of pressure to make our crime lab work. I was just doing a little troubleshooting before anything got out of hand."

"Our crime lab is functioning superbly. I think what is out of hand is gossipmongers and passive-aggressive bullies. I think you had better turn your attention to your stationhouse staff, who all appear to be preoccupied with pettiness and character assassination, and ask yourself why they are failing in their surveillance duties." Diane paused a moment. "If you can't tell, this makes me very angry."

"I can see."

"No . . . I mean it makes me *really* angry."

"I don't doubt you."

"The caller—on one of his calls when I was pushing for justifiable reasons for murder—he talked about gossip and bullying."

"What are you getting at?"

"He used those as examples. It must have been for a reason. What might a gossip do to someone who's on the edge? Whoever is calling me—if he's the killer, his motive was not the motive of a serial killer. I think it was more specific and focused. He wanted to get even. He seems obsessed with personal justice. If that's true, he probably knew the victim or victims—provided he really is the killer."

"So you're saying, if he killed the victims in Cobber's Wood, it had to do with revenge?"

"I suppose that's what I'm saying. Look, Frank is expecting me to come to his house for dinner with him and his daughter. I'd like to not be late. I've put in very long hours, and I'd like to take this evening off."

"Of course. I'm sorry for holding you up. And . . . I'm sorry for the other thing."

"Douglas, I think I know who's spreading this rumor. If it's who I think it is, he's a good friend of Frank. And since this person met me last year and heard those first unfounded rumors about me, he hasn't wanted to let go of the notion that I'm not good enough for Frank. If you talk to him, advise him of how appropriate it is to mind his own business. Pettiness has no place in what we're trying to do here.

"And speaking of what we're trying to do here, I got another E-mail from our friend. He wants to meet."

Garnett raised his eyebrows. "He wants to meet with you? How do you feel about that?"

"I'm thinking it might be a good idea, under the right controls."

"Let me think about it."

"It may be the only way we're going to catch this guy. Has Sheriff Braden made any headway?"

"We've sent the pictures out and searched missing persons. No hits. Of course, it's still early on getting anything back on the drawings. We're searching for similar murders across the country. Both Braden's men and mine have been asking around at truck stops for anyone suspicious, or anyone who may have talked about the murders, or anyone who has picked up hitchhikers that look like the drawings. We have a photograph of a waggoner's knot we've shown around at the stops. Found several guys who know what it is and use it, but so far no leads on our guy. We've tried to get a list of end buyers for that particular type of orange carpet, and that information, apparently, is simply not available."

"Strange. We have all that forensic evidence stacking up in my lab and absolutely no one to attach it to."

"It's frustrating, for sure. In the Chris Edwards and the Raymond Waller murders, we've canvassed the neighborhoods. We've talked with everyone they knew and worked with, including their families. We're doing the same with Kacie Beck. My gut still tells me it's Steven Mayberry for the Edwards and Beck murders. With what you told me about your talk with the journalism student—what was her name, Madison something?"

"Madison Foster."

"That's it. I'm convinced that Mayberry and Edwards were into something. Maybe Mayberry killed Kacie Beck to protect himself. He might feel that everyone thinks he's dead and he likes it that way. For Raymond Waller, it was someone after his collection. He didn't know any of the other victims. It was just a coincidence that he was Dr. Webber's assistant and worked on the hanging victims."

Everything Garnett said seemed plausible, and she was actually impressed with what he and the sheriff were doing.

"Then maybe what I should do is take the guy up on his offer to meet. I think maybe he wants to turn himself in and he just needs a push, and he's using me to push him into it."

"It will be very dangerous. You'd have to insist on meeting him on your terms, not his."

"I know. If he wants to come out in the open . . ."

"You really think he wants to get caught?"

"I don't know. It's possible, but ask the profiler."

Garnett looked at his watch. "I'll go to Kingsley's hotel tonight and have a talk with him. Have you responded to the guy yet?"

"No. I was waiting to talk with you first."

"I'm going to have to really think about this. Let's talk tomorrow."

Diane left the station house wondering what their faces would look like the next time she had to visit. It would be nice to have succeeded in wiping the smirks off them. One thing she was convinced of—she couldn't expect their help if she was in trouble.

Chapter 35

Star met Diane at the door and hugged her. Her hair was all one color—black—and was short. She had a ring in one nostril.

"Uncle Frank's heating up dinner. He brought home Chinese, which means we'll have Chinese leftovers for the rest of the week."

"Probably."

Frank's house was an old Queen Anne set off the road. It had polished hardwood floors, walls painted a light sand color, and oak and walnut furniture as substantial as the house. It always smelled like furniture polish and always shined. It was a comfortable house, a house much like Frank—traditional, reliable, solid.

"So, I hear you have a mummy. Can I see it?"

"Yes, we have a mummy and, yes, you can see it if you would like."

"Cool."

"Hey." Frank came in and gave her a peck on her lips. "How you doing?"

"I'm glad to be having a break."

"You look tired."

"I've had a string of long days."

"Sit down, relax. I'll get you a drink of wine."

"Can I have one?" Star was being mischievous.

"No," said Frank.

Star laughed.

Diane kicked off her shoes and curled her feet under her on the stuffed sofa. Star lay sideways across an overstuffed armchair.

"You can stay here some time," Star said. "You and Uncle Frank don't have to just get together when I'm out of the house."

"We're together now."

"You know what I mean."

"We're doing fine, Star."

"The two of you are so old-fashioned."

"Are we?"

"I'm almost grown, you know."

"I think *almost* is the operative word."

Frank came in with a glass of red wine for Diane. "We're having Chinese tonight. How does that sound?"

"Great. It's nice just to relax. How has your day been?"

"Slow. We're working on some identity thefts, and they are always tedious to track down. Unfortunately, we often *don't* track them down. Feel like eating?"

As Diane suspected, Frank had the dining room table spread with enough food to feed the whole neighborhood. It was a compulsive habit of his— always buying more food than anyone could possibly eat. He always said he liked everyone to have a choice. She helped herself to fried rice, Mongolian chicken and steamed vegetables.

"Want chopsticks?" asked Star.

"Fork will be fine," said Diane. "How's school?"

"Boring. So, tell me about the mummy."

Diane repeated everything they knew about the mummy so far. She included the Victorian pickle jar. Star almost fell out of her seat laughing.

"I've been talking to Star about going to college," said Frank.

"I really don't want to. I mean, I'll just have to take a bunch of dumb courses and stay bored to death for four years."

"You could take something you like."

"I like to listen to music and go to the movies. Do they have courses in that?"

"They have music, and I think they have a course or two in film."

"Don't you have to take a bunch of English and math?"

"Yes. You could learn to enjoy English and math."

Star looked at Diane like she'd grown a horn out of her forehead. "You're joking, aren't you?"

"No. Just think about what the courses do for you. What you'll learn."

"Yeah, like when am I ever going to use math?"

"I use it all the time, analyzing skeletons, exercising, cooking, working on the museum budget, hiring staff, balancing my checkbook. Most jobs require some math."

"Not all—hardly any."

Frank sat back eating his Chinese food, listening to Diane and Star have their conversation. Diane guessed that he and Star had repeated this same conversation many times.

"Why don't you give college a try for a year?" said Diane.

Star made a face like she'd suddenly bitten into something rotten.

"I'll tell you what. Try it for a year and keep at

least a two point seven grade point average, and with Frank's permission, I'll take you to Paris and buy you new clothes."

Star's eyes grew wide. "Are you kidding? I mean, you're not just saying that just to keep the conversation going?"

"No. I'm not just saying it. I mean it."

"Like a whole new wardrobe?"

"Yes. I'll have get used to life without an arm and a leg, but yeah, I'm talking about a lot of new clothes."

"Oh, wow. What do you say, Uncle Frank?"

Frank's eyes had grown as large and round as Star's on hearing Diane's offer. "Think you can meet the conditions?" he said.

"I'll need help with the math."

"You're in luck, then," said Frank. "I'm pretty good in math."

"And the museum is a good place to get help in a lot of subjects. Think about it."

"Wow. Just a year?"

"Just a year."

"Wow." She stood up. "I need to go use the phone."

When she left the table, Frank turned to Diane. "You know what you're doing?"

"I hope so. I thought some incentive might help. Who knows? She may like college."

Frank reached over and held on to her hand. "That was really nice. More than nice."

Diane helped Frank put the food in the refrigerator, and they retired to the living room sofa. Diane curled up against Frank and rested her head on his shoulder.

"Hard day?" Frank asked again.

"The mummy was fun. But I guess you heard, we had another murder."

"What!"

"This time it was the girlfriend of Chris Edwards, one of the guys who found the bodies in the woods."

Frank pulled back and looked Diane in the face. "My God. What *is* this about?"

"I don't know. The profiler thinks the murders aren't related."

"Three people dead, one missing, and another attacked—all of whom had something to do with three more bodies in the woods. Maybe he ought to take math."

"But what's the connection?"

They heard laughter filtering down from Star's room.

"You've really made her happy. That's not an easy thing to do."

"Everyone needs something to look forward to."

"Can I go with you to Paris?"

Diane chuckled. "Sure."

They sat in silence for a long time. Diane was glad for the rest. Frank was comfortable and safe.

"I have a great-looking red SUV I'm driving," Diane said.

"I saw that out the window when you drove up. That the loaner?"

"Yes. Nice. I rather like it. I might get one. Maybe not that color." She paused a moment, not sure whether to bring up the subject of Izzy. "Garnett called me in today to talk about my inappropriate behavior."

"Jesus. Now what?"

"Dating men half my age. I told him you are at least a couple of years older than me."

Frank didn't say anything for a minute. He pulled Diane closer. "I'm sorry," he whispered. "I know where that came from."

"So Izzy talked to you too."

"Yes. I told him he was being an ass. I see I should have used stronger words. I'll talk to him."

"No. I've dealt with it."

"Did Garnett give you much trouble?"

"Not really. I suspect when the story was told to him it was amplified with colorful derogatory words. When he cleaned up the language to explain to me why he called me in, the whole thing ended up sounding a little ridiculous."

"Diane, maybe we should talk about us."

"Us?"

"That's shorthand for you and me. I can't tell you how frightened I was the other night. It made me realize how much you mean to me."

"You mean a lot to me too, and I find that a little scary."

"Scary? How?"

"Ariel meant the world to me. She was my heart. Losing her was more than devastating. Caring about people is a risky business." Diane hesitated for a moment, searching for the right words, but no right words came. "The two of us are doing fine. You work in Atlanta, I work here, we see each other when we can. Life is good."

"True, but permanence is something to think about."

"Okay. We'll think about it."

Frank laughed. "I'm glad we got that settled."

Diane was about to kiss him when Star bounced into the room. "Jennifer wants me to go out to Wal-Mart and maybe a movie. Her mother says it's okay."

"Who else is going?"

"Maybe Jessica and Stephanie."

"Who's driving?"

"Jennifer. She's kind of on her way to pick me up."

"She kind of is, is she? Go ahead, but be back by ten forty-five, and no controlled substances."

"Uncle Frank, you know, that was funny the first thirty times you said it. I've never done drugs."

"No smoking of anything that I call a drug and you don't."

"I told you I gave that up. You know, I could just give you a glass of pee every time I come home."

"That's an idea. Have a good time, and don't be late."

Star already had a purse in hand, a small black crochet fringed thing she hung over her shoulder and across her chest. She'd changed from jeans and black tee-shirt into a short black skirt and black blouse. She kissed Frank on the cheek.

"I'll be here if you need me," he told her.

Star turned to Diane. "You really meant it, didn't you, about Paris and the clothes?"

"Yes."

She almost broke into giggles again. "Wow. Thanks. I mean it." She bounded out the door at the sound of a car horn.

"Star seems to be doing well."

"Most of the time she is. She cries at night sometimes. She doesn't want me to know."

Diane understood Star's grief. That was one reason she made the offer. Trying to deal with grief and get your life back is one of the hardest things to do. Star had lost both her parents and her brother to a murderer and had been accused of committing the crime herself. It was going to take her a long time before she stopped crying into her pillow.

*   *   *

It was after midnight before Diane returned home. Star had come home on time, and Diane had to confess, it was a relief to see her walk through the door. Diane tried to imagine what it would have been like waiting up for Ariel to come home from a date, and her eyes misted over. She sometimes still cried into her pillow too.

The policemen were on duty, parked in front of her house. She parked and got out with the coffee and doughnuts she'd gotten for them on the way back and handed them through the window.

"Thanks. We appreciate this."

One of the policeman walked her to her apartment, apologizing along the way. "Jim and I are just really sorry about the mix-up last night."

"This whole business has all of us baffled," said Diane. "I appreciate your being here."

He walked with her inside and to the stairs before going back to his car. Diane decided that there may be something to the theory about getting to a man's heart through his stomach.

She walked up to her apartment and went in. It was stuffy. She hated running the air-conditioning when she wasn't there, but this wasn't good either. She turned on the air and went to the bedroom, changed and settled into bed.

She was almost asleep when a voice out of the darkness said, "I really want to talk to you."

Chapter 36

Diane didn't realize she had shot out of bed until she was halfway out her bedroom door. She made it to the front door and grabbed at the safety latch. Too slow. He grabbed her from behind and held her in a tight grip. She got out half a scream before a hand clamped over her mouth.

"I just want to talk. I'm not going to hurt you."

Diane kicked, but with bare feet she did little damage. *Dammit, I'm stronger than this.* She wrenched her body around, throwing them both to the floor. She hit her head on the hard floor, stunning her for a second, but her body was on automatic. She scrambled to her feet and raced for the bedroom, intending to lock herself in and call 911. But he was too fast. Before she could close the door, he hit it with enough force to knock her backward. She fell to the floor and rolled under the bed.

She saw the shadow of him on his knees grabbing for her, sliding under the bed after her. She rolled out, got to her feet, grabbed the radio on her nightstand and brought it down on his head as he crawled out from under the bed.

His struggle to rise was hampered by still being half

under the bed. She hit him again, harder, dropped the radio and ran. The safety was unlatched from her first attempt at escape so all she had to do was turn the locks and bolt from her apartment. As she ran down the stairs, she hoped the police hadn't decided they had to go somewhere else. She ran down the walk and into the street, each step hurting her bare feet. Halfway across the street the police saw her.

"What is it?" they shouted.

"He's in my apartment."

"Stay here." They jumped from the car and Diane climbed in the backseat, breathing hard. Bile rose up in her throat and she felt sick to her stomach.

Diane wore a fleece short-sleeved nightshirt that came halfway between her knees and thighs. The last place she wanted to be was in the back of an unmarked police car dressed in sleepwear. Damn him.

A gunshot echoed through the air. Oh, God. She put a hand on the door and started to open it, then stopped. She was still undecided on whether to get out. One of the policemen came running.

"We got him. An ambulance is coming, but I'm not sure he'll make it."

Diane felt sick all over again. "Can he talk?"

"He's in and out."

"I need to ask him some questions."

"I don't know."

"In case he dies, I need to ask him some questions."

"Okay. I suppose it's all right. You are a member of the department, after all."

Diane thought he'd like to add *a rather troublesome member*. She ran back up to her apartment, where the other policeman had a towel on the intruder's chest.

Diane knelt down by his side. "Can you hear me?"

"Just wanted talk. Not a murderer. Exec . . ." His breathing was labored and he started to cough. "Can't trust the police." He closed his eyes and lapsed into unconsciousness.

He was still alive but unconscious when the ambulance came and took him to the hospital. Diane sat on her couch in a pair of jeans and the nightshirt, waiting for the police to ask her questions. When she came back to her apartment, she'd passed her landlady and several of her neighbors, including the Odells across the hall. She wondered if it was time to look for another place to live before she was asked to leave.

She was ministering to cuts on her feet when Garnett arrived. "You need medical?" he asked.

"Just a few cuts on the soles of my feet. How's the officer who shot . . ." She let the question trail off.

"He's all right. A shooting's always hard. He thought the guy was drawing a gun. It turned out it was his cell phone. Can you tell me what happened?"

Diane told him about going to bed and hearing the voice just as she was about to fall asleep. She told about the struggle as best she remembered and about hitting him in the head with the radio.

"I talked to him after he was shot. He said he just wanted to talk, that he wasn't a murderer."

Garnett shook his head. "Think he's our guy?"

"I don't know. He may be just a stalker."

"You can't come in here." The voice was from a policeman outside her door.

"Tell Dr. Fallon that Frank Duncan is here."

Diane recognized the calm voice even through the door.

"Ask them to let him in," she said.

Garnett obliged, and Frank came in and sat down beside Diane, putting an arm around her shoulder.

"What on earth happened?"

Garnett explained while Diane put a couple more Band-Aids on her feet.

"Is he the guy who attacked you last night?" asked Frank.

"I don't know," said Diane. "How did you know something happened?"

"Izzy called. I think he's trying to make up for being a horse's ass. Get some clothes and come spend the night at my house."

Diane nodded. That sounded safe. She was sure her neighbors would feel safer if she were gone. Her newest neighbors must think this kind of thing happened to her every night.

As she left, Veda Odell, the neighbor across the hall, stuck her head out. "Marvin says he'd rather have a load of cats living next door than you."

"Mrs. Odell," said Diane. "I can't say as I blame him."

Diane called Garnett the next morning from the crime lab the minute she arrived. "What's his status?"

"Critical. He seems to be hanging in there. Hasn't been conscious for more than a few minutes at a time. Won't talk when he is."

"Do you know who he is?"

"He had no identification on him. We found what we believe is his vehicle. Stolen plates, no registration. And like I said, he isn't talking. We're sending you a copy of his fingerprints."

"Here they are now."

David stood in front of her with an envelope in his

hand. David, Jin and Neva had been hanging around her desk as if she might disappear if they looked away for a moment. Jin was stretched out on the sofa. Neva perched on the edge of one of the chairs.

"These are fingerprints of the guy who came into my apartment last night. Check them against all our crime scene prints and every fingerprint database we have access to. We need a match if there's one out there."

"I'll get on it," said David. "I've just installed a new identification algorithm. I'm anxious to try it out."

"Jin. Find out how the GBI is doing with the shed hair project." She took a key off her key chain. "Go to my apartment and get some of his blood off my floor or on the towel they used to cover the wound, and take it with you to Atlanta. See if we can match it."

"Neva." Diane picked up a piece of paper from her desk. "This report from the bone samples came back yesterday. All of our victims grew up in the northeastern United States. Sheriff Braden isn't having any luck with missing persons. I want you to scan your drawings and save them as graphic files, JPEG, GIF, whatever works best on the Internet. I want you to locate a professional list serve, discussion board or whatever it's called for plastic surgeons. Post the drawings of Blue and Green Doe, and see if anyone recognizes either of them. Mention where they grew up, Green's heart condition and Blue's tattoo of a butterfly on her ankle."

"I could do the same thing with the tattoos," said Neva. "Look for a discussion board about tattoos. Might get something."

"Good idea. Okay, guys, you have your assignments." Diane stood up. "I'm going to be working in the museum if you need me."

"You seem hyper today," said David.

"Hand-to-hand combat does that to you."

"You weren't hurt, were you?" he asked.

"I'm fine. When I finally got to a safe bed, I got a good night's sleep."

"You've had some reporters calling," said Andie, eying Diane as she came through the office.

"What did you tell them?"

"That I didn't know what the heck they were talking about. What the heck were they talking about?"

Diane described the events of the previous evening, trying to make it sound casual, but failing miserably.

"He's in critical condition. Have no idea who he is."

Andie stared at her with her mouth open. "Is that the guy who sent the flowers?"

"Yes."

"How is it that you attract all these weirdos?"

"I have no idea. I'm contemplating hiring someone to steal that interview the TV station has on file so they can't play the damn thing again. I thought I was just giving generic answers, but they certainly seemed to set this guy off."

"He was in your bedroom all the while?"

"Apparently so."

"That's creepy, not to mention scary."

"I'm going to get some work done. I want only museum business calls. Send all reporters to the police for information."

"Dr. F." Korey stood in the doorway. "I've got something you need to see."

"What's that?"

"It's up in the conservation room."

Diane nodded. "Sure."

She walked with Korey to the conservation lab located on the second floor.

"How did our mummy fare on his outing?" she asked.

"He did fine. When we got him back, I went back in with the endoscope and took a sample of the tumor. That ought to be interesting."

Diane quickened her pace.

"You have the amulets up there?"

"Sure do. Great stuff. You haven't seen them?"

"No, and I would like to."

Korey grinned. "You're going to like this, then."

Mike Seger was in the conservation room looking at the amulets when Diane arrived.

"You tell her what you found?"

"Not yet. She wanted to see the amulets first."

"This sounds mysterious." Diane stopped at a table where twenty-one Egyptian artifacts were laid out on a piece of batting. "These are absolutely lovely."

They were small. The largest piece was a scarab about four inches long. Each piece had a card next to it saying what it was and what materials it was made from.

The scarab was alabaster and probably had been over his heart. Several small fish figurines made of alabaster and lapis lazuli lay in two rows. An inscribed cylinder of sandstone had the name Senusret III written on it, according to the card. There was another row of several limestone figurines and a figure made of black steatite that was labeled SHABTIS.

"That's a Get Out of Work Free card for the after-life," said Korey, as Diane picked up the shabtis and turned it over in her hand. "According to Jonas, the writing on the back is a spell to let the person send the shabtis in his place if he was ever asked to do work. It seems that's what the rich folk did in life too. When there was mandatory work to be done, they could send in a sub. The work they were opting out of was the hard labor variety. Seems that ancient Egypt had a big public works program. Very useful when the Nile flooded."

Two figures lying next to each other looked like colored glazed pottery. The card was labeled FAIENCE."

"Kendel says faience ceramic is made of lime, crushed quartz and alkali and makes a glaze when it's fired," said Korey. "She says a lot of their jewelry was made that way."

"These are wonderful," said Diane. "They'll make an incredible exhibit."

"The designers are already at it. I've just about had to run them out of here to get any work done. Can't blame them, though. This is really fine stuff."

"Now, what did you ask me up here for?"

"The lawyer for Raymond Waller called and asked us if we could make the arrangement to send the base-ball collection to the Negro Leagues Baseball Museum. I told him sure, we interact with museums all the time."

"Certainly, we can handle it. Is there a problem?"

"I think you need to call the lawyer and talk to him. I mean, in order to make sure what's supposed to go the museum and what's supposed to go to his heirs."

"I'm not following," said Diane.

"You will." Korey and Mike led her to the climate-controlled vault in the rear of the lab, where he stored the baseball collection.

Chapter 37

The vault was cool. Diane shivered and rubbed her hands over her bare forearms. It had rows of shelves filled with items that had to be stored in a stable environment, always kept at the same temperature and humidity. Some items never left the vault until Korey was sure they would not deteriorate outside. Some of the objects couldn't stand the normal museum environment and had been in the vault since the museum opened. The mummy was there, lying on a table, with the plastic wrapping removed.

"Alicia's working on the wrappings that came with him," said Korey, with a nod of his head toward another table holding the linen mummy wrappings. "It's in pretty bad shape, but we'd like to use it to rewrap him."

A large table in the center of the room held Raymond Waller's pride and joy—his collection of artifacts from the Negro Leagues. There was the bat that David mentioned, and the ball. In fact, there were several balls and bats. There were uniforms and pennants, stacks of photographs, cards, signs and newspaper clippings.

"I went ahead and deacidified the paper, checked

out the material. I figured you wouldn't mind me taking care of his stuff."

"Sure. That's fine."

Korey picked up a handkerchief that had something wrapped in it. "I was checking out the uniforms for moths and things and I found this stuffed in the pocket of the Birmingham Black Barons uniform with the number ten on it. That's significant."

"Korey."

"I'm getting to it."

He unwrapped the handkerchief. In the center were three crystals about the size of marbles, each shaped like two pyramids stuck together at their base. They looked like they were made of clear ice.

"When I found these, I called Mike."

"What are they?"

She looked at Mike, who had that amused glint in his eyes again.

"You tell me," he said.

"Are you saying these are diamonds?"

Mike nodded his head. "Good-quality, uncut diamonds. I've already mapped and photographed the internal structure—thought it'd be nice to have on file."

"How much are they worth?"

"Cut price, we're talking in a range over two hundred thousand dollars."

"For three rocks?" said Diane.

"Three very sweet rocks."

Diane shook her head. "You were right, Korey. We have to call the attorney back and let him know."

She took the stones and let them rest in the palm of her hand.

"Damn. This is what the thief was looking for.

Where in the world did Raymond get them?" she whispered almost to herself.

"There is a way to trace a diamond back to the mine of origin," said Mike.

Diane looked up at him sharply. "How?"

"Every diamond has a chemical signature that is specific to its origin. It would require drilling a microscopic hole in it with a laser beam. The only problem is that not all the world's mines have been cataloged. And there's also the problem of diamonds mined from alluvial plains that have been washed maybe hundreds of miles from their origin."

"I'll present that option to Mr. Waller's executor."

"It's a very new methodology. It was developed to help legitimate diamond dealers. There's a big black-market trade in blood diamonds. Those are the diamonds used to finance the various African civil wars, and most dealers want to make sure their diamonds aren't part of that trade."

Blood diamonds, thought Diane. She wondered if that would turn out to be an appropriate name for these stones if indeed they were what caused Raymond's death.

"I'm going to have to tell Garnett too." Diane started to put the diamonds back in the handkerchief.

"Here." Mike handed her a jeweler's box with depressions in which to fit each diamond. "Stones like these don't need to be knocking around against each other."

"You put them against black," she said, smiling.

"Well, since we already know the color, you might as well present them at their best." Mike put the box in a jeweler's bag and handed it to Diane.

"I feel like I need a guard to go back down to my office."

"I'd be happy to oblige," said Mike, holding out an arm for Diane to pass.

Diane walked with Korey and Mike out of the vault as Alicia, one of Korey's assistants, was entering.

"Dr. Fallon? Andie told me about last night. That must have been terrifying. Jeez, two nights in a row. You must be feeling besieged."

"I'm fine. Thanks, Alicia."

"You were attacked again?" asked Mike and Korey at the same time.

Diane gave them the briefest description of the events. The two of them gawked at her.

"A few cuts on the soles of my feet from having to flee the house without my shoes, but other than that, I'm fine."

"But they caught the guy?"

"Yes," said Diane. "They have him."

"You be careful, Dr. F.," said Korey when Diane and Mike left the conservation lab.

"Could you use that technique to compare the cut stone I was telling you about with these to see if they were from the same place?" Diane asked Mike.

"Yes, but that stone's already been cut. The owner might not want even a microscopic hole in it. You could ask her."

"No, I can't. She was murdered."

Mike stopped in his tracks. "Her diamond?"

"Gone."

"Damn, Boss. Do you think you should stay in your apartment?"

"I'm not. I'm staying with Frank."

"He's got a gun, right?"

Diane frowned. "It looks like they have the guy."

"He's the one doing all the killings?"

"That's what the crime lab is trying to determine."

"If there's anything you need . . ."

"Thanks, Mike. I'd like to relax in a nice, cool dark cave."

"Now you're talking. How about next weekend?"

"Sounds good. I'll tell Neva."

Mike escorted Diane to her office. She sat down behind her desk, found the business card for Russell Keating, Raymond Waller's attorney, and gave him a call.

"Mr. Keating, we've found items in the baseball memorabilia that probably don't belong with the baseball bequests. It may be the reason he was murdered, so I need to tell Chief Garnett about it too. Could you come to the museum this afternoon?"

"This is going to cause me problems with the twins, isn't it?"

"I think so."

"Lord have mercy." He paused and shuffled some of his papers on his desk. "I can be there at three thirty."

Russell Keating and Chief Douglas Garnett sat in front of Diane's desk staring at the stones she had in front of her.

"And you say these are worth how much?" asked Keating.

"Our geologist says they would be worth more than two hundred thousand dollars after they were cut."

"That's what his murderer was after," said Garnett. "It has to be. We'll have to hold these as evidence."

"Hold on now, evidence of what? Of your idea that this is what the murderer was after? You thought the murderer was after the collection and you didn't hold it as evidence. You told me you brought it to the museum for safekeeping."

"We don't know who the diamonds belong to," said Garnett.

"The hell we don't. They belong to Raymond Waller's estate. They were in his possession."

"Where did he get diamonds that valuable on his salary as a morgue assistant?"

"It doesn't matter," said Keating. "He could have found them in his backyard. He owned his house and property, including the mineral rights. These aren't cut diamonds. They are the way God made them."

"This is Georgia. We don't have diamonds just lying around," said Garnett.

Diane cleared her throat, and they both looked at her.

"According to Mike, in the 1800s when prospectors panned for gold in Georgia, occasionally they'd find small diamonds. It sparked a few diamond rushes, but no one has been able to find the source."

"So he could have found these in his backyard," said Keating.

"None has ever been found this large. I believe Mike told me the largest ever found was about two carats. I think it would be unlikely he'd find three significantly larger ones in his backyard."

"But not impossible," said lawyer Keating.

"Mr. Keating. Why don't you let us keep them in our safe for the time being? You have a good argument, and all things being equal, it will certainly hold up in court. However, Mr. Waller was murdered, and Chief Garnett wants to find out who did it. And these stones may very well belong to someone else—for instance, Mr. Waller may have been holding them for a friend."

"How would anyone else claim them?" asked Keating. "All three look alike. How would this hypothetical friend describe them to a court of law?"

"By the internal structure. It's like a fingerprint. Every diamond is unique."

"All right, then. I certainly don't want to keep them in my office."

"That's fine by me," said Garnett. "And I don't want to take anything that rightfully belongs to his heirs." He shook his head. "This is getting far too complicated."

"What are you complaining about?" said Keating. "You don't have to deal with the twins."

Chapter 38

Chief Garnett stayed after Russell Keating went back to his office. It was not the first time he'd been in Diane's museum office, but he hadn't paid any attention to the decor that first time, as Diane recalled. It had been strictly business. He stared at the photograph of her dangling at the end of a rope from the vertical entrance to a cave.

"This is what you do for fun?"

"Yes. It's very relaxing."

"If you say so. It doesn't look relaxing to me." He turned his attention to the Escher prints on the other wall—an impossible waterfall, a castle with its equally impossible ascending and descending staircase, and a tessellation of angels and devils. "I wonder what our profiler would think of all this," he said.

"How's he working out?"

"Actually, I don't find him very useful. He has to change his profile substantially every time we get a new bit of information. He was the commissioner's idea," he added.

"He'll have to change the profile again, after this. You realize we have two victims now with diamonds that they shouldn't have been able to afford."

"So you don't buy the backyard deal?" said Garnett with a tired smile.

"Of course not."

"Where did they get them?" He sat down again across from Diane and crossed his legs.

"The choices are: he bought them, he stole them, he found them, they were given to him," said Diane. "It seems unlikely that he bought them. He may have stolen them, but he didn't have theft in his background."

"A lot of money adds up to a lot of temptation."

"Yes, it does. Perhaps Raymond Waller, Chris Edwards and Steven Mayberry worked together," said Diane. "They got hold of the diamonds, had a falling-out and killed each other. Perhaps Steven Mayberry is the last man standing."

"For the first time, we're getting somewhere." Garnett unfolded his legs and leaned forward, his forearms on his knees.

Diane's mind was racing through possibilities. "There's another thing Chris and Raymond had in common besides having diamonds they couldn't afford—a direct connection to the Cobber's Wood victims."

"Coincidence," Garnett offered, as a counterargument.

"Maybe. Let's look at them for a moment. They were found hanging. That is a very uncommon way to murder someone. They were all dressed alike in clothes that didn't fit. In fact, all the clothes were the same size—extra-large coveralls."

"Were they?"

"It was in the report."

"That's right."

"That could have been to conceal their identities too," said Diane. "He wanted to get rid of their clothes, but he didn't want them naked." She shrugged.

Garnett pulled up his chair and leaned on Diane's desk. "And the tips of their fingers were cut off. That was either to thwart identification, or to collect a trophy."

"I can see why the profiler thinks it's a serial killer," said Diane. "That's what it looks like. The guy who was calling me certainly sounded like a nutcase. I would peg him as a candidate for a serial killer—I mean, the flowers, then attacking me."

"But he also suggested he was angry about some injustice. What was it—gossip, bullying—he talked about?"

"Yes, he did. Let's look at the killings another way," said Diane. "He said he is not a murderer. He seems obsessed with justice—and injustice. If he committed the Cobber's Wood murders, perhaps he hanged them for their real or imagined crimes, whatever they might have been. He dressed them up like prisoners. Perhaps he really believes himself to be their executioner for just cause, not their murderer. Their fingers were cut off to avoid them being identified if they were found."

"What if they'd been found before their faces rotted? They could have been identified that way."

Diane frowned for a moment. "Maybe there is a reason the fingerprints are a greater threat to identification than their faces or their teeth."

"How's that?" asked Garnett.

"They grew up in the northeast, not here. Maybe that's where they lived, and he thought being far away from home would delay identification."

"They grew up in the northeast? How do you know that?"

"We got back the chemical analysis on the bones. Different regions of the world have different chemicals in their soil and different kinds of air pollutions. These chemical combinations show up in bones. I sent the report to your office."

"I haven't seen it. You're thinking that he thought they might not be recognized down here, far away from home?"

"Yes. But he might have realized we'd put their fingerprints through a database and get a hit, so he cut their fingers off."

"Speaking of fingerprints," said Garnett.

"David hasn't gotten a hit off any of the fingerprints we've found and he's been through all the databases we have access to."

Diane realized that she hadn't yet told Garnett about the tasks she'd assigned to Jin and Neva. She explained her idea about the plastic surgery discussion boards and Neva's idea about the tattoo discussion boards.

"It's a long shot," she said.

"But that was a good idea. What did we do before the Internet?"

Diane ignored his comment and continued. "The DNA results on the shed hair may take a while, or it might not work. I haven't heard from Jin."

Garnett stood up. "I feel like we made some progress. It was good to talk it out." He sounded surprised as he said it, as if he hadn't really expected he could talk to Diane and get anywhere.

Diane's door swung open and Star peeked in.

"Star," said Frank. "Ever heard of knocking first?"

He came in behind Star and put his hands on her shoulders.

"It's all right. We're finished," said Diane.

Frank and Garnett shook hands. Star stood staring. She suddenly held out her hand to shake Garnett's.

"Hello, I know who you are. I'm the girl who didn't kill her family."

"Star!" said Frank and Diane together.

Garnett had a pained look on his face, muttered something about being sorry for her loss, said goodbye to Diane and hurried out.

"Well," said Star when he was gone. "When you use bad judgment, there are consequences. Isn't that what you are always telling me, Uncle Frank? So, can I see the mummy and the Victorian pickle jar?"

Frank and Diane looked at each other and sighed.

"The mummy's upstairs."

She took them up to the conservation lab and showed them the amulets and the mummy. Star was fascinated with both, but disappointed that the object in the pickle jar had been used to get blood and tissue samples. Frank was more interested in the baseball collection that Korey showed him. Afterward, they had dinner in the museum restaurant and Diane followed them home in her rental SUV.

Diane curled up on the couch with Frank and a glass of wine, hoping that there wouldn't be any murders tonight.

"This has been a nice evening," she said.

"We had a good time. Loved that baseball collection."

"I needed to slow down. Too much has been happening."

"I've planned for your relaxation," he said. "The

doors and windows are locked and barred. Star is staying in tonight, so all is well. Oh, and I caught two of my identity thieves today. Two seventeen-year-olds from upper-middle-class families. They would have just gotten a slap on the wrist, but one of the people whose identity they stole has a brother who is a state senator, so their butts are in trouble."

"Do you believe in coincidences?"

"They happen, but as a rule, no."

"As a rule, I don't either. And that's what is nagging at me. There doesn't appear to be any logic to the connections that Edwards, Mayberry and Waller had with the hanging victims. We can't figure out if it means anything. But the odds seem so much against pure coincidence."

"Don't think about it. Just let it relax in your brain and the answer will come to you."

"You're right. I'll just enjoy you and my wine."

Star came into the living room and sat cross-legged in a chair opposite them.

"I get to pick out the clothes, don't I? I mean, I know you're paying for them and all."

"You get to pick them out. Does this mean you are going to give college a try?"

"Jennifer's going to Bartram. Stephanie's going to the University of Georgia. If they can do it, I suppose I can give it a try. It's just a year, isn't it? I can do anything for a year—even prison time." She settled back in the chair. "I have a question."

"What's that?" asked Diane.

"Is it a whole year, like, I mean, most schools let out in the summer. Does a year mean I have to go to summer school too?"

"Star," began Frank. "It sounds like you're trying to figure out how to do as little as possible."

"No, I'm just trying to get the rules straight so I know what I have to do."

"One academic year. You don't have to go to summer school. But you do have to have a two point seven GPA."

"What if I work real hard and only have a two point six?"

"That would be tragic," said Diane.

"Okay." She unfolded herself and bounded out of the room.

"You know," said Frank, "family life can be nice."

Diane nodded, but the talk of family life always made her feel the sharp pain of Ariel's absence.

Chapter 39

Jin bopped into Diane's crime lab office and slammed a folder down on her desk.

"We did it, Boss. It's in there." He did a little dance and spun around.

"You're going to have to be a little more specific. We've got so many things working."

"The hair. The hair. They matched the hair," he sang.

"The shed hair protocol worked?"

"GBI came through. They're all very excited. It matched with the blood in your apartment perfectly—I'm talking nuclear DNA. This is exciting."

"Jin, you've earned your pay. Would you like to take a copy of the report to Garnett?"

Jin grinned. "Sure. I'd love showing him the kind of magic we can perform, and wipe some of those smirks off those guys downtown. Of course, most of them won't even realize what a feat it was to get readable nuclear DNA from shed hair."

"Do you get those smirks too? I thought it was just me," said Diane.

"No. We all get them. It's especially bad for Neva, since she used to be down there. They see us as geeks, I guess. However, there's more. The DNA was the cake, but I have some more evidence that lights the candles."

"I see you're on a roll. What's the other evidence?"

"Cheap orange carpet fibers."

"In Kacie's apartment?"

"No. Yours. I went over before I came here and did a sweep of your apartment." He stopped. "I hope you don't mind."

"No, of course not. I hope you vacuumed the whole place."

"By the way, you have some strange neighbors across the hall."

"Tell me about it. You don't know how strange."

"They asked me if I was moving in, did I have a cat. I told them no, that I was from the crime lab, and they asked me if I knew anything about the best funeral homes. What's that about?"

"It's their hobby. They love funerals. They go to funerals for people they don't even know."

Jin stood gawking at her. Apparently left speechless.

"The landlady told me they had seven children," said Diane. "All of whom died. They showed her photographs of their funerals."

"Now, that's downright scary. You live across the hall from those people?"

"Last year, when she thought I was harboring a cat her husband was allergic to, she lifted the landlady's keys and snuck into my apartment. I came home and found someone hiding behind the curtain and almost brained her with a cast iron skillet."

Jin was laughing now. "You're yanking my chain."

"No. It's true."

He put Diane's key on her desk. "The orange carpet fiber was on your couch, and on the bloody towel."

Jin frowned suddenly and pulled up a chair and sat

down, switching gears from his usual hyperactive mode.

"I've been looking at the evidence from Kacie Beck's scene. The rape kit was negative. He used a condom. I didn't find anything on the body that belonged to the perp. Her house was clean too. No prints, no fibers that we can identify—we got the same cotton fibers, but that's all. The guy skinned her fingers pretty bad getting the ring off. I'm betting he got some blood on him—clothes, gloves, something. Doesn't help us now, but it might later. You know, Boss?"

"What?"

"I've been thinking about a DNA lab."

"You have. Been thinking about the money to put one in?"

"No. Haven't been thinking about that. The Girl Scouts raise a lot of money selling those cookies. Maybe we could get some crime cookies—some shaped like a gun, a knife, a bone, maybe. The sandwich cookies could have red filling. What do you think about that?"

"I'm starting to think you don't have enough to do."

"How about tee-shirts? We could sell tee-shirts— *People are just dying to see us.*"

"Good-bye, Jin."

Diane watched him go out the door. She looked at her blank wall and decided she needed to do something to decorate this office—it seemed like she was spending a lot more time in it.

The reports her team generated were stacked up on her desk. She'd been through them several times hoping for a revelation. There was none, but it was the slowly trickling evidence that was taking the day. They were getting close—more than close. They could put whoever it was in the hospital with the hanging victims on two separate bits of evidence—the orange fibers and the DNA. That was a home run.

Her thoughts went to Raymond Waller. He seemed such an unlikely person to be involved in crime. But who knows? She'd really only met him a couple of times. Lynn Webber knew him, though. Worked with him every day. She'd trusted him. Diane shoved it out of her mind and stood up. All this was really in Garnett and Braden's purview.

She started back to her other office but made a detour to the rock lab and looked at Raymond's diamonds in the safe. Even uncut they shone against the black velvet.

The diamonds kept intruding into her thoughts. That must have been what Steven Mayberry meant when he said his ship had come in—and what Chris Edwards was so happy about. They must have gotten their hands on several valuable diamonds—not only the one in Kacie's ring. Bet they had more. Raymond had to be a part of it somehow. However unlikely a criminal ring the three of them seemed to be, they must have stumbled into something.

But how in the world did a serial killer fit into all of this? Unless he wasn't a serial killer. The other thing Chris, Steven and Raymond had in common was the hanging victims. Chris Edwards and Steven Mayberry found them. Raymond Waller helped with their autopsies. That connection was accidental. It came after the Cobber's Wood victims were dead—or did it, really? Maybe Edwards and Mayberry simply led the sheriff to the people they had killed—but then, how did the man in the hospital play into it? He was there too.

It hit Diane suddenly. Maybe he was supposed to be in the fourth noose, the forgotten victim—but what were the E-mail, phone calls, flowers and the attack in her apartment about? If he was a victim, why didn't he just walk into a police station instead of calling her?

No matter what scenario she came up with, there was always some part of it that didn't make sense. She gave up and went back to her museum office.

She'd been going over budget figures for an hour when Garnett called and asked her to meet him and Braden at the hospital.

"He might tell you something he hasn't told us," he said. "He was anxious to talk to you before."

"You're not talking to my client."

John Doe's court-appointed attorney stood in front of the door leading to critical care, barring Diane, Sheriff Braden and Chief Garnett from entering.

"Your client," said Sheriff Braden, "killed three young people barely out of their teens in my county. One of us is going to talk to him."

The attorney, Tim Preston, looking hardly out of his teens himself, stood with his arms folded, not moving.

"You don't know my client did any such thing."

"We have your client," said Garnett. "We've matched his DNA with DNA left with the Cobber's Wood hanging victims."

"Did you have a court order to take his DNA?"

"Didn't need one. He left his blood all over Dr. Fallon's apartment," said Sheriff Braden.

"What's his name?" asked Diane.

"I don't know."

"What do you mean, you don't know?" asked Braden.

Preston dropped his arms to his side. "I mean he's not talking to me either. My client is still in critical condition. If your policemen hadn't been so quick to shoot a man for holding a cell phone . . ."

"He broke into Dr. Fallon's apartment and attacked her. She barely escaped with her life. My men went in to get him and he drew something from a holster on his side that looked like a gun—after he was ordered to freeze. We aren't going to have any of this he-was-just-a-poor-innocent-victim business around here," said Garnett. "Now, we want to know who he is."

"He's not talking—not to you and not to me. That's the way it is. The doctors are giving his chances of recovery about fifty-fifty right now. If you want him to live to stand trial, leave him alone."

"We would like to know who the victims are so we can notify their families," said Diane.

"No. He's not talking. What part of that aren't you people getting?"

"Well, this is a hell of a note," said Sheriff Braden, as he, Diane and Garnett walked back to their cars. "We have him dead to rights, and can't even get the son of a bitch's name."

"We'll get it sooner or later," said Diane. She got in her car and drove back to the museum. As she was parking, her cell phone rang. It was Neva. "I got a hit on the plastic surgeons' list."

Chapter 40

Neva was sitting at the conference table in the crime lab when Diane arrived. She had several photographs in front of her, along with her drawings of the victims. David and Jin joined Diane at the table.

"What have you got?" said Diane.

"First, let me tell you, I bombed out on the tattoo lists. I didn't really handle it the right way. I cleaned up the photos of the tattoos so they didn't look like they were on a dead body, and I phrased my questions as if they were missing persons. Not a good idea with this group. They took the attitude that they had a right to be missing. I sort of got a lot of flames on that list.

"Thank goodness, the doctors were more forthcoming." Neva turned the photographs around. "I said from the start that I was trying to identify two sets of bones. I got a bite last night. A plastic surgeon in Buffalo, New York, E-mailed me to give him a call."

"He recognized the drawings?" asked Diane.

Neva nodded. "He said they looked like patients of his. I also included photographs of the nasal bone and spine of Blue Doe. I hope that was all right. I thought he might recognize his work, even . . . even though the nose wasn't there."

"Too bad he wasn't one of those surgeons who initials the bones of his patients," said Jin.

"Did he? Recognize his work?" asked Diane.

"He said he did a lot of rhinoplasty like the ones that showed up in the bones, and he said the drawings did resemble a particular patient of his. When he found out I was trying to identify bodies, he sent these photographs to my E-mail."

The four photographs were before and after shots of a young woman in side and front views. The photos looked startlingly like Neva's drawings.

"The interesting thing is," said Neva, "that he was scheduled to do her cousin. Here's his before shots."

Neva pushed two more photos across the table. Again, they looked to Diane like a match to Neva's drawings.

"You say he was scheduled for surgery?"

Neva nodded. "He didn't show up for pre-op. The doctor's office called his home and didn't get an answer. They called the cousin's home and the housekeeper said the family was gone on a trip. Isn't that interesting?"

"Yes, it is. Frankly, I'm amazed this worked. Good job, Neva. What are their names?"

"Ashlyn and Justin Hooten. Both live in Buffalo, New York. I have their addresses and phone numbers."

"Well done," Diane said again. "I'm going to call the sheriff."

Diane couldn't reach the sheriff or Garnett immediately. She left voice mail on their phones. She wondered if they went back to the hospital after she left them.

It was past lunchtime and she was hungry. She left the crime lab and went down to the restaurant, ordered herself a club sandwich and took it to her museum office.

Andie was eating at her desk with one of the docents, a young woman about Andie's age.

"Everything going well here?" Diane asked.

"All quiet. No strange E-mail, wandering snakes or anything else out of the ordinary."

"Good. I'm going to be eating in my office. I'd like some quiet time, so unless the museum catches fire . . ."

"Gotcha."

Diane went into the meeting room adjoining her office. She got a bottle of cold water from a small refrigerator she had there and sat down at her small conference table with her sandwich.

She felt like the note containing the information about the Hooten cousins was burning a hole in her pocket. She tried to ignore it. She was about half finished with the sandwich when she decided to make the call herself, without waiting to talk with Braden or Garnett. The identity of the victims was the key to everything. She walked into her office and picked up the phone.

She called Justin Hooten's number first and let it ring twenty-five rings. No answer. She dialed Ashlyn Hooten's number. Someone picked up on the third ring and announced that she had reached the Hooten residence.

"I'm Diane Fallon from the Rosewood Police Department in Georgia."

She decided that saying she was head of the crime lab might be too frightening. As much as the photographs and the drawings seemed to match, they may not be the right people.

"I'm looking for a possible witness. Is Ashlyn Hooten in?"

"No. She on vacation with her cousin family."

"Are her parents there?"

Diane heard another voice in the background. "Who is it, Nancy?"

"She say she the police. From Georgia."

"I'll take it. Hello. I'm Ashlyn's father, an attorney here in Buffalo. What is it you want?"

"When was the last time you saw Ashlyn?"

"What's this about? Look, I want you to stop harassing my daughter. You are not to call here again." He hung up.

"Well," Diane said aloud. "That went nowhere."

She tried both the sheriff and Garnett again. They still weren't answering their cells. She started back to the conference room to finish her sandwich when the door flew open and Lynn Webber stormed in. Andie flew in behind her.

"Dr. Fallon . . ." Andie was obviously helpless to slow down Lynn.

"It's all right, Andie." Andie backed out and closed the door.

"Just what are you and Garnett trying to do to Raymond?"

Diane sat down and motioned to the chair. "I don't know. What are we trying to do?"

"Don't act smart. I thought we were friends. I thought you liked Raymond."

"I thought so too, and I do like Raymond. If you tell me what you are talking about, maybe I can respond more coherently."

Lynn Webber dropped herself into the chair in front of Diane's desk.

"Garnett came to see me, insinuating that Raymond was a thief, asking me all kinds of questions about him knowing Chris Edwards and some other people I never heard of. He suggested that I might have had something to do with stolen diamonds. I don't even like diamonds. He said you and he cooked this up."

Diane was having a hard time making sense of Lynn's diatribe in terms of what Garnett might have actually said.

"Did he really use the work *cook*?"

"What? Are you taking this seriously?"

"I am. But since we 'cooked' nothing up, I'm having a hard time following. What exactly did he say that brought you here?"

"I can't remember his exact words. He said some diamonds were found among Raymond's possessions and he wanted to know where he got them and did I have any ideas. It was the way he asked if *I* had any ideas. I mean, would Garnett know a real diamond if he stepped on one?"

Diane was trying to measure what exactly to tell her in terms of what Garnett might have revealed to her. She didn't want to give anything away, but if he had mentioned the diamonds to Lynn, then he didn't mind her knowing about them.

"Diamonds were found among Raymond's things, and they are real. One of the geologists here at the museum verified that."

"Oh. Garnett said they're valuable."

"Yes, they are. Would you like to see them?"

"Well, yes, that would be interesting. If I'm suspected of stealing them, I'd like to see what it is I was supposed to have stolen."

"Did he really accuse you?"

"He kept asking if maybe Raymond found them in Chris Edwards' clothes."

"Chris Edwards wasn't wearing any clothes," said Diane.

"Don't think I didn't tell him that. He suggested that they may have been hidden in his shorts. Now, I ask you. I would have noticed if Raymond found anything in Chris Edwards' tighty whiteys. Then he asked me about the clothes on the hanging bodies. Well, I told him you were there for the first two, and there was nothing in Red's clothing."

Diane took Lynn to the second floor, and for the second time today she took the diamonds from the safe. She set them down on a table in the lab and opened the box and eyed Lynn closely.

"They don't look like diamonds."

"They're uncut," said Diane.

"They look large."

"They are."

"And these were in Raymond's things?"

"Yes."

"Oh, Raymond, what were you into?" she whispered.

Diane put the diamonds back in the safe and escorted Lynn to the lobby. By the time they got there, Lynn's anger had abated and she was all sugar again. Diane had about decided that the next flare-up, she wasn't going to coddle her anymore. As she opened the door for Lynn, Diane's cell rang.

Finally, she thought, as she looked at the display. Garnett had called back.

"John Doe is dead," he said, before she could tell him about the Hooten cousins. "It looks like someone killed him."

Chapter 41

"What happened?" Diane asked Garnett when she arrived at the hospital.

They sat in the waiting room near the critical care unit. Sheriff Braden was twirling his hat in his hands, not saying much.

"Apparently, someone came in and slit his throat," said Garnett. "The nurse had just left to check on another patient. She remembers an orderly. It must have happened quickly. When she got back, he was bleeding out. They tried to save him, but he had lost too much blood. And what with his other injury, well, he didn't make it."

"This is strange."

"That's one word to describe it," said Garnett. "Somebody is mighty desperate for something."

"If we can identify the victims," said Braden, "I can close this damn case. Are you any closer to finding out who they are?" he asked Garnett.

Garnett looked annoyed, and she guessed that he and Braden had had a disagreement. Cobber's Wood was the only one of the crime scenes in Braden's jurisdiction, and she got the idea he probably didn't care if Garnett solved his cases or not, even if they were all related.

"I may know who they are. I've been trying to call," said Diane.

This got Braden's attention.

"The sheriff and I were called back here as soon as we got back to our offices," said Garnett. "They made us turn off our cell phones inside the hospital, so we didn't get your call. You know who the victims were?"

"Maybe. I told you about the discussion boards and lists Neva was checking on the Internet. She got a hit from a plastic surgeon in upstate New York. He sent photos of two of his patients, and I have to tell you, they look a lot like our victims."

"She get names?"

"Yes." Diane related the entire story she got from Neva. "When I couldn't get you on the phone, I called the numbers the doctor gave her for them. Justin Hooten's family wasn't home. Ashlyn Hooten's father brushed me off. I think that they've had some dealings with the law before."

If Braden or Garnett were angry at her initiative, neither showed it, so she pressed on. "I'd like to try again."

"Be my guest," said the sheriff. "The sooner this is out of my hair, the better." He rose and stalked off toward the restrooms.

"What's that about?" asked Diane.

"I was pretty hard on Lynn Webber. I was thinking that maybe the diamonds were on Chris Edwards' person—hiding in his underwear, some place an intruder might not look. And then I thought, if not Edwards' clothes, why not the hanging victims'? She seemed to take offense at my tone of voice. She told him about it. I tell you, the guy's hopeless."

Diane was only half listening to what Garnett was

saying. What had caught her eye was a poster for colon cancer screening.

"She was saying," continued Garnett, "that you were there when they removed Blue and Green's clothes and you took them with you, and Red's clothes were bagged immediately. It seemed to me like a way to connect up Braden's murders with mine."

"And it was," said Diane, staring at the poster. "There was something Raymond did by himself that wasn't in sight of either me or Lynn Webber."

"What was that?"

"He cleaned the bones."

"What?"

"Before I do a thorough analysis of bones, they are cleaned by a process that dissolves all the flesh and cartilage. Raymond is the one who cleaned them. When he strained the solution to capture any of the small bones that might be trapped in it, that's where he found the diamonds. I'll bet one of the victims had swallowed the diamonds, maybe to smuggle them, like they do cocaine."

"You know, that makes sense. Raymond had never been in trouble, even as a teenager. It bothered me that he would suddenly turn to something this big. But if he found them, he probably counted himself lucky—poor fellow."

"That would also explain why he was targeted. Someone out there knew where the diamonds were hidden, and with a little asking around about what happens to bodies, could have figured out Raymond was the one who had them."

Diane felt more comfortable with this explanation of how Raymond Waller got the diamonds than she did with the idea of his being in league with Edwards

and Mayberry. She turned it over in her mind as she
drove back to the museum.

If Raymond happened upon diamonds, why not
Chris Edwards and Steven Mayberry? They were out
doing their timber cruises all over the woods for days.
From their explanation of what a timber cruise is, they
walked over every inch of ground. What if they also
had the misfortune of stumbling across more of the
diamonds? But if she were right and Blue, Green and
Red Doe had swallowed theirs, then where would the
ones have come from that Edwards and Mayberry
might have found?

Her head was beginning to ache. When she got back
to the museum, she changed into the running clothes
she kept in her museum office. If she was going caving
on the weekend, she needed to start exercising again.
She hadn't done anything in a week.

"Andie, I'm going for a run on the nature trail. Go
ahead and lock the offices when you leave. I have
a key."

"Sure. See you tomorrow."

The nature trail made a tangled loop a little over
half a mile long around the back of the museum. It
was an exhibit in itself and Diane considered it an
important part of a museum of natural history. It was
a wooded trail, full of more species of trees than
Diane could name. When the leaves turned in the fall,
it was dazzling. In the spring and summer, it was the
flowers and shrubs that shined: rhododendrons, aza-
leas, bluet, violets, trilliums. She tried to remember
the names as she passed the plants. Late summer, the
museum staff liked to pick blackberries that grew
along the trail, and Diane was thinking about having
a staff blackberry picnic in July. The crowning jewel
of the nature trail was the swan pond in the center—

a small, quiet lake that could have come from a
fairy tale.

She never tired of running the nature trail and she
always saw something she hadn't seen before. Nor-
mally, there were many people running in the evening,
but it had been so hot that a lot of people headed for
the treadmills in an air-conditioned gym. She was
mainly alone, only occasionally spotting a runner
through the trees.

She wanted to run five miles. That usually took her
anywhere from thirty-five to forty minutes, depending
on how leisurely she wanted to make it. She looked
at her watch. It wasn't too late.

Today, she felt like running fast. She sprinted
through the trail. Her heart beat fast. It felt good. She
thought she heard the steady rhythm of footfalls behind her. *Another runner,* she thought. It sounded like
a runner. She barely heard it, but she felt the rhythm.
She speeded up her pace. The rhythm was still there.
She glanced back, but she'd just passed a turn and the
trail behind her was hidden by rhododendrons.

Recent events had made her paranoid, and she was
starting to become a little worried. She rounded another turn, stopped and stepped behind a cluster of
forsythia bushes and waited for several seconds. She
heard the footfalls coming. She stepped back farther
in the bushes, ready to run. Around the turn, passing
her, ran Mike Seger.

"Mike," she called.

He stopped and turned, breathing hard.

"Dr. Fallon. Damn. You are hard to catch up with.
You run fast for an old lady. Andie told me you came
for a run. I run here every day too, but usually in
the morning."

Diane walked back onto the trail and started running again, but at a slower pace. He caught up with her.

"So, is this your second run today?" she asked.

"No, not today. I had to proctor a makeup exam at the university this morning. What are you doing out here by yourself anyway?"

"The guy who attacked me is dead."

"Oh."

They ran almost a half-mile loop without talking. While she ran, Diane's mind kept turning over the diamonds—cut and uncut.

"Tell me," Diane asked, "where's the closest place to have a diamond cut?"

"I'd say New York. No. There's a guy who teaches at the tech school. They have courses in diamond cutting. Just started last year, one of the very few places you can learn in the United States."

"What's his name?" asked Diane.

Mike thought a moment. "Joseph something. Joseph Isaacson. I think he's from Belgium."

"Thanks."

"In my car I have a map of the cave we are going to visit. I brought you a copy. I thought you might like to see it. It's just the easy section, but that's all we are doing this time. Maybe later we can map the wild sections. Like you said, that would be a good project for the club."

"Great. How far do you usually run?"

"I usually make about twenty laps."

"Then why are you breathing so hard?"

"I told you, trying to catch up with you. I have a friend opening up a new gym in town. It has a great rock-climbing wall. You might check it out."

"I might do that. I've let my weight training go this week."

"I wouldn't worry. You still have some pretty hard deltoids." He reached over and touched her bare shoulder.

Diane ran faster.

Chapter 42

While she waited for a decent time to call the Hooten household again, Diane sat at her desk, studying the map Mike had given her of the cave they were going to explore. It was not a particularly well-done map. In fact, it was amateurish. She should have suspected by his grin when he showed it to her. It had its own way of describing features, drops, slopes and escarpments, instead of using any of the normal mapping conventions. But it also had its own charm. It was sort of like an old-fashioned treasure map. Diane had to fight the urge to copy it off on parchment paper. But it did have entrances and branches clearly labeled, and it showed tunnels and passages in ways that were probably recognizable—with names such as Fish Scale Way, the Silo, Crawl-Belly Tunnel.

The section they were going to traverse included a half mile of easy cave. Neva was a novice, and Diane wanted it to be easy. But the easy part was still interesting. It included several turns and several different elevations. The mapper had clearly marked the branches that led to the wild parts—Abandon All Hope and There Be Dragons passages.

She looked at her watch—a little after 9:00 P.M. She

picked up the phone to call, but instead of dialing the Hooten residence, she thought better of it and got the number for the Buffalo police. She called and introduced herself and explained that she was trying to identify three bodies that she had reason to believe originally resided in Buffalo. The person on the other end listened patiently.

"Is there anyone there familiar with an Ashlyn or Justin Hooten?" she said finally.

"Hold the phone, ma'am."

She held the line for a full ten minutes. Finally, someone picked up. "Detective James LaSalle here. How can I help you?"

Detective LaSalle had a very friendly voice. Diane hoped that also meant he would be helpful. She explained again what she was after.

"I'm very familiar with little Ashlyn and Justin Hooten. Stereotypical ignored rich kids who get into trouble and their parents get them out, but other than that, don't pay any attention to them. They have the reputation of being bullies. You say you think they are dead?"

"I don't know. I'm trying to identify the remains of three individuals. Two of them fit their description. The bodies were badly decomposed and we did an artist's reconstruction of their faces. One had plastic surgery. That's how we got a lead."

"Nose job on Ashlyn, right?"

"Yes," said Diane.

"Damn, this doesn't look good."

Diane went on to describe the other characteristics they had discovered—tattoos, heart condition. She also described Red Doe, her tattoos, ballet, back problems and the fact she was probably half Asian.

"I realize I'm grabbing at straws here," she said.

"No, I don't think you are. They have a friend. Cathy Chu. She wore a back brace for a while. And you say the parents don't know they're missing. That's not surprising."

"I need some X-rays to make a positive identification. The plastic surgeon was very forthcoming, but as you can understand, he was reluctant to send X-rays without permission."

"I'll see that you get what you need. Jeez, what goes around comes around."

"What do you mean?"

"The father probably thought you were calling about an incident that happened a couple of years ago. I don't know exactly what happened—it was hushed up—but I can give you some good bits and pieces."

"Please do. We've had other murders that may be connected. Do you know if they were involved with uncut diamonds?"

"Oh, Jesus, they did get in over their heads. I knew it would happen. The three of them went to the University of Pennsylvania. Thought they were really slick customers. Got involved in smuggling contraband out of Canada. Small stuff at first—cigarettes, clothes. They thought they were really into a sophisticated racket. Had a few close calls with customs, but nothing their parents couldn't take care of.

"They started getting a little more daring and got involved with some dangerous people. This is where it gets a little murky. They got involved with something. Maybe it's diamonds. You have diamonds, then?"

"Yes."

"Well, damn. I thought it was tobacco. You know about Canadian diamonds?"

"Not really."

"There's a big diamond mine in Canada, the Ekati mine. Produces nice white diamonds, and the Canadian authorities work hard to keep organized crime out of the rough-diamond trade. But you never can completely. Rough diamonds are harder to identify and they are easy to smuggle. On top of that, they have a high profit-to-size ratio. A dream for organized crime."

"This is what they got into?" asked Diane.

"I'm not sure. It wouldn't surprise me. Like I said, I thought the big trouble two years ago was tobacco. What I do know is that something happened and they got in way over their heads. They may have tried to strike out on their own and crossed the wrong people. That's where Alice Littleton comes into the picture. She was a freshman at Penn—from Georgia. That's probably the connection their father made when you called him. From what I can tell, Alice was a little southern girl who was really impressed with the big-city sophisticates from New York, although Buffalo isn't exactly Manhattan. No offense."

"None taken."

"Like I said, I've had to piece together what happened. Alice wanted to fit in. Followed Ashlyn and her crowd around like a puppy. When Ashlyn, Justin and Cathy got into trouble, they sent little Alice in their place for some kind of delivery, and she got killed. Ashlyn and her friends got religion after that. They went to classes and played good. I thought maybe they had learned their lesson. It looks like they got themselves into deeper trouble. Diamonds. Jeez."

A thought struck Diane. "Did Alice Littleton have a brother?"

"Is he in this too? You bet she did. Everett Littleton.

That's why I know so much about it. The poor guy traveled back and forth from Pennsylvania to here, to Ontario and back, trying to find out what happened. Hounded us to death about the Hootens. But there was nothing we could do. Nothing that happened was in our jurisdiction. There's times I'd like to arrest people on general principles, but—how do you folks say it?—we didn't have a dog in that fight. Everett was several years older than Alice. Raised her after their parents died."

"Can you tell me what Everett looks like?"

"Sure. About six feet. Brown hair and eyes. About thirty-two. Drives a truck, as I recall—had his own private one-truck business."

"I think he was the one who killed Ashlyn and Justin Hooten, and Cathy Chu."

"You don't say? Took the law into his own hands. This thing was tragic all the way around."

"If I send you a picture, can you identify him?"

"Sure thing. Just JPEG it on up here." He gave her his E-mail address.

"Was there another person involved with them?" asked Diane.

"Besides the Hooten cousins and Cathy Chu? I don't know of any. Could've been, though. Why?"

"There was a fourth, unused noose where we found the bodies."

"A noose?"

"They were hanged."

"Jesus. Did it up right, did he? There might have been some known associates. You got a description?"

Diane almost said no, but she remembered her attacker. The right age, and identity unknown. "He might be about the same age. Roughly six feet. Dark hair. Muscular. Prone to violence. But could be someone different."

"I can ask around. I'm going to have to talk to the parents anyway. Give me your address and I'll send you X-rays, dental charts, whatever we can get."

Diane gave him her address at the crime lab. She also gave him contact information for Chief Detective Garnett and Sheriff Braden, as well as the plastic surgeon's name and address in Buffalo.

"He has X-rays of both Ashlyn and Justin. Thanks for talking to me. You've made a lot of things fall into place."

"Glad to do it. I'm just sorry this turned out so badly for everyone. Have you caught Everett?"

"Yes, it appears that we did. But he's been murdered also."

"I'll be damned. You do have yourselves a situation down there."

"That's a bit of an understatement."

"I'll contact the Canadians. Like I said, they want to keep crime out of their diamond field—and they'll want their diamonds back if they turn out to be stolen."

"Sure. Just have them call me or Chief Garnett. Thanks again."

Diane sent a JPEG photo of John Doe to Detective LaSalle, then called the tech school and left a message asking for an appointment to talk with Joseph Isaacson. On her way home, she called Garnett and repeated everything LaSalle had told her.

"So we know who they are and why they were killed. You were right. Our John Doe was angry. This was about revenge—or maybe justice, as he saw it. I'll call Braden and the profiler. He'll have to revise his profile again."

Diane heard him laughing as he hung up his phone.

*   *   *

Joseph Isaacson was a small man with short white hair and salt-and-pepper eyebrows and moustache. He walked with a slight stoop. Diane wondered if it was from years of bending over his work. He reminded her of their mummy—they called him a scribe, but he could have been an artisan like Joseph Isaacson. He spoke with a slight accent.

Isaacson closed the door to cut out the sound from the adjacent polishing and cutting equipment of the classroom, moved a stack of papers and invited her to sit.

His office was cluttered with books and papers. He had an old rolltop desk against the wall and a table in the middle. It was the table he actually used as a desk. Behind him was a photograph of a large sparkling diamond.

"I'm looking for someone who cut a diamond for a young man named Chris Edwards," she said. "He was a student at Bartram University."

Diane explained briefly that Edwards had been murdered, perhaps for the diamond.

"You think one of my students may be a murderer?"

"Oh, no. I'm hoping you or one of your students cut the diamond and can tell me about it."

"Aren't you the director of the museum?"

"Yes, and I run a crime lab."

"Such opposites."

"Often very complementary."

"A very yin and yang life you lead, my granddaughter would probably say. I did not cut a stone for the young man, but let's ask my students."

He rose, and the two of them walked into the classroom. He clapped his hands.

"Students, listen."

They stopped what they were doing and looked up.

"This nice woman is Dr. Diane Fallon of the River-Trail Museum of Natural History. She's looking for information. Did any of you cut a diamond for a man named Chris Edwards?"

The students looked at each other and back at the professor, except for one male student who kept looking at his work.

"Kurt. You look like you can help us."

"Yes, sir." His voice almost cracked.

Kurt looked very young and miserable as he followed them back into the office. He brought a leather notebook with him and he held it close to his body like a shield.

"Don't look so forlorn, Kurt. We just want to ask you some questions."

"I should have come forward sooner, sir, when I heard about Chris. I didn't know if his death had anything to do with the diamond, but it might have." He slumped into the chair Isaacson offered him.

"Sit up straight and answer Dr. Fallon's questions, Mr. Martin. She's not here to devour you."

Kurt straightened up in his chair.

"Tell me about the diamond," said Diane.

"I knew Chris Edwards. We lived in the same apartment building for a while until he moved. He called and said he had inherited a diamond from his grandmother and wanted it cut into a stone for his fiancée. Well, I said sure. But when I saw the diamond—well, I was afraid at first, but Chris insisted he wanted me to do it."

"You're doing fine, son," said his teacher.

"Mr. Isaacson, you should have seen it. It was beautiful. I've never seen a stone like that. I studied it for a couple of days and it was like you said—some stones just tell you how to cut them. The diamond yielded two one-carat stones. He wanted them round, so I did an ideal cut." He pulled out his notebook and took out several photographs and gave them to his teacher. "I took pictures."

Isaacson looked at the photographs, then looked at Kurt over his glasses. "You are right, this is a fine stone, Kurt. And you did a beautiful job. What did you name them?"

"The Star Princess and the Princess Kacie," he said, sitting straighter in the chair. Suddenly, he slumped again. "I suppose I should have said something to somebody. I knew they were valuable stones."

"It's all right. This is America, Kurt. We don't inform on people because they have nice things," said Isaacson.

"Did you believe he inherited it from his grandmother?" asked Diane. "Did you get any sense that it may have come from somewhere else?"

"Was it the museum's?" asked Kurt.

"No."

He looked relieved. "I sort of thought he probably did inherit it. I mean, he was a forestry student, not a world-class cat burglar. How could he possibly even steal a stone like that?"

"That's a good point," said Diane. "Thank you for your time."

"Am I in trouble?"

"No. The detective in charge of Chris's case may want to talk to you, but that's only to try to figure out how he acquired the stone."

"So it didn't come from his grandmother?"

"Probably not."

"May I keep the photos, Kurt?" asked Isaacson.

"Yes. I made copies for you. I was just trying to figure out how to tell you about it."

"You can go back to your work now."

"Thanks." Kurt hurried out the door as if Diane might change her mind at any moment and decide to devour him.

"He was not at fault," said Isaacson. "Diamonds are alive, you know, and they talk to you. Kurt's diamond spoke to him, and the temptation to cut such a stone is more than anyone can resist. See that stone?" He pointed to the photograph of the diamond that hung on the wall. "That is the Arctic Star. It's my stone." He shrugged. "Some Japanese businessman has it in a vault somewhere, but it will always be mine. I studied it, I cut it. Fifty-five carats. Stunning stone. Kurt isn't in any trouble, is he?"

"I would not think so."

"Where did the diamond come from? It was not a blood diamond, I hope."

"From Canada, I believe."

"Oh, the Ekati mine. Beautiful diamonds. Very white."

"Thank you for your time."

"My pleasure. You know, you could use some nicer stones in your gem collection at the museum."

"We're working on it."

Chapter 43

It was four in the morning, and in thirty minutes Diane would be getting up to go caving with Mike, Neva and Mike's friend who had gotten them access to the cave. She had her backpack ready and had checked her batteries and ropes.

"Would you like to go caving with me?" she said, giving Frank a kiss.

"No, nor do I want to go skydiving, bungee jumping, or solo climbing."

"You don't know what you're missing. There's no peace like the depth of a cave."

"You have a little bit of insanity running in your family, don't you?"

"Possibly. What are you going to be doing this weekend?"

"I'm taking Kevin and Star to the Atlanta Raceway."

"Now, see, that's crazy. Is Star looking forward to that?"

"Sure, she loves it. Star knows quite a bit about cars."

Diane got out of bed and put on her clothes. She was lacing up her boots when Frank put his arms around her waist and kissed her on her jaw. "Watch where you're going."

"Always."

She loaded her gear in the SUV and drove to pick up Neva. The two of them were dressed similarly— jeans, tee-shirts and flannel shirts over them, lace-up boots. Neva stored her gear in the back and got in the front with Diane.

"Excited?" said Diane.

"Very nervous. My parents think I'm crazy."

"Funny, I was just told that too. You'll do fine. Didn't I hear that you're into tai chi?"

Neva nodded. "I like it a lot. Very relaxing exercise."

"As I understand it, one of the objectives of tai chi is to develop a tranquil mind and become aware of your surroundings."

"A lot of people think you learn to zone things out. It's really just the opposite."

"That will really help you caving. You have to be constantly aware of your surroundings, notice where you've been and watch for hazards. Once you've had enough practice, it's second nature."

"In some of the caver meetings we discussed different methods of walking in caves so you don't get tired out," said Neva.

"It's good that you've done that. Fatigue is a major enemy. Remember to keep your head as high as you can as you walk. There's a natural tendency to want to stoop over inside a cave."

"Mike said we're going to start meeting at the museum."

"I thought it was a good idea. Up in the rock room, probably."

After a pause, Neva asked, "Who killed the man in the hospital? Everett Littleton, right?"

"It's still open. The nurse on duty has a vague memory of an orderly coming into the critical care unit. That's about all. Garnett likes Steven Mayberry for it."

"And you?"

"I don't know. It was someone who was bold and proficient, or reckless."

"Everett Littleton killed the three in the woods?"

"That's what it looks like. I think he tried to tell me he executed them, but with him dead, we may never know the whole story."

"Did he kill Chris, Kacie and Raymond too?"

"I don't know. Chief Garnett thinks either Everett Littleton or Steven Mayberry killed them."

"So Steven Mayberry went from forestry student to super ninja serial killer?" said Neva. "A lot of this just isn't tracking for me."

"Obviously, there are a lot of loose ends. But our part is over now. We've analyzed the crime scene evidence and turned in our reports. It's up to the police and the D.A. to figure it out and make a case, if there's anyone left to make a case against."

"So many dead, and no one to prosecute," Neva said.

Mike Seger and a slightly husky young man with a short straggly beard stood waiting at the curb in front of Mike's house.

"This is Dick MacGregor," said Mike. "His cousin owns the land the cave is on."

"Yeah, it's my favorite cave," said MacGregor. "Did you like my map? I started it when I was a kid. I don't know much about how cartographers do it, so I just did it my way, as the song says."

"The only thing that matters in a map is that it reflects what's there," said Diane.

Mike shot her a glance as he climbed in the backseat. Diane was not above flattery if it got her access to an interesting cave.

They drove for twenty minutes and MacGregor chatted the whole time. Diane hoped he would tone it down inside the cave.

"Mike told me you've done a lot of caving on rope," he said.

"Yes, I have."

"I haven't done much of that. I'd like to learn."

"Mike says he has a friend who just opened a gym with a good rock-climbing wall," said Diane. "That'd be a good place to start working on your climbing muscles."

It was just daylight when they arrived at the cave. They piled out of the car, and Diane left her customary note and map detailing where they were going. She had also told Frank, Andie, David and Jonas. She never went caving without several people knowing where she was going and how to find her.

They hiked through the woods, through a gate and up a trail. The cave entrance in the side of a rock outcrop was shielded by thick brush and vines growing out of the cracks in the rock face.

At the entrance, Diane hung her compass around her neck and took a reading. They put on their hard hats, turned on their helmet lights and arranged their backpacks comfortably. MacGregor went in first.

"Anybody has claustrophobia, now's the time to say something," he said, and laughed.

Diane followed him. Neva came right behind her, and Mike brought up the rear.

The entrance chamber was small and filled with detritus blown and washed in from the outside. The walls were steep solid rock that curved upward and inward to make a dome-shaped ceiling. The entrance didn't allow much sunlight to filter in, so the twilight zone— the dim area between the light of the outside world and the deep darkness of the cave—came quickly. Diane saw a black hole in the rear wall. She remembered on the map it led to a short passage and to a larger chamber beyond—the Tail of the Lizard, Mac-Gregor had labeled it.

"Now entering the twilight zone," said MacGregor, and he hummed the theme song from the TV program. Diane glanced in Mike's direction. He smiled and shrugged.

They had to duck low to enter the new passage. The limestone walls closed in with smooth, undulating shapes with bulges that curved gently like the beginnings of an arm carved eons ago. They were entering the realm of geologic time where the amassing of years was almost impossible for humans, who have been on earth the mere blink of an eye, to wrap their brains around.

Diane loved everything about caves—the ancientness, the wildness, the ornate shapes, the bejeweled and flowered mineral features, cave creatures and even the absolute velvet darkness. The lights from their headlamps made strange shadow puppets of the shapes and protrusions of the wall. Had any of them been overweight, the passage would have been a squeeze. She glanced briefly at Neva. She looked fine.

The tunnel was short. It led into a larger chamber strewn with boulders of various sizes, the largest being the size of a human. The rock face of one wall leaned toward the chamber, looking like it might fall over on top of them. They were in the dark zone now. Without their lights, they would be as blind as some of the creatures who lived there.

Diane turned and examined the tunnel they had just come through so she could recognize it from the opposite direction. You have to learn how to see in a cave. You can see only in the direction your head faces because your light is on top of your head and points straight ahead. And in the darkness of a cave, the light beam is quickly swallowed up. You don't get the panoramic view your peripheral vision gives you up in the world of sunlight.

She took another reading of the compass and marked it in her notebook. They all carried notebooks. Mike had a camera and snapped shots of the formations, making a quick burst of light with each picture. He wrote things in his notebook that looked like chemical notations, from the brief glimpse Diane got of them. Neva drew sketches in her notebook. MacGregor looked like he was writing a novel. Perhaps he was, and a cave was where his muse talked to him. Diane could understand that.

The easy trail through the cave was a succession of tunnels and rooms like beads on a string, frequently crossed by other passageways. MacGregor's chatty nature was useful inside the cave, for he freely explained what was down each passage they crossed.

"There's lots of mazes in this cave—little twisting passages that all look alike." He laughed, indicating that he'd just told a joke, or quoted something.

"*Zork,* an old computer game," Mike whispered to her.

Sometimes they took one of the cross tunnels when it was marked as part of the easy route. They came to a passage that MacGregor called Fish Scale passage and was just what Diane thought it would be—a tunnel that once had water moving through it, creating scallops in the ancient streambed as it flowed. The steep side of the scallops was the upstream direction from which the water had traveled. The small size of the scallops and the curviness of the passage told her that it had been a fast-moving stream. Mike snapped pictures, made measurements and explained the water movement to Neva as she rubbed her hand on the water-carved surface.

Diane continued taking compass readings as a prelude to mapping. Direction gave her an understanding of the cave. That was how she defined a cave—a directional space through rock. Her compass readings hardwired the cave system in her mind, giving her a visual image of it. That made it easy when she got down to actually drawing the maps. With every compass bearing she took a backsight from the opposite direction to check her first reading, in case the cave had magnetic rocks that influenced the compass, or in case she made an error.

Mike moved ahead. Neva followed, and MacGregor walked quickly to catch up with Mike. *Walk slowly in a cave,* thought Diane, but she didn't say anything. This particular tunnel was clear of breakdown, jutting or overhanging rocks. Not much to bump into or stumble over. They came to another cross passage. Diane tried to visualize it on the map. She walked slowly, looking at every feature of the tunnel.

Mike had taken the lead, following the things he was interested in, and they all followed him. He frequently checked the map to be sure they didn't stray into a wild zone. MacGregor seemed to be trying to regain leadership.

"There's a small chimney up here," said Mac-Gregor. "Are you game to give it a try, Neva?"

"I don't think so—not this time. Anyone notice that the lights are acting funny?"

"What do you mean?" asked Diane.

"I don't know. I think someone's light is flickering."

"It's not Mike snapping photographs?"

"Maybe."

"We better check out the headlamps," said Diane.

As they walked, the tunnel changed midstream, so to speak, from a rectangular passage to a rounded tunnel.

"Well, this is interesting," said Diane.

"Funny how the shape changes," said Neva.

"The slope too," said Diane.

"Yeah, I've always wondered about it," said MacGregor.

Mike was scrutinizing the walls. He took photos of the change.

"What do you make of it?" asked Diane.

Mike grinned. "I think it's a place that marks the change from phreatic water movement to vadose water movement. This is why I love caving. Where else would you get to see this?"

"Ooookay," said MacGregor, "I'm glad we cleared up that little mystery—yes, sir, I'll sleep well tonight. What the heck does that mean?"

Mike had started to explain, when Diane heard a sharp crack. The next thing she knew, MacGregor was staring at her, a puzzled look on his face.

Chapter 44

The first thing Diane saw after hearing the noise was blood dripping down MacGregor's shirtsleeve. He clutched at his arm and looked at the blood on his hand, confusion showing in his eyes.

"What the hell?" Mike saw him and took a step toward him.

"Gun!" yelled Diane. "Get out of this tunnel."

She grabbed MacGregor and pulled him into a side passage. Mike and Neva followed on her heels. The lights from their headlamps made chaotic swaths of light across the walls and ceiling. But she could see they were in a large chamber strewn with breakdown. Diane shoved MacGregor behind a large boulder.

"I'm bleeding. Is somebody shooting at us?"

"Who the hell are you?" yelled Mike. "Are you crazy?"

"Dr. Fallon, you're a hard woman to find. Good thing you left maps and directions for me."

The voice sounded familiar, but it was distorted by the echo effects of the large chamber they were in.

"What do you want?" she yelled.

"I want my goddamn fucking diamonds."

"Diamonds?" MacGregor's voice was approaching

a high-pitched squeak. "What's he talking about? There's no diamonds in this cave," he yelled. "I'd have found them already."

Diane turned off her headlamp and Mike and Neva followed suit. She reached over and turned off Mac-Gregor's. The eerie glow of a flashlight radiated around the corner from the passage they just left.

"I don't have your diamonds," said Diane.

"You know where they are, and I'm going to haul your ass back to get them."

"You know, it's not safe to shoot off a gun in a cave," said Diane.

"Then don't give me any trouble."

"Detective LaSalle?"

"Right on the first try."

"How did you get here so fast?"

"I never left."

He walked from around the corner, holding a flashlight in his left hand just above his left shoulder. He had a gun in his other hand.

"I'm on vacation. I told them at the station up in Buffalo that I was still working on little Alice Littleton's case, and to forward any calls about it to me. I figured if you ever ID'd the bodies, you'd call the Buffalo police."

Diane could see the faint figures of Neva and Mike slowly moving toward LaSalle, keeping out of the beam of his flashlight. *No,* she wanted to shout at them. *Don't try anything.* But they were moving. Damn.

"So you killed Ashlyn, Justin and Cathy?" Diane desperately wanted to keep his attention focused on her.

"No. Everett made that little mess."

Without warning, he fired and Mike fell.

"No!" yelled Diane. "Damn you!"

Diane rushed toward him as Neva jumped for La-Salle. He'd seen Neva coming, and with the force of his whole body behind it, met her head-on, knocking her flying across a large slab of sloping rock on the floor of the cave toward a black opening.

Neva started sliding. Diane switched on her head-lamp as she ran for her. Neva grabbed and scratched at the rocks as she slid over the edge of . . . of what?

Neva screamed. Diane ignored LaSalle shouting for her to stop. She scrambled across the rock and looked over the edge.

Her heart lurched in her chest. Neva had fallen into a narrow slit between vertical rock walls. She was slowly sinking, becoming more tightly wedged in the gap. Below her dangling feet lay only blackness. She was hanging in the opening above a cavern so large that the light from Diane's lamp did not penetrate it. Diane reached down and grabbed her hand.

"Help me," Diane yelled at LaSalle.

"Leave her and get over here."

"Hold on to the crack in the wall." Diane pulled Neva's hand toward a fissure to use as a handhold.

Neva's eyes were wide, frightened and panic-stricken. Diane pulled Neva's other hand upward until Neva's fingers grabbed into the fissure.

"Hold on."

Neva's fingers slipped out and she fell farther into the crack. Diane grabbed her wrist and pulled hard. She felt herself slowly sliding forward toward the edge. If she slipped into the opening headfirst, it would be over for all of them.

"Help me, damn you! You can't leave her like this!"

"I work for people who are going to cut me in two with a chain saw—before they kill me. Don't tell me what I can't do. I'm trying to survive here."

"I have to get some rope," she said to Neva. "Hold on."

Diane pushed back against the rock to keep from sliding.

"Please don't let me go," Neva pleaded

"Neva, you can do this. Hold on for just a couple of minutes while I get some rope. I'm letting go. Hold on to the rocks."

"I'm slipping. There's no place to hold on to."

"I have to get some rope."

"I am so scared. Oh, God."

"I'm going to get you out of this."

She let go of Neva's hand and scrambled off the huge slab lying on the edge of the crevice. She turned and faced LaSalle.

"We're going to get my diamonds," he said.

"I'm going to get her out of there."

"You get the hell over here, or so help me God, I'm going to shoot you."

"Okay, you win. Shoot me."

"You stupid . . ." LaSalle raised his gun at her and held it there for several seconds. He wavered, then dropped it to hip level. "Dammit, go ahead, get her out."

"I need help," said Diane.

"Well, you don't have any."

Diane glanced at Mike lying on the cave floor. He was trying to move. There was a growing dark stain on his shirt. It looked as if the bullet hit him in his side.

MacGregor was huddled against a rock, whispering a mantra of "Oh, God, oh, God, oh, God."

Diane ran for her backpack.

"Don't for a second think of trying anything," La-Salle said.

"With what? We have no weapons. Just rope and candy bars."

"Dick," she called at MacGregor. "Help Mike." He didn't move. "MacGregor!" That got his attention. "Mike needs help."

Dick MacGregor looked at her a moment, switched on his headlamp and crawled over to Mike.

"He's bleeding."

"Take off your shirt and apply pressure to his wound. Do it."

"Will you hurry up?" said LaSalle.

Diane didn't say anything, but pulled a tough, almost new nylon rope from her backpack. She uncoiled it and began tying foot slings on one end using a bowline on a bight, creating two nooses. She dressed and set the knot so the parts were properly aligned and very tight. Neva was about five feet six, and she needed several more feet for a harness. Diane tied handhold loops higher up on the rope.

"My patience is wearing thin."

"I'm hurrying as fast as I can. Your diamonds aren't going anywhere. You didn't call the Canadians, did you? Just didn't want me to call and alert them."

Diane fished candy out of her pack. "I'm throwing you a candy bar. Snack on that while you wait." She threw it toward his feet.

He actually said thanks.

Diane secured the other end of the rope around a boulder with a figure eight bend, tying it off with an overhand knot to keep the rope from slipping.

"I see you're good with knots," said LaSalle. "Everett Littleton was good with knots. His knots never got loose. He was one pissed-off son of a bitch. I told him I didn't have anything to do with his sister Alice's death. That was all Ashlyn and Justin trying their tobacco scam on the wrong people."

Diane didn't say anything. She remained focused on what she was doing. If the knots were tied incorrectly, they would reduce the strength of the rope or slip loose. With the rope anchored to the boulder, she went back to Neva, who was literally hanging on by her fingernails.

Neva was stuck at hip level. So far there was room around her chest for her to breathe. Diane had wanted to make a harness around Neva's chest, but she was too far down for Diane to reach safely without help, and LaSalle wasn't willing to help. Damn. She untied the handhold loop she had made and tied another one lower on the rope.

"Okay, Neva. I'm lowering the rope beside you, down through the opening. I want you to find the loops with your feet. There are two of them. If you can, put a foot in each loop. If not, put at least one foot in."

"I think maybe I broke my right leg." Neva's voice was very high-pitched and soft. "Please don't leave me hanging by my hands again."

"I'm going to get you out of this. The rope is going to support you."

Diane dropped the end of the rope down through the crevice in the rocks, stopping it with the end loop near Neva's left foot. Diane took off her flannel shirt and used it as a pad to protect the rope from being cut by the edge of the rock.

"Okay, Neva, find the loop. You need to raise your foot slightly."

Neva tried and missed the loop. She whimpered. "I don't want to die here."

"You're not going to. Concentrate on putting your foot in the loop."

Neva tried again. On the third try her foot found the loop.

"Now you can put your weight on the rope. Hold on to the handholds on the rope."

Neva pushed against the rope. "That's better. Maybe I can climb out."

She strained, pulling on the rope. Diane pulled as hard as she could on her end.

"I'm stuck." Neva started to cry. "It hurts."

"Okay, Neva, I want you to listen to me. Right now you are a cave creature and your only purpose in life is to hang on to this rope. No matter what happens, no matter how tired you get, no matter how much you hurt, the only thing you have to do is to hang on to this rope. You understand?"

"Yes." Her voice was barely a squeak.

"I will come back with help for you and for Mike and Dick. Trust me. I will."

Diane took a space blanket from her pack and tucked it around Neva as best she could without going over the edge herself.

"Okay, now let's go." LaSalle was insistent.

"I'm going to see about Mike, and then we'll go get your damn diamonds. I'll even give you some extra from the museum if you'll be a little patient. We have some fine gems."

"Well, a woman who knows how to bargain. I like that. Look at him, then. After that, we go."

Diane rushed to Mike. He was conscious and pale. His skin was cool to the touch, but the cave was cool.

She looked at his side. MacGregor started to lift his shirt from the wound.

"No. Keep it there. If you move it, you'll pull the clotted blood loose and start the bleeding again. It looks like it's slowed."

Diane folded parts of the shirt over the area to soak up more blood. She put a hand on Mike's back. He was bleeding from the exit wound. Damn. She fished out her first aid kit and tore open the gauze pads, stacked them up and pressed them against the wound. "Hold this," she told MacGregor. "When I finish, I'll look at your arm."

"Dammit, this isn't a hospital," LaSalle said angrily.

"You're the one shooting people. Just one of our stones at the museum is worth ten thousand dollars and we have lots of them. That's a lot of money when all you have to do is stand there and wait a minute or two."

Diane wrapped an Ace bandage tight around Mike's midsection. He had been silent so far. Now he looked at her as if he were trying to telegraph thoughts.

"He's going to kill you," he whispered so silently Diane had to read his lips, "and us."

"No," whispered Diane. "Trust me."

Mike's stare had an urgency as he looked at her. "He won't let you . . ."

"What are you two cooking up?"

"Nothing. I'm trying to comfort Mike. What could we possibly be cooking up? You have a gun, and three-quarters of us are incapacitated. I'm almost finished."

She looked deep into Mike's eyes. "Trust me and trust my love of caves." He looked at her, puzzled. "It's your job to stay alive."

Diane looked at MacGregor's wound. It wasn't bad, she was relieved to see. She put a bandage on it. She took another space blanket and draped it over Mike and MacGregor.

"Watch the others. I'll come back with help. Don't let Mike move. Talk to Neva occasionally. Tell some jokes. You have a captive audience." He gave her a weak smile. "I'm counting on you," she added.

Diane stood up. "I'm ready to go."

Chapter 45

"Well, finally. We can get out of this damn place." LaSalle worked his way around the rocks to Diane. "Move." He waved his pistol in the general direction from which he had entered the chamber.

Diane had walked in front of him for several steps when two shots went off behind her. MacGregor began screaming. Diane whirled around, dread filling her chest. Mike was halfway up, leaning toward MacGregor, who was screaming and sobbing. Blood was flowing from both his boots.

"You son of a bitch," Diane yelled at LaSalle.

Diane rushed to MacGregor and kneeled down beside him, but LaSalle pulled her up and began dragging her from the chamber. He dropped his flashlight and it clattered on the floor.

"See what you made me do." He shoved her to the ground.

Her hands stung as she broke her fall.

"I ought to just shoot you and cut my losses. Pick that up and hand it to me."

Diane picked up the light and handed it to LaSalle.

"Why did you have to shoot him? He was no threat to you."

"The hell he wasn't. He was just winged. After we left, what was to stop him from walking out and calling the police? He can wait and suffer with the rest of your group. Now, listen and understand this. I showed compassion by not putting a bullet in their heads. That's my show of good faith. Now it's your turn. We're going to get out of this fucking cave and get my diamonds. No more delays, no more problems. You got that?"

Diane turned to Mike and MacGregor. "Dick, don't take your boots off. Put pressure on your wounds. Stay warm and still. Keep that space blanket around the two of you. Talk to Neva occasionally, but don't strain yourself. I'll come back with help."

"Aren't you just the sweet little mother."

For the first time, Diane got a good look at LaSalle. His good looks were ruined by a mean expression. He had dark hair, sharp, well-defined features, muscular build. She thought she understood what the story was with Ashlyn and Justin. Two arrogant kids caught smuggling contraband, probably caught by him—a corrupt cop. He offered them a deal—working for him for a much bigger prize than cigarettes. Ashlyn probably fell for him.

Diane walked slowly out of the chamber and started up the passage. She remembered Everett's last words about not trusting policemen. At the time, she thought he was talking about the policeman who shot him. He had meant LaSalle.

"Did Everett find you out and think you were involved in his sister's death?" she said.

"Yeah, you figured that out, huh? I tried to explain to him all that happened before I met the little twits, but he wouldn't listen. Caught me off guard one night with this electric cattle prod. Damn thing hurt like hell. Before I could recover, he had me tied up like a pig and I was riding in a truck from New York to Georgia with those three sniffling kids. All of them tied tight like me. Cried and moaned the whole way. The worst thing was, he stole our diamonds. Stuffed three of them down the kids' throats before he hung them. He cut off their fingers while they were alive. God, he was a maniac."

He *was a maniac,* thought Diane. *You're doing a good impression of one.* She listened to him talking and kept walking and checking her compass.

"Can't you speed up?"

"This is a cave. As you witnessed, caves are dangerous. You walk at a slow pace in a cave. Why didn't you just wait for us to come out?"

"I got the stupid idea that I could deal with all of you and not have any witnesses. I didn't know this place was a hazard waiting for an accident. Why would anyone in their right mind come to a place like this?"

"It's fun," said Diane.

"You like it dangerous, huh? I can give you dangerous."

"Why did you rape Kacie?"

"Why? She had my stone. She belonged to me. That prick of a boyfriend of hers ruined my diamond."

"You're some piece of work."

"Just get us out of this cave. I'll show you what kind of piece of work I am."

"He didn't ruin your diamond, you know. I was told by an expert that it was a superb cut."

"He took it to an amateur."

"A very gifted amateur."

"Well, pardon me."

Diane had a plan, and it seemed like a good one, but it was looking less feasible now that she was alone with him. If she could just play for time. Keep him talking. Slow the pace.

"How did you escape from Everett?"

"Being the last in line for the hanging. Wait a minute. I'm not recognizing any landmarks."

Diane pulled the map from her pocket. "Would you like to lead?"

"No. Just don't shit with me or I'll just cut my losses and shoot you." He grabbed her hair. "I might fuck you first right here in the cave before I kill you, and I won't make it fun for you."

"I'm trying to get us out of here as quickly and safely as I can. Remember, I have friends I'm trying to save too."

"*You* just remember that."

"I will. Tell me the rest of your story."

"Why? You like to hear me talk?"

"I just want to know what happened. Will it kill you to satisfy my curiosity?"

What Diane desperately wanted was to distract him. So far, he proved to be a talker, but it wouldn't last forever.

"Everett Littleton was Judge Roy Bean with a Rube Goldberg device. When we got to Georgia he zapped us, drugged us until we were practically zombies, and stuffed us like sardines in the backseat of his truck. He unhitched the trailer, drove the truck into the woods. First thing he did was tie all the nooses around different tree limbs. Shit, the guy was crazy—all those ropes. He seemed to get some kind of satisfaction out of tying knots. He had this routine he did."

They came to the There Be Dragons Here passage and Diane turned down it and looked at her compass.

"What are you doing?" He pulled at the compass cord on her neck.

"I'm checking the compass reading. You want to get out of here, don't you? I've been doing this the whole time we've been walking."

He let go of the cord. "Why the hell you think this kind of thing is fun is beyond me."

LaSalle continued talking and hadn't noticed the change of route. She didn't think he would. All the passages probably looked alike to him. She guessed he had followed their voices and lights to locate them—and he obviously got his hands on a map that had the route marked on it. LaSalle struck her as resourceful.

"Everett pulled the first kid out and told her why she was being executed," LaSalle continued. "Then he cut off her fingers and hauled her up with a winch, her screaming like a wild animal. While she was dangling in the air, kicking and screaming, he climbed on top of the cab and put the noose around her neck, took off the rope from around her chest that he pulled her up by, and let her swing by the neck. Sick bastard said a prayer. He did the other two kids, one at a time. Each one of them having to watch what he did to the ones before them. By the time he got to me, I'd sobered up and managed to cut my rope on a file he had in the back of the truck. While he was doing the last kid, I got out of the truck and ran for the woods. He looked for me for a long time, but I found the road and got the hell as far away from there as I could. I jacked a car from somebody's front yard and got back to town. I got even with the son of a bitch, though. I got to slice his throat."

Diane was looking for a place that would put her at an advantage. She would have no more than one chance, and it had to work. She had to surprise him. If she didn't do it right, he'd kill her and the others. She wasn't under any delusions that he would let her go. He'd get the diamonds, kill her and come back and kill them. But she needed just the right place.

This tunnel was looking very different from the ones they had passed through. It was larger, with more breakdown littering the floor. The hydrology that had created it was different, and the shape of the tunnel was different. Would he notice? Diane searched for more conversation.

"What happened to Steven Mayberry?"

"Bastard almost got away—still trying to steal my diamonds. He'll be found by hunters one of these days."

"How did you know about Chris Edwards and Steven Mayberry?"

"I got lucky. I saw them being interviewed on television. I knew that Everett threw the pouch with the rest of the diamonds into the woods. I went back there to look for it, and it was gone. I figured maybe these guys found it. I discussed the possibility with them."

LaSalle stopped suddenly and looked around the tunnel, shining his flashlight on the walls and floor.

"Are you trying to distract me? I don't recognize this place. None of the tunnels were this big. Damn you, bitch, I told you not to shit with me."

He slapped her in the jaw with the side of the flashlight. Instead of recoiling, Diane lunged into him with her shoulder. Off balance, he stumbled over a rock, fell and hit his head on the floor. The gun and the flashlight went flying. The cave had done for her what she was searching for a way to do.

Stunned, he rose to his knees, shaking his head. She

switched off her headlamp. He scrambled in the dark for the thing that was most important to him, the thing he thought he couldn't live without—his gun. Diane scrambled for the thing he needed most in a cave— his flashlight. She got to her prize first and switched it off. They were plunged into absolute darkness. Diane silently picked a path several feet away to a large rock near the entrance to the passage, crouched behind it, and listened. She could hear him feeling for his gun.

"Okay. You've had your little laugh. Get the fuck over here with the flashlight."

Diane said nothing.

"Are you listening to me, bitch! Turn on the god-damn fucking light."

She was silent.

"If I have to find you, you won't like it."

Diane concentrated on breathing softly, hoping he couldn't hear her, hoping she wouldn't have to cough or sneeze. She waited, trying not to think of the others.

"Okay. You win. I'll help pull your friend out of the hole she's in. You know how to make deals. How's that for a deal?"

He was silent for several moments, as if he was waiting for Diane to ponder his offer.

"Look, you stupid bitch, you have to get out of here too. Did you think that far ahead?"

Yes, thought Diane. *I did.*

"You can't move. If I hear you I'll shoot, you have to know that. I'm a pretty good shot. I can aim by sound."

Diane heard him fumbling in the dark. He'd started walking, bumping against the rocks. She picked up a stone and threw it. He didn't fire.

"You didn't expect me to fall for that old trick, did you?"

Diane said nothing. She picked up another stone and threw it. Again, he didn't fire. This time she rose and slowly slipped out of the passage, and this time he fired—toward her.

The bullet pinged off the wall and echoed throughout the chamber. The cave was cold but she felt sweat trickling down her back and between her breasts. She started to shiver.

She heard him moving and fumbling through the breakdown. He cursed and yelled at her. In the dark, her plan seemed to have vanished with the light.

Focus on the task. You're a cave creature, she reminded herself.

Diane stuffed the flashlight in her pocket and felt along the walls, felt the scallops carved by water—steep slope of the scallop upstream. She focused on remembering the cave, the paces, the directions. She moved as quickly as she dared, feeling the wall along the way. The breakdown debris was the hardest. It slowed her passage as she felt for a firm footing with each step.

She came to a passage and stopped. She fished her small knife out of her jeans pocket and worked on prying the cover off her compass. She fumbled, searching for a place to put the point of her knife, trying not to slip and stab herself. It was stuck fast.

She stopped, took a deep breath and tried again. It moved. She stuck the knife in the widening crack, raising the cover. She broke it the rest of the way open and felt the compass inside with her fingers.

"I'm going to catch you, and when I do, you'll wish you'd never crossed me. You won't die quickly."

Diane let her compass rest level for a moment before she put her fingertips on it, feeling for the tiny raised arrow painted on one of the hands. She had succeeded in separating LaSalle and herself from her friends for the moment, but what if he found his way back to Mike and the others? There would be lights there. They and she would all be worse off than when they started. She'd promised them they'd be safe.

Off in the distance she occasionally heard a muffled cry. MacGregor, or Neva maybe. If LaSalle heard it he could home in on it—maybe, or maybe not, but she couldn't take the chance. If he found the right passage, he might eventually see the glow from their lights, unless they thought to turn them off. Mike might think of it, if he weren't so injured . . . if he weren't dead.

No! she shouted inside her head. *You are going to get everyone out of this mess.*

She wondered if she dared turn on the flashlight for just a moment to check her bearings. She leaned against the wall and listened. She heard him in the distance, stumbling over the rocks, cursing under his breath. He was not in this passage. Maybe he would pass it by—more likely he'd take each passage he came to. That plan would eventually lead him into bad trouble.

She needed to stay far enough away from him to stay out of his hearing but near enough to know the direction he was traveling.

"I'll make you a deal," he shouted. "I give you my word—on my father's grave, and I respected my father. Turn on the flashlight and we'll both get out of here and I'll go my separate way."

Yeah, right, thought Diane. She listened as he bypassed her tunnel and kept going straight. She doubled back, always keeping her hand on the wall, walking as quietly as she could, trying to get behind him. Time was passing, and Mike and Neva didn't have much of it. She was able to move more quickly than LaSalle. Even her effort to move quietly was faster than his stumbling, angry traverse through the cave.

She had formed another plan. She didn't like it, but she saw no other way. If she got close enough, she could hit him hard with a rock, turn on her light and take his gun.

She was closing the distance behind him. He stumbled and stopped dead still. Had he heard her, smelled her sweat? Her apple-scented shampoo? Was he just resting?

She stood still, holding her breath for long moments. When she did breathe, it was slow and silent. He still hadn't moved. Was he formulating a plan? He had sensed her somehow. It was a reckless plan she'd come up with.

He started walking again, but now back from where he had come. He was close now. She remained still and breathless. She heard him fumbling and jangling.

Almost before it happened, Diane realized what he'd thought of, what she hadn't thought of. A tiny light flickered, like the tail of a lightning bug. She was face-to-face with the most evil set of eyes she had ever seen.

Chapter 46

His breath was hot and angry, and the look in his eyes said he would like to cut her heart out. He put the gun to her head.

"Don't think you can bargain your way out of this. Let me tell you what's going to happen. We are going to get out of this cave. I'm going to stuff you in the trunk of my car and drive to the museum, and when it's dark you are going to get my diamonds. You know what happened to little Kacie. That's nothing compared to what I have planned for you. You'll lick my shoes like a dog and beg me to kill you. Then I'm going back and shoot your friends in the head—if they're not dead already. That is what is going to happen, and I'm going to enjoy every second."

He held the gun barrel so hard against her temple it was digging into her flesh. Diane said nothing. Oddly, all her fear had vanished. The rock wall at her back was cold and she felt frozen to it. Her legs were too weak to carry her weight. She wanted just to sit down and wait. . . . Wait for what?

He put his key light back in his pocket, grabbed the flashlight sticking from her pocket and switched it on. It flickered a moment, then went out.

"Damn, you fucking bitch. Look what you've done."

Her body was on some automatic will of its own. It knew what he was going to do before her brain did. She collapsed on her shaking legs just as he rammed his fist against the wall where her head had been. He yelled in pain. She grabbed the chin strap on her helmet, pulled it off her head, struck it hard against the rocks and heard the tinkling of her electric head-lamp breaking.

Diane grabbed the pant leg of his left ankle and stood up, using the power of her legs to lift with all her strength. As his foot came off the ground, he fell backward, grabbing her as he went down. The gunshot exploded loud near her ear and she felt the heat on her cheek. She tried to scramble away, but he pulled her legs out from under her. She felt a hand on her neck, squeezing fingers working their way to her throat. For all his previous grumbling, he was silent now, and that frightened her more. Diane reached out her hand, searching for a rock. They were all over the place—why couldn't her hand find one?

She grasped a sharp rock the size of a baseball and clutched it tight, trying to resist his efforts to force her on her back. He flipped her over and she struck with all her strength. He cried out and dropped the gun. She scrambled backwards walking crablike, trying to escape, still holding the rock. He'd let go of her throat, but he held on to her leg. He fished the key light from his pocket and flicked it on, illuminating a tiny area around them. She struck again hard on his temple and grabbed at the light as he fell over.

Diane squeezed the tiny light to turn it on. He was stunned, but still trying to rise. She turned around, searching for the gun. She saw it, nose down between two rocks. She went for it at the same time LaSalle came around enough to realize he needed to act. He scrambled across the rocks toward her and the gun. Diane put out the light and grabbed the gun. LaSalle swore at the darkness—and Diane.

"Okay, you got me," he began, but Diane could hear him moving, trying to regain the advantage.

She stepped back and squeezed the tiny key light. In the dim glow she could just make out LaSalle rising from the rocks like an evil demon that wouldn't die. She aimed the gun and shot once—not in the foot, where he had shot MacGregor. She shot him in the ankle where the tibia and fibula joined with the tarsal bones and where several important tendons were bundled together. He screamed and collapsed. She shot his other ankle, and his cries echoed throughout the chamber. She stood in the darkness listening, without emotion. When his cries died down to curses, she spoke.

"Now, let me tell you what's going to happen. You are going to sit here in the dark and wait for the police to come and haul you to jail. I suggest you don't try to crawl anywhere, but wrap yourself into a fetal position and stay until they arrive."

"Don't leave me here like this."

"I have no choice. Even if I could carry you, I can't trust you. I'll tell them where you are. It shouldn't be more than a few hours."

Diane retrieved her damaged helmet and picked up the flashlight. She shook it and tried the switch. It came on, shining a beam of light on LaSalle.

"Let that be a lesson to you."

She left him there calling after her and worked her

way through the passages to the mouth of the cave. She retrieved her phone from beneath her driver's seat and punched in 911.

Mike looked pale against the white hospital pillow. The bullet had nicked his intestines, but luckily did no organ or spinal damage.

"You were caving in the dark? God. What were you thinking—that you could feel your way through the cave?" He grinned at her. "You got guts."

"I thought I could negotiate in the dark better than he could," Diane said. "It barely worked."

"We could hear the gunshots. Didn't know what to think." He touched the bruise on her face left by the flashlight. "So how about it, Doc, willing to take care of a wounded friend?"

Diane grabbed his hand and held it. "I think the hospital's doing a fine job." She paused a moment. "Mike, I'm sorry."

He put a finger on her lips. "Not your fault, Doc. It'll make a good chapter in my caving journal."

MacGregor wheeled in in his wheelchair. Both feet were immobilized in casts and his arm was bandaged. La-Salle had shot him in the metatarsal portion of both feet. Bad enough, but they were injuries that were easier to deal with than had he hit the closely packed tarsal bones. Diane had expected MacGregor to be angry and never want to see them again. Instead, he'd bonded. He sat there and grinned at Diane, showing off the autographs on his casts.

"The doctor says I'll be in walking casts real soon. I'll be ready to go caving with you again in no time."

"We'll keep a guard at the entrance next time," said Diane. MacGregor cackled. "Take care," she said. "I'm going to check on Neva."

"She was a real trouper," said Mike. "Hung on to that rope like you told her to, didn't complain. That had to be scary."

"I hope it hasn't put her off caves," said Diane.

"We'll get her back out there as soon as our wounds heal."

Diane was silent for a moment watching Mike. "I'm glad you followed my instructions and stayed alive."

"You were pretty firm about that," he said.

Diane left them and walked down the hall to Neva's room. She was dozing. Jin and David were sitting in chairs by her bed.

"How's Mike and that fellow?" asked David.

"Doing well. Mike'll be back to work in about a month," said Diane. She gestured toward the bed.

"Good," said Jin. "Neva's doing just fine."

Neva's rescue had been complicated. The rescue team rigged a rope system for themselves so they would have the support needed to work in safety. Getting a harness around her chest was a big step. It gave her arms a rest. One of the rescuers had to hang over the edge with Neva and chisel out the rock from around her to free her so she could be pulled to safety.

Neva opened her eyes. "Hi," she said. "How are Mike and Dick?"

"They're doing fine. How about you?"

"Glad to be out of that crack."

"Think you'll want to try caving again?"

"I have to. I bought all that equipment—hard hat, backpack. I had five backup flashlights in my backpack." Neva sobered a moment. "Jin was telling me they didn't find LaSalle, just a trail of blood leading off to a wild part of the cave."

"The police are going back in to look for him. Garnett said a team of federal marshals who are also cavers are coming down to join the search."

"Jeez, that's scary. What do you suppose happened to him?"

"I can't imagine he got far, the way he was wounded. He couldn't have stood on his feet. I think he probably crawled somewhere and got into trouble."

"I can't say I have much sympathy," said Neva.

"No, I can't say I do either," said Diane.

Epilogue

The museum was closing for the day. Diane stood in the new Egyptian exhibit, taking another look before its opening the next day. It was in a small room on the second floor that suited the few artifacts on display and made it seem like a larger exhibit than it was. Also more personal.

The walls were painted in colorful but muted tones like the worn walls of an Egyptian tomb. The real star of the exhibit was Neva's sculpture, sitting cross-legged in the middle of the room. The entire face and body were a 3-D reconstruction made using the measurements gained from the CT scan.

Neva sculpted him from clay first. The museum then had experts from Madame Tussaud's make a wax figure. He looked so real Diane expected him to unfold his legs, take the papyrus lying in his lap and walk off his pedestal. They had concluded he was a scribe. Jonas figured him to be a royal scribe because of the position of the hands and some of the amulets that belonged to him.

Diane walked around the wax figure, viewing it from several angles. He had tan skin and a dark wig styled similar to figurines and wall paintings from the

times. He wore a simple white linen loincloth, and a
reed pen and pallette hung from his neck. An auto-
mated video beside the figure described his life and
the process the museum used to research the mummy.

The analysis of his tissue samples revealed that he
had several bacterial infections common in ancient
Egypt. Release of this information garnered Diane another mountain of mail wanting access to the mummy.
The analysis on his kidney tumor showed it to be be-
nign. When the report came in, Jonas and Andie were
relieved, somehow glad that the scribe hadn't died
of cancer.

The mummy himself was inside the anthromorphic
coffin that they still were unsure was really his. The
closed coffin was inside a glass case built just for the
mummy. Diane decided to exhibit the actual mummy
only a few times a year. But there were photographs
of him on the walls. A video documented his rewrap-
ping by Korey and his assistants, beginning with his
own wrappings and supplementing those with a substantial amount of modern linen.

The amulets were displayed under glass, each highlighted on its own pedestal. They decided not to display the Victorian pickle jar. The rest of the exhibit
included models based on life in twelfth-dynasty
Egypt. In one end of the exhibit, there was an entire
miniature Egyptian town, including a scribe's house.

Diane was pleased with the exhibit. From a small
number of artifacts, Jonas, Kendel and the exhibit designers had done a great job. The room dimmed as
the daytime lighting went off automatically and the
nighttime lighting came on. In the shadows of the dim
light, the wax figure looked as if he might indeed come
to life. She turned and left the room.

Diane walked out of the museum to her new SUV and, like she now did when she left the museum, or anywhere, she scanned the area looking for anything out of the ordinary or dangerous.

Beverly Connor is the author of the Diane Fallon Forensic Investigation series and the Lindsay Chamberlain Mystery series. Before she began her writing career, Beverly worked as an archaeologist in the Southeastern United States specializing in bone identification and analysis of stone tool debitage. She weaves her professional experiences from archaeology and her knowledge of the South into interlinked stories of the past and present. *One Grave Too Many* was the first book in the Diane Fallon series. Five of her titles have been translated into Dutch and are available in countries of the European Union.